The
Why
of
Things

Center Point
Large Print

**This Large Print Book carries the
Seal of Approval of N.A.V.H.**

The
Why
of
Things

❧

ELIZABETH
HARTLEY WINTHROP

CENTER POINT LARGE PRINT
THORNDIKE, MAINE

This Center Point Large Print edition is published
in the in the year 2013 by arrangement with
Simon & Schuster, Inc.

The text of this Large Print edition is unabridged.
In other aspects, this book may vary
from the original edition.
Printed in the United States of America
on permanent paper.
Set in 16-point Times New Roman type.

ISBN: 978-1-61173-921-3

Library of Congress Cataloging-in-Publication Data

Winthrop, Elizabeth Hartley, 1979–
The Why of things / Elizabeth Hartley Winthrop. — Large
   print edition.
pages ; cm.
ISBN 978-1-61173-921-3 (library binding : alk. paper)
1. Murder—Investigation—Fiction. 2. Domestic fiction.
   3. Psychological fiction. 4. Large type books. I. Title.
PS3623.I7W49 2013b
813′.6—dc23
                                                    2013021333

For my sisters

The
Why
of
Things

Prologue

They stand at the quarry's edge: Joan, Anders, and their youngest girls, Eve and Eloise, who will not go to bed. The water below them is black and looks thick as tar; reflections of light from the house are wavering rectangles on its surface: window, window, door. Now and then, debris will bob through the light. An empty beer can. A flip-flop. A plastic bag.

"A bubble," Eve says suddenly, and Joan has seen it, too, a single bubble breaking through the surface. "A bubble!" Eve says again, louder this time. She looks at her parents, demanding, expectant.

Joan touches her daughter's arm. "Shhh."

Behind them, in shadow, a handful of policemen lean against an ambulance and mutter, not about the tire marks that lead right to the quarry's edge, not about the gasoline slowly spreading across the surface of the water, not about flip-flops or beer cans. Joan hears the words *cheese steak,* and *cold one,* and then a snuffle of muted laughter. She grits her teeth and digs her elbow into Anders' side. "This is taking forever," she whispers.

"Shhh," Anders hushes her.

"But no one is doing anything."

"What can they do, Joan? All anyone can do at this point is wait for the divers."

"It's been an hour and a half."

"And it's nine o'clock, and the dive team is coming from Beverly." Anders looks at his watch. "Give them time."

"Time," Joan murmurs. She shifts her weight from one foot to the other. The day as it had passed seemed nothing but a blur of last-minute packing, of traffic jams and drive-throughs and tollbooths and endless highways that in her mind as the day of departure neared had come to symbolize escape. Now, though, looking back, Joan remembers the day as a detailed series of moments that at the time she hadn't known she was aware of, and this sudden clarity both surprises and unnerves her, as if these details were presenting themselves now for a reason, for examination.

There is an image in her mind of Eloise standing inside their house in Maryland, silhouetted by the stark sky outside, her little face pressed against the screen door as she watches Anders load the car. Their summer things had been piled on the porch above the driveway, and Anders had carried them down to the car, box by box, bag by bag, one load at a time. All that is left to be carried to the car, in this image, is a dry-cleaned suit, hanging against a column of the porch.

There is an image of Eve sitting sullen on the steps with headphones on, her hair with a hot pink streak that last week was red, the bangs she's growing out hanging in her face.

There is an image of the Sherpa cat bag by the door. Two bright green eyes blink slowly in its darkness.

There is an image of mist rising from wet pavement.

There is an image of traffic shimmering on the highway, Anders' hand draped over the steering wheel, and her daughters in the backseat of the car, side by side despite Anders' attempt to separate them with a duffel bag, which Eve had pushed into the window seat. That was still Sophie's seat, the girls had said, and both refused to sit there.

Thinking back on the day like this, this morning and Maryland seem like a lifetime ago. Today, as Eve has reminded them several times, is the summer solstice, the longest day of the year; truly, to Joan, it has felt like it.

"Bubble!" Eve says, pointing. "If someone's down there, time is running out!"

"Evie," Joan says. "Hush!" though the same has occurred to her, too.

"You hush," Eve says, and she swivels on her toe. Joan watches her go: she stalks toward the policemen leaning against the ambulance. The doors of their cruisers, which they have driven onto the grass, are open, and radio voices crackle from within. Eve passes through the beam of the headlights and then pauses before the policemen, as if considering whether to speak to them. But she continues past, around the quarry toward the house, which is a large, dark shape among the trees, only a few of the downstairs windows aglow. They hadn't yet even made it upstairs. Their car is parked beside the house, its tailgate open and the inside lights still on. She imagines she can hear the chirpy *ding ding ding* of the open door starting to whine as the battery slowly dies, but she is too tired to really care. Anders had been just about to start unloading an hour or two ago, after they'd finally arrived here for the summer, when Eve had called out from over here, where Joan is standing now. *Someone drove into the quarry!* she called, and of course it had seemed unlikely, impossible, even, but then Eve pointed out the tire tracks that ran over the lawn, and the bubbles, and the things slowly surfacing even as they watched from the shore: a gas can, beer cans, a piece of Styrofoam.

Eve disappears into the shadows by the house, and Joan returns her gaze to the quarry. Another bubble surfaces.

The tire tracks that lead directly to the quarry's edge run between two trees so closely spaced together that Eve would never think a car could fit between them, but the tracks are there, and recent; the flattened grass seems to have lifted itself a bit in the short time since she first noticed them. Eve squats before the larger of the trees, where each summer she and her sisters have upon arriving at the quarry carved their initials and the year. After they arrived tonight, as her father began unloading the car, Eve had gone directly to the tree, as if she thought that perhaps she would find this year's date already carved, Sophie's initials fresh in the bark. As if she thought that somehow Sophie would be waiting there inside the house for them.

But of course Eve had found on the tree no new markings other than a nick where she now imagines the side-view mirror bumped against the tree as it passed, and then she had noticed the tire tracks, and followed them to where they ended at the quarry's edge. No one believed her until they saw the tracks for themselves, of course, probably because they didn't want to. She wasn't surprised.

She traces their initials from last year with her finger now. It had been raining when they carved them, she remembers, and the bark had been slick. Sophie had gone first, and then she'd guided Eloise's small hand with her own. Eve, when it was her turn with the knife, had managed to cut her finger, which though it didn't hurt her began to bleed so heavily and immediately that Sophie had ripped a strip of material from her frayed cutoffs to wrap around it. Eve can see her sister clearly in her mind's eye, her thin shoulders hunched as she tied the denim as tightly as she could, her inquisitive expression when she was finished, asking Eve with her eyes, *is this all right?* Sophie hated pain, her own or anyone else's.

Eve examines her finger now, the pale indentation of the resulting scar, then stands up. Across the water, her parents and Eloise stand staring into the water, backlit by the headlights of the cruisers. The policemen behind them are vaguely familiar to Eve from encounters in past summers: the breakers-up of beach parties, the dispersers of crowds of kids gathered in the parking lot of the 7-Eleven. Those are the kinds of things they are good at, Eve thinks bitterly; when it comes to anything serious, like cars in quarries, they stand around uselessly waiting for someone else to do the dirty work. She casts an anxious glance in the direction of the driveway, wishing the divers would hurry up and get here.

Eve sighs, returning her attention to the tire tracks beneath her. She follows them back from the trees away from the water to where they disappear on the driveway, which leads out to one of the many dirt roads meandering around the various quarries on Cape Ann, theirs only one of the many silent scars of the granite days, filled with the rain of years, sometimes hundreds of feet in depth. She and her sisters have spent many summer hours on the sunbaked slabs along the quarry's edge, hazarding gruesome guesses as to what over the years may have accumulated in the deep. Now, their worst imagining has come true, and Sophie isn't even here to witness it.

Eve wanders down the driveway away from the house, and turns onto the road. She is barefoot, as she makes a point to be in summer, and though the grass of the lawn had felt cool and smooth beneath her feet, she walks gingerly on the road, wary of the pebbles and sticks that have not yet toughened up her soles. Only yards from the house, she finds herself in total darkness. It is not that there are no moon or stars, tonight; as she'd stood at the quarry's edge moments ago she had noticed Cassiopeia reclining on the horizon, and above it, the moon, and she'd wondered whether it was on the wax or the wane—and she should know this, she thinks now, widening her eyes against the darkness, blinking as if to blink it away. Sophie knew this. But it is one of those things that Eve herself can never remember. When the moon is facing left, is it growing, or has it already been full? She looks up; she can see nothing through the canopy of trees.

Tonight is the shortest night of the year, today the summer solstice. It is Eve's favorite day, because it's the longest, and it marks the start of summer, but it carries with it also just a tinge of sadness, because from here on out the days are only going to get shorter, start their slip-sliding decline into winter. This year, the actual solstice, the very moment the sun climbed to its farthest point north of the equator, and, for just a minute, stood still, was at 7:09 p.m. Eve had been anticipating the moment all day, urging her father to drive just a little faster so they'd get here in time to see it, but then, amid the excitement over the tire tracks and the stuff in the quarry and calling the police, she'd entirely forgotten. And now she's going to have to wait a whole year to have the chance to see it again. She sighs now with frustration, annoyed with herself for being so easily distracted.

It is dark, but she knows this road by heart; she doesn't need light to walk it. She imagines to her right the boulder that years ago someone painted as a frog, to her left the rusted chain that marks the entrance to a path through the woods. Soon, she knows the road will curve to the right and begin to slope downhill, past the Bakers' driveway and the edge of the Carvers' lawn. Eve pauses in the darkness when she hears the growing sound of an engine. The divers, she thinks, pleased at the thought of intercepting them and immensely relieved that they are finally here, but the headlights growing out of the darkness are accompanied by the sound of thudding music, and Eve steps out of the road, into a safe nook between a triangle of trees. Teenagers, she thinks nervously, as if the car-load of kids had earned the title through something other than age. She herself will be fifteen this summer, but would never consider herself a teenager in that way.

She stands in the shadow of the front-most tree so as to remain unseen as the car passes, its headlights bright and blinding, illuminating things in flashes as the car lurches over ruts: an overhanging vine, a roadside rock, a cracked and dried-out puddle.

Things are soft in the red glow of fading tail-lights, and Eve steps out from between her trees. She squints at that rock across the road in the dimming light and steps closer. Three cigarettes lie side by side on the rock, unsmoked. Though not a frequent smoker, she gathers them greedily—they are a rare find—and she has just put them carefully into the front pocket of her shirt when again headlights loom in the darkness.

"They're here," Anders says, both he and Joan hearing the sound of the divers' truck before its beams come up the driveway. He offers Joan Eloise's hand and all the sleepy weight attached, and she leads their daughter around the quarry to the house, blinded for a brief moment by the divers' high beams as they pass. She gestures into

17

the light with her free hand, a vague salute, and for some reason, the image of herself squinting and waving, Eloise in tow, now lines itself up with the other images of the day, the only one in which she is a subject.

She puts Eloise to bed; thankfully despite her adamance earlier in the evening that she not miss out on anything, she's too tired to put up a fight. Probably the mere possibilities of what might be dredged from the quarry's depths are terrifying enough; though she acts tough, Eloise is easily frightened, and has sense enough to know when to shut her eyes to things. *Don't leave the house,* she implores her mother from beneath her sheets, and Joan promises that she won't, and the fact of it is that she is glad not to go back, not to have to stand there wondering if Eve is right and there *is* some poor soul who died down there tonight. Though of course she's wondering anyway. She watches the scene unfolding across the quarry from afar, in brief glimpses as she unloads the car, bringing in their summer things and piling them in the house, where the furniture is still covered with sheets. The policemen across the water are faceless figures from this distance, the divers bizarre, black, rubber-limbed creatures lowering themselves into the dark water. She doesn't need to be any closer; Anders and her imagination will fill in the details, both wanted and unwanted, she is sure of that.

Despite the strangeness of this situation, the potential horror, Joan feels oddly detached from it all, even resigned. As they drove the final miles of their journey late this afternoon she had laid out the evening in her mind, the quarry still the refuge at the end of those symbolic highways, a place of normalcy. They would unload the car first. They would strip the sheets from the furniture and open all the windows to air out the house. While she unpacked their clothing, Anders would go into town and pick up a pizza for dinner, and he'd go to the grocery store for the basic things: milk, juice, water, something to eat for breakfast tomorrow. Eve, perhaps, would take Eloise down to the beach.

But then, only moments after they'd arrived, her plans had derailed; somehow, she was unsurprised. Nothing surprises her much, anymore. There is a car at the bottom of their quarry, possibly—likely—with a body inside. And perhaps this happens often—maybe there are cars in quarries all around the cape. They have had no dinner, aside from the saltines and peanut butter she gave to Eloise before putting her to bed, which were leftovers from the car ride. The bags are still packed, and the kitchen is empty. Nothing has gone as planned or imagined, which has only served to reaffirm her sense that it is better never to plan or imagine anything, better never to count on the future.

Sophie died on a Tuesday. The following weekend was Columbus Day weekend, a long one; she and Joan were meant to fly to Boston, rent a car, and drive a loop through New England, touring colleges. Instead, they held her funeral. For Thanksgiving, they had had plans to go to Joan's cousin's house in Delaware for a family reunion, which under the circumstances they abandoned, and for Christmas they were going to drive to Anders' sister's house in Vermont and ski, which they also failed to do. Joan had vaguely counted on going shopping with Sophie for a prom dress sometime in the spring, had counted on going to her soccer games, and taking her to see the World Cup in June, had counted on watching as graduation caps filled the air, so many black shapes against the sky. There are many things that she hadn't realized she was vaguely counting on; she has gone through the months since with the sense that she took a wrong turn somewhere, or that in some parallel universe another version of herself is leading the life she had expected.

She brings the last load in from the car: her computer and notes, though she hasn't written much of late. She had always considered herself lucky to be a novelist, to make a living writing books, but lately she has not been able to find much sense in it. It seems there is enough in the real world to worry about without creating a second one to fret over as well. She doesn't have the energy left to care about that second world, into which she has come to think she invested too much of herself over the years. Indeed, she'd been neck deep in the final edits of her last book when Sophie died, and up at night thinking about her characters and their problems rather than her own living children.

There is a scratching at the door; Joan looks up at the noise and sees through the screen on the dark porch two green eyes: Seymour. She opens the door; the cat darts inside as if chased. Joan steps out just as a neighborhood dog disappears into the shadows behind the house, the jingle of its collar fading into the distance. She leans in the darkness against a column of the porch, slips off a sandal, and scratches at her ankle with her toe; there are mosquitoes. She hears a shout from across the water. A dark, rubber-clad head surfaces, a bright headlamp attached, and then another and another, and then something else: a body, Joan is sure, though she had hoped and hoped that the car in their quarry was empty, a piece of junk abandoned like so much other junk, put into neutral and pushed. If there is a God, Joan thinks, he treats the world with the same irony as a writer treats her world; it is awful, she thinks, to find herself a character.

Anders watches as the divers leave the dead man on a sloping slab of granite, head side down, while the paramedics get the stretcher. The cops have mounted a powerful light to the roof of one of the cruisers, lighting the whole scene like a movie set. Anders stands near the ambulance, at the edge of the light, his hand on the back of Eve's neck. Nearby, he can hear two of the divers talking about the stuck seat belt, and how they'd had to cut through it with a knife. Apparently it's a pickup truck down there, nose down between some rocks. The third diver is sitting on a rock off to the side, his head in his hands.

Eve had escorted the divers in. When their truck finally pulled up the drive, Anders was surprised, when a door opened, to see his daughter emerge. He'd thought she was still beside him at the quarry's edge; he hadn't realized after Joan and Eloise had gone inside that aside from the policemen a few yards back he'd been standing there alone. The divers followed Eve up the grass to the quarry's edge. Anders was also surprised at the sight of them. They were wearing cargo shorts, T-shirts, and flip-flops; they were just regular guys, not one of them more than thirty, and they looked almost as if they'd been interrupted from a baseball game or a night at the bar. Anders thought there must be some mistake. He realized he'd half expected them to show up in wet suits and flippers, their air tanks already strapped to their backs. He'd expected divers, not people. They stripped down to the bathing suits they wore beneath their shorts and then pulled on their wet suits wordlessly; they looked afraid, and Anders didn't blame them. He didn't envy them their task.

Now two paramedics wheel a stretcher across the grass and collapse it beside the dead man. Silently, they slide a board beneath him, and they seem to Anders as careful with him as they would be if he were alive. They fasten him to the board with straps and hoist it onto the stretcher. When the ambulance had arrived with the policemen earlier tonight, Anders had wondered what the point was, since if anyone was in the quarry, surely they were dead, even as Eve kept pointing urgently to bubbles gurgling to the surface, *signs of life!* It had already been two hours, at the least. Anders gazes at the dead man now. He is young, like the divers, certainly no more than thirty. He is wearing khaki pants and a white T-shirt that is ripped in the armpit, no shoes. He has been maybe three days without a shave. Or he had been three days without a shave until he died, whenever that was. Anders rubs his chin vigorously; his own stubble is about three days old.

The dead man does not look asleep, as Anders imagined he might have, as other dead people he has seen have looked—his mother, and his father, who had passed out of this world as Anders watched, both of them softly overcome by a quiet stillness. What Sophie looked like he does not know, and it is not something he and Joan have talked about. Joan had had to go identify their daughter's body alone, while Anders was stuck in the airport in Rome, waiting. He had stared up at the armed guards patrolling on the balcony above him, the melodies of his students' songs repeating in his head as even at that moment they sang in St. Peter's Basilica without his direction.

No, this man does not look asleep, but decidedly dead. His skin is a faint blue, and his lips are very dark. His left eye is open just a bit. There is a leaf in his hair. Anders had watched as the divers swam the dead man to the quarry's edge, had seen that floating leaf catch in the dead man's hair. This is a detail he will have to remember to tell Joan. He studies the dead man carefully, wondering if he might be familiar in some way from summers past, trying to place him in the land of the living: in the aisle of the grocery store, or pumping gas at the Shell station downtown, or pouring a beer at their favorite local bar. It's surprising how easy it is to do, animating this lifeless form before him, and he is struck by the familiar bewilderment he feels of late whenever he considers the line between life and death, how permanent, yet how fine.

It is so much harder, he thinks regretfully, to imagine where the living go on the far side of that line—into the nothing where Sophie has forever disappeared.

He looks up from the dead man across the quarry toward their house. The windows are all lit now; the porch is dark but for the glowing tip of a cigarette: Joan, who smokes only when she's anxious. After the divers arrived and Anders wordlessly handed over Eloise, Joan had tapped her chin nervously, a superstitious tick that annoys Anders only because it makes him nervous, too, even when of his own accord he wouldn't otherwise be. He had thought that certainly whatever car was at the bottom of the quarry was an empty one, an old one; it is as if Joan worried this young man into it.

Eloise has been in bed for as long as it has taken to count to 4,873 before she hears a series of car doors slam and the light that has been casting looming shadows across her wall is finally shut off. Her jaw aches from clenching, and she knows that her fingernails will have left little moon-shaped marks where she has had them dug into her palm. It's hard to stop herself from counting now, as hard as it had been earlier to get herself to start, afraid that if she did not the fear that had left her voiceless might also force her mind to freeze and forget to tell her heart to beat.

The porch light outside turns on, and just as quickly off; she hears the screen door downstairs open. She waits for the usual sound of the springs slamming it shut, but it doesn't come. Her father must have caught the door behind him, and shut it quietly. Though he was probably trying not to wake her, the slam that never comes makes her feel even more unsettled, the way she feels when she cannot find an itch. She hopes that at least he has locked the door, locked all of the doors, even though they never lock anything in summer. But someone has driven into their quarry. Someone may have died in their quarry. There could be killers in the woods. Kidnappers. Thieves. Ghosts. Sophie's ghost, of which Eloise is ashamed to be afraid. There could be anything out in the woods. Anything, it seems, is possible.

One

Eve sleeps badly. She wakes up maybe a dozen times over the course of the night, each time at first unsure of where she is before slowly the room comes into focus: the iron rungs of her narrow bed, its rarely used twin across the room, the old white dresser in the corner, the wingbacked wicker chair where often the cat curls up to sleep. Every time she wakes and looks at the clock, she is incredulous to find that only half an hour has passed since she last looked, especially since each half hour is filled with dreams that seem hours long at least. In one, she's stuck in a tree that sways dangerously under her weight, threatening to break and leave her at the mercy of the bobcats that circle below, waiting. In another, she goes ice-skating in the grocery store. In yet another, she goes out with her father in a boat they don't even have, which he crashes into rocks that she tries over and over to point out to him, but that for some reason he can't see.

At six, she lets herself get up, amazed, horrified, and oddly thrilled to find that the events of the night before were not a dream, but beyond all that impatient to find out what exactly happened, and what will happen next. Murder, she is convinced of that. But who? And why?

And under what circumstances? It occurred to her sometime between dreams last night that the man in the quarry might have been killed and dumped into the water already dead, a much more comforting alternative to the notion of him trapped down there and dying while they stood waiting at the quarry's edge.

She dresses quickly, pulling on a bathing suit, shorts, and a T-shirt dug from the duffel she'd lugged upstairs and left in the corner of the room last night after the policemen and the divers had left. A few feet above the duffel, tacked to the slope of the wooden ceiling, are the familiar drawings of sailboats and sunsets and rainbows and trees, done by herself and Sophie years ago in now-faded Magic Marker. Eve studies these as she pulls her clothes on. What's funny, she thinks, is that she has no recollection of making them, even though half have her name scrawled in childish letters at the bottom, and the realization makes her feel oddly disconnected from herself, or a self she used to be. She finds herself wishing that someone, sometime, had taken the drawings down; she'd like to put up a Grateful Dead poster, or a poster of the constellations, or maybe a tapestry. Now, of course, it's too late.

Dressed, she hurries downstairs and outside to examine last night's scene by day. She pauses on the porch, which is still empty of the wicker furniture and the low-slung hammocks waiting to be brought out from the garage. The porch looks much larger to Eve, bare. Bird droppings have accumulated at the base of one of the columns. She looks up; there's a nest in the rafters. She can just see the edge of it, a crude, sturdy arrangement of straw and twig and dry leaf. Woven among all this, Eve notices a short, blue length of the same sort of string she used to make bracelets out of when she was younger. No bird appears to be home.

Eve drops her eyes from the nest to the quarry, a deep, misshapen pool about three hundred feet in length and half as wide. The water had seemed so black, last night; this morning, it seems to have no color of its own. It is instead a perfect mirror of the sky, of the rocky ledges that contain it, of the slender trees that grow stories high at its edge. In the far corner of the quarry, where on ordinary days blown leaves and bits of grass collect, drawn there by some mysterious current, a slick of gasoline has gathered, leaked from the pickup truck that even now sits somewhere at the bottom. The beer cans and the gas can and the other debris that had surfaced last night float there, too. It seems strange to Eve that no one has collected this stuff, as evidence, strange that they have not roped off the quarry with crime scene tape, or stationed officers to keep watch. As far as Eve could tell, no one last night did much of anything except stand around and wait for the divers to bring the body up from the quarry floor—the body that as they waited might still have been a living person.

She takes the porch steps two at a time down to the grass, which is still wet with dew. Blades of it catch in her toes as she makes her way to the edge of the driveway, where she first noticed the tire tracks last night. The tracks on the grass are barely visible now, but Eve can still just make them out, leading up onto the grass from the driveway, and then across the lawn about twenty unwavering meters to the quarry's edge. Eve walks in the middle of the tracks, scanning the grass for any sort of clue as to what might have happened: a cigarette butt tossed out the window, a candy wrapper, anything. She pauses when she comes to the tree where her and her sisters' initials are carved, where the truck left a nick as it passed. In the daylight, she is even more amazed that a truck was able to maneuver between this tree and the next one over.

Eve frowns and follows the tracks up a small slope of grass to the ledge from which the truck plunged into the water. This strikes Eve; it's the quarry's tallest, about ten feet in height, and the one she and Sophie have always jumped from for the greatest thrill. She gazes across the water toward where the gasoline and debris have drifted; aside from these things, it's almost as if nothing happened here at all. A row of lilies send up unbloomed stalks, their spider leaves dangling over the quarry's edge, and leaves drift as they always do among the insects on the water's surface. She wonders, if the incident had taken place a few months earlier, whether anyone would have ever known. The gasoline might have gradually disappeared. They might have thought the garbage was just that: beer cans left behind by partiers one winter night. They might have gone swimming this summer just yards above a dead body, strapped into his truck.

She leaps down onto a lower ledge—the ledge where they laid the dead man last night—and touches the rock's surface tentatively, as if it might hold some memory of the body, those clammy limbs. She realizes that this is how she will always think of the ledge from now on—the ledge where they laid the dead man—though she has sunbathed on it hundreds of times, and eaten picnic lunches there, and it is also the spot where she had her first kiss, with Evan Arnolds four summer ago. She peers down into the water; at first, she sees nothing but darkness, but then she can just make out a vague, wavering shape in the depths, like a large, white jellyfish; it calls to her irresistibly. She looks across the quarry toward the house, wooden and rambling. Sunlight glints on the windowpanes. Soon, if they're not already, her family will be getting up. She strips down to her bathing suit, and before she has time to think herself out of it, think of what else might be down there and what exactly she's diving toward, she flings herself headlong into the water.

Beneath the surface, the water seems to eat up even light; the sunlight, which above was bright with early morning, here is a struggling yellow haze. It isn't that there is murk in the water, none of the wavering bits of algae that float in a lake, no specks of dirt. The water is perfectly clear; Eve has collected it in glass jars, looked at drops of it under a microscope, and it is even more clear than water she collected for comparison from the sea. It is something invisible, she thinks, that breaks the sunlight down, or maybe what it is is visible darkness. Eve swims down, holding her arms at her sides so as to make herself as streamlined as possible; she lets her feet do the work. The water, which on the surface was so warm it seemed without temperature, grows colder and colder as she descends. She swims past a jagged ledge, and then a crevice where two boulders come together, and then another ledge, keeping her eye on the vague white shape, and she is just about to run out of air when the thing is finally within her reach. Without ascertaining what it is, she snatches it from where it sits half on an underwater ledge, half fluttering in the depths. She can feel that it's fabric of some sort, heavy in her hands as she swims for the surface as quickly as she can.

She bursts into daylight, gasping for air. After the silence underwater, the sounds around her now seem magnified: the water dripping from her ears and hair, the intake of her breath, a dog barking in the distance. She swims to the quarry's edge, grasps the ledge, and spreads the white thing out. It is a man's T-shirt, dripping, stained, and heavy with water. Beneath the cartoonish image of a pint of beer, faded lettering reads: I Get My Kicks at Vic's.

Joan and Anders get up not long after Eve. Joan wakes up when she feels the mattress sink beneath her weight as Anders gets out of bed, as if it were a water bed. Her heart sinks in much the same way when reality floods onto the briefly, blissfully blank slate of her mind, when she remembers the truck in the quarry, the covered furniture, the bags and crates in the hallway. And of course, like every morning, Sophie. She wonders when she'll ever shake that feeling.

She doesn't like transitions, and as has been true every summer they've spent in this house, since long before the girls were born, she knows she cannot possibly feel settled here until their clothing is unpacked, their things put away, and, this year, that poor man's truck pulled from the quarry floor. At least, she thinks, they have gotten the body out. She's not sure she could live with that. She puts on yesterday's clothes, which she

33

left folded on the bench at the foot of the bed, and goes downstairs, leaving Anders in the bathroom brushing his teeth.

The first floor of the house, aside from the kitchen, is one large, open space divided into the suggestion of proper rooms by the arrangement of furniture. A couch and two large armchairs are gathered around a sturdy coffee table trunk in the evocation of a living room. A dining table resides by the large, multipaned bay window that looks out over the quarry. Bookcases line the far wall, in front of which is an Oriental carpet—the only carpet to cover the room's otherwise bare, wooden floorboards. There are beanbag chairs and pillows on the carpet, which is where some days in the past the girls have built their Lincoln Log villages and set up their train tracks, and where on other days they have curled up to read.

Joan wanders through the room, pulling off the sheets that have covered the furniture all winter. It smells musty; the house isn't winterized, and a good deal of moisture seems to have accumulated this year. They have been talking about winterizing the house for the twenty years they've owned it, but for various reasons they've never had it done. The house had originally belonged to an eccentric sculptor who would spend his summers here. Joan has heard he kept seals and swans in the quarry, and threw parties at which musicians performed on a floating stage. When he died, he left the house to his housekeeper, who let it fall into disrepair as she aged; by the time she died, it was in bad enough shape that Joan and Anders were able to buy it for a steal, along with several odds and ends inside—the Oriental carpet, the coffee table trunk, a gaudy set of crystal plates, all of which raise more questions than they answer about the man, and oftentimes have made Joan feel as if they're living with a ghost. Joan had spent her childhood summers on Cape Ann in a house that her grandmother owned, and that to Joan's dismay had to be sold upon her death to cover various debts, and so, when on a nostalgic visit here she and Anders accidentally discovered this house, Joan could hardly resist. It required a lot of work to slowly restore it, and Joan had always envisioned winterization as the point of completion to their efforts. But then one year the house in Maryland needed a new roof, and another year they thought they might be moving to London, and then they had three girls to get through school. Joan has always wanted to see the quarry frozen, a football field of smooth black ice, but she never has; the few times they have been able to come up in winter have always been too warm.

She brings the sheets to the laundry room and kneels down behind the washing machine to hook it up for the season when she hears Anders' footsteps behind her.

"I thought I'd go get donuts," he says.

"Oh, don't do that," Joan says. She is hooking up the dryer now, trying to fit the stubborn plug into its socket. "Let's go out when the girls get up. I could use something substantial." She crawls backward on her knees out from behind the machines and stands up, brushing her hands off on her thighs. "We could go to George's."

Anders helps her push the washer and the dryer back against the wall. He, too, is wearing yesterday's clothes, Joan sees, and he has had a shave. A small white square of toilet paper clings to his neck, and something about this, the vulnerability it suggests, strikes Joan's heart with a bolt of distress. Anders has aged since October, the manifestation of a sadness that Joan is both desperate and helpless to ease. And the facts of his graying hair, his deepening wrinkles, have propelled her imagination through the years to consider a time when she might be without him. She frowns.

"You cut yourself," she comments.

Anders touches the spot. "Last year's razor. Somehow I managed to forget mine."

"I hate to think what I've forgotten," Joan says. She sighs, giving the dryer a final push into place with her backside. She goes to the sink to wash her hands, which are dusty from the tubes and wires behind the machines.

"They're coming with a towing rig later today

to bring the car up," Anders says, over the sound of the water. "Truck, rather. Apparently it was a pickup. They're coming from Rowley, I guess."

"Right, you said last night." Joan rinses her hands. That it was a pickup in their quarry was one of the few things Anders had said last night, after he had come to bed. They hadn't talked about the irony of what had happened, though it seems impossible to Joan that he hadn't been thinking about it, too.

She shuts off the tap and turns around. "I hoped at first when I woke up it was a dream." She gives a laugh. "I wish."

"Hmm," Anders says. "Talk about a welcome."

"What time are they coming?"

"They said between two and four. Whatever that means."

Joan bends down to retrieve the laundry detergent from the cabinet beneath the sink, shaking her head. "The whole thing is just sort of hard to believe," she says, standing. "I don't even want to think about it, really. It makes me feel ill."

"Well. There's a book in it for you, anyway."

Joan regards her husband reproachfully. "Maybe someday." She wants to wonder aloud about the young man's reasoning for driving himself into their quarry, if that's what happened, about the family he may have left behind. She wants to acknowledge the parallels between what happened with Sophie and what may have happened here. "I'm going to run the washer," she says instead, holding back because she is afraid of dwelling with him there too much. "Would you bring the bags upstairs, and whatever else? Then maybe the girls will be up, and we can go. I'm starving."

Joan listens to Anders' footsteps on the stairs as she dumps detergent into the washing machine. They are slow and plodding, ponderous. She imagines him carrying up not one or two bags at a time, but laboring up the stairs with as many duffels as he can carry at once, bending under their weight; she imagines them as physical manifestations of his sadness. She sets the washing machine running and watches water cascade over the lip of the agitator and onto the dusty white sheets, waiting until it has filled before shutting the door. She spreads her hands on top of the machine, letting its vibrations travel through her body as it begins to wash, listening to the creak of the floorboards overhead as Anders deposits a suitcase here, a duffel there, settling them in.

She is thirsty. She goes into the kitchen and takes a glass from the cabinet. The glass is dirty; there is a dead spider at the bottom, traces of dust and cobwebs. She sets this glass aside and takes another; this one, too, is filthy. She scans the glasses in the cabinet; all of them have spent the winter right-side up, the receptacles of dirt, dust, and insects.

Her automatic assumption is to blame Anders, who is usually the one to put the house away, covering the indoor furniture with sheets and bringing the outdoor furniture to the garage, unhooking the washer and dryer, and overturning the glasses in the cabinet, while Joan herself packs up their things for the trip home, strips the beds, and cleans out the refrigerator. But just as quickly as she leaps to blame him, she remembers that he hadn't been in charge of these things last year. He'd had to go back to Maryland early for a music seminar, and packing up had been left to her and the girls alone.

She thinks back to the day of their departure, and how the oppressive heat of the week had finally given way to Sunday's torrential rain. In her mind's eye, she can see Eve and Sophie at either end of a wicker couch, their shorts and T-shirts pasted to their bodies. Eloise, she remembers, was upstairs howling in pain from swimmer's ear whenever the effect of her eardrops wore off, which was frequently. The roof in the upstairs bathroom had developed a leak, and one of the car tires was flat. Joan had been hassled, cranky; Sophie and Eve were quietly helpful, tiptoeing around their mother, carrying furniture through the rain, covering their duffels with garbage bags to get them dryly to the car, performing tasks she hadn't even asked them to do. And then Joan remembers—she had been unplugging the washer and dryer in the laundry room when she had heard a glass break. In the kitchen, Sophie had just begun the process of turning over the glasses when she'd let one slip, and this small accident was, for Joan, the final straw. She remembers cursing. *Jesus Christ, Sophie,* she'd said. *Try to be a little more careful.* She remembers angrily taking the broom from the closet to sweep up the shards of glass. *It's a glass, Mom,* Sophie had said. She reached for another glass, and then she shook her head. *Forget it. You can do it.* And with that she'd left the room.

It was just a glass, Joan thinks now, feeling punished by the memory. At the time, there was Eloise wailing upstairs, and Anders gone, and the rain, and the roof, and the flat tire on the car. But it was just a glass.

Joan brings the dirty glass in her hands now to the sink to wash it out. At home in Maryland, these types of memories—ones triggered by objects, by certain articles of clothing, by stains on a rug or drawings on the wall—have been visited and visited again each time the object or the stain or the drawing is encountered, and finally their potency has begun to fade. In Maryland, Sophie's absence has slowly woven itself into the fabric of reality. Not so here, Joan realizes. Here they are encountering her absence for the first time. Here they will have to endure the pain of losing her all over again.

Eve stands barefoot on the pedals of her bike as she coasts downhill on the unpaved road that leads away from their house through the woods toward the main road and the local variety store, where she'll pick up the paper for her parents as she does most summer mornings, though usually with Sophie. She can feel her cheeks trembling as she speeds over ruts and rocks, and the wind makes tears roll back from the corners of her eyes. Her hair is still wet, and her shorts and T-shirt are dampened by her wet bathing suit underneath. The T-shirt she found in the quarry she has left drying on a ledge in the sun—on the ledge where its presumed owner was laid last night, a vessel forever emptied of the body that used to fill it. Eve shudders with a morbid excitement to consider it; though grim, the discovery is electrifying.

She skids to a stop where the dirt road spills out onto the main road that circumnavigates the cape, tracing the coastline. From here, she can see all of Ipswich Bay spreading goblet shaped before her. She pedals across the street to the edge of the road, sets a foot down for balance. Below her, at the water's edge, crabs scuttle the mud, and egrets stand patiently, still, flightless.

Out across the bay, Hog Island hulks on the horizon, a dark shape against the sky. She can smell low tide, rotten and fresh at once, and she is filled suddenly with a longing ache, though she doesn't need to long for this place anymore; she is here, at last. But the ache remains, because it is not the same; she is here, at last, but alone.

She takes her free foot from where it rests on the pedal of her bike and angrily kicks a rock, cringing at the pain in her bare toe. The rock, though hardly bigger than a grape, makes a loud splash in the shallows, startling the egrets into stiff and labored flight. They resettle only yards from where they were, sink again into the mud and their heavy-lidded waiting. Eve glances down at her toe; a flap of skin has peeled away from its tip, and the raw skin beneath is still white the way a wound is before it realizes itself and begins to bleed. "Fuck," Eve says. This toe will be stubbed all summer now.

Anders has deposited each bag and crate where it belongs, the final bag his own. This he has put down in front of his dresser, where a brochure from the local dive shop sits among the seashells and driftwood and old anniversary cards that have collected there over the years, beside his wallet and planner and the contact card of one of the officers from last night. Anders brings the brochure over to the window, the many panes of which are breaking the early sunlight into bright squares across the floor, and then, when he opens the brochure, across its glossy surface. The brochure features photographs of divers gathered on a beach before a dive, of a red and white flag bobbing on the surface of the water, of various sea creatures: orange starfish, sea anemone, a shark.

For Father's Day, his family—Joan, really—has given Anders scuba diving lessons. She'd folded into his Father's Day card this brochure, which describes the various diving classes offered, and she had circled the one she'd signed him up for: a two-part group course, with six students, which meets twice a week for the first six weeks of summer. The first class is on Monday, the day after tomorrow. Anders is ambivalent about the prospect. He does vaguely remember expressing curiosity about diving one night this spring, as they watched some deep-sea program on TV, but it seems to him that swimming among coral reefs and exotic fish is one thing; getting into a wet suit and gathering around the edge of some pool with a group of strangers is another entirely. And it isn't just wet suits; he thinks of the divers last night, with their masks and fins and tanks and weight belts and regulators and all the other gadgets they'd had to strap to their bodies. Anders is generally wary of activities that require so much gear. But beyond that, the idea of scuba diving has always somewhat terrified him. To be willingly separated from one's own death by virtue of only a fallible oxygen tank seems crazy to him. He has read of more than a few local divers over the years who have drowned in the waters off Cape Ann, and his imagination always brings him to those last horrifying moments without air even as a world of it lies only meters above.

Since October, Joan has signed Anders up for other classes in addition to this one, as if he were a child she had to keep occupied. She signed him up for a watercolor class this winter that met every Tuesday evening at a local gallery. This spring, she signed him up for a cooking class that met on Saturday afternoons. She encouraged him to join her yoga class, though she didn't actually sign him up for it, and he didn't go. Anders knows what his wife is doing; she makes no effort to disguise her motives. She believes that he's been depressed since Sophie died, and that these new activities will somehow distract him from his sadness. Privately Anders thinks it's natural that he should be melancholy, and he has gone to these classes not so much for therapeutic reasons as much as he has to placate his wife. Joan has also tried to get him to join a group for grieving fathers, similar to the one she attends for mothers, but this he has refused to do. He doesn't want to share his grief with strangers.

Anders rubs his eyes with the fingers of one

hand, thinking vaguely of the irony of the fact that Joan, in trying to distract him from death with this latest class, is actually bringing him closer to a confrontation with what to him represents such proximity to it. He folds the brochure and slips it into his pocket, looks out the window. The breeze is silvering the leaves of the birch trees behind the garden, where his roses appear to be struggling. Some of them have bloomed, though not as many as usual for this time of year, and Anders can tell by the scarcity of leaves that something isn't right. He planted the rose garden nearly a decade ago, each bush with blooms a different color: pink, red, yellow, white, burgundy. And pink-tipped peach, Sophie's favorite. He frowns.

Often the fact that his daughter has died does not seem real to Anders. When he left for Rome with the high school choral group that Monday morning in October the week that Sophie died, he left behind a very different life from the one he would return to just days later, and he has been left with the feeling that he missed out on the most transformative event of his life. His experience was not, as Joan's was, of phone calls from the police, of hospitals and morgues and bodies and other things that would have both insisted and affirmed that what was happening was real. His experience was instead of waiting three hours in line to get through security at the airport, and then of waiting for a flight that was seven hours delayed. His experience was of sitting at the gate next to a woman who had tried to show him pictures of her new grandchild, of being offered peanuts—peanuts!—on the plane. He had felt acutely as if the world were somehow mocking him as he tried to navigate the everyday mundane while carrying the unfathomable burden of his daughter's death. When finally he arrived home, it was to a life that had, without warning, been radically altered in his absence, and he wonders, if he'd been there to experience the awful nuts and bolts of the change, whether it might somehow make more sense.

Anders rubs his eyes again. He can hear through the floorboards the sound of glasses clinking in the kitchen below, and he turns from the window to go downstairs. After standing in the bright light of the window, it takes a moment for his eyes to adjust to the darkness of the hallway. His and Joan's bedroom is at the end of the hall; he passes the bathroom on his right, and to his left, the door to Eve's, then Eloise's room. In front of Sophie's room, he pauses, and after a moment of hesitation, pushes open the door and looks within. He is aware that the room is exactly how she left it, tidy and bare but for a magazine on the corner of her desk, a handful of pencils in an I♥NY mug, a pair of earrings affixed to the shade of the lamp on her dresser, and, above this, a photo of all three girls after one of Sophie's soccer games tucked into the corner of the mirror frame. He gazes around the room, frowning, and then, gently, he shuts the door and quietly continues down the hall.

"No shoes?"

Arthur sits behind the counter, his black head of hair bent down over a newspaper. His voice is gruff. His voice is always gruff. Eve stands in the doorway of the store and looks down at her bare feet; she holds her stubbed toe up off the floor so as not to track any blood on the linoleum tiles, which are always vaguely dirty anyway. The store, and Arthur, have been here for as long as Eve can remember, selling the usual variety store assortment of soda, chips, juice, and candy, and behind the counter, cigarettes, travel-sized toiletries, batteries, and film. It also supplies basic things—peanut butter, toilet paper, white bread, ketchup, and an assortment of canned goods that have sat on the shelves untouched for so long that a layer of dust has settled on their lids.

"I never wear shoes," she says.

"I know," Arthur says, still looking down at the paper. "And I've told you about my neighbor growing up who rode his bike barefoot."

"And his foot slipped back into the spokes and his heel sliced off."

"Happy summer," Arthur says, lifting his eyes from the paper for the first time. "I was wondering when you were going to appear."

"How did you know it was me, anyway?"

"A hunch."

Eve rolls her eyes. She crosses the room to the refrigerator for a drink, and as she peruses her options, she can hear Arthur turning the pages of the newspaper.

"So tell me about this suicide," he says.

Eve feels herself grow suddenly hot. "What?" she says, too quickly. She turns around.

He lifts the paper and waves it in front of him. "The guy in your quarry," he says.

Eve blinks. "Oh," she says, though she can feel the flush still in her cheeks. She pulls out a lemonade and then slides the door shut. Arthur flips the paper around and spreads it out on the counter, and Eve steps over to look at it.

Inside, there is a small picture of the divers pulling the man from the water. In the photograph, you cannot see the man's face, but the image is etched firmly in Eve's mind: bluish skin, bruised cheek. She shudders. Behind the divers, back near the ambulance, she and her father stand awkwardly, both of them looking a little lost, near unrecognizable. She stares at the image, unhappily revisited by the sensation she had this morning of feeling wholly disconnected from a former self, and this one only from last night. "Suicide," she repeats, finally. "Is that what they're calling it?"

Arthur shrugs. "Accident, suicide," he says, as if these were one and the same.

Eve swallows her protest. "I'm surprised it made it into the paper," she says, instead. "That was just last night."

"Well, they managed to slip it in," Arthur says.

"Evidently." Eve blurs her eyes at the photograph until it is out of focus. She is aware of Arthur's gaze upon her, which makes her acutely uncomfortable. She doesn't know whether he knows what has happened with Sophie and is looking at her with a sympathy she doesn't want, or if he doesn't know and is beginning to register the fact that she has appeared at the store this morning uncharacteristically alone. She prefers neither alternative; she doesn't want to be the object of pity, nor does she want to have to explain.

"Anyway," she says, to ward off further conversation, hastily grabbing a paper from the rack and putting it under her arm. She takes a few wet bills from her shorts pocket and puts them on the counter. "See you, Arthur," she calls over her shoulder as she bolts.

Eve leaves her bike lying on its side in the grass at the edge of the driveway. She can see through the kitchen window that her family is up. Or her parents, anyway. Her father is sitting at the kitchen table, and her mother is at the sink. As Eve crosses the grass, steam from the water fogs the window, slowly obscuring her parents from view.

When she lets the screen door slam behind her, her mother shoots her a look. "Your sister's sleeping," she says.

"It's eight-fifteen!"

"And she was up well past her bedtime. You know she'll be a grouch otherwise."

Eve rolls her eyes and tosses the newspaper onto the table. "I brought the paper," she says. "You're welcome. It's most interesting, today."

"Thank you, Eve." Her mother turns off the faucet and dries her hands on her shorts.

Eve pulls out a chair at the kitchen table and sits down across from her father, who reaches for the newspaper, sliding away from him a brochure that Eve recognizes from the photographs on the front.

Eve lifts it from the table. "So, time to cash in," she comments.

"Or else wimp out," Joan says, leaning back against the counter.

"What do you mean?"

"Your father's waffling."

"What do you mean he's waffling? What's there to waffle about?"

"He thinks he's too old to take up things like scuba diving."

"I am," Anders says, opening the paper.

"You are not," Eve says. "You weren't too old to take up snowboarding last year."

"That was last year." Anders looks out from behind the paper. "And I broke my wrist!"

"Come on, Dad! It says here that the prerequisites are: *'the ability to swim, good health, a love for being in the ocean. Minimum age, twelve years.'* It doesn't say anything about a maximum age."

"Good health," Anders says, and grins halfheartedly. "I have acid reflux."

" *'Good health,'* " Eve reads. "They define it. *'Normal, healthy heart, lungs, ears, and sinuses. Circulatory and respiratory systems and body air spaces are healthy and normal. No severe emotional or neurological problems.'* It doesn't say anything about acid reflux."

Anders sighs. "We'll see," he says. He lowers the paper onto the table. "They made quick work of our body."

"It's in the paper?" Joan asks. "What does it say?" She comes around the table to look over her husband's shoulder.

Anders snaps the paper straight again. "Not much, at this point," he says. " *'Body retrieved from quarry,'* " he reads. " *'Authorities say the body of a Gloucester man was pulled last night from a private quarry in Lanesville. Officials confirmed it was the body of James P. Favazza, twenty-seven, who was reportedly last seen at his mother's apartment on Magnolia Street late Friday morning. It appears that Mr. Favazza drove his car into the quarry sometime Friday afternoon. Officials said Favazza's wallet, including cash, were on him when he was pulled from the water. Officials believe that there was no foul play involved in the incident, although an autopsy will be conducted to determine the cause of death.'"*

Eve sits back and folds her arms across her chest. "I don't understand why they rule out foul play right out of hand," she says. "I mean, think about it. It's kind of a big mistake to 'accidentally' drive into a quarry. And there are a lot of other, easier ways to off yourself, if that's what they're thinking." *Like driving onto the train tracks,* she almost says, but she stops herself. "But there *aren't* a lot of convenient places to dump a body," she finishes instead.

"Eve," Joan says.

"It's true. You have this secluded quarry where nobody's been for months. Who even *knows* how many bodies could be down there?"

"Eve," Joan says again.

"Plus they're doing an autopsy. Why would they bother doing an autopsy if they're so sure there was no foul play?"

"I'd say it's probably a matter of procedure," Anders says. "They need to be one hundred percent sure. And they probably want to check for other things—I'd imagine they'd do a toxicology report, for instance, to see whether there were drugs in his system, or alcohol, which would suggest, you know, maybe a drunken accident."

"But if they need an autopsy to be one hundred percent sure, that means they aren't one hundred percent sure. What if it comes back that he went into the quarry already dead? From, I don't know, blunt trauma to the head or something? It's going to be too late to figure out what really happened. They should at least investigate a *little.* I mean, there was a *body* in our *quarry.*"

"A body?" Joan, Eve, and Anders turn; Eloise has appeared in the doorway, still dressed in her Pluto nightshirt, a look of distress on her face. "A *body?* I am *never* going in the quarry again!"

Two

Years ago, when they'd first bought the house, Anders spent a summer building a stone wall to run along the back edge of what would later become his rose garden. He hired a local guy with a flatbed truck and a block and tackle rig to help him transport rocks from the woods to the yard. They stacked the rocks waist high against the incline of the hill at the back of the garden, assembling the wall in such a way that it looks not so much like it's leaning against the hillside as much as it's holding the hillside in. Over the years, Anders has wedged various trinkets into the wall's nooks and crannies, so that the wall itself has almost become a piece of art. There are old porcelain dolls, small rounded stones collected from the beach, bits of pipe, a clay rabbit made by Eloise one year in a summer art class, an old glass Coke bottle, seashells, a thin length of metal bent into the curling shape of a treble clef. There is an army of old tin soldiers that Joan once found antiquing. They are confederates, by the faded look of their painted uniforms, but Anders split the army into two and arranged them in opposing battle formation among the stones, leaving them on the perpetual brink of war. His wall is somewhere between a family joke and a legend;

in any case, it has made him a frequent recipient of random trinkets. It is rare for a birthday or Christmas to go by without his receiving something meant to be added to the wall.

This year for Christmas, Eve gave him a copper compass rose, about the diameter of a tennis ball. He and his daughter stand in front of the garden now, looking over the tops of the roses at the wall and trying to decide where the compass rose would fit best. Joan has taken Eloise to the beach while Eve and Anders wait for the tow truck and more divers to come retrieve James Favazza's truck from the quarry.

Anders holds the compass rose out at arm's length. "Over there, you think?" he asks.

"Mmm." Eve sounds uncertain. "Over, I think. To the right."

Anders moves his arm. "There?"

"Over more."

Anders moves his arm farther. "Good?"

"I'll show you." Eve picks her way through the roses and points to a spot between a small black wishing stone and a marble. She points. "Here," she says.

Anders nods and walks carefully through the roses himself. Their leaves, he notices with dismay, are covered with brown and black spots, which can't be a good thing. He squats down before the wall. "I suppose up should be north," he says.

"I guess."

Anders nestles the compass rose into the nook that Eve has chosen. "There," he says. He looks up at his daughter for approval. But she is looking out over the quarry, her face concerned.

"There's more gas," she says. "The truck's still leaking gas. There's more than there was this morning."

"It may still be," Anders says thoughtfully. He stands, brushes his hands off on his thighs. "But even if it is, the truck's coming out now, anyway."

"Where *are* they, anyway?" Eve lets out an impatient breath and turns to leave the garden. Anders watches her go, seemingly oblivious to the scratch of thorns against her bare legs, though he can't imagine that she doesn't feel them. She walks to the far edge of the quarry, where the gas slick has gathered, and crouches down.

Anders frowns. He has spent most of the day with Eve. After breakfast at George's, while Eloise and Joan took the station wagon to the grocery store, Eve had chosen to accompany Anders in the old Buick to the Building Center. He had thought the Buick, a convertible that spent the winter underneath a tarp in the garage and that Joan and Eloise have now taken to the beach, would lighten Eve's mood, but as Anders did his errands, Eve had only trailed behind him wordlessly, clearly preoccupied. He tried to talk to her about how she felt about tenth grade, and whether she thought she'd go out for varsity lacrosse this year; she shrugged. He tried to talk to her about what she planned to do this summer, since at the last minute she'd opted out of the program she'd been enrolled in, building houses in South America; she shot him a look and wondered aloud whether Joan had put him up to the question. The only topic she showed an interest in discussing was the truck in their quarry, and how it may have come to be there.

Eve has always been free spirited, independent, and tough, but lately that toughness has become impenetrable, sometimes abrasive. Anders understands that Sophie's death has left her reeling, but it is not something she is willing to discuss. Anders isn't sure, even if she were willing, what he would say, and the niggling knowledge that he should fills him with a dual sense of responsibility and failure.

Anders turns around, bends down to make sure the compass rose is securely in place before leaving the garden. He pauses, unsure of whether to go to his daughter, who is still crouched down at the water's edge, or to leave her be and start bringing out the rest of the porch furniture from the garage. He has, he feels, nothing to offer her—no solace, no understanding or explanation—as much as he wishes that he did. Before he can decide one way or the other, suddenly Eve stands, and then Anders can hear what has gotten his daughter's attention: the growing sound of crunching gravel. The tow truck is finally making its way up the drive.

Their local beach is at the head of a rocky cove, and at high tide is just a small strip of sand. This afternoon the tide is out; lines of pebbles and seaweed stripe the beach, making it look as if the tide has gone out in discrete steps instead of gradually receding, every stripe a record of what each retreating wave has left behind. Joan has rarely seen the tide so low; off the point, clammers are out on mudflats she didn't know existed, their cuffed pants like bells around their legs, and the sandbar extends beyond its normal bounds into the bay.

Eloise has spent the past half hour burying her mother; Joan lies in a trough covered by sand. Her daughter has carefully sculpted her body into the shape of a mermaid, her lower half neatly scaled with mussel shells, her wrists adorned with seaweed bracelets. Eloise has also built her two large breasts, the nipples of which she has covered with sand dollars. Or maybe the sand dollars *are* her nipples; Joan isn't sure. Right now, Eloise is at the edge of the beach, among the rocks, in search of other objects with which to decorate her mermaid mother.

The sand feels good. It is a cool and reassuring weight, and though part of her is curious about what is going on at the quarry, Joan is just as glad to be here. For a weekend, the beach is quiet; there are a handful of teenage girls sunbathing, and a young couple with a naked baby, and a very large woman who has been effortlessly floating since they arrived almost an hour ago, her body its own raft. Her endurance is impressive; Joan felt the water with her toe when they first arrived, and it is frigid.

There is a small plane performing stunts overhead, barrel rolls and loop-the-loops. Joan watches it anxiously, remembering the time when Sophie and Eve were young, before Eloise, when they saw from the beach a stunt plane like this one fall from the sky. Typical, she thinks, if today of all days, this year of all years, this should happen to happen again.

Suddenly Eloise appears above her, eclipsing the sun. Joan squints up at her daughter. "What have you got for me now?" she asks.

"This," Eloise says angrily, thrusting forward a dead seagull by its rubbery webbed foot.

"Oh, Eloise! Put that down!"

Eloise deposits the bird on the sand beside her mother. Though Joan's impulse would ordinarily be to move away, she stays put beneath her mermaid skin. The gull is small, and Joan can tell by the soft brown of its feathers that it is very young. It is newly dead; it has not yet been scavenged by bugs or other birds, nor does it have the deflated appearance that the carcasses of small creatures usually seem to have. It is completely tangled in fishing line; the clear wire is wrapped around its legs, its beak, and even around one of its wings, which suggests to Joan that the more the creature tried to free itself, the more mired it became.

"It was next to a tide pool," Eloise says. "Some stupid fisherman littered and now it's dead." She sits down, props her elbows on her knees and her cheeks in her hands.

Joan sits up, knocking the sand from her torso. "It doesn't seem fair, does it."

"It's *not* fair."

Joan wiggles her legs free of sand. Mussel shells go sliding. She wraps her arms loosely around her knees and studies her daughter, who is staring intently into the sand. "Maybe we should give it a burial," Joan suggests.

Eloise digs her heels into the sand. "Maybe we should just throw it into the quarry," she says.

Eloise has been quietly thoughtful since she learned this morning that there indeed had been a body in the quarry, no doubt carefully processing the information, and likely coming up with all sorts of horror stories to explain the event. Joan has not pushed her to share her thoughts, but now she nudges her daughter gently. "Hey," she says. "What are you thinking?"

Eloise lets out a weary breath. "I want to go back to Maryland."

"We're here, though," Joan says. "It was a terrible thing to arrive to, but we can't let it ruin the summer."

"What if we're haunted now?"

"We won't be haunted."

"How do you know?"

Joan takes a breath. When their old dog, Buster, died last summer, Joan had made what she now fears may have been a mistake by telling Eloise to imagine that Buster's spirit would always be with them. She'd said it was like having an invisible dog. She hadn't meant to inspire a belief in ghosts. After Sophie died, Eloise had asked seriously if it was like having an invisible sister now, and when Joan said that in a way it was, she saw a distinct glimmer of fear pass across her daughter's face. "So, Sophie is a ghost?" Eloise had asked. Joan had quickly tried to differentiate between spirits and ghosts, but she's not sure she made the distinction clear enough. In the end, it was Eve's quietly brutal reasoning that seemed to placate Eloise most; why, Eve had pointed out, would Sophie come back as a ghost when her whole purpose in dying was to get away?

"I just know," Joan says now, finally, loathe to invoke Eve's logic again.

Eloise rubs her eye. "Why did he have to pick *our* quarry?"

"I don't know. I don't think we'll ever know." Joan can think of nothing that might offer comfort. It occurs to her momentarily to point out that probably people have died on this very beach, and that they drive by spots where people have died every day on the highway, and Eloise doesn't consider these places haunted. But she thinks better of this; she understands that observations like these would hardly make her daughter feel more secure. "Let's go do something to get our mind off things. What do you feel like doing?"

Eloise sighs, and then gives her mother a serious look. Joan waits for the impossible, like "going back to Maryland," but, "Ice cream," Eloise finally says. "Can we go to Salah's?"

Once it finally arrives, the tow truck is unlike any Eve has ever seen. It's enormous, with a large crane folded on the back, giving the whole rig the leggy look of a cricket or a praying mantis. The driver—the tag sewn onto his shirt reads Tim—has backed it over the grass to the edge of the quarry, where Anders has directed him, and is now getting everything ready for the task at hand. He presses a button and flaps extend from either side of the truck, two near the back wheels, two near the front.

Eve asks Tim what the flaps are for, and in response, he presses a second button that lowers the flaps to the ground. "Stability," he says. He pulls down on a lever. The crane begins to extend.

Eve watches, cringing at the sound of metal sliding against metal. "How high does it go?" she asks.

"Forty feet." Tim rotates the base of the crane just a bit so that it's angled out over the water. "Longest stage two rotator in the industry. Fifty-ton capacity."

"That's a lot," Eve says, absently pulling up clumps of grass with her bare toes. "What would you ever need to lift that's fifty tons?"

"You never know," Tim says. He disappears around the other side of the truck. Eve can hear gears shifting and the hissing sound of hydraulics, but she doesn't see anything happening.

"What are you doing, anyway?"

The rig emits a few more sounds before Tim answers. "Prepping the drag winch," he says. "You ask a lot of questions."

Eve flattens her mouth. She looks across the grass to where her father stands talking with the policeman who has also finally arrived, and two divers, who are not the same divers as last night. She is disappointed—she'd have liked to ask them what else they saw down there—but she isn't surprised. Eve supposes you couldn't pay them to dive here again.

Tim reappears around the side of the truck. He leans back against the rig, rolling his shoulders with a grimace. He sniffs, then folds his arms. He seems vaguely bored to Eve, which annoys her. She thinks of all the boring jobs he could have been called to do today, towing cars that have broken down on the side of the highway, or that are illegally parked and blocking driveways or fire hydrants. "You *don't* ask a lot of questions," she comments.

Tim looks at her.

"Aren't you curious why you're pulling a pickup truck from the bottom of a quarry?"

Tim moves his jaw from side to side as if he has to give the question some thought before answering. But he never answers, and shifts his attention to Anders and the divers and the policeman, who are walking across the grass toward them.

Anders motions to Eve to get out of the way as Tim begins to give the divers basic instructions on how to connect the cable to the tow hook, and where to find the tow hook underneath the body of the pickup. The policeman stands off to the side, filling out paperwork on a clipboard.

"Shouldn't they have sent a detective?" Eve asks her father in a low voice. "Aren't policemen more like first responders?"

"I don't know," Anders says. "I don't know what they'd send a detective for."

"Right. Because there was so obviously no foul play."

Anders doesn't answer.

The divers put on their masks and headlamps and flippers. One gets into the water, and the other guides the cable in his direction, which Tim is lowering using controls on the side of the truck. The first diver grabs hold of the hook at the end of the cable and waits for the second diver to climb into the water.

Eve gives her father a nudge in the side. "Do you think the divers from last night didn't want to come back, or do you think it's just a different shift?" she whispers.

"I'd say probably both," Anders whispers back.

"If this happens next year, *you* can dive down," she jokes. "Actually, Dad," she continues, her whisper growing louder with excitement, "you really *should,* anyway. I mean—"

"Shhh," Anders hushes her, gesturing with his chin toward the divers, two black heads bobbing on the water.

In a moment, they disappear beneath the surface, and then there is just the sound of the lowering cable and a steady stream of small bubbles. Anders and Eve stand together at the edge of the quarry, watching, and this suddenly makes Eve think of the photograph in the paper, because in it, she and her father are standing in just the same way.

"Dad," she says.

"Yuh."

"That picture," she says. "In the paper."

"What about it?"

"How do you think it got there? I mean, who took it? I didn't see any photographers or reporters or anything, did you?"

Anders considers this. "No," he says, after a pause. "I didn't. I suppose it might have been one of the policemen. I guess it wouldn't be unusual for them to want to document something like that."

Eve thinks of the policemen last night, how they'd stood around telling jokes and talking about beer. She doesn't think any of them could have been bothered with a photograph. She frowns and squats down, stares at the surface of the water, waiting. The cable has been reeled out as far as it needs to go; it moves slightly this way, and then that, as the divers, a hundred feet below, struggle in the darkness to affix it to the car. Eve watches, wondering about that photograph and how it might have come to be taken, if not by any of the cops. Maybe, it occurs to her, if this really was a murder, it was taken by the killer himself; she has heard about criminals who do that sort of thing, in books and movies—send in pictures of their own crime scenes.

Suddenly, the cable is still, and after several, seemingly endless minutes, the divers resurface. One of them gives Tim two thumbs-up, and, on the shore, Tim pulls a lever. The cable groans slowly upward for two or three minutes before Eve can see a disturbance in the water, and finally the shape of the pickup itself just beneath the surface. Tim adjusts the crane so he can raise the truck without it swinging against the rocks at the edge of the quarry. The pickup comes swelling slowly up through the surface: headlights, hood, then body.

Eve stands, takes a breath as the truck emerges fully from the water. It is an old, red Ford, with rusted spots on the door. The front bumper, Eve notices, is dented, and the back right taillight case is broken, a Red Sox bumper sticker above it. Water cascades from the pickup as it dangles. It pours out of the cab through the driver's-side window, which is smashed, and around the frame of the doors.

"Dad," Eve says, suddenly. "Why is the window smashed?"

"Probably because the divers last night couldn't open the door."

"But if you were going to kill yourself by driving into the water, wouldn't you do it with the car windows open?"

"I don't know, Eve," her father says. "Maybe he wasn't thinking rationally. Or maybe it was accidental. I just don't know." He glances at Eve, and his expression suggests that he is tiring of her suspicions. Eve crosses her arms, says nothing more.

The old Buick has always vaguely reminded Joan of a boat, something about its thudding engine, or its beamy interior; two or maybe even three more people could fit on the bench seat where she and Eloise sit now, their hair whipping about their faces as they follow the shoreline around the cape into town for ice cream. The Buick is a 1982 Riviera convertible, the same car that she and Anders drove cross country the summer before they were married and that any mention of selling in the past has elicited howls of protest from the girls. It is a totally impractical car, and at this point it could never withstand a lengthy drive, but each summer, after a jump start, to Joan's surprise the old thing still runs. And the truth is she loves to drive it, with its enormous, padded steering wheel, its wide leather seats, the gear shift coming from the steering column, the vintage radio.

It is just a few miles from the beach into town, and Joan drives slowly, careful to avoid potholes and dips in the pavement around the frequent drainage grates. Between the houses off to the right, she can catch glimpses of the two-mouthed river that separates the island where they live from the mainland of the cape, running between Ipswich Bay to the north and Gloucester Harbor to the south, crowded as usual on a summer Saturday with boats motoring in both directions.

Beside her, Eloise sits Indian style, peering

every now and then over her shoulder at the dead seagull, which lies on a towel in the backseat. That was the other thing that Eloise said would make her feel better: to bring the seagull home and give it a proper burial. Joan had tried to convince her that it would be a better idea to bury it on the beach, but Eloise insisted that the tide would only uncover it, that it would be swept to sea and eaten by fish or else caught up in the propeller of a boat, and in the end Joan found it easier to give in.

"Mom," Eloise says now.

Joan glances at her daughter.

"There's a lot of gas in the quarry. Evie said before that it was leaking all night."

"There is gas in the quarry, that's true."

"That's really bad, Mom. Once in Alaska a tanker crashed and all these birds had tons of oil all over their feathers and they couldn't fly. We saw it in science class."

Joan slows down as they approach the rotary. "That was different," she says, watching for a gap in traffic. "And it was gallons and gallons of oil. Hundreds and thousands of gallons. There's just a little bit of gas in our quarry. And we don't have birds who live there." She pulls into the rotary, waving thanks to a driver who has slowed to let them in.

Eloise frowns. "What about the turtles?"

"The turtles will be fine," Joan says. She sets

her blinker and takes the exit for downtown. "They know to stay away from it. And right now, maybe even as we speak, a huge tow truck is pulling the truck out of the quarry, so it won't be able to leak anymore. And we'll get people to come clean up the gas this week, and things will be good as new."

Eloise gazes out the window, her brow knit. "No," she says. "They won't."

Joan sighs and steers onto a side street, meandering along their way. She likes the backstreets of Gloucester, which are narrow and haphazard, crowded with old, two-story, bevel-sided houses with small front stoops and fenced-in side yards.

"Where are we going?" Eloise asks. "Aren't we getting ice cream?"

"Yes, but we're taking the long way," Joan says. "Looking around. Reminding ourselves, since we haven't been here in a year."

Eloise seems to accept this explanation, and in a way Joan supposes it's the truth. When she arrived here for the summer growing up, she would do the same thing, crisscrossing the town on her bicycle, revisiting all the places that by the summer's end she'd again take for granted, but that after a winter away had gained a certain magic. She'd do the same with her grandmother's house, wandering through every room and examining as if for the first time the oddities that had cluttered the house for years: a small chest in whose every drawer were pinned rows of boldly patterned butterflies; a large copper compass that was missing its needle; the huge, toothlike gears of the grandfather clock, which she'd set ticking. Her parents, both doctors in New York City, only came up to Gloucester on the occasional weekends when they could get away, and so Joan, an only child, spent the summers largely alone with her grandmother. She was generally shy, and more inclined to stay at home with her books or take solitary bike rides or explore the endless cabinets and closets of the house than she was to hang out with the local kids her age, who all already knew each other and seemed grouped into specific circles she didn't have the nerve to enter.

She supposes that if what she was really doing now was revisiting, she would drive past her grandmother's house where it sits by the harbor. But before she gets to the waterfront, she sees the street she has all along been vaguely looking for, even if she hadn't entirely admitted it to herself.

She slows down at the next small intersection and peers up at the crooked street sign that tells her she has found Magnolia Street. She sets her blinker and turns left, following the street slowly up a steep incline toward the top of Portuguese Hill. It is the highest point in Gloucester, and so of course Joan has ascended it before, which is why Magnolia Street, as one of the several ways up, would have rung a bell.

"I thought we were going to get ice cream," Eloise says.

"And we are," Joan says, gazing at the houses that line the street, and wondering which is James Favazza's mother's. The houses are all variations of the same: small, boxy colonials, some with aluminum awnings over their small stoops, all with hinged outer doors whose upper halves, which now are screen, in winter would be storm glass. They are slightly smaller than the houses in other parts of town, and they come up nearly flush to the sidewalk, with barely room for even a small front yard. In one driveway, a man is giving his car a wash, and on the sidewalk opposite, some kids about Eloise's age are squatted down drawing on the concrete with fat sticks of chalk. A cat sits on a sunny stoop, grooming itself, and a woman with a wide hat is watering the flowers in her window boxes. It strikes Joan that James Favazza was on this very street just yesterday, alive, and that behind one of these front doors today, his mother is living through the unthinkable. There is nothing to suggest it, though Joan hadn't really expected there to be. She can remember sitting numbly in the living room the morning after Sophie died, wondering when anything would ever seem of consequence again; food and coffee and cleanliness and the fact that sometime she had lost a contact lens and couldn't rightly see all seemed insignificant details, and yet the world outside carried on: every half hour, a bus pulled up at the stop across the street, planes crisscrossed overhead, a garbage truck lumbered groaning down the street. Sometimes it briefly occurred to her the things she'd be doing, too—how she had dry cleaning to pick up, and a dentist appointment to get a crown replaced. She runs her tongue over the uncapped tooth now; she'd never bothered to reschedule, as if waiting for the time when that sort of thing *did* seem of consequence again. She's not sure it ever will, entirely; sometimes still she'll pause in the middle of vacuuming or putting gas into the car during a busy morning of errands, overcome without warning by an exhausted sense of pointlessness, and it's all she can do to carry on going through what are suddenly revealed as empty motions.

"Mom?"

Joan blinks, realizing that she has let the car slow to a stop.

"Are you okay?"

"Of course," Joan says. "I'm okay. I was just remembering things." She steps lightly on the gas.

"Like what?"

"Oh, I don't know. Being a girl here in the summers, like you. Getting ice cream."

"From Salah's?"

"It was from Salah's, actually. It was about half the size that it is now, though."

"What flavor did you get?"

"Coffee. With jimmies."

"But that's what you get now," Eloise says, sounding mildly confused.

"Well, yes, it is. But I'm still the same person, right?"

Anders has been digging for half an hour, working to get a hole deep enough to bury the seagull Eloise has brought home from the beach. For the third time, he encounters a rock that blocks him from digging any deeper, but he knows it has to be at least another foot deeper to prevent fisher cats from digging the carcass up. When Buster died last summer, they buried him in the woods not far from here, and when Anders came outside the following morning he found the grave plundered, the dog's remains picked clean just yards away from where they'd laid him. Anders reburied what was left and never told his family what had happened.

He tries to find the edges of the rock, but it is far too large. He thrusts his shovel into the dirt, stands up straight, and wipes his brow. No wonder his roses are dying, he thinks, a miracle that they have lasted as long as they have in soil as rocky as this.

"Another rock in the way," he calls over to Eloise.

Eloise sits on the low branch of a nearby tree, blowing at a blade of grass between her thumbs, trying to get it to whistle. Finally she gives up and lets the grass flutter to the ground, where the seagull sits at the base of the tree in a plastic bag. "Maybe we should try somewhere else. Like on the lawn," she says.

They have taken the seagull with them a few yards into the woods for burial, and Eloise is right, the soil is probably rockier here than it is on the lawn. Anders looks over his shoulder toward the house, where he can see Joan arranging the porch furniture. "I don't think your mother would appreciate that," he says, though the tow truck has made so much of a mess of the lawn that a small seagull's grave would hardly make a difference. There are deep, muddy ruts from the tow truck's tires, and the stabilizing flaps have left large rectangular gouges in the grass. And as the crane maneuvered it from out over the water and onto the grass, James Favazza's pickup truck knocked a sizable branch from the dogwood tree, though it is still jaggedly attached. Anders tried to yank the branch free, thinking to drag it off into the woods before Joan saw the damage, but it's going to take a saw to make the break complete.

When the truck first rose from the quarry, as it hung there, slowly spinning, and they waited what seemed endlessly for the cab to empty of water, the scene had jogged a memory Anders had forgotten he had, one from his early youth, when his father had been in Vietnam and his mother had taken Anders and his sister to live at their grandparents' farm in upstate New York. He can't remember what the circumstances were, but in the memory he is alone in his grandfather's pickup truck. It is dark, and raining, and through the windshield he can see his grandfather working in the light of the pickup's headlight beams, using a scalpel to peel the hide from a deer strung above a pit. The deer hangs upside down from ropes twisted around ankles that are thin and fragile as a woman's wrist, and its naked body looks like muscles in a book, all red and ribbed and lined with white ribbons of fat. The pit beneath the deer steams in the rain.

He has no notion of the memory's context, and in this sense it is more of a snapshot than an actual memory; he does not know what came before, or what happened after. Nonetheless, at the sight of the truck dangling over the water, the image of the deer flashed into his mind, and he stood at the quarry's edge, briefly and entirely transported. He finds that memories *happen* to him this way often these days, vivid and, like dreams, unbidden. Some are familiar; others, like this one, he didn't know he had. It is an odd feeling to remember them; it gives him the sensation he gets from that dream in which you discover in your house rooms you didn't know were there.

Anders stares out at the mess of the lawn, and the spot where the truck earlier dangled. At the far end of the quarry, Eve is gathering up the beer cans and other debris, pulling these objects toward her with a long stick. The day, which had started cloudless and sunny, has darkened; he can see thunderheads beginning to gather on the horizon.

Anders turns around and grips the shovel. "Okay," he says, refilling the half-dug hole with dirt. "Let's give this another try before the rain."

It does indeed start to rain not long after Anders and Eloise finally get the seagull buried, and it continues on into the evening. It is not a steady rain, but a series of loud and battering summer thunderstorms that subside just as quickly as they begin. During each one, Eve stands at the window looking out at the quarry, imagining with growing agitation bits of evidence being washed away with every downpour. For dinner, Anders cooks hamburgers on the grill in a lull between storms, and they have homemade brownies for dessert. Afterward, Eloise brings out the old Monopoly board, and they play a marathon game, which Eve wins handily, putting up hotels on all her properties and bankrupting the rest of her family.

After everyone has gone to bed, Eve pulls out from under her bed all of the artifacts she's collected from the quarry and lays everything out across the floor. The T-shirt from Vic's has dried. It is size extra large, and stained with flecks of deep green paint. She has looked up Vic's in the phone book and discovered that it is a bar in downtown Gloucester, and the fact that he had a T-shirt from there suggests to her that James Favazza must have been a regular. In any case, she knows he definitely liked to drink, given the number of empty beer cans and bottles that she collected from the water. The cans are all Budweiser, but there are two kinds of bottles, both specialty beers that Eve has never heard of before.

Eve has also collected a cooler bag, which is mildewed on the inside and smells, unsurprisingly, of beer. The name L. Stephens is written on the side of the bag in permanent marker. She found several Stephenses in the phone book—Donald Stephens, M. Stephens, and Bertrand and Faye Stephens—but there was no listing for any Stephens whose first name begins with L. It occurred to her that L. Stephens could be the son or daughter of any of these other Stephenses, but she's not sure how to find out. If she knew what L. stood for—Liam or Lucy or Lars—she could call the other Stephens households and ask for someone by that name, but she can't very well call up and ask for L. But whoever L. is, she's decided, he could be an important piece of the puzzle. A drinking buddy, she's inclined to think, and very possibly aware of who might have wanted James Favazza dead.

In addition to the beer bottles, the T-shirt, the gas can, and the cooler, Eve has found a plastic purple bowl—the disposable kind you might take on a picnic—a beat-up water bottle from Eastern Mountain Sports, and a single blue men's flip-flop. She frowns, squats down in front of the flip-flop. It is well worn, particularly on the inside edge; the padding beneath the big toe and the heel has been worn down so much that it is only about a quarter of an inch thick. It feels strange to be able to see so clearly the imprint of James Favazza's foot. Tentatively, she slides the flip-flop onto her own foot. The arch is much higher than her own arch, and the pressure of it makes her feel oddly as if she were somehow foot to foot with James. She shudders and slips the sandal off again, and then she gathers the beer cans and the flip-flop and the T-shirt and every-thing else and puts it all into the cooler bag, which she zips and puts underneath her bed.

She stands and gazes around her bedroom. Though it's getting late, she isn't remotely tired; she feels restless and edgy. She opens the window and puts her head outside. It has stopped raining for good, it seems; she can see the moon flashing through the drifting clouds, and every now and then, a star. She pulls her head inside and crosses the room to her bedside table, where she stashed the cigarettes she found lying on the rock by the side of the road last night. They are Marlboro Reds, which she doesn't really like, but she figures they're better than the menthol cigarettes her mother keeps in her pocketbook and smokes so infrequently that they are more often than not old and stale.

Quietly, she goes downstairs and outside. The storms have cooled things off considerably; Eve shivers as she crosses the lawn, but she doesn't bother to go back inside for a sweatshirt. Instead, she walks around the quarry to its far side and proceeds a few dozen meters into the woods, where a large pyramid of unclaimed chunks of granite rises among the trees. Carefully, she makes her way around the base of the rocky pyramid and settles down in the crevice on its far side, where the rocks come together in the suggestion of a lawn chair. This is the spot where Sophie used to come and smoke in the summer, like the spot up in the limbs of the oak tree in Maryland. She didn't smoke often, and of course no one knew about it—their parents, or teachers, who all thought she was perfect—and her secret was safe with Eve. Only when she happened to feel like it, she said, or when she was feeling particularly thoughtful, which, Eve realizes now, was more and more often in the days and weeks leading up to her death; many nights when Eve looked out the window she saw a glowing ember up among the oak leaves. Eve wishes she knew what her sister had been feeling so thoughtful about. But.

In front of her, the woods stretch darkly away, loud with crickets and cicadas, and even though the house isn't far behind her, in the darkness Eve feels remote from everyone and everything. She lights a cigarette with a match, grimacing as she inhales, wishing that she liked smoking more than she does, but wanting to smoke anyway, so that she's not just sitting here in the dark. Sophie would kill her if she knew. She leans back and pulls her knees to her chest, tilts her head to look up at the rocks rising above her, black shapes against what sky she can make out through the canopy of trees. The moon, she sees, when the rolling clouds reveal it, is larger than it was last night, which means that a leftward-facing moon is on the wax. She tries to think of a way to make this solid in her memory, though she suspects that it will always be one of those things she can never remember, like the number of c's in *necessary* or *successful,* or how many feet there are in a mile.

After a minute, she is aware of the distant sound of footsteps in the woods; she freezes, listening, her eyes fixed on the glowing end of her cigarette. There are many paths that meander through the trees, circumventing the various quarries and firepits in the middle of Cape Ann, and oftentimes at night local kids will gather in the woods. But they travel in loud groups, their movement punctuated by shouts and laughter; these are solitary footsteps, accompanied only by the sounds of night bugs, the residual drip of water from the leaves. Hastily, yet carefully, Eve puts her cigarette out. She knows there's nothing really to be afraid of, but her heart is pounding nonetheless, and she keeps very still, listening intently, trying to stop herself from thinking about the potential murderer. The footsteps pause, then continue, picking their way carefully along. Part of her wants to get up and run to the house, but her own movement will surely be heard just as clearly as she can hear the movements of whoever is in the woods now, and so she stays where she is, waiting for the footsteps to pass.

But instead of passing, the footsteps grow louder, and then suddenly Eve sees the shape of a figure in the woods, much closer than she'd expected from the sound. She scrambles from her seat, tripping over a fallen branch as she tries to flee. She cries out, terrified, and has just gotten to her feet again when she hears someone call out her name.

"Eve!"

She turns around, her pulse still ticking wildly in her neck, though she immediately recognizes the voice.

"Saul?" she says, catching her breath, a little bit angry now and embarrassed by her terror.

"Hey." Saul turns on a flashlight, the beam bobbing in her direction as he steps closer. "I didn't mean to scare you."

"Then why the hell did you sneak up on me like that?"

"I didn't sneak up," he says.

"You didn't have your flashlight on. You didn't call out. You just . . . crept. I didn't know it was you."

"And I didn't know it was you. All I saw was the end of a cigarette. I thought it might be your mother."

Saul is standing in front of her now, and the fact of his presence is mildly disconcerting. She realizes that she hadn't expected to see him this summer, that in her mind it was almost as if he had died along with Sophie. And yet, here he is, utterly familiar and real.

"Well it was me," Eve says finally.

"And it was me. And I'm sorry if I scared you."

Eve climbs back onto her perch and looks at Saul suspiciously. "What are you doing here anyway?"

"Walking," he says.

"Walking?"

"Walking. Thinking. I wanted to get outside, after the rain." Saul sits down next to her. "I didn't know you smoked."

"I don't really," Eve says, feeling caught. "Just when I feel like it." She glances over at Saul, thinking that just as he has caught her, she has caught him, too, in a way. She wonders how much time he spends wandering around here, thinking about Sophie, remembering, and it makes her almost uncomfortable to consider. An image appears in her mind of Saul at Sophie's funeral, his eyes red and hollow, his shoulders slumped, as if the awkward suit he wore were a great weight. It made her uncomfortable to see him that way, too, beaten and defeated, in such contrast to the Saul she knew, almost as if she were seeing him naked. "Do you walk around here a lot?" she asks.

"Just when I feel like it."

Eve hugs her knees to her chest, wishing she had gotten a sweatshirt after all; her clothes are damp from sitting on wet rock. Despite her initial irritation and surprise, she is glad to see Saul, glad for the company. "Did you feel like it last night?" she asks.

"No. I was working last night. Why?"

"Well," Eve says, delighted to share the story. "A pickup truck drove into our quarry."

"What do you mean, a pickup truck drove into your quarry?"

"I don't really know. I mean, it ended up in there somehow. When we got here yesterday I saw tire tracks on the grass, and they ended at the edge of the quarry, right at the high ledge, and then the police came and divers came and they found a body."

"Oh, wow," Saul mutters.

"Yeah, it was a guy, like thirty or so. No one knows what happened, exactly. But they're saying in the paper that there was no foul play, which I guess means they're assuming either accident or suicide."

The word hangs between them heavily.

"Jesus," Saul says. "That's creepy."

"I know." Eve is quiet for a minute, considering. "I don't see how someone could accidentally drive into a quarry. I mean, that's a pretty big accident. But I don't think it was a suicide, necessarily, either," she says.

"Well why do they think it might have been?" he asks, looking at her carefully.

"I don't know, really. I guess it's just the easiest answer and they're too lazy to bother with anything else."

"So what makes you think it wasn't?"

Eve pauses a moment, worried that confessing she thinks it's murder sounds childish. "I don't necessarily think it *wasn't,* just that it might *not* have been. I mean, for one thing, his windows were up. Wouldn't he have rolled his windows down?"

"Probably."

"Exactly." Eve lets out a frustrated breath,

pulls her legs up. "I guess it just bothers me that they're jumping to conclusions without looking into things a little more."

"How do you know they're not?"

"Well, it certainly doesn't look like they are, as far as I can tell."

"Huh." Saul runs a hand through his hair. "Who was the guy, do they know?"

"James P. Favazza."

"James Favazza."

Eve looks at Saul. "Do you know him?"

"Know him?" Saul shakes his head. "No. What else do you know about him?"

"Nothing really. Just what was in the paper, which was that he was twenty-seven, that his wallet and cash were on him, and that he was last seen at his mother's house on Magnolia Street. And that he liked to drink beer."

"That was in the paper?"

"No. But there were a lot of beer cans and beer bottles in the truck. And a cooler bag. And a T-shirt from some bar. I collected it all from the quarry, since no one else was. I have it all inside."

"Huh. What bar?"

"On the T-shirt? Someplace called Vic's. It's in the phone book."

"I know Vic's. That place is a dump."

This piques Eve's attention. "You've been to Vic's?" she asks.

"Once. Once was enough. You know the place. It's kind of across from the grocery store and the CVS?"

Eve tries to picture the various buildings that stand opposite the grocery store and CVS; the only two she can conjure clearly are Steve's sub shop and Salah's ice cream, because she's been inside both of these, but the rest appear in her mind as vague shapes that have held no relevance in her life. "Yeah, I guess," she says uncertainly.

There are footsteps in the distance, a shout, laughter. Eve and Saul listen.

"Maybe he was drunk," Saul says when it is quiet again. "And he drove in accidentally."

"Yeah, I know. But the thing is, the truck drove between two trees that are so close together it would be hard to do it even sober. Not to mention maneuvering his way up these roads and down our driveway in the first place. I don't know. If he was a good enough drunk driver that he got all the way to the quarry I don't know why he'd suddenly turn into such a bad drunk driver that he'd drive right in."

"Which would suggest suicide."

"I'm not convinced," Eve says flatly.

They sit quietly for a minute. Eve pulls a twig from a bush and rolls it between her palms, thinking. "Oh, and the autopsy," she says. "They're doing one, even though they're saying there wasn't foul play, which is a little weird."

"I don't know about that," Saul says. "I think that's probably a matter of procedure."

Eve shoots him a look. "You sound exactly like my father."

They are quiet for a minute. "How is your dad?" Saul asks finally.

Eve shrugs in the darkness.

Saul turns to look at her, questioning.

"He's fine," Eve says.

"Your mom?"

"She's fine. Eloise is fine. I'm fine. We're all fine."

"I'm just asking, Eve."

"And I'm just answering. What am I supposed to say?"

"Jesus, I don't know."

Eve puts a chin on her knee. "How are you?" she asks, after a moment, feeling a little as if she is somehow giving in.

"I'm fine."

"See? It's a perfectly acceptable answer."

"Fair enough."

"How's college?"

"Okay. I'm taking next year off."

"What are you going to do?"

"South America, I think. Teaching English."

"I was supposed to go to South America this summer," Eve says. "And build houses."

"Why didn't you?"

Eve considers this. There are many answers.

She didn't want to leave her family so soon after Sophie died, feeling more needy for them—despite herself—than she has since she was a little girl. She worried that something might happen to one of them while she was gone. She couldn't face spending a summer with a bunch of kids her age who have come to seem almost alien to her. Or perhaps, she thinks, she feels like the alien; she hasn't called any of her own friends since arriving here, nor does she really want to. "I don't know," she says finally. She prods at her stubbed toe and sighs, feeling suddenly drained. "I'm tired," she says. She gets up off the rock, clutching her arms around her. "And freezing."

Saul gets up, too. "Yeah," he says. "I've got to get up early. I have to check my traps. I just set them out last week."

Last summer was the first time Saul and Sophie had let Eve come with them in the boat to check his lobster traps. Eve wonders if she'll ever get to help him again, and thinks probably not. She sniffs. "Where'd you park?" she asks.

"By the gate to the public quarry. Not far. Do you want an escort home?"

"Please," Eve says. "The house is two seconds away. I think I'll make it." She rubs her hands up over her arms to warm them. "Thanks, though," she adds.

"Sure. I'll see you, Eve," Saul says, touching

her lightly on the shoulder before turning away.

Eve watches him start to walk away, and she wonders when she will see him again—he who had been such a summer constant—and how, if at all, he will factor into their lives now. "Hey, Saul," she calls.

Saul turns around.

"You should stop by sometime," she says. "Probably everyone would want to see you. If you want."

"Yeah, I will. It would be good to see your family." He raises a hand. "Night, Eve."

"Night, Saul."

Joan and Anders lie side by side in bed beneath sheets that feel damp after all the evening's rain. They have just turned off the lights when they hear the distant sound of a car engine passing down the dirt road beyond the house. The sound gets louder, almost as if the car might come up the driveway, and in the pocket of time before it begins to fade the question Joan has been struggling to avoid all day finally presents itself to her, and there is no denying it. She props her head on her hand and looks at her husband. "What if we'd been here?" she asks. "Like Eve said?"

"What?"

"What if we'd been here? What if we'd gotten here on Thursday, instead, or even just a few hours earlier?"

Anders turns his head and looks Joan in the eye. He isn't surprised by her question. He knows Eve has brought it up to them both. "We didn't," he says quietly.

Joan isn't surprised by his answer. She sighs and drops back onto her pillow. "I know it doesn't do any good to wonder, but I can't help it. It's hard not to think that the outcome might have been different if we'd been here."

"And it might not have," Anders says. "It might have all been worse."

Joan ponders this. Anders is right; they could have seen the whole thing happen and been unable to do anything about it, and this *would* have been worse. "Maybe," she says. "Still." She lets her eyes wander over the water stain on the ceiling, absently tracing its familiar, turtle-shaped outline, just visible in the darkness.

The door downstairs opens, shuts, and then they hear Eve's footsteps on the stairs, then in the hall, the reverse sequence of the sounds they'd listened to her make half an hour before.

"What do you suppose she's been up to?"

"Something to do with the quarry, I'm sure," Anders says. "She's fixated."

Joan sighs. "I know it. I can't say that I totally blame her." She pulls the sheets farther up her chest. "Do you think she's okay?"

"Eve? I don't know," Anders says. He looks at his wife; he can see moonlight glinting in her eyes as she gazes at the ceiling. "I think she is, as much as she can be."

Joan is quiet for a minute. "I do worry about her. She's so . . . tough. I wish she would let her guard down. Or I wish that she felt she could. I wish she would talk to someone."

Anders knows where Joan will go next, and says nothing. He looks up at the ceiling himself.

"I wish you would talk to someone, too," Joan says, turning her head.

She slides her hand across the sheets toward him, slips it in the hollow beneath his back. "But you know that."

Anders breathes in slowly through his nose, feeling Joan's gaze upon him. He is acutely aware of her hand beneath him, and he knows that this is partly a gesture, that one time upon feeling her hand there, he would have next rolled toward her and pulled her against him, and that things would have proceeded from there according to an intimate, unspoken choreography. He doesn't move. Somewhere nearby, a dog is barking, and he finds himself counting the number of barks.

"Don't you?"

"Yuh," he says. "I know."

Joan returns her gaze to the ceiling. "But I know I can't force you."

"No," Anders says.

When, a moment later, Joan glances over at Anders again, he has closed his eyes. She studies his profile, the shadows of his cheekbones, the jut of his Adam's apple, and even though he is right there beside her, she feels as if there is a giant space between them. He seems very far away, or buried deep within himself; she would give anything to reach inside and yank him out, and her powerlessness to do so fills her with panic, as if time were somehow of the essence and slipping quickly away.

"Anders," she whispers. "Anders."

But Anders has fallen asleep. For a moment, Joan watches the rise and fall of his chest in the moonlight, her chest tight with a mixture of love and sadness. And then she turns her head, closes her eyes; and though her fingers have begun to tingle beneath her husband's back, she leaves her hand where it is.

Three

Anders wakes on Monday morning in the blue light of dawn, which creeps like fog over the windowsills and spreads across the floorboards, rustling the curtains and bluing the tangled sheets. Outside, the night bugs are chirping less and less, their argument lost to the morning birds, whose songs are growing bolder. For a moment, he only lies there with his eyes closed, hoping that he will fall back to sleep even as he understands that he will not; his eyelids twitch and tremble as thoughts begin to tumble in, many small ones at a time, and about nothing in particular—just noisy enough to keep sleep at bay.

After several minutes, he opens his eyes again, amazed by the process of dawn, by how quickly morning happens; objects in the room that only moments before were grainy and undefined have gathered themselves, taken distinct shape, as if their particles had strayed by night and are returning now in the brightening light. Quietly, he gets out of bed and goes into the bathroom to get dressed, where it is dark enough yet that his face is just a shadow in the mirror; still, he does not turn the lights on.

He passes barefoot around the bed, where Joan

lies sleeping on her side; she stirs at the creak of floorboards, and Anders pauses in the doorway. Then he pulls the door shut behind him. He passes Eve's room first as he makes his way to the stairs. Her door is cracked open; when he looks inside he can see her splayed out across the mattress, one arm dangling over an edge, a foot sticking out from beneath the sheets. The door to Eloise's room is closed; quietly he turns the knob, compelled to check in on his daughter even if he risks waking her. Eloise is curled on her side, facing away from the door, cocooned in sheets he tucked at her insistence as tightly as possible around her little body last night, as she demands he do every night after he has finished reading her the latest chapter in whatever book they're reading, which right now is *Alice in Wonderland*. Anders vividly remembers reading this years ago to the older girls, as he lay against pillows on the floor between their beds in Maryland. The familiarity of the text as he reads this book to Eloise now has a curious effect, making him feel as if no time has passed at all since last he read the book, and at the same time very old when he compares his present self to the person he was then. Gently, he shuts her door again and continues down the hall to Sophie's room.

As he did yesterday, at first, after pushing open the door, he only stands on the threshold, surveying the room and the few objects his oldest daughter left behind: magazine, photograph, earrings, mug. Then he enters the room and wanders over to the desk, where he sits down in the chair and leans on his elbows, his hands clasped and the backs of his thumbs to his lips. He lets his eyes wander to the magazine, an old copy of *Scientific American*, and from there across the grain of the wood-top desk to the pencils in the I♥NY mug, their erasers hard with age, Sophie's name etched in gold along their sides.

It comforts him to know the origins of each item before him—the pencils a gift from Joan's sister, bestowed to each niece upon the start of kindergarten in such abundance they can still be found all around the house in Maryland, ready writing instruments if only they were ever sharpened. The mug was from a trip Anders took with the older girls to New York City the year that Eloise was born. It was the souvenir Sophie had chosen from the gift shop at the Statue of Liberty, where she'd tripped on the lobby floor and chipped her front tooth. Given the choice, she'd opted not to fix it, just as she'd decided against braces, insisting that she liked the teeth she had, as if to fix them in any way were akin to getting new ones. She was always loyal to a fault. The magazine was a gift subscription from her parents for Christmas her freshman year; science was her favorite subject. Ever since she was little, she'd loved to examine the way things worked, from the inside of Anders' old watch to the way the waves changed as the tide came in, inching ever closer up the shoreline.

Anders sighs. Absently, he pulls open the desk's topmost drawer, where he finds a pad of Post-it Notes, a few loose paperclips, masking tape, and a smooth, orange seashell, which, after a pause, he slips into his pocket. The bottom drawer is empty, though the wastebasket below is not; there is a Twizzler's wrapper at the bottom, a balled-up Kleenex, a movie ticket stub, which when he takes it from the basket he sees is from August 12, for a matinee of *Citizen Kane* playing at the arts cinema in Rockport. He remembers Saul coming to pick her up that afternoon. There is a crumpled scrap of paper with doodled stars around a street address in Beverly—588 Cabot —a chewed toothpick, a broken barrette.

Anders lines these things up before him on the desk, takes a deep breath. It is light outside now, the birds in noisy chorus in the trees; early sunlight glints in beads of moisture gathered on the windowpane. For a moment, Anders only gazes out past these, watching foliage tremble in the gentle morning breezes. And then he looks away, slowly slides the magazine across the desk toward him, and, imagining his daughter doing the same, he lets it fall open where it will and starts to read.

● ● ●

Eve also rises early, pleased when she looks out the window to see that the day is perfectly clear. It is as if yesterday's rain has cleansed the air of a layer of scum that had somehow been blurring things since they arrived; her bike lies gleaming in wait in the grass, her chariot for today's mission.

L. Stephens, it turns out, lives in Georgetown, which is two towns up the coast and one over from Gloucester, about twenty miles away. Yesterday afternoon, while her family played yet another game of Monopoly, Eve had been looking through the phone book for any other Favazzas when it occurred to her that their phone book is local, covering Gloucester alone, and that the elusive L. Stephens may well live somewhere else. It was raining hard outside, and since the power was briefly out and she couldn't investigate on-line, Eve put on a poncho and rode down to Arthur's store. She propped her bike against a telephone pole and went inside, the useless yellow plastic of her poncho clinging to her skin.

Arthur was sitting behind the counter, flipping through a magazine.

"I need a phone book," Eve said.

Arthur looked up at her. "You look like a drowned rat," he commented.

"Thanks. But I need a phone book," Eve repeated.

"I don't sell phone books."

Eve rolled her eyes. "I need to *look* at a phone book. Not just local. You have one?"

Arthur studied her, then pulled a fat phone book out from a shelf under the counter. To her excitement, Eve found an L. among the Stephenses, whose information she greedily copied down, her mind racing.

Now, hurriedly, she gets dressed, and then takes the cooler bag filled with all that she has collected from the quarry from underneath her bed. She empties the contents into a plastic bag, which she puts back beneath her bed; last, as sacrilegious as it seems to her to do in summer, she puts on a pair of sneakers, which she ties tightly, tucking the loose ends of the laces beneath the tongues. Even she'll admit that Georgetown is too far away to ride barefoot.

Joan isn't concerned when she wakes to find herself alone in bed; she assumes that Anders has gone down early to make coffee, or else gone for a walk while the morning is still cool. She pulls her clothes on absently, making a mental list of the things she'd like to get done today, like getting that painting she'd bought last summer framed, and buying flowers for around the house, and organizing her study—and her brain—and figuring out how to get these things done while dealing with logistics, like ferrying Eloise to camp and home again, and dealing with the oil cleanup people who are scheduled to come this afternoon.

She wakes Eloise and leaves her in her room to choose clothes; she is on her way downstairs when she notices that the door to Sophie's room, which yesterday was closed, is open. She pauses, then continues slowly down the hall, pausing again when she comes to the open door. Inside the room, she sees Anders at their daughter's desk, his head down on folded arms atop an open magazine; Joan can tell by the rise and fall of his back that he is sleeping. She wonders how long he has been there, how much of the night she might have spent alone. She considers waking him, but she does not, thinking that perhaps he'd not have wanted to be found, that he came here by night purposefully, to mourn privately, and alone, and she respects this even as it heightens her own sense of isolation.

When Anders comes downstairs, he finds Eloise and Joan already in the kitchen. Eloise is sitting sullenly at the table, absently stirring the few bloated Cheerios that remain in her bowl. Joan is leaning against the counter with a mug of coffee. "And one year," she is saying when Anders appears in the doorway, "Evie's group sailed up the river to Richdale and bought candy." She slides over so that Anders can get to the coffee machine on the counter. A mug waits for him beside it.

"I still don't want to go."

Anders fills his mug and taps in a fine dusting of fake sugar from an open packet.

"You know," Joan says after a moment, "Daddy feels just the way you do. It's his first day of camp, too, did you know that?"

Anders pours cream into his coffee, watches as the white ribbons of it swirl into the dark liquid before it all clouds into a single color.

"He's feeling anxious about it, but he's going to give it a try anyway and see how it goes. Isn't that right, Dad?"

Anders turns around. "That's right," he says, "I am." It's true that the first of his scuba classes meets today, but he has not yet in fact committed to going, as Joan well knows. He takes a large sip of coffee. It burns his tongue.

Eloise peers up at her father suspiciously. "You're going to camp?" she asks.

"Well," Anders says. "Kind of." He puts a slice of bread into the toaster and pulls out a chair across from his daughter. He sits, leans forward on his elbows. "It's a scuba diving class. It's sort of like camp."

"Do you know anyone there?"

"Nope."

"Are you scared?"

"Not scared. Maybe just a little anxious, like Mom said. A little nervous."

"You see?" Joan says. "It's natural to be nervous when you're about to do something for the first time. But if you let that frighten you out of trying things, you'd end up never doing anything!" The toaster pings. Joan puts a hand on Anders' shoulder before he can start to get up. "I'll get it."

Anders glances at Joan over his shoulder, then returns his attention to Eloise. "Your mom's right," he says. "I remember you were very nervous about swimming lessons when you were little. And imagine if you hadn't gone!"

Eloise narrows her eyes. "I was nervous about swimming?"

"You were," Anders says. "You even hid in the closet."

"I did?"

Joan sets Anders' toast down before him, spread with butter and honey.

"And think about what a fish you are, now," Anders says.

Eloise seems to consider this.

Standing above them, Joan brings her hands together. "Lunch," she says. "Peanut butter or ham?"

Eloise spoons up a single soggy Cheerio and chews it thoughtfully. "Ham," she says. She looks at her father as Joan begins to rummage through the fridge. "What kind of sandwich are you going to have?" she asks.

"Oh, I don't need a sandwich," he says.

"Yes, you do. What will you have for lunch?"

"They have food at Daddy's camp," Joan calls over her shoulder. "He'll be able to get his lunch there."

Eloise lifts the final two Cheerios from her bowl, decides against eating them. She pushes the bowl away and sits back in her chair, regarding her father as he eats his toast. "Are you going to have to wear a wet suit?" she asks.

Anders holds up a finger as he chews, savoring the salty sweetness of the butter and honey. He nods as he swallows. "I imagine so," he says.

"Are you going to have to wear flippers?"

"I imagine I'll have to wear flippers, too."

"I know how to walk in flippers. Do you know how?"

Anders shakes his head. "Tell me," he says, taking his last bite of toast.

"You have to walk backward," she says. "Otherwise you'll trip and fall."

"Backward." Anders nods again. "I'll remember that. Thanks for the pointer."

Joan returns to the table with a fat brown bag. "Lunch. Ham sandwich, peanut butter crackers, grapes, and a brownie. And apple juice." She looks at the clock above the door. "It's eight- thirty now, which means we need to be out of here in about ten minutes. Eloise, why don't you and I go get your things together, and then we can hit the road."

"Okay," Eloise says. She starts to get up, then pauses. "Are you going to pack, Dad? They gave me a list of what I have to bring. Did they give you a list?"

"I think I probably just have to bring a bathing suit and a towel," Anders says, getting up from the table. "Not too much packing for me to do, so I'll stay here and do the dishes while you two get ready."

Joan and Eloise go upstairs. Anders brings his plate and mug and Eloise's bowl over to the sink. He does the breakfast dishes and the few remaining dishes from dinner last night. He glances through the window to the empty spot of grass where Eve's bike usually sits at the edge of the driveway. He wonders where she's already gone off to.

He puts the last dish in the rack, shakes the excess water from his hands, and then dries them on his shorts. As he turns around, Eloise and Joan reenter the room. Joan is carrying Eloise's new tote bag. Eloise is wearing one of her sisters' old life jackets. She puts a towel and a pair of Anders' trunks on the kitchen table. "I got your things for you," she says.

Anders glances at Joan, who gives him an almost imperceptible wink, then looks at his daughter. "Well, thank you very much, Eloise," he says. He looks at his wife again. "Where's Evie?" he asks.

Joan shrugs. "Her note was cryptic. But it assured she'd be back before dinner. And when I called her phone, I heard it ringing in her bedroom."

"What a surprise," Anders says.

Joan looks up at the clock and then puts her hand on Eloise's head. "Ready, Freddy?"

Eloise looks at the floor, seeming a bit to lose her resolve. "I guess," she says.

Joan goes to the door and holds it open. Eloise looks at her father. "Aren't you going to camp?" she asks.

"My camp doesn't start for a little while," he explains. This is true; whether or not he decides in the end to go, the diving class doesn't start until eleven.

Eloise's face falls. "Oh," she says. She looks toward her mother. "Mom, I really don't know if I want to go!"

"It's going to be fun!" Joan says with forced brightness. "It's okay to be nervous, but you'll have a great time."

Eloise lets her shoulders slump.

"Hey," Anders says. "Look, I'll leave at the same time as you guys, if it'll make you feel better." He shrugs. "I'll just get there a little early, it's no big deal. But we can all go off to camp together this way."

Eloise seems to hesitate, but she doesn't argue.

"Does that sound like a good plan?" Joan asks from the doorway.

Eloise nods, and Anders extends his hand to her, to walk together to the door. Just as they are about to step through the threshold, Eloise stops short, looks at her father incredulously. "Your *things,* Dad," she says.

Anders bats his brow with a palm. "Of course!" he says. "Silly me."

He returns to the table to get his towel and trunks where Eloise has laid them, then follows his wife and daughter outside, where he finds them waiting for him beside the station wagon. "Well," he says. He bends down to give his daughter a kiss. "Have fun," he instructs.

"You have fun, too," she says. "Are you still nervous?"

"A little bit," he says. "But I'm looking forward to it, too."

He stands and leans in to give his wife a kiss. "Bye," he says. Joan gives his hand a squeeze, winks again. Then Anders walks down the driveway to the Buick, which is parked behind the station wagon, blocking it in. He'll go to the nursery, he decides, and find out what can be done about his roses.

He has just put his trunks and towel into the backseat and found the old sunglasses he keeps in the glove box when Eloise appears at his door.

"Here," she says. She holds out her brownie.

Saran Wrap glistens in the sun. "In case the food is gross."

Anders takes a breath; Eloise may as well have wrapped her little fist around his heart. "Keep your brownie," he says. "You'll be hungry, and I'm sure the food will be fine."

"No, Dad, take it!" Eloise insists, and Anders understands that there will be no fighting her.

"Thank you, sweetheart," he says. He takes the brownie and puts it on the seat beside him. "That's very generous of you."

Eloise runs back to the station wagon, and Anders backs the Buick down the drive to a spot where he can turn around. When he glances in the rearview mirror, Joan and Eloise are two small figures waving in the glass. Anders raises his own hand in response as he drives away, and holds it up until he rounds a bend in the drive and has passed out of sight.

A little more than an hour after she has left the house, Eve arrives in Essex, a small strip of a town one over from Gloucester, with marsh on either side. She lets her bike coast into the town, breathing heavily. There are more than thirty antique stores in Essex, and three clam shacks, and while ordinarily during a summer day the town is crowded with antiquers and tourists waiting in endless lines for fried clams, it's early enough in the morning that things are still quiet, the causeway empty of traffic, except for the occasional car and a produce truck making a delivery. A pair of dogs trot purposefully down the street.

Eve pulls her bike up outside a donut shop along the causeway; though she ate before she left the house, she is hungry again, and she still has miles to go. She buys two donuts, one chocolate honey-dipped and one Boston cream, which she eats sitting atop one of several picnic tables beside a low-slung clam shack looking out over the marsh. The restaurant won't open for a few more hours, but the smell of fried food mixes with the sulfurous odor of low tide. Eve gazes out at the view as she eats, following the twists of the tidal river through marsh grass to where it meets the bay, across which she can just make out the contours of Cape Ann. She finds the water tower on the horizon and uses this to approximate just about where their own house lies. She imagines her family there having a breakfast of their own, Joan and Anders and Eloise at the kitchen table, and she is struck, suddenly, by a strange and surprising pang of loneliness.

She frowns as she reaches into her pocket for James Favazza's obituary, which she clipped from yesterday's paper. It is disappointingly sparse, and although Eve has read it enough times that she practically knows it by heart, she scans it again anyway.

James Favazza, 27, of Gloucester, died unexpectedly on Friday evening. He was born in Gloucester on Feb. 3, 1983, son of Elizabeth Favazza of Gloucester and the late Gordon Favazza. He attended Gloucester High School. James was employed at Gorton's Fish Company in Gloucester. James was a quiet, caring person and was very loyal and well liked by all of his friends and he also enjoyed bowling. He loved his family very much and will be missed by all who knew him. He is survived by his mother, Elizabeth Favazza; two older sisters, Benedetta "Bunny" Favazza of Quincy and Jocelyn Favazza Trupiano and her husband, George Trupiano, also of Quincy; and one younger brother, Billy Favazza, of Gloucester.

Arrangements: His funeral Mass will be held at St. Ann's Church on Wednesday, June 26, at 11 a.m. Relatives and friends are cordially invited to attend. Visiting hours will be held at the Greely Funeral Home, 212 Washington Street, Gloucester, on Tuesday from 5 to 7 p.m. In lieu of flowers, contributions can be made to the family, c/o Elizabeth Favazza, 932 Magnolia Street, Gloucester, MA 01930.

There is a photograph of James Favazza beside the text, about the size of a postage stamp. Eve has studied this carefully. It is cropped so that you can only see his face, but she can tell by the horizontal slats behind him that he is standing in front of someone's house. He is looking directly at the camera, and it seems to Eve that he was just about to speak when the shutter clicked; his mouth is parted, and his eyes are animated, focused, his neck craned slightly forward. He is wearing glasses, too—rectangular glasses with dark rims—and the shadows they cast across his cheek suggest that the sun was directly overhead. Eve wonders if he wore glasses all the time, and if they are now somewhere on the quarry floor.

She takes her second donut from its bag and eats it slowly, breaking off small bits at a time. She wonders what L. Stephens will be able to tell her about James Favazza. She wonders if he will be distraught or shocked at the sight of the bag, and whether or not he knew that his cooler bag was in the truck at all. She wonders how much time L. Stephens spent with James Favazza in that very truck that would be James Favazza's grave, drinking beers from the cooler bag propped open on the seat between them.

A seagull coasts in from over the marsh and settles in the dirt only yards away from where Eve sits. She breaks off a piece of her donut and pretends to toss it in the bird's direction. The bird starts and skitters to snatch up the scrap, but finds nothing there.

"Greedy," Eve says, putting the piece of donut into her own mouth. Instantly she feels guilty. She swallows, looks at the bird. "Fine," she says, tossing a crumb, which the seagull throws down its gullet in a single gulp. Eve narrows her eyes. "You didn't even savor that, you jerk."

The bird regards her closely, waiting for more, its unblinking yellow eyes hard and glassy, like marbles set into its skull. Eve looks back, and for just a fraction of a second she thinks of Sophie, as if her sister might somehow inhabit the bird. But she quashes the thought before she's even allowed it to really occur; it's a seagull before her, greedy and bold, nothing more. She puts the last of the donut into her mouth and lunges at the bird, arms raised; it takes to the air, cawing, and Eve stands at the edge of the marsh, watching as it flies away.

Anders drives unhurriedly in the direction of the nursery, mesmerized by the flickering of sunlight through the canopy of trees overhead, splotches of it flashing like so many Rorschach inkblots across the car hood as he goes. He thinks of the article in the magazine on Sophie's desk that he read this morning, which for some reason he cannot get out of his head. It was about the Tunguska event of 1908, when some kind of meteor or comet crashed above Siberia. Anders had never heard of this event before, but something about it struck him as he read, and as he thinks about it now. The force of the explosion washed over the land like a giant roaring wave of heat, knocking people off their feet and breaking windows in villages hundreds of miles away. In the days that followed, the night skies glowed so brightly that people as far away as London could read the newspaper by their light. If it had happened earlier or later, the magazine said, with the world at any other point on its axis, it could have been a disaster. New York or London could have been obliterated. If it had happened over the ocean, it would have made tidal waves big enough to destroy coastlines. It could have been the worst disaster in human history, but humanity was spared; what boggles Anders' mind is that so few people know about it.

The nursery is a few miles down the main road and another half mile up a back road like their own. Anders follows the road to where it dead-ends at a dirt lot among the trees. He parks in the shade at the edge of the lot, looks up at the trees above him, silhouetted starkly against the sky. Trees, he thinks, were the main casualty of the whole event, eighty million of them toppled, fanning out in the shape of a butterfly. In the magazine, there were pictures of the trees, grainy old sepia images of them scattered like pickup sticks. What struck Anders most were the trees at ground zero; though their limbs and bark had been stripped away, they were still standing, though it seemed to him that the trees were not so much resolute as uncertain which way they should fall.

The trees now overhead sway dizzyingly against the clouds, and Anders drops his gaze, blinks, returns his attention to the task at hand. On one side of the lot where he has parked is the gate to Bay View Auto Recycling, an odd junkyard of a place set a ways back out of sight in the woods; on the other side is the nursery, a warehouse-type structure with a large greenhouse attached to the back. Anders parks in the shade at the edge of the lot, and walks toward the nursery through the cloud of dust kicked up by his arrival.

The bells on the door jangle behind him as he enters, the sound loud in the relative silence of the place. Shovels, trowels, spades, and bulb planters hang along one wall. Underneath these, coiled hoses are neatly piled. A flotilla of wheelbarrows is arranged in one corner of the room, near a large rack of seed packets. There's no sign of any person. Anders glances at his watch, thinking that the nursery might not yet be open, but it is well after nine. He walks softly through the room to the back, where a door gives onto the greenhouse. Anders cups a hand to the glass, looking in, and though he sees nobody there among the rows of plants, either, he steps inside.

To enter into the greenhouse is to enter a

different atmosphere. It is warm and moist, and the mingling smells of earth and fertilizer permeate the air, though when Anders bends close to a lily, he is overwhelmed by its sweet scent. He gazes into the single open blossom. A deep, flecked pink stains each petal at its center, fading toward a crisp white edge. Glowing orange anthers, powdery with pollen, tremble at the ends of delicate filaments. Four other flowers on the plant have not yet bloomed; they rise from the stalk like hands held together in prayer. Anders' mother always said that if anything could persuade her there was a God, it would be the design of flowers, and looking at this lily now, Anders thinks that it maybe could persuade him, too, if anything at this point could. Perhaps, he thinks, half joking, instead of scuba diving he should look into some gardening classes—he might have a better chance at finding the solace Joan's hoping for.

"Can I help you?"

Anders looks up. A man has come in from outside, where endless trays of perennials sit out on tables in the shade. His hands and even his bare forearms are thoroughly stained with dirt. He scratches his cheek, which then has dirt on it, too. Anders recognizes the man as the nursery owner, the same person who sold him his roses nearly a decade ago, though he hasn't changed over the years; it would be impossible, Anders thinks, for the lines in his face to deepen, his hair to grow more white. But while he is familiar to Anders, Anders doubts if he himself would be familiar to the man, being just one of so many customers.

"Yes," Anders says. "I'm having some trouble with my roses. They seem to be losing their leaves."

"Are they blooming?"

"Yes, they're blooming. But maybe not quite as well as usual. And I noticed dark splotches on the leaves that haven't fallen."

"Ah. Sounds like black spot," the man says matter-of-factly.

"Black spot?"

"It's a fungus. Diplocarpon rosae."

"Oh." This means nothing to Anders.

"When did you begin to notice the defoliation?"

"This weekend, but that's only because we just arrived here for the summer. So I don't know how long it's been happening."

The man scratches his head. "If they're still blooming, that's a good thing. Heavy leaf shed will interfere with flower production. But all the rain won't help."

"What can I do?"

"Black spot's a toughie. Common enough, but pretty damaging. The fallen leaves carry the fungus, and the spores get to the healthy leaves via wind and rain. Very contagious, especially with the rain we've been having, as I said. But you can give fungicide a try."

Anders nods. "Whatever I have to do. You're sure it's black spot?"

"Sounds like it. Could also possibly be Cercospora leaf spot, but around here it's not likely. And you'd do the same for that. Fungicide." The man gestures toward the front room of the nursery. "I've got what you need in the store."

Anders steps aside to let the man pass and follows him back into the store, where he crouches down before a shelf of bottles and sprays.

"You could do chlorothalonil," the man says, taking a bottle from the shelf. He pats at his pocket for a pair of glasses, which he holds above the writing on the bottle like a magnifying glass, rather than putting them on. "It's a general garden fungicide, but pretty potent. Or," he says, taking another bottle from the shelf, "you could do propiconazol, which is a systemic fungicide."

The man looks up, questioningly.

Anders shrugs. "Whatever you think is best."

"Personally, I'd go with the propiconazol." He stands up; Anders can hear his knee pop as he rises. "It'll cost you a little more, but if you want to beat this thing."

"I do," Anders says. It makes his heart fall to consider that he might *not* be able to beat this thing.

The man brings the bottle to the register. Anders follows.

"You want to mix two tablespoons per gallon of water, and apply it to the leaves every five to seven days. Evening's best; otherwise on a hot, sunny day it'll burn the rose foliage."

As Anders pays the man, the bells on the door jangle. The man glances up, over Anders' shoulder. "You're late," he says.

"I'm so sorry, Nestor!" a girl's voice says. "I couldn't get my car to start, so I had to bike! I swear it won't happen again."

The man—Nestor—cocks an eyebrow. "Hope not. I'm understaffed as it is." He puts the fungicide into a plastic bag, which he hands to Anders. "Here you go. Good luck."

"Thank you," Anders says. He begins to walk to the door, where the girl is busy tying an apron around her waist. She is a featureless shape against the bright sky outside, so Anders doesn't recognize her, at first. But she says his name as he approaches.

"Mr. Jacobs," she says.

It is Josie Saunders, one of Sophie's friends. Anders is caught off guard, and feels himself wince at the sight of her; he hadn't been prepared for such an encounter.

"Josie," he says, smiling weakly, though he feels utterly unmoored. He clears his throat. "I didn't know you worked here."

"I just started," she says. "It's only my second week."

"That's great."

"Did you guys just get up here?"

"Friday."

Josie nods. She completes the knot on the apron. "Well, welcome."

"Thank you." Anders tries to smile again, thinking that it would be natural next for him ask after her brother, her parents, her year, but that then it would be natural for her to reciprocate, which would inevitably lead to their having to acknowledge the unspoken thing obviously looming between them, and he's not sure he has it in him. But almost before this familiar mental calculus is even complete, before he has had a chance to turn for the door, Josie speaks.

"I'm really sorry about what happened," she says. She looks him directly in the eye, and her expression is more serious than sad or sympathetic, for which Anders is grateful; he is never sure what to do with pity.

He nods at her, and instead of giving the customary thanks, "Yeah," he says. "Me, too."

When Joan pulls into the driveway after leaving Eloise at camp, she is surprised not to see the Buick parked there; she'd thought that Anders would have turned around a mile or so after driving off this morning and returned to the house just minutes after he'd left. She turns off the engine and sits for a moment in the driveway, puzzled and mildly disappointed that her husband isn't home, for no good reason except that she'd expected him to be. The house looms empty before her. Beyond it, the water in the quarry glints almost teasingly in the sunlight, its surface rippled by gusts of a warm breeze, and birds chatter in the trees overhead.

She gets out of the car, taking with her the bouquets of flowers she picked up from the florist on her way home—long stalks of pink gladiola, large-fisted peonies, sunflowers. These she brings into the kitchen, where she trims their ends and sets them into vases that she distributes around the house, carrying the final vase upstairs with her to her study, which she resolves that finally she'll unpack, a gesture toward getting at least some writing done this summer, though the prospect makes her glum. She hadn't bothered finishing her edits after Sophie died, just delivered the manuscript as it was, half finished. Since then she has barely touched the keyboard, unable to go on with this central part of her life even as she has urged her family to carry on with their own. More paralyzing than the lack of inspiration—nothing has seemed important or worthy enough, and writing itself a pointless exercise—is the guilt she feels over the attention she paid to her work, especially in October, when it mattered most. That the book did well only makes this feeling worse, the novel still prominently displayed in bookstore windows—mockingly, it seems to Joan, as if to remind her at what cost.

Her study is an upstairs room at the front of the house, looking out over the quarry. It is a sparsely furnished little room. Anders, she sees, has deposited her box of notebooks and her computer beside the old rotary telephone atop her desk, which is a small round table beneath the window. There is a bookshelf lined with the old books that came with the house, left behind by the sculptor who owned it before them; they are mostly pulp romances written in the sixties, from which Joan imagines the older girls have likely derived many questionable ideas about sex over the years. In the corner of the room, by the papasan chair, is a half-finished bust of a young man also left behind by the sculptor. When she looks at it, Joan always has the distinct impression that the unrealized half of his face exists already formed somewhere in the stone, and that if she just chipped away it would quite easily reveal itself.

She crosses the room to the window, where she sees a spider has woven a large and intricate web just inside the frame. It is beautiful, a shimmering silver maze of silk that Joan thinks will be a shame to have to destroy, and then she decides she won't; there's no spider at home, and she doesn't mind sharing space with a web.

Suddenly, she is aware of the growing sound of crunching gravel: a car making its way up the drive. She looks toward the place where the car will soon emerge from the trees, expecting to see Anders in the Buick. But instead, it's a car she doesn't recognize, a maroon sedan. It slows, then stops, idling there. Joan frowns, peering down at the car; she cannot make out whoever is inside through the glare on the windshield. After about ten seconds, the car starts to back down the driveway, and then disappears again into the trees.

She stands at the window, looking intently toward the spot where the car has vanished as if waiting for it to emerge again. She feels somewhat unnerved, though she has no real reason to be. Probably someone turned into the wrong driveway accidentally. Or somebody was simply exploring the back roads of Cape Ann and wound up here. Still, it seemed to her that the car had been approaching with purpose, as if it were routine, stopping in its tracks only at the unaccustomed sight of their car in the driveway. And perhaps it *had* approached with purpose, she tells herself—perhaps the driver was scoping out the house to see whether anyone is home so that he could take a swim; in the past they have sometimes come home to discover kids making use of their quarry, and she has no doubt that people must gather here in the off-season when no one is around. It doesn't really bother her, though perhaps it should.

The phone rings on the desk beneath her, loud and sudden, startling Joan; she feels her heart begin to race. She brings a hand to the base of her neck and takes a deep breath, letting the phone ring once more before answering as she tries to settle herself. She clears her throat, then lifts the phone. "Hello?" she asks.

She is more relieved than she cares to admit to hear Anders' voice on the other end of the line, though she's not sure exactly whom or what she was expecting. "Hi," he says.

Joan lets out an audible breath. "What's up?"

"What's the matter?"

"What?"

"You sound—I don't know—is everything okay?"

"Yes, I was just . . . the phone startled me. Where are you?"

"I went to the nursery to ask about the roses, but I wanted to let you know I think I may go to the scuba class after all."

"You *are!*" Joan says, glad for this. "Good. I can deal with the gas people, that's no problem."

"Oh, no, never mind, then. I forgot the gas people were coming. I'll skip the class, I should—"

"No, no!" Joan says. "You should go. Definitely."

"If you're sure," Anders says, sounding uncertain. "I guess it's done around three, so I should be home after that."

"We'll be here." Joan gazes out the window, where she can see Anders' rose garden half in shade, his ever-growing wall behind it. "What did they say about your roses?" she asks.

She hears Anders sigh. "Eh. The guy said it's probably black spot. Some kind of fungus. I don't think it's very good."

"Is there anything you can do?"

"I got some fungicide. We'll see."

"Hmm." Joan frowns. It makes her sad to think of the roses dying, not so much for the plants themselves as for the fact that Anders had planted them and cared for them and even loved them, in his way.

"Well, I'll see you later."

"Have fun," Joan says.

Anders clicks his tongue. "I'll try."

The Paul J. Lydon Aquatic Center is a windowless brick building set back behind the mall in Danvers, which is only a twenty-minute drive from Gloucester, but after even only a weekend on Cape Ann feels worlds away. The sight of the building fills Anders with the same sense of dread he had when, after New Year, his father would drive him back to boarding school and they'd turn up the drive, at the end of which he could see the dark shapes of the dormitories and the library and the dining hall, those buildings that would imprison him for the months to come.

Anders gazes at the center through the windshield, listening to the Buick's engine tick beneath the hood. He doesn't have to be here, he understands this; it's the brownie that's done it, as difficult as it is for him to explain even to himself. But when he got into the car after the nursery, feeling utterly derailed from the tentative track of his day, the sight of the brownie on the seat beside him made his lungs shrink to the size of pebbles. He pictured Eloise, her arm outstretched over the car door, her face a study of stubborn concern as she offered him the brownie, and then he imagined her at camp without it, and he was overcome by a combination of guilt and love that made him want to weep. He is here, he supposes, to legitimize the gift—to earn it, as little sense as that might seem to make.

He looks at his watch; the class begins in five minutes. He reaches for his swim trunks and his towel and makes his way across the hot pavement to the building. The woman behind the reception desk points him not to the locker rooms, as he'd expected, but to a classroom off the lobby.

It is a windowless room, the walls off-white cinder block and the floor scratched linoleum tile.

Maybe a dozen plastic chairs with arm-desks attached are arranged in a circle, but only three of these are filled. A teenage girl sits in one, doodling in a notebook, her hair a dark curtain around her face. In another chair is a young man with close-cropped hair. He wears fatigues, boots, and a tight-fitting white T-shirt, which makes Anders think that he must be in the military. Finally, there is a woman about Anders' age, which he finds comforting, given the relative youth of the other two. She smiles at Anders as he takes a seat, grimacing as the legs of his chair shriek against the tiles.

The four of them sit in silence for several minutes. A clock ticks loudly on the wall, and the fluorescent lights flicker. Anders is just beginning to think that it may well be a mistake to be here after all and that it's not too late to leave when the door partially opens, and he hears a man's voice calling out something to someone on the other side. There is the sound of laughter, and then the man enters the room and closes the door behind him.

"Sorry I'm late," he says. He lifts a stack of papers into the air, as evidence, before putting the pile down on a desk at the front of the room. "The Xerox machine doesn't like me." He is a young man, with a short ponytail, sun-weathered skin, and bloodshot eyes, a typical outdoorsy type, reminding Anders of a ski instructor or a kayak guide. He smiles at them all broadly. "So," he says. "I'm Dave, and I'm going to be your scuba instructor. First thing, how about let's all introduce ourselves, so we're not strangers." He turns to the middle-aged woman. "Ma'am?"

"Well," she says, sitting up straighter in her seat. "I'm Mary Alice Arnold."

"And where are you from, Mary Alice?"

"I live in Rockport. My husband and I just moved from Maine."

"I grew up in Portland," Dave says. "Maine's a great state."

"It is a great state. Although so far we're happy here, too."

"Good to hear," Dave says. "Great diving off Rockport."

"That's what I've heard," she says. "And I left my job when we moved, so I've got lots of time on my hands."

Anders scratches his forehead, wishing Dave would just get started; this is exactly the type of thing he had dreaded, preferring anonymity to this sort of forced camaraderie.

The teenage girl, they learn next, is named Caroline, and she is from Gloucester. She has just graduated from high school, and before she starts college she is spending a year in East Timor, which is why she wants to be certified. Anders has never associated East Timor with scuba diving, but Dave is wildly enthusiastic. Anders

126

studies her seriously—she is exactly Sophie's age —but she reminds Anders more of Eve than of his eldest daughter, her slouched demeanor typically teenage.

The military-looking guy is named Pete Brown, from Essex, and he doesn't say much more than that. Dave doesn't press him to elaborate.

"And, Mr. Jacobs, you and I have met," Dave says, turning to Anders last.

Anders looks at Dave blankly.

"This weekend. Quarry. Tow truck."

"Oh," Anders says, recognizing him now as one of the two divers who came to pull the pickup from the bottom of the quarry. "Of course. I'm not great with faces, I'm sorry."

"I shaved," Dave says, drawing his fingers across his cheeks, pinching his chin. "I had some serious scruff going." He squints in Anders' direction. "Your first name is?"

"Anders."

"Anders. Nice to remeet you." He tilts his head and winks. "It may not be East Timor, but you've actually got some interesting diving right in your backyard. Literally."

Joan is in the garage folding the tarps that have covered the porch furniture all year when the oil- and gas-removal people arrive. She stands in the open garage door and watches as a small caravan of vehicles pulls up the driveway: first a flatbed truck, then a utility vehicle with a trailer, and finally a pickup with its own trailer, on which sits a blue, rectangular structure about the size of a gas pump.

The driver of the flatbed truck gets out, leaving the engine running.

"Goodness," Joan says as he approaches, overwhelmed by all the equipment.

"Ma'am," the driver acknowledges, nodding.

"Joan Jacobs," Joan says, extending her hand.

"Roscoe McWilliams," he says. "We spoke on the phone."

"Yes. Nice to meet you."

Roscoe McWilliams gestures toward the quarry. "Mind if I take a look before we get started?"

"Of course not." Joan leads him around the quarry to its far side, where James Favazza's truck went in, and points to the shiny rainbow slick, which covers no more than a hundred square feet. "It's just that," she says. "Just what leaked from a car. Pickup, rather."

Roscoe McWilliams looks at the water, nodding. He turns, then, whistles loudly, and beckons the other vehicles over. The trucks make their way across the lawn. In their wake is a wiry gray dog, sniffing across the grass, its collar tinkling with every step.

"What you've got," Roscoe McWilliams says, "is a gasoline sheen. Much harder to remove than heavy oil."

"So what do you do?" Joan asks.

"Gotta pump the oily water out into that," he says, pointing toward the rectangular blue structure. "A water-oil separator. Does exactly what it sounds like. Then we give you your clear water back."

Joan nods.

"But what we're gonna do first," Roscoe says, "is set up a boom to contain the sheen." He gestures toward the trailer, where another man is slowly unwinding a large reel of yellow neoprene. "Compactible boom. Very simple, very durable, highly buoyant."

Joan nods.

Roscoe shrugs. "Should just be a couple days."

He crosses his arms, watches the men work. One runs the hydraulics on the trailer, feeding the boom out, and another guides the boom into the water. A third has tied a rope to the end of the boom and stands on the other side of the quarry, pulling the boom across. The dog runs excitedly back and forth along the quarry's edge, marking the boom's progress across the water.

"If you don't mind me asking," Roscoe says, "how'd you end up with a pickup in your quarry?"

Joan sighs and shakes her head. "Ehh," she says. "I don't really know. I mean," she shrugs, "somebody drove in."

Roscoe looks at her in surprise. "There was someone in it? He get out in time?"

Joan shakes her head, thinking to say that that probably wasn't quite the point. "No," she says quietly instead.

Roscoe McWilliams does not reply, and they watch the men in silence. After a minute, the dog leaves its post at the edge of the quarry and approaches the spot where they are standing. Roscoe McWilliams crouches down to greet it. The man on the far side of the quarry gives a shout, signaling to the man by the trailer, and then there is a loud hissing sound as the boom inflates. Roscoe looks up and says something Joan can't hear over the noise.

"Sorry?" she asks.

"The dog," he calls, and then the hissing sound suddenly stops. He clears his throat. "The dog," he repeats, in his normal voice. "What's his name?"

Joan shakes her head in surprise. "I don't know," she says. "I thought he belonged to you."

"Nope," Roscoe stands, brushes his hands together. "Cute little fellow, though."

Joan and Roscoe watch together as the dog sniffs its way toward the woods, following whatever scent it's on into the trees.

Eve's legs feel like rubber by the time she gets to Georgetown around midday. Inland, it is much hotter than it was on the coast; the air is heavy with humidity. She knew before she came that she was unfamiliar with Georgetown, but she thought she must have driven through at least once or twice before with her parents on their way to someplace else. When she arrives, though, she doesn't recognize a thing, and she begins to question whether she's ever actually been here at all.

There's not much to the town: a hardware store shares a lot with a pharmacy, across from which is a medium-size grocery store. A single-story strip of stores a little farther down the road houses a pizzeria, a bar, and a barbershop. Two of the units in this strip are empty, their windows papered over. Across the street is a small fire station, and a gas station and minimart.

L. Stephens lives at 16 Pine Street. Eve suddenly realizes that she has no idea where this is, and she feels a flash of irritation at herself that this had not occurred to her earlier. She's not sure what she was thinking—or maybe she just wasn't thinking at all. She supposes she'd expected Georgetown to be a neat grid of streets that she could bike up and down until she found Pine. But in actuality the streets branch off haphazardly from the center of town, and smaller streets branch off of these, and Eve understands that it could take hours before she happens to stumble upon the street she's looking for.

She decides to ask at the gas station for directions and pulls into the parking lot. She props her bike against a Dumpster off to the side of the store, where a cat sits delicately licking its haunches. It stops at the sound of Eve's bike clanking against the Dumpster's metal and looks at her almost accusingly, annoyed at the interruption. Eve looks back. "Resume," she says, and in a moment the cat does.

The convenience store smells like stale cigarette smoke and bleach, but it is blissfully cool. Eve pauses just inside the door and lets the air-conditioning wash over her, feeling as if she has just climbed out of a stew, and realizing suddenly how thirsty she is. She crosses the room and gets a large bottle of water from the refrigerator, which she guzzles immediately, stopping only to gasp for air and to wince at the sudden blinding stab of cold pain behind her eyes.

"Thirsty?"

Eve looks toward the counter, where a man sits partially obscured from view by a large lottery ticket dispenser.

"Yeah," Eve says, wiping her mouth. "Very." She screws the cap back onto the bottle and brings it to the counter to pay, noticing the World Cup game playing on the small TV behind the man. "Who's playing?" she asks, though she realizes she only cares because Sophie would have.

"Spain-U.K. Scoreless." The man gestures

toward her water. "Anything else?" he asks.

Eve shakes her head. "That's all," she says. "Except I'm wondering if you can tell me where Pine Street is."

"Pine?" He takes her money. "You're close to it. Head north out of town, it's the third street on your right. Come to an intersection you've gone too far."

It doesn't take Eve long to find it. Pine is a narrow, rutted street that leads through tall trees, among which nestles the occasional ranch-style house. Eve lets her bike coast down the street's slight incline, peering at each house she passes, looking for number 16. In the yard of one house, a couple of kids stare at her from a swing set. An old man sleeps in his rocker on the porch of another. Off in the trees, Eve can see some fort-like structure that strikes her as somehow ominous, less a child's play place than some-where dead bodies might be stored.

Not four hundred yards from where it begins, Pine Street dead-ends at a lake, and here she finds number 16. She sits on her bike and surveys the place, one foot on the ground. The house is a rickety-looking structure sitting up on wooden stilts. Underneath it is a wheelbarrow covered with plastic sheeting, a basketball hoop lying on its side, a few metal garbage cans, a canoe filled with cobwebs and dead, soggy leaves. There are rusted barrels in the yard, and a tattered

American flag hangs from the rafters of the porch. Beyond the house, the lake meets the yard with reedy graduality, cattails and canary grass marching up from the water like a small army. An old blue Camaro, which she recognizes because her Aunt Sam drives one, is parked out front, with a Red Sox bumper sticker—like the one on James Favazza's truck—and New Hampshire license plates, which still depict the state's famous man in the mountain, even though the overhang that formed his profile was in real life destroyed. Eve has often wondered if they'll ever change the license plates and the state's centennial quarter; evidently no one's gotten around to it yet.

Eve surveys her surroundings with interest, wondering whether James Favazza might have hung out here. She imagines his pickup parked beside the Camaro, James and L. sitting drinking beer as they sat out in the porch's rocking chairs, enjoying a summer evening. It's possible, she thinks, eyeing the chairs and the lopsided table between them.

Suddenly, the screen door opens and a man steps out onto the porch, a cigarette between his fingers. He is wearing a short-sleeved plaid button-down shirt with a pair of swim trunks, as if he had been about to replace either the button-down with a T-shirt or the swim trunks with a pair of khakis when he noticed Eve out at the edge of his yard. The screen door slowly swings shut behind him, hitting the frame in a diminishing series of whaps before finally coming to rest. He takes a long drag of his cigarette.

"Can I help you?" he asks then, exhaling. He is maybe thirty-five or forty, and Eve notices when he steps out from the shadows of the porch that he has a large, deep scar running from his eye several inches down the left side of his face.

Eve swallows. "Mr. Stephens?"

"Who's that?"

"Does a Mr. Stephens live here?"

"I'm Larry Stephens. I mean who are you?"

Eve unstraddles her bike and balances it against her thigh, begins to untie the cooler from the rack where she's strapped it down, her hands shaking. She realizes in panic—again too late—that she isn't sure exactly what she'd planned to say to L. Stephens when she saw him. "Um, I'm Eve. I just"—she fumbles with the strap—"I think I have something that belongs to you."

Larry Stephens comes slowly down the porch stairs. He takes a final drag of his cigarette and flicks the butt onto the ground.

Eve drops her bike onto the grass and squats beside it so that she can better work the cooler bag free, eyeing the smoldering butt with distracted disapproval; it is only one among many that have been strewn and flattened on the grass. "It's, well . . ." She finally gets the bag free and stands up. "I think this is your cooler bag." She takes a step toward Larry Stephens, holding the bag out before her.

Larry Stephens frowns, eyeing the bag, which Eve suddenly sees for what it is: stained and smelly, the shoulder strap frayed.

"It has your name on it," Eve explains, desperate to fill the silence. "Is it yours?"

Larry raises his eyebrows and shrugs, flashing his palms. "I guess it is," he says. "If it has my name on it." But he makes no move to take it.

"I thought you might want it back," Eve says. "I—I found it."

Larry takes the cooler bag from her hands. "Thanks," he says, and nods at her.

But Eve is not yet ready to turn away, determined to elicit more of a reaction; she stands her ground, staring at Larry Stephens. He gives her a bemused half smile.

"I found it," Eve says, "in our quarry." She speaks slowly, carefully enunciating each word. She clears her throat. "In Lanesville." She gives Larry Stephens a somber look, waiting for a flash of recognition, but he only looks at her evenly.

"Thanks," he says again.

Eve takes a breath. "The quarry where they found James Favazza's body," she says finally, playing her final card. "Your bag was in his truck."

Larry Stephens bunches his brow. "Who?" Eve can't tell whether he's pretending or not.

"James Favazza." Again, Eve speaks slowly, with emphasis, as dramatically as she can.

Larry Stephens shakes his head. "Don't know him."

Eve blinks at him, bewildered. "You don't?"

Again, Larry Stephens shakes his head. "Nope. Not even sure this is even my bag, tell you the truth."

"But—" Eve swallows hard; this seems impossible to her. "Oh," she finally manages. "Then how—" she breaks off, frowning.

Larry Stephens holds the cooler bag up in the air. "But hey, kid, thanks for this, anyway," he says, turning away.

Eve watches him climb back up the porch stairs and disappear inside. She doesn't even move to protest. The door whaps behind him. Somewhere in the trees overhead, a crow calls out, and hot bugs buzz. Eve bats at the mosquitoes around her ears, whose murmur she knows she will continue to hear long after she has left this place.

After Roscoe McWilliams and his crew have left, Joan goes into town to drop the painting off at the framer's and stop by the liquor store before picking up Eloise from camp. She finishes her errands with half an hour to go until camp has ended, and in the time she has to kill she finds herself turning once again onto Magnolia Street. She peers out the car window at the numbers on the houses, and when she reaches 932 Magnolia Street, she brings the car to a stop. It's an off-white, two-story house with vinyl siding, and like most of the houses on the street, it comes up flush to the sidewalk, which slopes steeply enough that the exposed brick foundation is a foot taller on the right side of the house than on the left. Three small steps lead down to the sidewalk from the front door; above the stoop is an aluminum awning, from which a set of wind chimes hangs.

This is where James Favazza's mother lives. Elizabeth Favazza. Joan knew in the back of her mind from the moment she first saw the address printed in the obituary that she would end up back here, though she's not sure exactly why; she doesn't fully understand her own motives. There isn't, after all, really anything to see. If she were a character in a book, she thinks, something of consequence would happen right now: visitors would solemnly arrive, and Joan would be able to catch a glimpse through the door as they went inside, or else Elizabeth Favazza herself would come out. Or maybe Joan would go knock on the door, and she would say to Elizabeth Favazza . . . what? She isn't sure.

Joan sighs and puts the car into gear. In the group she goes to in Maryland, there is one mother who lost two children in a fire, and another whose daughter was killed in a car accident. Two mothers lost their sons to cancer,

138

and one woman's daughter was murdered. Joan is grateful for the group, but she also feels as if she doesn't quite belong, or that she isn't worthy; her daughter took her own life. Joan can't help but feel that this is a reflection of her own failures as a mother, and that while these other mothers' children were taken from them, she somehow had a hand in losing her own child. Elizabeth Favazza, she imagines, might feel the same.

She follows the backstreets down to Washington, where she comes to a stop, her blinker ticking, pensive and uneasy. The last image she has of Sophie is at the breakfast table the morning that she died. When Joan came down to the kitchen that morning to set coffee brewing, she found Sophie already awake and dressed—although maybe, it occurred to Joan later, she had been there all night. She was sitting in her usual spot at the table, her hands cupped around a mug of tea. Sunlight slanted through the window, illuminating one side of Sophie's face and casting shadows across the other, catching in the steam that twisted slowly upward from the mug between her hands. *You're up early,* Joan had said, or something to that effect, thinking that Sophie had soccer practice, or a meeting for the photography journal that she coedited. She can't remember exactly how Sophie responded; Joan was groggy and unfocused, on early morning autopilot. She ought to have been paying better attention, she thinks again now, as she has thought many times since. Indeed, she's haunted by that image, which has come to represent the moment where she missed her chance. She suspects it will trouble her forever: her daughter at seventeen, beautiful and sad, that curl of steam, the sunlight in her eye and on her face, cast by an autumn sun frozen there against the sky, standing still there as if for all time. This is the moment, for Joan, where life separated from itself.

The traffic is crawling on Washington Street, with cars backed up in line for the rotary, and Joan wishes she had taken the back way to Eloise's camp; even if it takes longer, at least she would be moving. She watches the cars around her waver in the heat as she remembers. Many times she has returned to that image of Sophie to try to find something that she may have missed —in Sophie's posture, or expression, anything. She wonders what would have happened if, instead of dumping coffee grounds and water into the machine and hurrying upstairs to get dressed, to wake up Eve, to get Eloise ready for school, she had taken the time to sit down across from her daughter and talk to her. It has occurred to her that perhaps Sophie was there waiting for her, knowing that she'd come down early, hoping to catch her mother before she was caught up in the momentum of the day. But even at that hour

Joan was already caught up in it. She was so caught up in the momentum of life that although she clearly recognized that Sophie was depressed, she failed to comprehend that her daughter had reached a point at which life no longer felt worth living.

She considers the fact that James Favazza was last seen here, at his mother's house. Was it to say good-bye, she wonders? Had he known already what he was later going to do—if in fact what happened was a suicide? What might have the visit been like, and is Elizabeth Favazza being haunted by it just as Joan is haunted by the memory of Sophie at the breakfast table? Had Elizabeth sensed that anything was wrong? Is she obsessively replaying the image of her son's truck receding down the street three days ago? Will she wish forever that she had waved to him and called him back?

Behind Joan, a car honks. The traffic has moved on; there are maybe five or six car lengths between her car and the car ahead of her. She blinks hard, returning herself to the day, and puts her foot gently on the gas.

There are two ways onto the island part of Cape Ann, one by a highway that crosses the river proper over a large-spanned bridge, and the other by a smaller road that crosses the river's narrow cut over a drawbridge. Anders takes the highway, since it is a straight shot to Gloucester from Danvers. For the sake of the Buick, he takes it slow, cruising along in the traveling lane. The warm air has quickly dried his hair, which was wet from the pool and now stands up on end, windblown and stiff with chlorine.

They spent only the second half of the class actually in the pool; the first half took place in the classroom, going over the general vocabulary and principles of scuba diving, and learning how all the equipment works—regulator, cylinder, mask, pressure gauge, depth gauge, and buoyancy control device, or BCD, which is a sort of inflatable jacket that divers wear and that Anders had never been aware of. Afterward, Dave distributed booklets about diving for them to read as homework before class meets again, and then he outfitted them each with gear of their own, which they will keep until the class ends. When they finally got to the pool, they practiced breathing exercises and learned basic skills, like how to get water out of your mask, and how to recover your regulator if it comes out of your mouth. They also learned how to do something called a fin pivot, which involves kneeling at the bottom of the pool, your BCD empty of air, and then inflating the BCD just enough that you achieve neutral buoyancy, the force of the weights in your belt equal to the force of the added air. It was difficult to find that balance—at first Anders kept adding so much air to his BCD that he rose to the surface. But once he achieved it, the sensation was almost magical, unlike anything he'd experienced before, similar to what he imagines it would be like to exist in a world without gravity. Though he is still wary of the prospect of an ocean dive, today wasn't bad, he has to admit.

He reaches over and turns the car radio on, glancing back and forth between the road and the thin orange line moving across the radio's cracked face as he tunes it. The antenna, he discovers, is broken, bent at the top perhaps by the weight of the tarp that covered it all winter, and the stations crackle in and out. He carefully adjusts the knob, and he's almost got a station playing the Beatles to come in clearly when he glances up at the road and sees out of the corner of his eye a bicyclist riding on the highway's shoulder. He sees the person only as a passing flash, but something tells him with visceral certainty that it is Eve; this is confirmed by a quick look in the rearview mirror. Anders' eyes widen in disbelief, and he pulls the Buick onto the shoulder of the highway, turns the engine off.

He stares into the rearview mirror, watching as his daughter pedals closer. She is not yet aware of him; she is looking down at the pavement just beneath her tires instead of looking at the road ahead. She pedals wearily, each pump a seeming effort. About twenty yards behind him she finally looks up, and at the sight of her father in the Buick she stops her bike. She puts a foot on the ground and lifts a hand from the handlebar, pushes the loose hairs from her face.

Anders waits. For a minute, Eve just stands there, as if considering her options. Cars whiz by. Finally, she lifts her foot from the ground and slowly starts to pedal up behind him. They look at each other in the rearview mirror until she has reached the car and pulled up alongside it.

"Hi," she says.

Anders gives her a hard look. She is sweaty, and there are faint smears of dirt across her face. She looks at him with a combination of uncertainty and boldness, as if both dreading rebuke and inviting a challenge. "Hi," he finally says. He gets out of the car and comes around to the other side, opens the passenger door. "Get in."

Eve does as he instructs, and Anders lifts her bike into the backseat before getting back into the car himself. Beside him, Eve stares straight ahead.

"Eve," he says finally. "Your mother and I give you an awful lot of freedom, because we trust you to use your head. But the highway? You know better than to ride your bike on the highway."

"I had no choice," Eve says.

Anders raises an eyebrow. "Oh?"

"I didn't! The drawbridge was stuck open. This was the only way to get back."

"To get back," Anders repeats. "Eve. You know better than to ride your bike on the highway, *particularly* without a helmet, and you know better than to leave Cape Ann in the first place."

Eve is silent.

"Don't you?"

"I had to."

"Why?"

Eve folds her arms across her chest.

Anders waits. "Hmm?" he asks when she says nothing.

"You wouldn't get it."

"Try me."

Eve takes a deep breath, then slowly lets it out. "There was a cooler bag in the quarry and it had the person's name on it and I wanted to return it so I did."

Anders sucks air through his teeth. "Ah," he says. "Straightforward enough."

Eve shrugs.

"And where did you need to return it?"

"Georgetown."

"*Georgetown!* Jesus, Evie."

"It's not *that* far."

"It's over twenty miles! Thirty, maybe!" It makes Anders' heart leap to consider his helmet-less daughter riding her five-speed bike all the way to Georgetown, and he is glad that he didn't know about it until now that she is safe in the car beside him. "Did it occur to you that your mother or I would have driven you over?"

Eve looks at him like he's crazy. "No, you wouldn't have," she says. "It was a crappy old cooler bag and it was falling apart and you would have said I was nuts."

She's probably right. Anders regards his daughter. "And so why did you want to return it?"

Eve takes another deep breath, in and out. "Just because," she says at last, instead of really explaining. She would, if she'd had any success, but she hadn't learned a single thing from Larry, either about James Favazza or who the murderer might be. "I don't even know if it was really even his. And my helmet," she adds, turning to her father, "might fit if my head was the size of an apple."

Anders sighs. "Well, we'll have to get you a new one," he says, hiding a smile. He turns the key in the ignition, and after a few cranks the engine sputters to life. He waits for a gap in traffic, and then pulls out onto the road. They ride in silence until the highway soars up over the bridge, from which height they can see dark clouds gathering over the bay.

"Looks like it might rain again," Anders comments then, dismayed to think of his roses, whose situation isn't helped by rain.

"Good thing I ran into you," Eve says. Anders

slows the car as they approach the rotary at the highway's end. "Where were you coming from, anyway?" Eve asks. She looks sidelong at her father, bracing herself against the door as they come around the rotary's curve.

"Danvers," Anders answers. "I had my first scuba session."

Eve turns in her seat, excited. "Oooh!" she says. "You went? How was it?"

"It was okay." Anders rubs an eye, taking their exit.

Eve narrows her eyes. "It was just *okay?*"

"It wasn't bad," he concedes. "The instructor was actually one of the divers from Saturday."

Eve's eyes go from slits to circles. "He was? What did he say? What's down there? What did he see? Did you ask?"

Anders shrugs. "He didn't say much," he says. "I mean, he said it was—interesting, I think he said, whatever that means."

"Interesting?" Eve repeats, incredulously. "Interesting how? Why? What did he say?"

"Nothing," Anders says. "He didn't. He was just—you know. One lady lives in Rockport, and he said that was good diving, one girl is going—I forget where, East Timor—but he said there was good diving there, too. I think he was just trying to include me."

"Yeah, but *Dad,*" Eve says. "Come *on.* *Think* about all the stuff that could be down there. I can't *believe* you didn't ask." She slumps against the seat. She looks at her father again. "Will you *ask* next time?"

Anders doesn't respond, thinking that with all this quarry business it is going to be a long summer. He hadn't meant to add fuel to Eve's fire.

"Will you? For me?"

"Yes, Eve. For you, I'll ask."

Eloise brings a dead chipmunk home with her from camp. Joan does not know this at first, but in the car on the way home Eloise insists on holding her tote bag in her lap, and after Joan notices her daughter continuously peering into it she finally asks her what's inside. Eloise doesn't answer, but at the next stop sign she tips the bag toward her mother, displaying the small body of a chipmunk resting on the towel at the bottom of her bag.

"I found it behind a shrub. In the parking lot, while I was waiting for you."

Joan takes a breath. "Oh. And you thought you'd bring it home?"

"It needs a burial."

Joan nods. "We can give it a burial," she says, as if it is perfectly normal; she figures it's best to simply bury the creature as a matter of course rather than make an issue of the fact that her daughter has brought a dead animal home with her from camp, two days after she brought a dead bird home from the beach.

When they get back to the house, they find Saul Collins there waiting on the back porch. He is sitting on the stairs, stroking the cat, which he has always done even though he is allergic.

Eloise sees him first. "Saul!" she cries, breaking into a run as she crosses the grass to the house.

Saul stands. "Hey, Eloise!" he says.

Eloise slows as she approaches him, suddenly bashful, and looks over her shoulder toward her mother, who is following her across the lawn.

"Saul," Joan says. She is glad to see him, as inevitably painful as it is. Saul was the only boy that Sophie was ever involved with, and, as with everything Sophie was involved with, the involvement was thorough—four years at least, Joan thinks, and, knowing Sophie, it probably would have been forever. She forces a smile and gives Saul a hug. "It's good to see you." She means it.

"Hey, Mrs. Jacobs," he says.

"How are you?"

Saul nods. "I'm doing okay. I hope you don't mind me just dropping in. I bumped into Eve, and she said to stop by." He gestures toward a large cooler he's left on the porch. "I brought some lobsters," he says.

"Lobsters! Saul!"

"I hauled them this morning."

"Well you've got to let me pay you for them," Joan insists.

"Nah, they're for you. Really."

Joan smiles. "Thank you, Saul. You're too generous."

"It's no problem."

"Look at what I found," Eloise says. She solemnly extends her bag, holding it open so that Saul can see what's inside. "A dead chipmunk."

"Oh, no! What happened to it?"

Eloise shrugs. "I don't know. I found it behind a shrub. I think it's a baby. And this weekend I found a dead baby seagull."

Joan puts her hand on Eloise's head. "We seem to be starting a small animal graveyard." She frowns and looks up at the sky. "And we should probably get that buried sooner rather than later, speaking of. It looks to me like it's about to rain."

Saul offers to get a shovel from the garage while Joan brings Eloise's life jacket and the wine she's bought from the liquor store into the house, and then the three of them together walk a short distance into the trees behind the house, where the seagull's grave is marked by a couple of sticks lashed together into the shape of a cross and stuck into the ground.

Saul thrusts the head of the shovel into the earth.

"It's kind of rocky," Eloise says. "This weekend

Daddy had to try four places because rocks kept getting in the way."

Saul heaves a shovelful of soggy leaves and dirt aside. "So far so good," he says, ramming the shovel into the earth again. "So where'd you find the seagull?" he asks Eloise as he digs.

"The beach. It was all tangled up in fishing wire."

"That's sad."

"I know. And you know what else?"

"What else?"

"A car drove into our quarry. And there was a body inside."

Saul straightens and stands the shovel upright in the dirt. He draws the back of his arm across his brow. "Yes," he says. "I heard that." He glances at Joan, but he doesn't ask what happened, and Joan is grateful. Saul nods at the grave he's dug. "I think that should do it."

Eloise kneels down and gently places the chipmunk into the ground. "Rest in peace, chipmunk," she says. "I hope you had a very good life and died of natural causes and didn't get attacked by a cat or something scary." She looks up at Saul and nods. "Okay," she says.

Saul dumps a shovelful of dirt on top of the creature, and another, and he has just about finished filling the grave when the same gray dog from earlier appears from out of the woods, its collar jingling as it trots along.

"A dog!" Eloise cries. The dog runs up to Eloise, who unreservedly lets it lick her face, the nub of its tail twitching with excitement.

The dog turns in circles and then goes to Saul. He squats down to say hello, prompting the thing to throw itself belly-up on the ground for a rub. Saul obliges. Gravity pulls away the skin around the dog's mouth, exposing a jagged set of teeth.

"It's smiling," Eloise says. And then her face clouds over. "Do you think it's lost?"

"Oh, I don't think so," Joan says. "He was hanging around here earlier. I think he must live in the neighborhood."

"He's got a collar," Saul says, reaching for the tag attached. "His name is Henry." He flips the tag over. "No address, though."

"Is there a number?" Eloise asks.

"There is a number," Saul says.

"Do you think we should call it?" Eloise asks.

"I don't think we need to," Joan says. "I bet he'll take himself home."

"But what if he's lost?"

"Let's give it a little while and see what happens," Joan says, feeling on her shoulders the first drops of rain.

Anders and Eve pull off the road only miles from home to crank the roof up on the Buick; as much of a chore as it is, Anders doesn't want to risk soaking the leather seats. They get the roof up just in the nick of time and drive the final stretch of road home beneath its canvas dome, the wipers thwumping across the windshield's glass. When they have pulled into the driveway, Anders turns the engine off, but he doesn't get out of the car. Eve stays where she is beside him, waiting. Raindrops batter the roof, and water cascades in sheets down the windshield.

Anders turns to face his daughter. "I won't mention Georgetown to your mother," he says, "*if* you promise never to do something like that again. No leaving Cape Ann, unless you let us know first. And unless you bring your phone. You have it for a reason."

"Okay," Eve says dully. Unlike most teenagers, Eve can rarely be bothered with her phone.

"*And,* from now on, I want you to wear a helmet."

Eve doesn't respond.

"Okay?"

"I haven't worn a helmet since I was, like, ten."

"Eve."

"Fine."

"I mean it."

"Fine, okay, I will."

Anders peers out the window. "Someone's here," he says, noticing a car parked beside the station wagon.

Eve follows her father's gaze, and feels her

pulse give an excited rush. "It's Saul!" she says.

She grips the door handle, looking at her father for approval. "Can I?"

Anders nods. Eve gets out of the car and darts through the rain to the house. She sees through the window that her mother is in the kitchen, but she doesn't feel like answering questions, and so she goes around to the old wooden door that leads into the main room. It is a door they hardly ever use, made of thick boards canyoned with weathered grooves. Eve tries the heavy brass door handle, but it doesn't budge. She doesn't bother knocking, knowing that the rap of her knuckle would never be heard through the wood, and instead goes around to the paned bay window at the front of the house. She is no longer hurrying; by now she has surrendered to the rain, which has pasted her shirt to her back and shoulders. She cups her eyes to the windowpane and peers inside, thinking she'll tap on the glass to get somebody's attention.

She sees Saul and Eloise through the glass, sitting on the floor beside a dog she figures must be Saul's. They are playing a card game—Spit, it looks like, from the speed and intensity with which they're handling the cards. Saul is cross-legged and hunched forward, flipping his cards over with calm determination. Eloise is sitting on her heels, and unlike Saul's neat piles of cards, hers are scattered and haphazard, tossed in reckless haste. Eve watches them play until they come to the end of the hand, and Eloise slaps a pile; Saul has let her win.

Outside, Eve blinks. Rain has started to trickle down her back and into her eyes, beading on her lashes. She feels suddenly exhausted, flooded with a dual sense of loss and inadequacy, but mostly she is overcome by the piercing understanding that has washed over her again and again in the past months, with decreasing frequency but no less force, that things will never be the same. The most unexpected things do this to her, and always take her by surprise: a song on the radio, the smell of pine needles or split pea soup, the sight of icicles hanging from the gutter, or of Saul and Eloise playing cards on the floor, where Sophie should be, too. Instead of tapping on the glass, Eve turns away from the window and walks to the edge of the quarry, to that highest ledge. Raindrops bounce on the dimpled surface of the water, relentless and unslanting.

Eve stands at the quarry's edge and squints through the rain, staring into the endless depths, wondering, if her mother is right and it was suicide, what darkness could ever lead someone to want to be submerged in them forever, just as she's stood on the tracks in Maryland on the small back road where Sophie drove her car into the path of that train, trying to understand. The tracks run along a ridge, like a giant version of the mole tunnels that ravage their yard each spring, and coarse clumps of grass push their way through the gray stones on either side. The tracks themselves are old rusted steel; they stain your fingers brown if you touch them, and some of the wooden beams over which they run are also old enough that in places the wood is so soft with rot it sinks beneath a foot. Their father many times took her and Sophie as young girls to the tracks where they pass through downtown to set down pennies and nickels that after a train had blasted past were thin, oblong disks, George and Abe's faces flattened out of recognition. Eve and Sophie had always stood halfway behind their father as the train approached, hands over their ears to block the sound of its shrill horn, and even the yards away their father kept them from it they could feel the breeze of its passing.

Since October, Eve has visited the tracks, though not always the very spot where Sophie died, at hours when she knows a train will come, and tried to imagine what her sister had been thinking. She wishes she could think it was an accident, some sort of a mistake, but her sister was too careful; she didn't do anything she didn't mean to do. And so Eve's wondered: Had Sophie gone there with a purpose, a plan, and driven her beloved old VW Fox onto the tracks without a second thought? Or had she driven to that small back road and idled yards away from the crossing, uncertain of whether she would really do this thing? Had she gone there before, and turned away, returned to the family as if they all hadn't just escaped the unthinkable? Had she been afraid? Had she sat stiffly at the tracks' edge as the train approached, at first nothing more than a vibration in the steel, and then a distant whistle, and then a black thing growing like dread on the horizon? Eve has stood there by the tracks and let those trains blow by, and she has watched them speed away until they are nothing more than silent specks of smoke in the distance, and she cannot understand what the person she thought she understood best in the world had been thinking. All that Sophie said in the note she left behind was that she loved them, and that she was sorry. But sorry isn't good enough for Eve; sorry isn't *why.*

Eve lifts a rock from the quarry's edge and hurls it into the water, watches as the ripples spread until they are indistinguishable from the ripples of the rain.

Anders brings Eve's bike from the Buick to the garage before going into the house. He hurries through the rain with the bike over his shoulder and steps into the cavernous shadows of the garage, and when he goes to stand it up he finally understands why his daughter always leaves it on its side: the kickstand is broken. He leans the

157

bike against a worktable and squats down to examine the thing, which he finds isn't actually broken, but stuck in the up position, thoroughly rusted into place. Anders stands up, thinking that he'll come out and fix it later, after he's gone inside and greeted Joan, but at the sight of Saul's car in the driveway, he hesitates, remembering his encounter with Josie Saunders this morning.

Instead of going inside, he turns back into the garage and finds a can of WD-40 on a shelf among other cans of paint and primer and various types of cleaning fluid that have been there for who knows how many years. After he has successfully lubricated the kickstand so that it goes down, he decides that while he's at it he'll lube the chain. And then he notices that the tires of the bike could use some air, and he has just affixed the nozzle of the pump to the valve on the rear tire when he hears the muttering of a car engine. He looks up and sees through the garage door Saul behind the wheel of his car. Anders lifts a hand in salute, feeling caught, only realizing after Saul has started to carefully back his car down the drive that he is hidden in shadow and can't, after all, be seen. He lowers his hand, watches as Saul's car disappears into the trees.

Eve is furious with herself for not having come in sooner when she finally does enter the house and discovers that Saul has left. She is also deeply disappointed—and increasingly unsettled—by her encounter with L. Stephens, exhausted by her trip to Georgetown, and generally so out of sorts that at dinnertime she can hardly even enjoy her lobster, and this only heightens her annoyance, because she loves lobster.

She takes herself to bed early, ready for today to be over, but she cannot fall asleep; her mind won't stop racing. Again and again she goes over the details of her meeting with Larry Stephens, trying to remember every word he uttered, every expression that passed across his face. Looking back, she is certain that she found the right man, and the cooler bag was without a doubt his. He was clearly nervous, she thinks. The way he paused at the top of the porch stairs before coming down onto the lawn—there was something to that hesitation. The way he said he "guessed" the cooler bag was his, as if he wasn't sure whether to admit it. And the way that once he finally acknowledged that it might be, he didn't move to take it right away. It was as if he was afraid to touch the thing. And then, once she'd mentioned James Favazza's name, he was back to denying ownership again. Eve doesn't buy it for a minute, now that she really thinks about it; the bag, after all, was clearly marked with his name. Nor does she believe for a minute that he doesn't know who James Favazza is, if his cooler bag was in James Favazza's truck. What she can't understand is why he would deny it, unless he has something to hide. Unless he was there the day that James Favazza died. Was he a murderous foe instead of the friend she'd initially imagined him to be? That must be it, she decides. Larry Stephens must have played a role in James Favazza's death. That would explain everything—the cooler bag with his name in James' truck, his strange reaction when he saw Eve with the bag. He even *looks* like the murdering type, with that badass scar—and living at the end of that creepy street . . .

As soon as it's formulated, Eve's theory takes on the weight of truth in her mind. On the one hand, she's glad it hadn't occurred to her earlier, or she might have lost her nerve and not gone to Georgetown at all. But on the other hand, what now seems so obvious—of course he had something to do with the death!—makes her wants to tear her hair out with frustration that she hadn't gone about things differently, planned things out instead of being so impulsive, thought through clearly what she was going to say to Larry Stephens, and how. But now it's too late; she's blown her chance.

She's been in bed for about an hour when she gives up on sleep. She swings herself out of bed and pulls on a pair of shorts and a sweatshirt, and then she takes one of the two remaining cigarettes she found the other night and a book of matches from her bedside drawer and puts these into her pocket. She goes downstairs as quietly as she can, walking at the edge of the staircase where the steps give less. In the big room, she finds her father asleep on the couch, cast in a dim orange glow from the reading lamp above him, which is the only light on in the room. His reading glasses are on the floor, and a book is lying open across his chest. The sight of him makes Eve pause. She wonders if she should wake him and send him to bed, but she also doesn't want to be discovered. For a moment, she studies her father, watching the steady rise and fall of his chest, almost sadly, though she doesn't fully understand why the sight of him should make her sad. She decides to leave him where he is, and passes quietly through the room and outside, easing the door shut behind her.

The wood of the porch floor is cool and wet beneath her bare feet. A single lit bulb hangs from the ceiling. Moths and June bugs flit and whir around it, and a string dangling from its switch sways gently in the space beneath. Beyond the porch is darkness; Eve can see nothing out there, though when she steps into the night the objects around her slowly begin to take shape: the trees through which James Favazza's car passed, the dogwood tree, the rocks at the quarry's edge, and across the quarry, the hoselike boom floating on the surface of the water. Eve walks around the quarry and picks her way a short distance into the woods, to the far side of the rock pile where she sat last night. She climbs up onto a rock and lights her cigarette, and then she lies back, looks upward through the trees. A balloon is caught in the topmost branches, a black and listless bobbing shape, the helium having surrendered in its struggle to rise. Eve wonders briefly what child might have let it go, and when and where, and if the balloon had been there the other night, too, but she hadn't noticed. She wonders if it was there the night that James Favazza died. A satellite blinks into view; as she smokes, Eve follows its slow path across the sky.

When her cigarette has burned down to its filter, Eve stabs it out against the rock, and slips it into her pocket instead of tossing it onto the ground, loathe to litter it in the same way Larry Stephens did. She pictures his smoldering butt, the tan speckled filter and the half-burned gold lettering—and here she suddenly sits up straight, because it was a Marlboro, like this one and the other two she found on the rock the other night! She brings her hands to her head, incredulous that she hadn't considered that those three cigarettes might be linked to James Favazza's death, wishing deeply that she had not already smoked two of them. She's more sure than ever now of Larry Stephens' involvement.

She sighs, wishing Saul would appear again.

Part of her, she knows, came out here hoping that he would, just so that she'd have somebody to talk to. It's possible that he's out here, she thinks. It's possible that he is wandering sadly through the woods as she has imagined him doing night after night. She pulls herself upright, deciding that instead of going back inside she will go to the gate to the public quarry, a short walk away, which is where Saul parked last night, to see if his car is there.

Eve gets carefully off the rock and walks slowly through the trees, leaving the house behind her. Fallen leaves are soggy and cold between her toes, but she is warm in her sweatshirt. She reaches out to touch each tree she passes, as if for balance, or a sense of continuity, willing herself not to be frightened by the snapping sound of a breaking branch, or the distant howl of coyotes, or the hoot of an owl. If it were daylight, she reminds herself, she wouldn't think twice about walking here. Still, it is with no small sense of relief that she finally reaches the road, even if its rocks and pebbles are sharp against the cold bottoms of her feet. She decides that instead of returning home through the woods, she will take the longer route, following this road to where it meets up with the one that leads to the house.

She walks gingerly along the road, cringing but unsurprised when she restubs her wounded toe on a stone. When she comes around a bend in the

163

road, she pauses. She can see the gate from here. Six or seven cars are parked nearby, ominous dark shapes hulking quietly along the edge of the road. The inside light of one of the cars suddenly goes on, and Eve steps quickly behind a tree. She peers out from behind it. Through the windshield of the car, she can see illuminated the faces of a girl and guy, and then she hears a distant chiming as the car doors open and four people get out— the girl and the guy, and two other guys from the backseat, whom she hadn't seen at first. Smoke drifts lazily from the open doors, which they shut behind them, one at a time. The driver points a key at the car, and it locks with a chirp.

One of the guys says something Eve can't make out, and the girl laughs loudly. The four of them climb over the metal gate that marks the path to the public quarry. Eve steps out from behind her tree, watching as the foursome's flashlights bounce away into the darkness. She walks down the road in the direction of the cars, among which she can make out Saul's brown Volvo as she approaches. So he is out here after all, she thinks. In front of the gate she pauses again, curious, and no longer frightened; there are clearly many people out in the woods tonight, gathered somewhere at the public quarry's edge, and the fact of their presence emboldens Eve, seems to cancel out what otherwise imagined thing might threaten. She puts her hands on the gate and hurtles nimbly over it, setting off down the path herself.

She knows this path well, from games of capture the flag, and blueberry picking, and searching for wildflowers. She has rarely spent time back here after dark, as Sophie did, though the glass and cans and bottles and the remnants of fires often present by day testify to what goes on at night.

The path leads about half a mile through the woods to the quarry, where it splits and loops around the quarry's edge. Eve pauses at the intersection, scanning the water's circumference for firelight. And sure enough, she sees a flickering glow across the water, silhouetting a bush and illuminating the trunk of a large tree, beneath which she can make out several small figures gathered in a clearing. A shout travels across the water, followed by distant laughter.

Eve follows the path clockwise around the quarry for about ten minutes, and hears the murmur of voices before she has actually reached the clearing. She slows down, approaching carefully, then crouches down behind a bush in the shadows about ten yards away, where she can watch unseen.

There are about a dozen people gathered in the clearing, which is really a large slab of granite about twenty feet above the water. Two logs have been rolled into place as benches, and between these a fire burns. Two girls sit on one log, one of them resting a head on the other's shoulder and drunkenly swirling the dregs of her beer. Another girl sits on the ground, leaning back between the legs of a guy, who is frowning in concentration as he seals a joint with his tongue. Three people are sitting along the quarry's edge, their feet dangling over the side. One girl has climbed into the tree above the clearing; she sits cross-legged in the cleavage of its lowest branches. Eve recognizes this girl as the one from the car, and she recognizes, too, the boy who comes out of the shadows with an armful of branches, one of which he tosses onto the fire, sending up a bright shower of sparks. And then she sees Saul, lying with his head in the lap of a girl Eve doesn't recognize, gazing up at her as she drags the end of her long brown braid across his forehead.

Eve stands in the shadows and stares; the sight takes her breath away. She wants to run into the circle of light and pummel them both, yank the girl's braid off, scream and shout at this betrayal. But she is tired suddenly; she feels defeated, and oddly physically drained. It is all she can do to turn away, to disappear into the night.

Joan wakes up not long after she has gone to bed, roused by something that seems at first urgent and specific—like the sudden memory of something forgotten in the oven, or a bath left running

—but that she cannot identify. She looks at the clock; though she feels as if she has been sleeping already for hours, she has been in bed for just shy of one. The bed beside her is empty, and she can tell by the smooth sheets that Anders' absence is not because he has slipped into the bathroom, but because he has not yet come to bed. She is not surprised, just as this morning she was not surprised to find herself similarly alone. She has grown accustomed to feeling alone; not to *being* alone, necessarily—there has not been a night she and Anders have been separated since he returned home from Italy—but to feeling it. She remembers that first night after Sophie's death, longing for his presence as she lay alone in bed watching the progression of moonlight across the ceiling, but even after he had returned home the following day, it was as if he had lost some part of himself along the way, and she couldn't find the comfort she'd counted on in his presence beside her, almost as if he were simply too lost in his own despair.

She wonders how Elizabeth Favazza is spending her first nights. If, like Joan was, she is lying awake in bed, listening not to the hiss of buses kneeling to the curb on Chestnut Street in Maryland, but perhaps instead to the rev of a car engine making its way up Magnolia, or the distant tolling of the fog horn. She wonders if Elizabeth Favazza is running through endless what-ifs in her mind, wondering what she could have done differently, wondering, above all, *why*.

Joan sighs and brings her hands to her temples; the headache she's been vaguely aware of all day has started to pulse more insistently. She swings herself out of bed and goes into the bathroom, rummages for aspirin in the medicine cabinet, but she finds nothing useful behind the mirror, just leftovers from who knows when—witch hazel for bug bites, a bottle of calamine lotion crusted pink around the cap, a faded box of Band-Aids. She searches next through her pocket-book, which she has left hanging over the bathroom chair, but she cleaned it out before the trip. She checks last in the drawer of her bedside table; it is not unusual for her that headaches strike at night, and she knows she's kept a stash there in the past.

The drawer catches on something, and she has to jiggle it open. Inside, there is the usual assortment of random items—a miniature flashlight, a deck of cards, a bookmark, loose change, and, wedged up at the top of the drawer, an old postcard from Happy, Texas, the evident culprit. She takes this from the drawer with wonder; she's surprised the postcard has been in here all these years, kept, yet long forgotten. It is faded, and bent at the edges, with the photograph of a wide main street lined by low-slung buildings and the words "Happy, Texas: The town without a frown."

She flips the postcard over, remembering the day they spent near Happy, eight thousand miles into their thirteen-thousand-mile journey the summer before they married. The Buick had blown a tire, forcing them to stop at an old Exxon station in the Texan desert just south of the nothing town, and in the time they had to fill while they waited for the delivery of a new tire from Amarillo, they fatefully decided to have lunch, a giant pulled-pork gas station burrito, which that night came back to haunt them; it was while she and Anders hung in mutual misery over a motel toilet's porcelain rim that after months of hesitation, Joan finally agreed to marry him. It wasn't that he'd proposed before and she'd declined; the subject of their marriage was simply an ongoing discussion that for her was not yet resolved—though why she should have reached a resolution while sweating wretchedly on a motel bathroom floor she isn't even sure herself. Often they have wondered, jokingly, about what might have happened if it hadn't been for that burrito, whether they'd be living completely different lives. The infamous burrito; the stuff of legend, though really, Joan thinks, if you were going to blame the burrito, you might as well blame the piece of pipe in the road that blew their tire out in the first place, or the faulty alarm clock at the motel the morning before, which had gotten them on the road hours late.

All those little switches in the rails were simply sending them slightly different ways toward the same inevitable end, not changing their ultimate journey. She's never for a moment thought they wouldn't be married now if they'd shared a bag of chips for lunch instead.

Joan lowers the postcard into her lap, realizing how much easier it is for her to apply this logic to her life with Anders than to Sophie's death, wishing that she could, and so find some sense of absolution. Sometimes Joan drives herself mad analyzing specific events, moments, conversations, searching for the blame in each, wishing that she had spoken differently, acted differently, held her temper, remembered to say good-bye, as if any of these individual modifications would have steered the course of events along an entirely different path, like mythical poison burritos, just as she imagines Elizabeth Favazza doing right now as she lies alone in bed. And perhaps, she thinks, returning to that last morning at the kitchen table, that image of her daughter there, they might have. Although when she really considers it, by the same logic as she applies to her life with Anders—burritos, chips, or burgers made no difference—instead of absolution the awful alternative to blaming a moment is to accept that she should have gone about things differently in *every* way, that her cumulative performance as a mother led to how things are today. Either way she cuts it, she blames herself.

She gazes out the window, where she can see the bright lights of a low-flying plane blinking across the sky, each blink begging the question *Why? Why? Why?*

Four

On Wednesday morning, after Joan has left to take Eloise to camp, Anders goes out to the garden to tend to his roses. Today is the first day since they arrived here that isn't meant to bring rain, so finally this evening he will have a chance to spray them with the fungicide he bought earlier in the week. Fungicide, Anders has learned, is a misleading term; the stuff doesn't actually kill fungus, but rather protects foliage from fungus' infection. The instructions are very clear: Anders must remove all of the infected leaves from the roses, and only after that spray the healthy ones that remain.

The leaf removal pains him; there are more infected leaves than healthy ones, and halfway through the garden his plastic bag is nearly filled with leaves, and the bushes he's left in his wake have the scrawniness of wet kittens. Yesterday Anders did some research on black spot, and he's learned that it is actually quite a common problem. When he entered the term into the computer, the results produced were endless; rose gardens and black spot are apparently as associated as dogs and fleas. It surprises him that his roses have never suffered in the decade since he planted them; he would have been more grateful if he'd known all along how lucky he'd been to have avoided the blight. But this is always the way, he thinks; you never know how lucky you were until you aren't anymore.

He pulls the final leaf from a particularly devastated bush and drops it into the bag, pausing before he moves on to the next bush to look up at a small plane buzzing overhead. He thinks of the framed photograph they have in Maryland, likely taken from a plane such as the one above Anders now. It is an aerial view of the quarry and its surrounds, the ground a green nubbled carpet of trees scarred with the odd black shapes of quarries. Anders wonders, if the photograph were taken at this minute, whether he would factor into it at all, the top of his head a small brown dot. Probably not, he thinks; or if he did, he would probably go unnoticed. He has scanned their own photograph for signs of life before—a runner on the street, or someone mowing a lawn—and found none, though he can't imagine that nobody was outside when the photo was taken.

Anders moves on to the next bush, which he finds to be in comparably good shape to the one before, for which he makes a point to feel grateful. He has just started in on the garden's final bush when he hears the jangling sound of a collar above him; he looks up and sees on the rise at the top of the garden wall the same gray dog that has been hanging around all week—Henry, according to the name on the tag. The dog looks down at Anders, its eyes warm black globes peering out through the wiry gray fur of its brows, its nose a third black ball to match. Anders is not surprised; since the dog first appeared the other day, Eloise, certain that it is lost, has been providing it with a constant supply of treats, standing on the lawn and calling it by name until it appears.

"Hello," Anders says, and the dog runs the length of the wall and down the swell of ground to the edge of the garden, where it stands, looking at Anders expectantly, its nublike tail twitching. Anders frowns, wondering if it's just hanging around because of the treats, or if in fact Eloise is right, and the dog is lost. Anders leaves the last bush unplucked and picks his way through the roses to where the dog is standing in the grass. He crouches down to read the tag on the collar, thinking he'll give the owners a call. Two summers ago, after Buster had started to go blind, he was lost for several days before finally someone noticed him hanging around and thought to call them. Anders makes a mental note of the number on Henry's tag, which he recites to himself over and over again as he strides across the lawn, the dog not far behind him.

He finds Eve in the kitchen beside a bowl of cereal, her eyes slits and her cheeks creased by her sheets. The newspaper is spread out before her; he'd had to go down to Arthur's store this morning to get it himself, as Eve was still asleep, to his surprise. She looks up as her father enters, and lifts a hand in greeting. Anders waves back, pointing toward the dog as he lifts the old rotary telephone from the wall. "The owners," he explains as he dials, the disk clattering around the face in a way that Anders has always found satisfying.

The line rings once, twice, three times. Anders shifts the phone from one ear to the other, aware of his daughter's gaze upon him, even as his own eyes are on the dog, who has settled in the corner of the room. After the fourth ring, a machine answers, one of those automated voices instructing him to leave a message. Anders glances toward Eve, who has set her chin in her hands and watches her father curiously. He leaves his brief message and hangs up.

"So now you're thinking he's lost?" Eve asks.

Anders pulls out a chair at the kitchen table. "Maybe," he says. "It's hard to say. What do you think?"

Eve looks down at the dog and shrugs. "Maybe," she says.

"He doesn't *look* lost," Anders says.

"But what does lost look like?"

"You have a point."

"Plus it'd be impossible for him to get skinny with all Eloise has been feeding him."

"I suppose that's right."

Eve gazes balefully down at the newspaper spread before her, and closes it with a sigh. "Nothing new," she says glumly.

Anders shrugs. "I thought the fire in Essex was pretty interesting."

"I mean about James. James Favazza."

"Ah." Anders folds his arms. "Of course."

Eve pushes her cereal bowl away, leans forward on her elbows.

"Not hungry?" Anders asks her.

"I am," she sighs. "Just not for Cheerios."

"Me neither," Anders says. "I could eat at George's, though. You?"

Saul was right: Vic's is indeed among the buildings clustered haphazardly across from the grocery store and CVS, where three streets intersect to form a sort of triangle, with a self-service car wash in the middle. Eve sits inside George's at a table by the window, waiting for her father to return from the ATM across the street, and stares at its awning, shocked by her own blindness. She realizes that of course she must have seen the bar before; she's helped her father wash the Buick at that very car wash, and she's gone for ice cream countless times at Salah's, nearby. But she's never before registered the bar's presence; nor, she realizes now, her eyes roaming from one building to the next, has she ever really registered the presence of the thrift store also across the way, or the frame shop, or the Polarity Center. She supposes she's been vaguely aware of these places, but they have existed only on the periphery of her experience, which has centered around the car wash, around Salah's, around Steve's sub shop next to that. Seeing these other places as if for the first time unnerves her; she wonders what else she's been oblivious to all these years.

A man steps out of a side door of the frame shop, which Eve would guess leads up to the residence above. She wonders what *he* thinks of when he thinks of this area, whether she would recognize his Gloucester if she had access to his mind, or vice versa. She watches him walk down the street, her eyes tracking him as far as the bar, where they come to rest even as the man carries on.

Vic's is housed in a low, rectangular building of pale brown brick, a style at odds with the more colonial architecture of the frame shop and thrift store on either side of it, yet in keeping with the look of the car wash and the grocery store. Steam lifts from a raised, round vent on the roof, where a fat seagull sits perched on a ledge. Letters affixed to the bricks above the entrance spell out the bar's name, though the S hangs crookedly, half fallen. Weeds sprout up from the crack where the brick foundation meets the sidewalk. The seagull on the roof cries out, takes flight. A bus lumbers down the street, briefly obscuring the bar from view.

Eve pictures James Favazza's pickup parked out front, just as yesterday she pictured it in front of Larry Stephens' house. She wonders just how much time he actually spent there, and what it might be like inside—it does look a little like a dump, like Saul said.

"You order?" her father asks, pulling out a chair and sitting down across from her.

Eve glances at him; she hadn't noticed him come in.

"Yeah," she says.

Eve takes an assortment of jelly containers from the small rack on the table and lines them up before her. She briefly considers asking her father if he knows anything about the bar, or informing him of its significance, but she somehow doubts it's the sort of place her parents would ever go, and after the Georgetown incident yesterday she is wary of broaching the subject of James Favazza too insistently. She looks up at her father. "How would you rate them?" she asks. "Best to worst."

"The jellies?"

Eve nods.

Her father looks down at the small plastic

containers lined up on the table. "I like them all," he says.

"That's a boring answer. If you had to choose."

Her father sighs. He looks down at the jelly containers again and slides them into his own arrangement, with orange marmalade in the "worst" spot and apple in the "best." "There," he says.

Eve wrinkles her nose. "Apple jelly's the best? Blah."

The waitress comes over with their drinks, sloshing Anders' coffee onto the table and then swiping at the spill with a dishrag tucked into her apron. "Thank you," Anders says.

Eve takes a long sip of chocolate milk, sucking in her cheeks around the straw.

Anders puts cream and fake sugar into his coffee, eyeing his daughter, feeling he ought to take advantage of this moment to bring up what she's going to do with herself this summer. Joan knows a woman who is a wedding photographer, whom she learned yesterday is looking for an assistant for the summer, and Anders has been dispatched to float this idea. Joan knows that if the suggestion comes from her, Eve won't entertain it for a minute. Eve has grown increasingly intolerant of Joan, impatient and often short-fused, whether part of her reaction to her sister's death or a stage of adolescence. Anders suspects that it has to do with the former, that it's a way of warding off discussion of Sophie's death, and Joan's almost desperate insistence on "checking in" and promoting openness. While Anders himself is usually reticent on the subject, he knows that especially in the early days Joan felt no need to hold back, inquiring how they each were feeling, what they were thinking, if they wanted to talk.

He stirs his coffee and clears his throat, but before he can say anything, Eve speaks.

"So," she says thoughtfully, pushing her drink away from her and settling her chin into her palm, her eyes trained out the window. "How long would you say it usually takes for autopsy results to come back?" She cannot help herself.

Anders takes a sip of his coffee, unsurprised. "Well," he says, "generally speaking, I think a complete autopsy can take a couple of weeks. But they can probably make preliminary findings pretty quickly."

"Preliminary findings being . . ."

"Assuming we're talking about the body, I think they'd be able to tell pretty quickly if he drowned, if that's what you're getting at. Also if he had drugs or alcohol in his system."

"So do you think by now they know all that stuff?"

"I'd say there's a good possibility."

"In which case he must have drowned."

Anders looks at his daughter, puzzled by her logic, even if her conclusion is sound.

"As opposed to being killed some other way and then the body being dumped into the water. Because otherwise they would have to investigate and stuff."

"I suppose that's right."

Eve frowns. "But don't you think they should investigate *anyway?* I mean, just because he drowned doesn't mean he drowned himself, right? He could have been driven into the water by someone else. Well, driven *to* the quarry and pushed in. It *is* a possibility, you have to admit it."

Anders flattens his mouth. "I suppose anything is possible. But I think they're probably handling the matter in the way they think is best. And we don't actually know what's going on."

"I know we don't. I want to. You'd think since it happened in our quarry they would keep us informed."

"Maybe there's nothing to inform us of."

"Well, there is. The autopsy results, for one thing. Or the *preliminary findings.*" Eve lifts her straw wrapper from the table and twists it absently between her fingers, gazing out the window. Outside, an old man is making his slow way down the opposite sidewalk. "What do you think it's like to drown, anyway?" she asks.

Anders raises his eyebrows, unwilling to admit the detail with which he's considered the question. "I imagine it's not very pleasant."

"If you had to choose, would you rather drown or burn to death?"

Anders looks over Eve's shoulder for just a moment, looks back. "Thankfully," he says, "I don't have to choose."

"But if you did?"

"I don't."

"I think I'd rather burn to death. It would be less . . . frantic, maybe. You'd probably just pass right out because of the pain. But drowning, God. I *hate* when I can't breathe. That would be the worst."

She has twisted the straw wrapper into a rope, which she ties carefully into a knot. "If I had to pick a way to die, like if the world were going to end tomorrow, I would want to take a running start and jump off a really tall cliff. For a second I bet it would feel like flying." Then she looks her father sharply in the eye. "Not that I would ever do that," she says.

Just then the waitress arrives with Eve's pancakes and toast on two separate plates, which she sets loudly on the table, and by the time she has left again it feels too late for Anders to respond to his daughter's remark; that moment in their conversation has passed.

Eve lifts one of the jelly containers still lined up on the table and peels back the flap. Anders watches as she spreads her toast with jelly as they wait for the rest of the food.

"Mixed fruit," he comments.

"What?" Eve looks up.

"Mixed fruit. That's your favorite?"

"Usually I like strawberry. I'm just in a mixed fruit sort of mood today."

After the waitress has returned with the rest of their breakfast, they eat in silence for several minutes, both intent on their food. Anders has just opened his mouth to broach the subject of jobs when Eve starts in again. "Do you think we can find out about, whatever, the preliminary findings?"

"Eve," Anders says.

"Just out of curiosity. I think we have a right to know."

"Eve," Anders says firmly. "You cannot fixate on this all summer long."

"I'm not *fixating,*" she says through her mouthful.

"You're going to have to figure out another way to occupy your time. You need to do something with your summer. See some of your friends. Did you ever call Abby back?"

Eve looks away.

"You know, Mom's friend," Anders ventures, "what's-her-name, the photographer? She photographs weddings? She's looking for an assistant for the summer. You could do that."

Eve looks at her father with disdain. "Wedding photography?"

"It wouldn't be a bad gig. And think about it—weddings are on Saturdays. It's one day a week. But it would be something to do. And it would earn you some money."

"*Wedding* photography," Eve repeats.

"Do you have another idea?"

"Prostitution would be preferable."

The waitress comes over to the table and freshens Anders' coffee. When they are alone again, Eve sighs. "You shouldn't worry. I'm not going to just sit around all summer. I never have before, have I?"

Anders regards his daughter; it is true, when she grew out of camp, she was a counselor-in-training for two summers, and last summer she worked in the shipbuilding museum in Essex, helping to restore an old sloop.

"I'll find *something,*" Eve continues, spreading jelly onto another piece of toast.

Anders pours cream into his coffee, stirs it thoughtfully. "It just occurred to me," he says; his dirt-stained fingertips have reminded him. "When I was at the nursery the other day I heard the owner mention they were understaffed." He shrugs. "Just a thought."

Eve pulls her mouth to the side, contemplating this. "I'd do that," she says finally.

Anders glances up at her. "Really," she continues. "I'll go *today* if it would make you feel better."

"It might make *you* feel better," Anders says,

lifting his fork to resume eating, "to have something to do."

"I'm just fine, thanks." Eve stabs a home fry. "Except for one thing."

Anders lifts a piece of bacon. "What's that?" he asks before taking a bite.

"Can we make a deal?" Eve asks. "If I agree to go to the nursery today?" An impish look is spreading across her face, and Anders responds warily.

"I don't know. What kind of deal are we talking?"

"A fair deal," Eve says. "I only ever make fair deals."

St. Ann's Church is in a residential neighborhood of Gloucester, in the midst of a zigzagging network of narrow, one-way streets. Joan stands at the bottom of the stone steps that lead to the heavy church door, looking up at the building, which seems to sway as above it high white clouds race across the sky. A pair of pigeons is perched at the edge of the steeple's base, facing into the wind.

This, according to his obituary in the paper, is where James Favazza's funeral will be held in a few hours' time. While it has crossed her mind, Joan does not plan to attend; it would be strange to go to the funeral of somebody she didn't know, an infringement, somehow, to sit in on other people's grief. Still, she feels drawn to the church, wanting to pay respect in her own private way. She puts her hand on the cool metal rail of the banister and climbs the steps to the large wooden door, a small rectangle of which is propped open. Tentatively, she steps inside.

It is cool in the church, and smells of incense and old books. It is dark, too, and it takes a moment for her eyes to adjust. Funeral programs are already laid out on a table by the door; Joan slips one into her purse, then gazes around her. She has driven by this church many times, but she has never been inside, and she is surprised by its size. She feels small beneath the high, vaulted ceiling; the nave could seat a thousand people at least. For a brief moment Joan worries that even if a good number of people show up later for the funeral, the church will still feel empty.

It is not quite empty now; there is an older woman in a pew up front, and a middle-aged man in another pew about halfway up, praying on his knees. At the very front of the church, in the sanctuary, the choir is gathered in the choir stall, though at the moment, only one man is singing, a melancholy Latin hymn. Joan walks quietly to a back pew. She feels almost as if she ought to kneel and cross herself before sidling in, but she also feels this would be fraudulent, done in imitation and not out of faith.

The pews are wooden, box-style pews, more typical of a colonial New England meeting house than a Catholic church, and the kneeler is so wide that there is very little foot room, as if designed to force worshippers to their knees. Joan sits quietly, her hands clasped together in her lap, and listens to the man sing. He has a low, deep voice, and though Joan cannot understand the words, at the mournful tenor of the melody her eyes begin to well with tears.

She has never been a religious person, though she does believe in something, and she finds a humbling comfort in a church—not in the institution, but in the physical structure. When, years ago, she and Anders took a trip to Europe, what struck her most—more than the art or the food or the cities—were the massive stone cathedrals. Their elaborate architecture, and impossible size, and the fact that they each took generations to build seemed to Joan to bespeak a faith that she feels *must* be based in something real, even if she simultaneously feels that she does not quite have access to whatever that thing is.

Strangely, she feels closer to it since Sophie's death. In the days immediately following, there were moments, between crippling waves of grief, that she was possessed by an exhausted and necessary numbness. In these moments, she felt as if she were looking down at herself from a great height, and she was filled with wonder that she was able to endure, able to go on living. But also in these moments, she understood that others had lived through this, too, and had survived intact, and that this, the experience of loss, was part of what it meant to be alive. These moments, of course, were brief, but the knowledge they allowed gave her the strength to withstand the next battering wave of anguish, and they made her more acutely aware than she had ever been of the common, and humbling, experience of living. Later, she found a quote by Mark Twain about his own daughter's death that articulated just what she had marveled at. *It is one of the mysteries of our nature,* he wrote, *that a man, all unprepared, can receive a thunderstroke like that and live.* Perhaps this is where her faith lies, Joan thinks— in the essence and endurance of humanity.

She draws a breath. The man's singing slows as he comes to the end of the hymn. His voice rests on the last, long note, and fades.

Joan sits quietly for several minutes more and then rises; soon the mourners will begin to gather, and she has the day to attend to. From inside the church, the rectangle of the open door is blinding with daylight, and Joan finds herself dreading reentry into the bright, white world beyond. But when she steps out through the doorway, the brightness softens, and the world is tolerable after all, and as always it continues to go on. A car drives slowly down the street, stopping to let two children cross. Overhead, a seagull caws, and in the distance, Joan can hear the whistle of a train.

"I'll wait here," Anders says, parking the Buick in the shade of the trees at the edge of the nursery lot. He shuts the engine off, but leaves the key turned in the ignition partway so that he can listen to the radio; there is a call-in program about aliens and outer space, the only station that today the antenna will pick up.

Eve gives her father a beseeching look; Anders pulls a business card out of his wallet, a reminder of the deal they made at breakfast. Eve narrows her eyes. "What's that?" she asks.

"Officer Baldwin's card," Anders says. "One of the cops from the other night."

"He left you a card?"

"Just so we'd have a contact."

"He left you a *card?*" Eve repeats. "So we'd have a *contact?* You had a contact all along and you didn't tell me? And why would we need to have a contact anyway if everything is just so cut and dry, no foul play, case closed?"

Anders lifts his hands in the air: I don't know.

"Did you just roll your eyes?" Eve demands.

"Me? Never." He suppresses a smile.

"You think I'm obsessed."

Anders does not respond, and Eve sighs heavily, hoists herself from the front seat, and leaps over the car door. She turns around on the other side and looks her father in the eye. "I'm not obsessed, Dad. I'm simply understandably curious."

"You are that."

This time, it is Eve who does not respond; instead, she spins around and makes her way across the dusty lot without a backward look. Anders watches her go, her feet bare and her jean shorts tattered, the pink streak in her hair catching the sun. He can just hear the bells hanging from the nursery door jangle tinnily as she disappears inside, and then, when they are silent, he is left with the sounds of birds overhead, with the *beep-beep-beep* of a flatbed truck backing up the hill across the lot, with voices speaking of infinity, the boundless nature of outer space.

The nursery is cool, compared with the sun outside. Eve blows some loose hairs from her face. When her eyes adjust to the shadows, she sees the place is relatively empty; a man stands by the seed rack, reading the back of a seed packet, and a woman is comparing various spades and trowels where they hang along a wall. The quiet puts Eve in mind of a library or a museum or a church; moving quietly herself, she approaches the counter, where a man is intently examining sheets of paperwork, a pair of dirty rimless glasses low on his nose.

"Excuse me," Eve whispers.

The man raises a finger, his eyes still on the

papers before him, holds it there in the air; it is stained with dirt, soil caking the short, ridged nail. Eve waits, watching the man's eyes dart back and forth across the page. He is a tall man, with dark, deeply lined skin and a shock of white hair; he seems to Eve somehow ageless, both youthful and ancient at once. He is wearing a short-sleeved, checkered button-down with a second pair of glasses in his breast pocket nestled alongside a small, worn notepad; a white, wormy scar runs the length of his muscled forearm, from wrist to elbow. Eve stares, both intimidated and intrigued.

The man takes a long breath through his nose, and finally looks up. "May I help you?"

"Um, yes," she begins; she'd half forgotten why she came here. "I'm here about the job?"

The man blinks at her. "What job?"

Eve frowns. "I thought you were hiring."

"And what led you to believe that?"

"My dad. He said you said you were understaffed. Or something."

"I am understaffed. But I'm not hiring."

For a moment, Eve is speechless. "Oh," she says, finally. "Are you sure?"

The man looks at her, his face without expression.

"I mean—Oh."

The man holds her gaze; Eve feels frozen by his eyes into place until finally, at the sound of the back door opening, he looks away, and Eve does, too.

Josie Saunders is standing in the doorway, brushing her hands off on a filthy white apron. Anders had mentioned that Josie worked here, which meant nothing to Eve. Though Sophie and Josie were friends, Eve has never known Josie well—she's always just been one of any number of the older girls who might have come over to sunbathe, or swim, or sit around sucking on freeze pops while Eve and her own friends spied from the woods—the friends, like Abby, who so far this summer she has gone out of her way not to see. The mystery of James Favazza's death has been quite enough, anyway, to keep her occupied. Josie smiles at her now. "Hey, Eve," she says.

Eve waves, gives a quick smile, not particularly eager to engage, and wishing at this point that she were anywhere but here.

"Are you finished with the mulch?" the man asks Josie.

"Yeah, I'm done. Except for the shrubs near the treeline. I didn't know if you wanted me to do them."

"I do." He turns back to Eve. "You see I've got a helper already," he says.

Eve nods; she can hear the rush of embarrassed blood coursing through her veins. "Prostitution it is then," she mutters before she can stop herself; the man raises an eyebrow, but he doesn't respond, and, blindly, Eve turns to leave.

She feels acutely self-conscious as she goes,

and when she realizes too late that in her desperation to get out of here she has headed for the back door rather than the door through which she entered, she continues anyway, and soon she finds herself outside again, not in the dust of a parking lot but among the rows of plants on tables set up out back; at the sight, she comes to a grateful stop.

She hasn't been to this nursery in years, but she can remember coming here as a little girl when her parents needed fertilizer, or mulch, or plants to line the border of the quarry, and running among these rows, which then seemed infinite in number, a giant maze, but that, when she looks at them now, don't live up to the memory. She remembers one time running headlong into a man she thought was her father and wrapping herself around his leg, and the horror she felt when she realized that the leg belonged to someone else; she wonders if it was the man's behind the counter. She does not remember being impressed by the individual plants themselves—except for the strawberry plants, and the warm, soft fruit that she and Sophie would sneak when they thought nobody was looking—though now she finds herself admiring the structure of the leaves, the delicate blooms. One in particular catches her eye; it is large and flowering, with bright, trumpet-shaped blooms, the crepelike petals opening around a long, seeded pistil. She pauses before it, watches as a butterfly hovers.

"Hibiscus. Latin, from the Greek for swamp mallow."

Eve turns around; the man from inside has appeared behind her, silent as a ghost.

"You see its flowers?"

Eve turns back to the plant, nods.

"They live only for a day. That plant will have produced new flowers by tomorrow."

Eve looks at the plant with interest, finding it a peculiar notion to think of a plant's appearance changing overnight, the positioning of flowers completely rearranged.

"Can you be here at seven o'clock?"

Eve turns to the man. "Me?"

"Yes, you."

"In the morning?"

"Yes. You. Here. In the morning. Seven o'clock. It's the most efficient time of day to water. Evening the plants stay damp and risk getting fungal disease. Midday's so warm that most of the water evaporates. If you can be here at seven to water, the job is yours. One less thing for me to worry about."

"Really?"

"I'd hate to see a young girl like you resort to prostitution," he says; almost imperceptibly, he winks.

On her way home from St. Ann's, Joan picks up a head of lettuce and a frozen pizza for supper for the girls tonight; it is trivia night at the Widow's

Walk, a bar and restaurant in downtown Gloucester. The food at the Widow's Walk has gone downhill over the years, and the owner who emcees the evening grows less and less coherent the more and more he drinks, which is more and more each year, but it has been Joan and Anders' tradition to go to trivia night every year they've come here for the summer. She hadn't really expected that they'd go—in Maryland, they'd abandoned their tradition of going out for Italian on Wednesday nights—but Anders mentioned it this morning as if their going were a given. Joan was both surprised and hopeful.

When she gets home, she puts the groceries away. She skipped breakfast, and now she is hungry, so she takes a yogurt from the fridge. This she eats standing at the kitchen counter, absently scanning a newspaper from the small stack piled there, waiting to be recycled. Three flat-screen TVs were stolen from vacant rooms in a Rockport hotel, and a Byfield man was sentenced for selling pot in Gloucester. Commercial and residential fishermen are appealing for congressional relief. A new charter arts school is bidding for students. It is Sunday's paper, she notices, and she flips to the obituary section. The familiar spot where James Favazza's obituary used to be is now a hole. Eve has clipped it: she's not surprised. She has read the obituary enough times anyway to know what it says.

Joan frowns. She tosses her yogurt container into the garbage, sets her spoon in the sink, aware suddenly of faint noises coming from behind the laundry room door. She looks at the door warily, imagining a raccoon or a squirrel or a rat or a bat trapped on the other side. She should wait for Anders to be home, she thinks, before she opens the door and risks loosing whatever creature it is into the house. But then she hears a whine, and a scrape against the door, and the throaty sound that precedes a bark—the unmistakable sounds of a dog. Peering through the door she sees the gray dog that lately seems to have made itself a fixture in their yard.

"What are *you* doing here?" she asks it, releasing the creature, which runs twice around the kitchen table, clearly delighted to be free. After the second lap, it returns to Joan and leans heavily against her, its tail wagging. Joan pats its head, noticing for the first time the note on the kitchen table, which she hadn't seen beneath the vase of flowers that holds it down. She lifts the note and reads it. *Gone to George's. Back soon. Dog in laundry room—will explain when we return. Love, A and E.* Joan feels a flash of jealousy; Eve would never agree to go to breakfast with her mother. The dog sits at her feet, looking up at her expectantly.

There is the sound, then, of gravel on the driveway, and Joan looks out the window above the kitchen sink, expecting to see Anders and Eve in the Buick, back from breakfast, but instead what emerges through the trees is the same maroon car that had come up the driveway the other day. Joan's limbs grow cold. As uneasy as the car had made her feel the other day, she hasn't thought of it since, but the sight of it here again now fills her with anxious apprehension. She takes a step back, out of the sunlight filtering through the window and into the shadows of the kitchen, where she hopes she can't be seen. The dog runs to the door and peers through the screen; Joan beckons it away, but it pays no attention. She wills it not to push through the door.

The other day, she hadn't been able to see through the windshield for the glare of reflected sunlight; today, she can easily make out the driver behind the wheel. He is a young man, perhaps in his twenties, and he is wearing a T-shirt and a baseball cap that is tilted upward at such an angle that his features are visible: pointed nose, hollow, unshaven cheeks, deep-set eyes. He is skinny, with a sharp jawline and a jutting Adam's apple that seems to bob nervously in his throat. He looks at the house, squinting, and then lowers his neck and peers out at the quarry. He doesn't look particularly threatening, and part of Joan feels she ought to simply go outside and find out what he's doing here. If Anders were home, she would. If Anders were home she wouldn't think twice about it. But aside from the dog, which has thankfully lost interest in the car and is now sniffing around the garbage can, she is alone, and so she doesn't dare.

After half a minute, the man turns around in his seat and begins to back his car down the driveway. Joan wishes that he would turn the car around so that she could read the license plate; mounted to the front is a plate with the big red B of the Red Sox logo.

Joan watches the car until it is out of sight. She wonders if its presence has anything to do with James Favazza, and regrets her trepidation; her curiosity now that the car has gone is more compelling than her fear. She should have just gone out there, she thinks, frustrated with herself. She wonders what she should do if he returns, and finds herself almost hoping that he will.

There is a crashing sound in the corner of the room; the dog has knocked the garbage can over, strewing the contents across the kitchen floor. Joan's yogurt container rolls out across the tiles among several balled-up paper towels, an empty container of orange juice, a soggy coffee filter. She feels a flash of frustration, and then it's gone. Distractedly, she rights the bin and picks up the refuse, letting the dog lick up the splattered remnants of her yogurt from the tiles. When a moment later she hears a car coming up the driveway, her eyes dart to the window, her heart racing. But it is the Buick that emerges from the trees; Anders and Eve are home.

The car doors open simultaneously, like a set of wings; Anders closes his behind him, but Eve leaves hers open, marching directly across the driveway to a pair of trees at the edge of the lawn. Anders follows. Eve points at the trees, her mouth moving rapidly; she is clearly worked up about something. Anders nods his agreement in a manner that seems both tolerant and weary. It's clear that whatever's got Eve worked up has to do with James. Eve turns and marches toward the house. Anders follows, shutting the Buick's open passenger door as he passes the car in the driveway.

"You're back," Joan says when they enter.

"We are indeed," Anders replies. He gives his wife a kiss and leans back against the counter.

Eve pulls out a chair and sits down with a plunk; the dog runs to her and jumps up, resting its front paws on Eve's thighs. She scratches it between the eyes.

"As is the dog, I see," Joan continues. The dog hops off of Eve's legs and gives its head a flapping shake that jangles its collar loudly. Joan looks at Anders questioningly.

"Yuh," Anders says. "It's back. We were worried that it might be lost after all. I left a message on the owner's machine, letting whoever it is know that we have him."

Joan nods. "I see."

"Obviously they didn't call back?"

"I've only been home a few minutes," Joan says. "But I didn't check the machine."

"I'll do it." Anders passes through the kitchen and into the main room, where the answering machine sits in the room's far corner, often neglected.

"Mom," Eve says, when her father has left the room. "You will never guess what we found out."

"What did you find out?" Joan doesn't even bother asking who they're discussing.

"Well, he did die of drowning, we learned that, so it wasn't like someone poisoned or bludgeoned him then dumped him in. *But,* here's the thing." She looks at her mother hard. "He was shit-faced."

Joan opens her mouth to scold Eve for her language, but stops herself.

"His blood alcohol level was *five times* above the legal limit."

"And how did you learn this?" she asks.

"Dad called the police station. After breakfast. He called up and found out."

"He did?"

"Yes, we had a deal, but—" Eve waves her mother off. "But *five times,* Mom. *Five times* the legal limit."

"That's a lot," Joan says. She is not sure why this has Eve so excited.

Eve stands and goes to the kitchen door. "See those two trees?" she asks her mother, gesturing.

"Yes."

"The truck drove *in between* those trees. Look how close together they are! You couldn't do that *sober!*" Eve returns to her seat and plunks down. "So I was right! Doesn't it seem possible, even *likely,* that he was driven in? Pushed in? I mean, maybe he was drinking with friends and passed out and they, I don't know, *thought* that he was dead, so they freaked out and drove him up here and dumped the body. Or else he was flat-out *killed.*"

Anders has reappeared in the doorway; he clears his throat and leans against the door frame. "I think," he says, "it was probably more likely an accident."

Joan finds herself wondering about this, wondering about the man just now in the maroon car, wondering who James Favazza really was. His image from the obituary flashes through her mind, somber and distracted. She's not sure *what* has happened here, but she decides to keep quiet.

Eve frowns. She crosses her arms, her brow furrowed in thought. "And," she says slowly, after a moment, "I just thought of another thing. According to the paper, he was last seen at his mother's house at eleven in the morning. Was he drunk then? I doubt it. I mean, don't you think his mother would have mentioned it?" Eve takes a deep breath. "Which means," she says, "he had to go *somewhere* to drink *after* he left his mother's house. Someone *must* have seen him. But they're not speaking up. A little weird, huh?"

No one responds. Outside, there is the sound of a helicopter somewhere overhead, and in the distance, the barking of a dog, which reminds Joan of the creature they are sheltering now, which has curled up in the corner of the room. She looks over at it, and then at her husband, who is looking at it, too. "No messages?" she asks.

Anders shakes his head. "No messages."

Five

She is lying on the beach, her heels dug into the cool, wet sand at the end of her towel. Though the water is just steps away, the noise of the sea is a distant, lulling murmur. Joan's eyes are closed, but she can tell when a cloud is passing before the sun; the screen of her eyelids dims from bright red to a deeper, rustlike color, and her body will have just begun to cool when suddenly the cloud passes and it is bright again—more bright, it seems, than it was before, if only because she had grown accustomed to the dimmer light.

When another cloud eclipses the sun, she waits for the sudden light, and as she waits, she gradually becomes aware of a distant cawing sound—one of many gulls in an inbound trawler's wake, she'd guess, but she doesn't hear a motor's throaty sound, and instead of passing harborbound and fading, the cawing remains constant, as does this cloud before the sun. Puzzled, she opens her eyes, lifts her head from the sand.

Before her, the sea and sky are impossible shades of blue but for the white of spraying wave tips and the gray-bottomed clouds that float across the sky, and the massive one now passing the sun. She recognizes the day as one of those end-of-summer days after the season has snapped; summer's haze has lifted overnight, revealing the forgotten shapes of islands on the far horizon. She realizes with horror that somehow, summer has passed without her knowledge, and her heart begins to race to consider all that she has missed, all that she has not done that she meant to do, and all that she is not prepared for.

She sits upright on her towel, runs a nervous hand through her hair, seeing for the first time the source of that mournful cawing: a seagull is staggering along the shoreline, its wing ensnared in fishing wire. The bird's eyes are yellow and wild, and it lets out strangled cries as it stumbles along, dragging its wing across the sand. She looks desperately around her, for what she isn't sure—some way to help the creature—and then to her relief she sees Anders walking with Sophie at the far end of the beach. She waves in their direction, but uselessly, for their backs are toward her; when she tries to call out, she cannot get her voice to work. Finally, Anders turns, not to look at her but to gaze up at the shadowing cloud, and when he does this she sees that it is not Anders at all, but the young man from the maroon car, the one who came up the driveway today.

It is only then that Joan understands that she is dreaming, and with effort she extracts herself from slumber, aware as she often is when emerging from a dream what a thin line exists between wakefulness and sleep. She can still feel the beach's gusting breeze; this is the evening draft coming in through the open window of her office. She can still hear the cawing of the wounded gull; this is the yammering of birds that have gathered in the trees somewhere outside. She opens her eyes to find that she has fallen asleep in the papasan chair in which she'd been reading; the patch of sunlight in which she'd positioned the chair some time ago has not been shadowed by a giant cloud, but has only made its way across the floor, and now illuminates the half-finished bust in the corner of the room. She gazes at the face emerging from the block of marble: the high, smooth cheekbone of the right-hand side, the intricate curls, the hollow of the eye, all of this informing what the left side might have been.

Joan rubs her eyes. She feels unsettled, less rested than she would be if she hadn't slept. And she hadn't meant to fall asleep at all, hadn't consciously chosen to set her book down and shut her eyes, and this makes her feel worse.

She gets up and goes to shut the open window, before which the empty spider's web she left intact some days ago has begun to unravel in the breeze. Beyond it, outside, she can see Eve on the far side of the quarry, inspecting the skimmer that still hums away at the water's edge. On the lawn below, Eloise is playing with the dog, holding an old pig toy of Buster's just beyond its reach and luring it in circles. Anders, she sees, is in his rose garden, his shirtsleeves rolled and a spray bottle in his hand.

Joan looks at her watch; it is already after six o'clock, and they are meant to leave for the Widow's Walk in less than half an hour. Eloise by now should have bathed—Anders, too, if he was planning on it. She wonders what would have happened if she hadn't woken up, how long they'd have carried on, oblivious to time and planning. She takes a breath, slides the window shut, and leaves the room; behind her, dust motes lifted by the window's closing shimmer unnoticed in a sunbeam.

Half an hour later, Eve watches from her bedroom window as her parents disappear down the driveway in the Buick. She has just showered, and is wrapped in a towel; she has left Eloise playing with Funny Foam in the bath. When the car is out of sight, she turns and goes to her bureau, where she discovers she is down to her last clean T-shirt, and as she's taking it out of the drawer, she accidentally lifts the paper lining as well; underneath, she finds several dozen small notes, all addressed to her in Sophie's eleven-year-old hand.

During the summer Eve was eight, Sophie left

notes every day under Eve's pillow from Hobbster, a magical Hobbit who lived on a star, to whom Eve would unfailingly respond. For her, their correspondence was nothing short of miraculous. Even when she had nothing specific to ask of Hobbster, or to report, she was sure to leave a note every morning in the bathroom laundry hamper, which served as Hobbster's mailbox, and all day she looked forward to the evening, when she knew she would find his response beneath her pillow. It made each day as exhilarating as Christmas, and it made her feel supremely special; no one else she knew had a magical friend.

Eve takes the notes with her and sits down on the edge of her bed. She hasn't read them in years; she'd all but forgotten they were even there. She reads them now as if for the first time; while she clearly remembers the existence of Hobbster, she remembers none of the notes specifically. Most of them respond to daily events Eve must have reported in her own letters: a ride at a carnival, a trip to the beach, a really long traffic jam. One offers advice about an argument Eve can't remember having with Phoebe Alexander, and one offers advice about an argument she'd had with Sophie herself. In some of the notes, Hobbster responds to Eve's queries about his own life: his favorite food is pizza, he has no siblings, he has a miniature pet dragon named Kermit who eats pebbles.

Eve sets the note down, gazes absently at the old drawings hanging on the wall before her, their origins, like the contents of the Hobbster notes, which she's sure she once knew by heart, also forgotten, and she wishes fervently that memory weren't such a fickle thing. She lies back across the bed and blinks up at the drawings, thinking of all the memories she doesn't have in the weeks and days and even hours immediately preceding her sister's death, when she didn't realize she ought to be paying attention. She doesn't remember the last thing Sophie said to her that morning, or the last thing she said to Sophie, though she tried hard for weeks. She doesn't remember the last time Sophie braided her hair. She doesn't remember the last argument they had. She doesn't remember what they talked about the last time she lay in the dark at the foot of Sophie's bed, as she sometimes did. She's not sure if she remembered to tell Sophie a joke she thought she'd love, even though she remembers the joke, which was about a nun who gets tricked into sleeping with a hippy. Dumb, in retrospect. Everything up to the days of Sophie's death is, in Eve's memory, a blur; everything thereafter is burned into her mind with laser clarity and detail, awful, haunting snapshots.

Like the memory of Eloise's orange soda, and how when their mother told them the news, it had slipped from her hands onto the living room floor, where it left an orange stain on the carpet that's still there.

Or the memory of sitting across from her mother at the kitchen table late at night the night that Sophie died, trying to eat cone-shaped frozen yogurt snacks from the freezer, and how the only light on was the light above the stove, and how it smelled vaguely like smoke from a house fire somewhere in the neighborhood. Her father was somewhere in an airport or the air, trying to get home from Italy. Eloise was upstairs in bed, and Aunt Sam had retired to the guest room, leaving Eve and Joan downstairs alone. It was awkward, sitting there. This is what Eve remembers most. She didn't know what to say. Her mother didn't seem to know, either. They held their cones absently, letting the pink yogurt melt and drip down the sides, each alone in their own numb stupor, each overtaken intermittently by waves of grief that, when they happened to her, felt to Eve very much like nausea, and that when they crippled her mother, made her nauseous all over again. Finally, she got up and threw her cone away. Joan did the same, poured herself a glass of wine instead.

Or the memory of her parents' embrace when her father finally got home late Wednesday night, and how both of them seemed to hold each other up while at the same time weighing each other down, and how the rain visible through the open door behind them fell like silver needles through the streetlamp's glow, and how the house smelled like garlic from whatever dish it was someone had brought for dinner.

Or the memory of lying on her back in the drying grass at the base of the maple in their lawn, staring up at the web of branches overhead whose pattern she came to know by heart, and the clouds passing beyond, blown by an unseasonably cold and blustering wind that over the course of a week stripped the maple bare of leaves. And the way the sidewalk turned into a passing blur beneath her feet when, stiff from lying beneath the tree, she'd walk, and the squirrel she passed each day, hanging by its mouth from telephone wires, undone by an electric bite.

Eve shuts her eyes, lets her limbs splay heavily across the bed. The squirrel was there before the day that Sophie died; she does remember this. Susan Baker had pointed it out from the backseat of the Bakers' car on their way to the Upton Carnival, which she chose to go to instead of going with Sophie to see *La Vie en Rose* at the movies because she didn't feel like reading subtitles. That's what she remembers of the days before her sister's death.

Eve opens her eyes, looks up at the old faded drawing of a rainbow, which, upside down, is a mocking grin. She should have gone to *La Vie en Rose*, she thinks, and for a few moments she only lies there, listening to the sounds of Eloise sloshing around in the bath, wishing, wishing, wishing that she had been a better sister. Finally, she pulls herself upright and off the bed. She retrieves a pen and piece of paper from her mother's study, then sits down on her bedroom floor, and starts to write.

Anders catches intermittent glimpses of the river between roadside houses as they drive around the cape into town. Across the river, the marsh is so swollen with the tide he can hardly make out its mazelike contours; only the very tips of the marsh grass haven't been submerged. He scans the evening sky to gauge the fullness of the moon, but it has not risen, or if it has, the sun is still so high that it is yet too bright to see. It is hard for Anders to imagine that in winter, by now it has already been dark for hours; even at seven o'clock he can still feel warmth from the sun, which, like the river, he can see off to the right in flashes between houses and trees, though its image hovers multiplied in his vision even after he has looked away.

Anders pulls absently at a hangnail on his thumb, letting his eyes skim over the passing landscape: house, tree, river, house, river, sun, tree, sun, all of it blipping by like images in a cartoon flip book. The Buick's engine thrums, the note of its sound making an oddly pleasant chord with the tinny sound of an outboard he can just see winding through the marsh, dragging an inner tube in its wake. Suddenly an image of the girls flashes into his mind, all three of them lifejacketed and suntanned, their hair wild and wet, their faces wide and bright with excited terror. This was a Christmas card from three or four years ago, Anders remembers, and he wonders why he should recall it now so vividly; he hadn't realized how firmly he'd unwittingly committed it to memory. He tries to remember other Christmas cards, as an exercise of sorts; he can conjure only two others specifically, and both, curiously, are faceless, taken from behind. One is of Sophie and Eve maybe a dozen years ago, sitting naked after a bath before the fire, the tips of their hair wetted into clumps, their small bodies white and round. The other is of Joan, himself, and between them, Sophie, an unsteady toddler holding each of her parents' hands as they make their way away from the camera down the street. He can't remember the circumstances under which the photograph was taken, whether it was posed, or just a snapshot, and, if a snapshot, who might have taken it, and where it was they might have been going.

Anders gives his hangnail a final yank, wincing as the skin comes away too deep. He looks down at his thumb, watching as a bead of blood begins to well. He resists the urge to bring his thumb to his mouth and suck the blood away; his hands are stained with dirt, and still covered in fungicide he didn't have the chance to wash away. It took him longer than he'd imagined it would to spray the roses, though he was determined to finish every bush tonight, before they left and despite the hour, so that all the bushes would be on the same schedule—even though as he tended to the final one Joan sat waiting behind the wheel of the Buick, the engine already running.

He looks over at his wife now. Her hair is tied back into a loose ponytail. Wisps have come free and flutter in the passing wind, which sends ripples through the white linen of her button-down. She is gripping the wheel with both hands, and firmly, he can tell by the way the skin is stretched over her knuckles, and by the muscled ridges of her forearms. Her eyes are slightly narrowed in focus, as if she were studying a difficult text, and she's pulled her lips in tight between her teeth. Anders wonders what she is thinking about, but he does not ask; he does not want to have to.

He frowns. Earlier this afternoon, when he went upstairs to find the pair of gardening gloves he thought he'd left in his bedroom closet, he caught a glimpse of Joan through the open door of her office, asleep in the sunlight on her large round chair—Anders can never remember what it's called—and something about the sight made him pause there in the darkened hallway. There was something about the way that she was sleeping, curled in the sun, her hands held as if in prayer beneath her cheek, that made Anders' heart surge. What it was, he realizes, was the rare and frank vulnerability it revealed—one he suspects she goes to lengths to conceal. As he looks at her now, even as she is gathered, upright and composed, that aura seems to linger about her still, filling him with a quiet sense of urgency that even he cannot quite understand, a desire to *do* something to help her, even as it seems that there is nothing to be done.

When they arrive at the Widow's Walk, Anders goes directly to the men's room to wash his hands while Joan scopes out a table; she's not surprised to see that there is only one left, at the very back of the room. She hurries over to secure it, and orders each of them a Widow Maker—a strong, fruity rum drink, a specialty of the Widow's Walk. The trivia has not yet begun, and the room is noisy with clashing conversations that are punctuated by occasional raucous shouts of laughter. Tier curtains hang across the lower half of each window, blocking what little sunlight makes it beneath the broad awning outside, and so it is dimly monochromatic aside from the small pockets of flickering light cast by candles on every table and the neon glow of the flat-screen TV above the bar, which is showing a World Cup soccer game. Joan's mind leaps immediately to the thought that she would be there now with Sophie if life had gone as she'd expected, and she realizes suddenly that this event—the World Cup—was as far ahead as she'd concretely envisioned or planned, before things changed. This was where her life fully diverged from that other, imagined, happier one—this was the last place she might ever be able to locate that self living the parallel life in which Sophie was alive.

Shaking away the thought, she pulls the candle on their table toward her and cups her hands around it, out of habit rather than cold, absently touching the hot, soft wax at the rim with her fingertips. Her dream has left her out of sorts, with the awful, panicked sense of having lost a chunk of time, helplessness about the wounded gull, alarm at the transformation of Anders into the man from the maroon car. But she is bothered most of all by the appearance of Sophie in her dream, because as always, when her daughter does infrequently appear in her dreams, it was as if it were an absolutely ordinary thing. When Joan dreamed about her mother after her mother's death, her dream-self knew that her mother had died, and so it was with wonder and with joy that she encountered the woman in her dreams. Not so with Sophie; when Sophie appears, Joan doesn't recognize the gift of it until too late, and she has already woken up, and by that time, it is no longer a gift at all, but a missed opportunity to be blissfully fooled. Her dream-self takes her daughter's presence entirely for granted, and Joan can't help but feel that this must be a reflection of how things were in life.

Soon the waitress returns with their drinks, dropping four tickets on the table; you get a prize ticket for every drink you buy at trivia night, and for every Widow Maker, you get two. The usual prizes you can win if your ticket stub is drawn at the evening's end include small, hand-painted fish carved out of two-by-fours, or Widow Maker T-shirts, or a coupon for a Widow's Walk lobster roll at a future trivia night, or whatever is the evening's raffle giveaway. Joan arranges their tickets into a tidy row; she has accumulated four of the wooden fish over the years and is ever hoping to enlarge her school, which hangs above the wet bar off the kitchen in Maryland, a joking homage to the bar here.

She sits back then, and gazes around her. Not much has changed from last year; Joan recognizes most of the faces, though she knows few names. The schedule of nightly entertainment is taped to the door, a microphone and speakers are set up in the front, and the specials are written on a chalkboard propped against a column by the bar, behind which the margarita machine tirelessly churns its neon liquid. The only thing different that Joan can see is the soccer ball hanging from the ceiling—Adidas, of course, which was Sophie's brand of choice—evidently tonight's big raffle giveaway, apropos of the World Cup on TV. It spins beneath the fan above her like a taunt.

She notices Anders making his way through the room; she watches him shoulder his way through the noisy crowd, flat-mouthed and apologetic, and she resolves to pull herself together. "My hands seem to have been cided," he says, sitting down.

"Cided?"

"Like little fungi." He extends his hands, which are blotched with red. "I should have maybe waited until I had some gloves."

"Anders, ouch." Joan grimaces. "I could have told you that."

"Well," he says. "Lesson learned." He pulls his Widow Maker toward him, and tilts it toward Joan before taking a sip. "Cheers."

Joan touches his glass with the rim of hers and drinks, grateful for the electric shock of rum, feeling it spread warmly through her chest.

Anders lifts the menus from where they stand pinned between the salt and pepper shakers at the side of the table and hands one to Joan. As she looks it over, she feels Anders' eyes upon her. After a moment, he is studying her still, and she lifts her gaze; as soon as she has, Anders drops his own. Joan regards him for a moment, and then returns her attention to the menu, on which only the prices have changed; handwritten stickers with new numbers have been stuck over the older, lower prices of last year.

"Joan," Anders begins. Joan looks up at him again. He seems to hesitate, and then he says, "You can tell me, you know, if there's something on your mind."

Joan returns his gaze, looking into one eye, then the next, and though part of her would like to, she realizes that she is afraid to tell him about her dream. She is afraid to tell him about her visit to the church this morning, too, and her drives by Elizabeth Favazza's house; to verbalize these things seems too much of an admission, one by which they all might come unmoored. She smiles at Anders with a mixture of gratitude and sadness, and realizing, too, that in the face of such an offer her sense of isolation is really no one's fault but her own. "Of course I know," she says. "I know."

The girls eat their pizza outside, at a table Eve has dragged down onto the grass from the porch. She has poured their milk into wineglasses, and she's gotten out the formal crystal plates instead of the Make-A-Plate plastic plates they usually use, decorated with the girls' old artwork. She'd been disappointed earlier to discover the lettuce already washed and spun in the fridge, the tomato sliced, and the dressing made, thinking of the times when Sophie was left in charge, and how she'd actually cook, fixing them things like breakfast for dinner, or her special homemade pasta sauce, or macaroni and cheese with hot dogs sliced into coins. Feeling underestimated, she'd resolved to make the meal special in her own way, slicing pineapple and scrambling hamburger as toppings, and making a garlic butter dipping sauce for the crust, and setting the table fancily outside.

They eat quietly, and though Eloise is gobbling her dinner happily, Eve herself makes a point of eating slowly, wanting to protract the meal and make it an event, rather than a feeding. She is filled with a rare sense of well-being and contentment; she is pleased by her sister's evident joy, pleased to be responsible for it.

It is the best time of day, in her opinion. The sun's light has taken on a warm and somehow lazy orange glow, and it filters through the overhanging leaves in hazy, slanting rays, not in the starkly dappled pattern of midday, but instead diffused, hovering like a glowing mist above the lawn, where Henry is sniffing about at the quarry's edge. The air smells like cut grass and dust and things grilling, and the temperature is, in Eve's opinion, perfect, such that it is almost difficult for her to tell where her body ends and the air begins. She glances westward. It will be a quiet sunset; it's one of those cloudless evenings, when the sun slips without ceremony beneath the horizon and the sky slowly fades to black, a few minutes earlier tonight than last, and a degree or two over to the left, to her chagrin; though summer has only just started, already the days are waning.

Suddenly, a cry from Eloise breaks the peace. "Evie!" she screams, jumping out of her seat and racing to the quarry's edge, where Eve sees that Henry has gotten into the water. "Get him out! Get him *out!*"

"He's fine!" Eve says, following her sister to the water; and it is true, Henry is swimming quite competently along. "Look at him, he's just gone for a swim."

"Get him *out,* Evie! Out, out, out! Henry, come! Come!" She looks at her sister with desperation. *"Evie!"*

"Eloise! He's fine! He just wanted to cool off. Look!"

Eloise looks out at the water, her face stricken; Henry has started to swim back toward them.

"See? He's a good swimmer."

"I *know* he's a good swimmer," Eloise moans. "But the *quarry*. It's dis*gusting*."

"It's fine, it's clean over here." Eve points. "See

the bright yellow thing? That's keeping all the oil over there. And by now there's probably not much oil left at all. But over here, it's perfectly clean."

Henry has swum right up to them by now; he's got his front paws up on the low ledge where they're standing and is scrabbling to get his haunches up; Eve reaches down and hoists him out of the water by his collar. The dog gives a vigorous shake; Eloise recoils from the spray. "It is *not* perfectly clean," she says. "It's perfectly *disgusting* and it's always going to be."

Eloise looks down at the dog balefully, and Eve understands that her sister's concern is not the oil and gas, but the stain of death. "Eloise," she says. Eloise looks up at her expectantly; though her mind is racing, Eve can think of nothing right to say. "It's okay," she finally says.

"No," Eloise says. "It's not. *Nothing* is okay." She turns and starts to walk across the grass toward the house. Eve watches her. Their elegant dinner sits abandoned in the grass.

By the time they have finished their cheese-urgers and the trivia section of the night has concluded, Joan and Anders have four tickets each for the drawing that brings the evening to an end. There is ordinarily an interlude of about fifteen minutes between the time the trivia ends and the prize drawing begins, during which

221

background music is again turned on and the din of conversation resumes. When the waitress comes to take their plates away, Anders asks her for one more Widow Maker for himself and Joan to share, and she drops two new tickets on the table. Anders slides these toward his wife and watches as she neatly lines them up beside the other four she's arranged into a row.

Their winnings this evening are impressive: they have won two new glasses, a Widow's Walk visor, and a Styrofoam key chain with the logo of one of the marine shops downtown. *Music* was one of the evening's trivia categories, so Anders did especially well, although after answering three of the questions correctly, he began to feel a bit like he was cheating, and he stopped raising his hand. He lifts the key chain from the table now and turns it over in his hands, finding it a somewhat arbitrary prize. It was what Joan won for knowing the full name of King George VI. "What was his name again?" Anders asks.

"Albert Frederick Arthur George."

"How do you know that, anyway?"

Joan considers this. "I have no idea," she says. She laughs. "It's sort of a useless piece of information, isn't it?"

"Well, it did get you a West Marine key chain," Anders reminds her. He sets the key chain down.

The waitress returns with their Widow Maker and two new straws; Anders peels the wrappers from both and puts the straws into the drink, angling one in Joan's direction. He takes a small sip and sits back. "It's hard to believe there was a time when we could drink, what, four of these apiece."

"I know it," Joan says. "And then happily drive home." She begins to push her tickets around the table, rearranging the order. "Five times," she says, thoughtfully.

"What?"

Joan looks up at her husband. "Five times above the legal limit. It *is* pretty drunk."

"Oh," Anders says. "The body."

"James."

"Yuh."

"Don't you think? I mean, five times."

"I do."

Joan frowns, watching the emcee fiddle with the microphone, which has occasionally screeched throughout the evening. "What do *you* think happened?"

Anders breathes deeply. He shrugs. "I don't know."

"I just assumed it was suicide. Right from the beginning." The emcee taps the microphone; a thud echoes. Joan pictures the man in the maroon car, pondering how, if at all, he might be involved. But, like all the other things she cannot bring herself to mention, she does not mention him, though part of her had intended to as soon as Anders and Eve returned. "But now I'm not so sure. I just don't know. I mean, even if it was intentional, how intentional can anything be, really, if you're that drunk?" She bites her lip, aware of how similar she sounds to Eve.

The lights go down; in the dimness, Anders shakes his head. "Whatever it was, I'm not sure that it matters," he says. "The outcome is the same."

The girls leave dinner where it is and give the dog a bath, which Eve is pleased serves as adequate balm to soothe her sister's distress. They play a game of Chinese checkers after that, which she allows Eloise to win; by then it is time for Eloise to go to bed. She does not want to read on in *Alice in Wonderland* without her father, so Eve tells her a made-up bedtime story about a mouse named Steve who gets stuck overnight in a refrigerator; after eating his way through the food on every shelf, finally Steve falls asleep in the cheese drawer. "And so even though he was scared to be stuck at first, in the end he was as happy as if he had died and gone to heaven."

Eloise peers over the edge of the bed with concern, the light from the hallway glinting in her eyes. "But he *is* going to die."

"What do you mean? He's in seventh heaven. It's like if you got stuck in a Moose Tracks ice cream factory overnight."

"No, Evie, there's no oxygen in a refrigerator. You suffocate if you get in one. That's what Mrs. Wilson said. Refrigerators make you suffocate, and if you put a plastic bag over your head you suffocate, too."

Eve takes a breath. "Well," she says. "In this particular instance, a mouse takes up very little oxygen. So there was still plenty by morning, when the owner of the house opened the fridge to get out his breakfast."

"So Steve got out?"

"Yes."

"Did the owner notice? Because then what if he set a trap?"

"He didn't notice. See, he opened up the fridge and the phone rang at the same time, so while he was reaching for the phone Steve made his escape."

Eloise seems satisfied by this. Eve gets up from the floor and tucks her sister into bed, pulling the sheets as tight as she can get them and pinning them beneath the mattress, as Eloise requires, thrilled to think of the note she's left beneath her sister's pillow.

When she has pulled Eloise's door shut behind her, Eve goes out to the lawn to collect the dinner dishes from the table in the grass. Now that dusk has gathered, the daytime sounds of lawn-mowers and the distant cries of playing children have been replaced by the sound of night bugs beginning to swell, like an orchestra warming up, and the gentle rustling of an evening breeze. She pauses in the grass, cocks her ear, listening also for the sounds of car doors slamming, shouts in the woods, anything to suggest that the usual revelers might be out there. She wonders if Saul is out there tonight, as he has been the past few, and what he might be up to. If Sophie were alive, she thinks, Saul would *not* be out there; he'd be here at the house. Instead of clearing the dinner dishes alone, she'd be hanging out in the kitchen helping Saul and Sophie tidy up, or maybe they'd all be making ice cream sundaes, or maybe she'd be setting up the backgammon board for a tournament that would last until her parents came home. Or maybe she'd just be up in her room with a book, alone but secure in the knowledge that Saul and Sophie were downstairs, or sitting out by the quarry—knowing that wherever they were, they were around, and that she and Eloise were not alone. The thought fills her with loneliness and longing, for her sister, for Saul, for the way things used to be.

She brings the dishes in to the kitchen and washes them carefully, sets them to dry in the rack. Afterward, she goes upstairs to her room, and, as has become her habit, pulls out from underneath her bed the bag with all of the stuff from James Favazza's truck: the single blue flip-flop, the purple plastic bowl, the EMS water bottle, the Vic's T-shirt, the beer bottles and beer cans. She gets a piece of paper and makes a list of all these things, including L. Stephens' cooler bag, even if it's not in her possession anymore. Beneath the list of things she's found she draws a diagram of the quarry and the lawn, making arrows to show the route the truck followed through the trees and across the grass. On the back side of the paper, she writes down all of the facts she knows, which are that *supposedly* James Favazza was "last seen" at 11 a.m. outside of his mother's house on Magnolia Street, that the window of the truck had to be smashed in order to open the door to get him out, that he died of drowning, that his blood alcohol level was five times the legal limit.

Five times. Eve cannot get that figure out of her head. She scans the beer bottles and cans before her on the floor, wondering if these were the very beers that contributed to his intoxication the day he died. She lines the beer cans up along the floor, and behind these she lines up the bottles, noticing for the first time that there is an even number of each. This suggests to Eve that there must have been two drinkers, one who preferred Bud, and one who preferred the fancy stuff, and that they kept up with each other beer for beer. She lifts one of the bottles, thoughtfully turns it around in her hand. Tuckerman's Headwall Ale, she reads, Brewed in New Hampshire. She blinks.

New Hampshire! An image flashes through her mind of Larry Stephens' blue Camaro parked lakeside on that creepy street in Georgetown, surrounded by none other than Marlboros butts, with none other than *New Hampshire plates.* She lifts the other kind of bottle, this one a beer called Smuttynose: it is also brewed in New Hampshire.

She sets the beer bottle back into place, mulling over this new piece of evidence; it only goes to further cement in her mind the idea that Larry Stephens was without a doubt present the day of James Favazza's death. Though she's been certain of it all along, his presence definitely rules out suicide, because who kills himself in front of his friend, and what friend lets it happen? Her father, if presented with this evidence, would probably still insist it was an accident, and she can see his case, up to a point. She imagines Larry Stephens and James Favazza drinking together in the truck where they'd parked at the quarry's edge—they must have arrived sober to get between those trees—Larry drinking the New Hampshire brews, James downing the Buds, Larry's cooler bag on the seat between them. She imagines, after a time, Larry getting out of the truck for a piss, James putting the truck into gear, thinking he'd start to drive off and strand his friend at the quarry, a drunken joke, and accidentally driving into the quarry instead; on a gearshift, drive and reverse are just slight clicks away. But if this had happened, why wouldn't Larry have called for help? And why deny ownership of the bag, and knowing James Favazza at all?

She tries out another scenario: again, Larry gets out, this time to smoke one of his Marlboros, and while he's gone, James—at five times drunker than the legal limit—passes out in the truck. When Larry comes back, he thinks his friend is dead, and he's so drunk himself and fearful of the consequences he can think of nothing else to do but put the truck into neutral and push it in! But she's not sure that a friend, no matter how drunk, would react that way. More likely, she thinks, returning to her original theory of murder, they got into some kind of a drunken fight, maybe Larry hit James and knocked him out—but didn't kill him—and then pushed the truck in. The question that remains is *why*.

Eve sighs and slumps back against her bed, letting her eyes wander from the lined-up beers to the T-shirt neatly folded beside them on the floor. Vic's. Vic's is another ingredient in the whole equation. She pictures the bar, that seagull on the roof, the forlorn lettering. If James was a regular there and they were drinking buddies, it makes sense that Larry is, too. Eve scratches at a mosquito bite on her chin, deliberating, then hoists herself with purpose from the floor. She hurries from her bedroom, closing the door behind her, and takes the steps two at a time downstairs. It has only recently become dark, and there are no lights turned on downstairs, but Eve doesn't bother to turn them on now, instead passing through the darkness to the telephone desk in the far corner of the room, where the telephone sits along with a phone book and their lumbering old answering machine. Eve pulls the chair out and spreads the phone book across the table of her thighs, her bare heels hugging the chair's thin wooden rung. She finds Vic's in the directory and dials the number, her heart going like a hummingbird.

The phone is picked up after the second ring. At first, she can only hear the background noises of a bar: muddled voices, tinny music, the occasional shout, glasses clinking. And then she can also hear the voice of whoever has answered the phone—the bartender, she assumes—and though she imagines that he is holding the phone to his ear, maybe has it tucked handless between ear and shoulder, he continues a conversation with someone else. *Yuh,* she hears him say. *Yuh, exactly, that's my point. That's exactly—wait a minute, would you?*

"*Hell*-o," he says, his voice suddenly loud in Eve's ear.

"Hi." Eve clears her throat. "Have I reached Vic's?"

"This is Vic's." She hears a clink, and the distinct sound of liquid pouring, the mutter of voices in the background.

"Yes, I'm wondering if you can help me with something."

"Yeah, I ah—you're going to have to speak up, I can't quite hear you," he says loudly.

"I—" Eve clears her throat. "Yes, I—ah, I'm looking for James Favazza. Is he there?" She winces, waiting for a response.

"You're looking for who? Mazzo? Mazzo's not here." Eve can hear tumbling ice, a whoop, chants of *Nomar! Nomar!*

"No," Eve says loudly. "Favazza. James Favazza."

For a moment, there is no response. "Who is this?"

"Sorry?"

"Who's calling?"

"Um, Joan," Eve says. "Joan Anders . . . son." Again, she winces.

There is another pause on the other end of the line, which seems to Eve pregnant with unsaid things. She holds her breath. "He's not here," the man finally says, and before Eve has a chance to reply, the line goes dead.

Eve sits for a moment, wide-eyed in the darkness, the phone forgotten at her ear until it begins to angrily buzz. She sets it down, going over the whole exchange in her mind. There was something to it, she thinks. His hesitation. His silence. Those words: *He's not here.* He didn't say, *Who?* Or, *He's not here right now.* So clearly, the bartender knew who James Favazza was, and also knows that he isn't ever coming back. So James *was* a regular there, and Larry, too. Then the people at Vic's, she thinks, are a whole new font of information . . . tipsy locals who can tell her what she wants to know about these guys, or at least more than she knows right now, like what they might have been fighting about—a bet, maybe, or a girl. The key is just getting in there—but how, without an ID? She looks out into the darkness, scheming, and before she has time to think better of it, or to remember Eloise asleep upstairs, she hurries outside and leaps off the porch, races into the night.

Anders drives them home when trivia night has ended, their winnings laid out on the seat between them: the cups and visors, the key chain, and finally, the World Cup soccer ball, which Joan won in the drawing. It rolls across the seat with every turn in the road, reminding each, as it hits a thigh, of Sophie.

They drive in silence, each staring intently into the pocket of light the headlights afford, watching the yellow line of the road disappear behind the car as if it were being reeled in. The night is mild, the heat of the day still emanating from the metal of the car, which is warm beneath Anders' arm where it rests on the frame of the door. Sometime over the winter small stretches of the road were repaved; the wheels whir over the old sections, whoosh over the new ones, *whirrrrr, whooosh, whirrrrr, whooosh.* Joan reaches over to turn the radio on; she turns the knob, crackles through static, turns it off again.

"Antenna's broken," Anders says.

Joan does not reply. Anders steers through a curve in the road; the soccer ball rolls across the seat. Anders picks it up, drops it over his shoulder onto the floor of the backseat. He saw Joan's face when her number was called, and does not need to ask what she is thinking.

They pull up the driveway soon after. Anders turns the engine off and sets the key in the ashtray, and for a moment, neither of them gets out of the car. A gentle breeze rustles in the topmost branches of the trees, and somewhere at the quarry's edge a frog is ribbiting away. Before them, the downstairs windows of the house are dark, though the light above the stove in the kitchen has been left on, and the windows of Eve's room are still aglow.

"Home again, home again," Anders says.

Joan gathers their prizes from the front seat of the car, and they go in through the kitchen door. Anders turns off the light above the stove and flips the overhead lights on; they flicker and buzz to life. "Remarkable," he says, noticing the dishes gleaming in the dish rack. "The dishes have been done."

Joan raises an eyebrow. "The sculptor's crystal, no less."

Joan sets the glasses and key chain on the table and hooks the visor on the edge of a chair, then leaves Anders in the kitchen putting the dishes away and goes upstairs to check on the girls. She comes first to Eloise's room; behind the door she can hear her daughter whimpering. She frowns, and cracks the door open; a triangle of light falls across the floor.

"Eloise?" she asks, pushing the door open all the way. "What's the matter, sweetie?"

At this, her daughter's cries grow louder, and Joan crosses the room and kneels beside her bed, where Eloise lies in a ball.

"I have a stomachache," she cries. "It really hurts."

"Show me where it hurts," Joan says, and Eloise uncurls herself to point. "We'll get you some Pepto, okay?"

"What's the matter?"

Joan turns; Anders has appeared in the doorway, silhouetted by the hall light. "Tummyache," she reports.

"I'll get the Pepto," Anders says. He walks down the hall toward the bathroom, pausing in front of Eve's room to tap on the door. When he gets no response, he taps again, and calls her name through the door. "Evie," he says, "we're home." Again, he hears nothing. He frowns, reaching for the handle of the door, and when he eases it open, he finds that his daughter is not in fact within, and having just passed through both the kitchen and the main room downstairs, he knows that she isn't down there, either. He sighs, looking into the room, where there are several beer bottles and beer cans lined up on the floor, along with an assortment of other junk that Anders has no doubt came from the quarry, and he understands quickly that she can only be off on some related mission. He goes into the room and puts his hands on his hips, surveying it all, and in a moment he hears Joan's voice calling his name as she comes down the hall. He turns around as she appears in the doorway.

"Oh, no," she says, her face falling.

"Oh, yes," he says. "No Eve. I think we have a problem."

Saul's brown Volvo is parked a few car lengths down from the gate to the public quarry, where three other cars have parked so far tonight. Eve makes it through the woods from the house to the road in record time, dodging limbs and leaping over fallen trees in her haste, no longer nervous amid the dark trees. When she reaches the gate, she pauses, breathing heavily, and wipes the sweat from her forehead with the back of her arm. She listens for the sound of voices, but it is quiet aside from the clicking timbals of cicadas and, in the distance, a barred owl asking over and over again what sounds to Eve like "Who cooks for *you?* Who cooks for *you?*" She gazes over the gate and down the path, anxiously remembering the other night, and the ring of people gathered around the fire at the quarry's edge that she'll somehow have to penetrate tonight, and who might balk to see her there. But. She swallows, and looks again toward Saul's car, reminding herself of why she's come here at all. She needs him to take her to Vic's.

The car is parked in a patch of mottled moonlight along the side of the road, and it faces away from Eve, so she can see the collection of bumper stickers pasted to the tailgate. Momentarily distracted by these, she wanders the short distance down the road to where Saul's car is parked. She crouches down behind it, her elbows on her knees, and lets her eyes skim over the various stickers. U.S. Sailing. I'm Going Nuckin' Futs. Old Crow Medicine Show. Keep Tahoe Blue. Cat: The Other White Meat.

And then Eve comes to the one that she is looking for: Consciousness: That Annoying Time Between Naps. She picked this one out with Sophie at a rest stop on I-93 two summers ago, on their way back from Canobie Lake Park, where Saul and Sophie had driven Eve and her friend Debbie Wasson for the day. Or Sophie had driven; Saul slept the whole drive up and the whole drive back. Eve and Sophie and Debbie had watched him, laughing at the way his head tilted slowly forward then jerked up again, and the way when he held his head back against the seat a throaty purr escaped his slightly open mouth. At the rest stop, the girls left him sleeping in the car, and inside, as they waited in line to pay for drinks, they surveyed a rack of bumper stickers and couldn't resist getting this one.

Eve had thought that maybe Saul might have peeled the sticker off. She thinks of the other night, and the way he had his head resting in that other girl's lap, the way he allowed her to drag her braid across his forehead . . . but the sticker is still there, and for that Eve feels a certain triumph on her sister's behalf.

As she crouches there, remembering, she is startled by the cluck of a car door and then another unlatching, and suddenly she finds herself bathed in yellow light streaming from the Volvo's interior. Instinctively, she lowers her head, and briefly considers dropping down and rolling beneath the car to hide, but before she has time to act, one of the car doors has closed, and she hears a gasp above her. She looks up; illuminated by the light of the car's interior, she can see the body of a girl in cutoff denim shorts and a T-shirt with the drop-mouthed logo of the Rolling Stones. The girl's head is in the darkness above the pocket of warm light shining through the window, but Eve knows who it is; the end of a long, brown braid hangs down across her chest. The second car door closes then, and the inside light goes off; instead of blissfully disappearing into darkness, Eve finds herself instead still clearly visible in the moonlight, as suddenly the girl in her entirety is, too, and Saul, when he steps around the side of the car.

"Evie!" he says, when he sees her crouching there.

"You know her?" the girl asks.

"Yeah," Saul says. He frowns at Eve, the look on his face a muddle of confusion, annoyance, and surprise. "What are you *doing* here?"

"I—" she begins, mortified to realize how unbelievable the truth will seem; no matter *what* the two of them were doing in there—and Eve hates to even consider it—they will think that she was spying. "I didn't realize you were in the car. I swear. I was—" She sighs in defeat. "I was looking at your bumper stickers."

Saul runs a hand through his hair.

"I know you probably don't believe me but it's true. I swear." On Sophie's life, she wants to say, but she holds her tongue.

"Saul?" the girl asks, her voice tight. "What is going on?"

Saul touches the girl gently on the shoulder. "Just hang on a minute." He takes a step forward and extends a hand to Eve, who had hardly even realized that she was still crouched down on the ground. She lets him pull her up, acutely aware of his hand, which is big and firm around her own. "And you were out here because . . ." he prompts her, once she's standing and he has let her hand go.

Eve narrows her eyes, feeling suddenly defensive; why *shouldn't* she be out here? "I was *walking*," she says, just as Saul had said to her the other night.

Saul looks at her. "Okay," he finally says. "Fair enough." He gives her a slight nod.

Eve blinks back at him.

Saul turns to the girl. "Should we go?" he asks, gesturing toward the gate.

"Yeah," the girl says, slowly, skeptically. "Let's."

Saul takes the girl's hand, and the two start to walk up the road. Eve watches them flash in and out of moonlight as they go, and they have just reached the gate when Eve remembers her whole purpose for coming out here in the first place. "Wait!" she calls. "Saul!"

Saul turns around, and Eve takes a few steps in his direction. "That's not really why I was out here. I wasn't really just walking."

Saul waits.

"I—" Eve glances at the girl, then looks back at Saul. "Can I talk to you for a second?"

Saul takes a breath, then nods. "Yeah," he says.

"Hang on." He turns to the girl; they exchange words in low voices. Then he helps her over the gate and watches for a moment as she disappears down the path toward the quarry. Finally, he faces Eve, beckons her over, and she obeys.

"So why were you out here," he asks, but without the inflection of a question.

"I was looking for you," she says.

"And why were you looking for me?"

Eve frowns; whatever thought process propelled her out here with such urgency seems suddenly jumbled and unclear. "I—It's kind of hard to explain," she begins. "But the other night . . ."

"Yeah?"

"After it was raining and you snuck up on me in the woods?"

"I didn't sneak—never mind. What about the other night?"

"Remember I was telling you about the quarry? The guy that drove in? Or supposedly drove in?"

"Yes," Saul says. "I remember."

"And the T-shirt I told you I found?"

"The T-shirt?"

"The Vic's T-shirt?"

"Oh, right. Yeah?"

"And you said Vic's was a dump."

"Uh-huh."

"Which means you've been there."

"Once, maybe twice."

"But, so, what was it like?"

"I don't know. Nothing special."

"That's it?"

Saul shrugs. "I don't know what you want me to say. I've been to Vic's, it wasn't great, I probably won't go back."

Eve sighs. "But you *could*."

"If I was so inclined."

"And you're not twenty-one."

"I'm not following you."

"You got into Vic's, but you're not twenty-one."

"There are a lot of bars in this town that don't really care about that," Saul says.

"Do you have a fake ID?"

"Eve, did you really come out into the woods at night to ask me this stuff?"

"Yes, actually. I did. Do you have a fake ID?"

"I do, yes."

"Did you have to show it to get in to Vic's?"

Saul lets out a breath that suggests growing impatience. "You're not going to like my answer, Evie, but I honestly don't remember."

"Well, anyway, I need you to take me there."

"To Vic's?"

"Yeah."

"Tonight?"

"Yeah."

"Evie, first of all, even if they didn't card me, I don't think they're going to let you in. Second of all—"

"I don't even need to go in! You can go in and just ask a couple questions for me!"

"Second of all, I already *have* plans for the night."

Eve does not answer. She slaps at a mosquito on her arm, wishing, too late, that she had not come out here at all. "Dammit," she says, studying the smear of blood on her palm. Saul, she can tell, is watching her closely; she looks at him, hard. "What?" she demands.

"I don't know what this is all about, Evie. I don't know exactly what you're after, but I hope you're not going to get yourself into any trouble."

Eve flattens her mouth, feeling suddenly foolish, lonely, and deeply misunderstood. But then again, here in the woods, part of her isn't sure what she's after herself. She looks at the ground, noticing the way the pebbles are casting shadows in the moonlight. She kicks one in Saul's direction, then looks up. "I'm not going to get myself in any trouble, thank you very much," she says. "Anyway, forget about it. I shouldn't have come and bugged you. And your *girlfriend*."

Saul frowns. "Evie."

Eve shrugs. She looks off into the woods, letting her eyes blur. She takes a deep breath, in and out, then refocuses her vision. "Anyway," she says, blinking. "Like I said. Forget about it. I should go. And *you* should go."

"I should," Saul agrees. He hesitates. "You okay, Eve?"

"Fine," Eve says shortly.

"You sure?"

"I'm fine."

"All right," Saul says. He puts an arm around her, pulls her to his chest, which is solid and warm and makes Eve want to shut her eyes right there and go to sleep, and the uncomfortable realization dawns on her that maybe it was *this* that she was after, not a way into Vic's at all, which she now sees as the harebrained idea that it is. "I'll see you around," he says after a moment, letting her go.

"Yeah," Eve says, glumly. She swallows. "See you." She watches as he vaults over the gate. "Saul!" she calls after him, and he turns. "I really was just reading your bumper stickers. I swear it."

He nods, and half smiles in the moonlight. "I believe you," he says. He turns away again, disappears down the path.

Eve stands in the road, looks up through the leaves and branches, which are black against the sky, and beyond them at the moon, whose face looks distinctly as if it is laughing at her. "Who cooks for *you!*" the owl hoots in the distance, and she thinks of Sophie, and suddenly she thinks with a sinking feeling of Eloise, asleep at the house alone. "Who cooks for *you!*"

Six

Somewhere up in the attic Joan is certain there is an old typewriter, which she has decided to search out to see how the process of writing might change if she cannot so easily press delete; this week alone she's generated countless pages that all have vanished with the swipe of a finger. It is early—not yet seven o'clock—but she has been up for hours, unable to sleep for the yammering of starlings gathered in the trees outside and the oddly empty racing of her mind, so she's decided to give in, get up, and start the day.

It is the first day of what is forecasted to be a heat wave; when Joan pulls down the attic's hatch door, she can immediately sense the sweltering air above, which makes the hallway seem cool by comparison. She extends the rickety folding ladder and carefully climbs up; her heart falls when she emerges through the hatch and looks around. She can't recall the last time she was up here, but it is more crowded than she remembers. What used to be an attic at their house in Maryland was converted into a bedroom by the people who owned the house before Joan and Anders moved in seventeen years ago, and so everything of theirs that one might keep in an attic is kept here, and the space is filled to capacity. Trunks and boxes are piled in the middle of the room, where the ceiling is highest. A narrow path leads around this pile, lined on its other side by the smaller items that are stored in the space where the sloped ceiling meets the floor, and against the back wall, shelves are filled from top to bottom. Joan has no idea where among all this stuff the typewriter might be.

A single lightbulb hangs from the ceiling just beyond the hatch; Joan pulls the string attached, and is unsurprised to find that the bulb has burned out. She doesn't bother to go down to get a new bulb to replace it; there are pie-shaped windows at the attic's either end, which are scratched and somewhat clouded, yet still let in a haze of light that is enough for her to see by. She wanders down the narrow path, scanning the labels of boxes in the center of the room to her right and peering into the low shadows at the loose things piled on her left.

There are several boxes of old clothes, one that contains suits of Anders' from the eighties, one that contains baby clothes, and one labeled Winter Stuff. There is a box labeled Shoes, and another Grad School Stuff, whether Anders' or her own she isn't sure, nor does she bother to find out. There are all sorts of items tucked beneath the low slope of ceiling to her left. A pair of roller skates. Rusted cross-country skis. A folded stroller. A cardboard heart covered in purple velvet, which Joan made for Anders when he had surgery to remove a benign tumor from his lung before they were even married. A pair of tennis rackets so old that they resemble lollipops, with long, thin necks and small, round heads. A castle made of cardboard (Sophie's), and another made of sponge (Eve's). These were third-grade social studies projects done while the class studied medieval times—an assignment partially for parents, Joan thinks, remembering the hours Anders spent on both girls' castles, the girls themselves the slightly distracted scissor holders and glue passers and snack getters. Eloise, it occurs to her, will be in the third grade this year; soon another castle will join these castles' ranks.

When she reaches the back of the attic, she spies the typewriter on the topmost shelf against the wall, between a dusty swivel-necked fan and a lamp that is missing its shade, and she is grateful, given the attic's stifling heat, at how easy it was to find. The typewriter is not quite beyond her reach, but it is high enough that she worries it might topple as she tries to coax it down, so she looks around for something to stand on, opting in the end for a metal box that she recognizes as Anders' old tool kit, which sits on the floor beneath the window. She goes to get it, pausing at the window to gaze out at everything below. It is early enough that the trees still cast shadows like fallen versions of themselves across the grass, on which dewdrops glint in the sunlight. The shape of the quarry looks different from this height, less like a rectangle, as she usually thinks of it, than a lima bean, but with sharp contours. The water's surface is glassy still, though suddenly, as Joan is looking, slight rings of ripples start to spread from the nearest corner—the disturbance of a turtle, Joan thinks, or a frog leaping in from the edge.

She lets her eyes skim over the lawn, which looks much more badly rutted from this perspective than it does from the ground; they'll have to till the soil and reseed, she imagines, and it will be some time before all traces of the incident have vanished from the lawn. Roscoe McWilliams and his crew are coming at noon to remove the boom and skimmer, which will leave even more ruts, though at least the yellow tubing will be gone, the quarry clean. And she hopes—she touches the wood of the wall—there will be no cause for any other vehicles—police cars, ambulances, tow trucks, or otherwise—to drive across the lawn again.

She is about to turn from the window when she sees a flash of red out of the corner of her eye; below her, Eve has emerged from the garage, dragging a garbage bag behind her, Henry the dog not far behind. Joan watches. Eve is wearing a pair of ratty cutoff shorts and a Red Sox T-shirt with the sleeves cut off, and she's got a blue bandanna tied around her head. Halfway across the driveway, she turns around and begins to walk backward so she can lug the garbage bag more easily. She has almost reached the driveway's edge, where two garbage cans have been set out for pickup, when the bag's plastic succumbs to the driveway's graveled surface and the contents—a ruined paintbrush, an empty can, a few small scraps of wood, one of which the dog snatches up and brings with it to the grass—begin to spill through a tear in the bottom. Eve lets the bag go and puts her hands on her hips. Joan sees her daughter's shoulders rise and fall in a sigh. And then, instead of going in to get a second garbage bag, Eve turns the bag over so the hole is facing up, squats down, and with visible effort hoists the entire thing and carries it the remaining distance to the garbage cans. She knocks the lid off one with a bare foot, and drops the bag in.

After they had gotten home from the Widow's Walk the other night, Anders had put Eve's collection of quarry-related items into a bag that they took out with them to the porch, where they sat in the darkness to wait for Eve to return home. They didn't have to wait for long; it was not even ten minutes after they'd settled into the old wooden rocking chairs when she appeared out of the shadows, breathless and sweaty. In the brief time that they'd had to wait, they'd discussed possible punishments without much enthusiasm; what was most important to them both was that Eve understand that she had been unacceptably irresponsible. But she already seemed to know it. She climbed the porch steps wearily, and when she saw her parents waiting there it was without much surprise. "I know it," Eve said, nodding. "I'm the worst. I am. Ground me."

Anders and Joan had never grounded any of their children before, and in truth neither had a clear grasp on what grounding should entail. In the end, they decided to forbid any postdark outings for two weeks, and to tax half the earnings from her nursery job, which sum would go to funding payment of any baby-sitters they had to hire in the future. Oddly, she seemed less upset by the curfew or the money than she did by the idea of a baby-sitter other than herself.

"So," she asked, as if what she'd been told were difficult to comprehend, "I don't get to baby-sit again?"

"Clearly," Anders said, "you aren't to be trusted." And the way she seemed to shrink at the words made Joan feel as if they alone were almost punishment enough.

In the five days since, Eve has taken it upon herself to wash both cars, to vacuum the entire house, to organize the bookshelves, and now, evidently, and even at this early hour, to clean out the garage, some of the contents of which Joan can see out in the driveway: a foosball table with several missing players, a box of lobster pots collected from the beach, and an old kayak that belongs to Anders' brother. While part of Joan is compelled to tell Eve that it's okay, that she can stop, another part of her feels as if to do so would somehow be belittling, and that she should simply let this run its course. Besides, Eve would certainly bristle at her mother's interference.

Below her, in the driveway, Eve turns from the garbage can and makes her way to where her bike is lying in the grass. She crouches down to give Henry a pat good-bye, then lifts the bike, straddles it, and pedals off down the driveway.

When Eve arrives at the nursery, she sees Nestor outside among the rows of plant-strewn tables, tying a tall, blue-flowering plant to a stake. She stands there for a minute at the edge of the lot, observing him as she catches her breath, and then she props her bike against a tree and starts across the dirt and gravel. Nestor glances up at her, but continues to work as she approaches.

"Delphinium Consolida," he says, tying twine into a knot around the stem. "From the Greek word *delphis*." He straightens up and looks Eve in the eye. "Do you know why?"

"No."

"*Delphis*. Dolphin." He points to one of the many blue, bell-shaped flowers. "The shape of the flower resembles the bottlelike nose of a dolphin, does it not?"

Eve frowns. "Kind of."

"Well." Nestor regards the plant. "It is also known as the larkspur. And it's highly poisonous."

"Poisonous?"

"All parts of the plant contain delphinine. A toxic alkaloid." He turns and points to another flowering plant, similar to the delphinium, but pink. "And this is?"

"Foxglove," Eve replies; foxglove was the plant on which he'd schooled her yesterday, hollyhock two days before.

"Or?"

"Digitalis purpurea."

Nestor nods once, down and up, approvingly. "And once again, this is?" He looks down at the delphinium.

"Delphinium . . . Consolida?"

"Very good." Nestor folds his arms across his chest; for all the dirt on his hands and arms he looks as if he were wearing gloves. "You're late."

"I know. I'm sorry."

"Reason?"

Eve opens her mouth. "I lost track of time," she says. "I—I was cleaning out the garage."

Nestor cocks an eyebrow. "At this hour?"

"Yes," Eve says. "At this hour." She shrugs. "It's kind of hard to explain. And anyway, I like

251

mornings." She squints an eye at Nestor, curiously. "What time do *you* get here in the morning, anyway?"

For a moment, Nestor only looks at her, unblinking. "I don't leave," he says finally.

"Oh." This is all Eve can think to reply. She looks around her. "What should I water today?"

Nestor brushes his hands together and clears his throat. "Today," he turns and points to the trays of flowers set out on tables behind the greenhouse, "most of these perennials over here are thirsty." Eve follows Nestor to the plants in question. "See here? Touch the soil." Eve does. "How does that feel?"

"Dry."

"As I've said, that's the only real way to know when to water. Soil moisture. If it's dry in the top four or five inches, it's time to water. Soon, I won't have to show you. You'll know what needs water when."

"How much should I give these guys?"

"For these, twenty, thirty seconds at the base of each plant. Now. What's the difference between an annual and a perennial?"

"How long they live?"

"That's right. Annuals, you will remember from yesterday, live for how long?"

"A year."

"And *bi*ennials?"

"Two years."

"And then we have perennials. *Per,* through, *annus,* year. Through the years. They bloom in the summer, die back in the winter, and return from their rootstock, again and again. As opposed to annuals, which seed themselves."

"So," Eve ventures, "roses would be perennials, right?"

"They would. But unlike some perennials, like the delphinium," he gestures toward the plant he'd earlier been staking, "which lasts only a few years, the rose can have impressive staying power." He looks at Eve thoughtfully. "The oldest rose in the world lives in Germany, on the wall of Hildesheim Cathedral. Do you know how long it's flourished?"

Eve shakes her head.

"Over a thousand years."

Eve's eyes widen; this seems, to her, impossible. "Have you seen it?" she asks.

Nestor smiles. "Of course I have. *Nestor.* Greek for traveler."

After he has left Eloise at camp, Anders drives to Plum Cove, where his diving class is scheduled to meet for their first real dive. At their last pool session last week, Dave gave each of them a test to ensure their readiness to move on to open water, which all four students passed, and sent each of them home with a video to watch in advance of today's meeting, which covered every aspect of diving: the basics of diving techniques, diving safety, equipment selection and maintenance, dive planning, and how diving affects your body. Eve watched the video with Anders, and she found particularly fascinating a somewhat alarming phenomenon that occurs when diving to greater depths than they will ever attempt in this class—something called nitrogen narcosis, a state of intoxication nicknamed "rapture of the deep," which makes it seem almost appealing, except for the fact that it can cause a diver to drown.

Plum Cove is a sheltered half-moon, with a beach at its head, which Dave said he has chosen for their first open-water swim because it is shallow, with an easy, sandy entry; there are no slippery boulders to navigate, or much sea swell, or strong tides. Anders parks along the side of the road. He gets his wet suit, fins, BCD, and mask from the back of the car and lays them out on the hood, preferring to wait for the rest of the class in the shade of the roadside trees. It is still early enough that the beach is not crowded despite the day's heat, to which everything seems to have surrendered; haze sits heavily on the horizon, and the bay is flat and glassy. A sailboat bobs a short ways out, its sails flapping listlessly as it drifts out with the tide.

Anders leans back against the car, looking out at the cove. Often he has seen groups of divers gathered on the shore, or the red flags that signal divers are below, but he has never actually considered what they might be seeing down there. He associates scuba diving with coral reefs and exotic fish and turquoise waters; the waters here are dark and cold, and in truth he has never wondered much what lies beneath the surface. Now he looks out curiously, if not without some trepidation. He'd had several dreams about drowning last night, and this morning he'd half decided to bow out of today's dive, but he couldn't think of how he'd explain himself to his family. And so he's here: it's as simple as that.

Soon he hears a car approaching, and a van pulls up behind him.

"It's a hot one!" Dave calls, climbing out of the van. "Perfect day for diving. You psyched?"

"I'm looking forward to it," Anders says, trying to sound enthusiastic.

Dave goes around to the back of the van and swings the doors open, reappears with a cylinder tank of oxygen under either arm.

"Can I give you a hand?" Anders asks.

"There are a couple more back there," Dave says, repositioning one tank beneath his arm. "If you want to get those it'd be great."

With the two remaining cylinders he follows Dave down onto the beach. They set the cylinders on the sand not far from the water's edge.

"Only four?" Anders asks; there are four people in the class, five including Dave.

"We've lost Mary Alice, I'm afraid."

"Ah." Anders nods. He is not entirely surprised; at the last session he and Mary Alice had been assigned as buddies while they practiced gas-sharing, in the event that during a dive one buddy's tank should fail, and she had seemed neither comfortable nor enthusiastic. Still, her absence makes him feel even more anxious; no one else aside from Mary Alice in the class is over thirty, and Anders took a certain comfort in her presence; if she could do it, he could do it. Now he feels as if he has lost an ally.

Soon after Anders and Dave have brought the tanks down to the beach and returned to the shade, Pete and Caroline arrive. All four of them put their wet suits on by their respective cars, and then they trudge down to the water's edge. Dave supervises them as they prepare their equipment, as they have been taught to do. Anders works carefully, recognizing that in this activity, more than most others, there is no room for error. He can't help but think of Eve's query the other morning about whether he'd rather burn to death or drown; he'd have to agree with her that drowning would be worse, and he finds himself thinking of all the things that could cause him to drown today—he could have a heart attack; or his tank could fail; or, once he's at the bottom, he could panic and forget everything he's learned to do. And then what? He doesn't know, and when he reconsiders the endless, lonely darkness death represents, he is dumbfounded all over again that it is something Sophie chose to face, and worse, that it is something he has lost her to.

After Dave has carefully double-checked everyone's equipment, they put on their weight belts and help each other on with their tanks. Beneath his wet suit, Anders by this time has long been soaked in sweat, whether more from nerves or from heat he's unsure. Dave points in the direction of the reef they'll be exploring, goes over the basics one more time, and assigns buddies: Pete and Caroline are a pair, and Anders, to his relief, is buddies with Dave. "I can't stress it enough, you guys," Dave says. "Know where your buddy is at all times. Got it?"

They nod.

"Let's do it."

They put their masks on and their regulators into their mouths, and, fins in hand, they enter the water. Even though the plastic of Anders' mask is clear, through it the world seems very far away; this sense of distance is only heightened by the thick skin of his wet suit and the hoodie tight around his head. He listens to his pulse thrumming in his ears and concentrates on his breathing, taking a breath with every wading step he makes into the water. When he is waist deep, he pauses with the rest of the group to put his fins on and inflate his BCD.

Dave removes the regulator from his mouth. "Everyone good?" he asks, and when he sees each of them nod, he returns the regulator to his mouth, gives a thumbs-up sign, and falls backward into the water.

Anders looks up, fixing his gaze on a single wisp of cloud streaked like a brushstroke through the sky, and lets himself fall back. Suddenly the sky above him is replaced by a wavery green shot through with shards of shattered light, and bubbles racing up toward the surface. Anders watches them until they cease, feeling the cold water seep into his wet suit, and then he turns over, so that he is floating facedown, and begins to swim in the direction of the reef.

Eve is home from the nursery by nine. She drops her bike in the driveway and heads straight for the garage, wanting to finish cleaning it out so she can begin whatever task she decides to tackle next; since Trivia Night, she has been determined to redeem herself; she screwed up in a way that Sophie *never* would. When she returned to the house that night and her mother asked her what on earth she'd been thinking, it was difficult for her to articulate. She explained about the two types of beer, and about the cooler bag and Larry Stephens, and the Vic's

T-shirt, and the bartender's response when she called him up, and how certain she felt that she could learn something possibly vital at the bar. She had tried valiantly to get her parents to see, but even as she uttered her justification, it was clear to her—and had already become so, out in the woods—how flimsy it was.

"And why," her father asked, when she had finished speaking, "even if you are correct in your assumptions, did you have to try to get to Vic's *tonight?* Vic's isn't going anywhere. Saul isn't going anywhere. Could it not have waited until tomorrow?"

Eve opened her mouth to reply, but she was at a loss for words. "It could have," she finally agreed.

"All right, then, Evie," her father had said, and he had given her a firm look. "Listen to me, okay? Enough is enough. Got it?"

"Yeah," she'd said. "Okay."

She has tried to moderate her preoccupation with James Favazza in the days since; she hasn't brought up the incident with her parents or anyone else, and she has tried to keep busy with other things. Of course she does still think about it—she cannot help herself—and in the evenings, in the privacy of her bedroom, she allows herself to speculate over James Favazza's things. But she keeps all conjecture to herself, and she has refrained from any active sleuthing that might get her into trouble.

She steps now into the shadows of the garage, where it is cool compared to the sun outside. She surveys the space, pleased by her progress. She's stored the paints and glues and sprays she deemed worth saving underneath the worktable, in an old glass aquarium that used to hold the Siamese fighting fish they kept when they were younger, which died all at once from poison algae growth. She's gotten rid of junk from the standing closet, too, and reorganized the remaining contents: fishing poles and tackle (which have not been used in years), a set of oars, extension cords of various colors and lengths. There are only a few more boxes to go through, which she'd left out in the middle of room before going to the nursery this morning.

She sorts through these now. One box is filled with old electronics—wires and cables and other devices she doesn't recognize and so can't decide whether to keep or throw away; this box she sets aside for her father to take a look at. In the next box, she finds all sorts of tools—chisels and files and wire modeling tools that she recognizes from ceramics class; these must have belonged to the sculptor who lived here before them.

In the last box, she discovers a transistor radio, an old VCR, and, housed in a sturdy case, a boxy old manual Pentax camera and two used rolls of film. She takes the camera out of its case with interest. Though it clearly hasn't been used in years, it appears to be functional; it clicks obediently when she presses the shutter release, and when she winds the dial, the film inside advances. She looks at the camera curiously, wondering whose it is, how old the film might be, what pictures might be on it, and on the other rolls, too.

She takes the camera with her out to the quarry and sits down on a ledge. The zoom, she discovers, is impressive; peering through the viewfinder, she traces the quarry's edge, adjusting the focus as she goes, amazed by the camera's ability to capture each crevice up close, and the bits of pollen, and the water bugs afloat on the surface of the water. She looks at the high ledge where James Favazza's car went in, as if she might see something she has not seen before —a shard of glass from a taillight, maybe—but there is nothing there worth noting. She focuses in on her father's roses, where, through the camera, she can see a bee hovering above one. She zooms in on the starlings overhead, which have been swarming noisily in the trees all day. Up close, they look decidedly more purple than black, though it is hard for her to focus on one for any length of time before it swoops out of view.

Still peering through the lens, she lowers the camera; suddenly she sees her mother's face: lined, pensive, staring off into some distance. Eve hadn't realized her mother was even home. She watches her, sees a flinch of muscle along the side of her mouth, the blink of an eye, the absent parting of lips; studied this way, suddenly her mother looks entirely and oddly unfamiliar, in the way that a word will start to sound strange when you say it over and over again: number, number, number, number. Eve lowers the camera, unsettled; with her bare eyes, her mother is just a figure across the quarry, standing on the porch with a watering can in hand; with her bare eyes, her mother is just her mother again.

But then Joan notices Eve; she lifts a hand, smiles and waves. Eve waves back, and then both of them look up at a heightened chatter in the trees; as if on cue, the starlings clustered overhead rise at once and swarm into the sky, where they seem to become a single swirling entity against the blue.

The reef is about a hundred yards out past the entrance to the cove and runs parallel to the shore; they have to descend only twenty feet or so to reach it. Anders had imagined the reef would be covered with a thin green film of algae, barnacles, perhaps a few starfish, but it is in fact like an underwater garden; there is the furlike wavering green that Anders had expected, and the clinging starfish, but there are also fist-size pink anemones, and clusters of what look like fragile heads of lettuce, the leaves nearly tranlucent. There is one sort of plant that looks like a soft green fan, a sheep's ear of the sea, and one part of the reef is covered with a growth that looks like purple lace.

Anders had thought maybe they'd see a lobster here, a flounder there, perhaps a skate or two skimming the bottom, but there is in fact a whole society of creatures gathered by the reef, coexisting like members of a small city. There are giant hermit crabs, their shells and legs covered with hairlike algae, that seem to creep almost tentatively along, testing each step with a leg before they take it, like blind men tapping with their canes. There are other crabs that look like purple spiders, from which Anders keeps a wary distance, and the more traditionally shaped crabs, with shells spotted like a leopard's skin. Sitting bloated at the bottom in the shade of a rocky ledge there is a creature the likes of which he has never seen before, a bright red lump of a fish with lazy eyes and a large, O-shaped mouth, which to Anders looks decidedly bored. At the far end of the reef, somewhat removed from the other creatures, there is a pair of squid, hovering pink and electric, their eyes like large round mirrors and their tentacles aglow, as if wrapped around some purple neon current. Anders swims slowly, surveying all of this with amazement, and sometimes, as with the squid and the purple spider-crabs, mild alarm. It is hard for him to believe that all of this is here, and has been here all along; he feels as if he has been presented with a color he never knew existed.

They have almost swum the length of the reef and back when Anders finds himself above a sandy stretch of seafloor, where he notices camouflaged against the sand a flat fish, which is almost invisible but for the faintest trace of its outline. Anders pauses, and for a moment simply hovers, gazing down. The fish is about the size of a dinner plate, with a delicate tendrilled fringe and round black eyes that seem to study Anders as curiously as he is studying the fish. When he looks more closely, he sees that the fish is actually more transparent than colored like the sand, as he'd originally thought; if he held it up to the light he is sure he would be able to see all its countless fragile bones. After a moment, the fish gives a flick of its tail and slowly swims away, leaving in its wake a slight and quickly settling plume of sand, and a second later, Anders feels a tap on his shoulder. He turns; Dave is signaling that it is time to go up. He looks upward, where Caroline and Pete are already small figures overhead, and then back at Dave, whom he realizes that against diving protocol he had all but forgotten. Dave looks at him questioningly, with two thumbs up. Anders nods. He obediently inflates his BCD and propels himself toward the surface, feeling like a kid on a carnival ride that has come to an end.

Breaking through the surface is like waking from a pleasant dream; the real world seems vaguely disappointing by comparison. He blinks into the day's bright light, which is almost blinding after the cavelike dimness of the deep. Everything is the same as it was an hour ago when they descended, though Anders has the odd sense that it shouldn't be. The bay is still windless and glassy, the sky still a nearly cloudless blue, though he imagines that the day has gotten even hotter than it was; when he looks toward the shore, the beach is shimmering with heat.

He turns around, looks out again at the bay, where the bell buoy tilts slowly in the gentle rolling swell, mournfully tolling, and where, a few feet away, a cormorant is floating on the surface. Anders lowers his face so his mask is half in the water, half out, and he can see below the waterline, where the cormorant's legs are tucked against its undersides. They give a kick here, a kick there, and then, while Anders is watching, the cormorant gathers itself and dives. Anders puts his face into the water entirely, and watches as the cormorant swims down, and down, until finally it has disappeared from view, and though he would like to follow it, Anders turns and follows the rest of the class toward the shore.

. . .

Roscoe McWilliams and his crew arrive promptly at noon to remove the boom and skimmer from the quarry. After greeting them, Joan goes inside and up to her office to pack her computer away and replace it with the typewriter, which she discovers, when she feeds an experimental sheet of paper into the thing and tries to type, needs a new ribbon. She removes the lid, and she is just about to lift the spool from its posts when the phone on her desk begins to ring. She glances at it with annoyance, but she answers anyway.

"Hello?" she asks, not meaning to sound quite as hassled as she does.

A woman's voice somewhat timidly replies. "Hello, I'm calling for—Anders Jacobs?"

Joan frowns. "May I say who's calling?"

"Yes, my name is Elizabeth Favazza. I'm returning his call about a dog he found? He called several days ago."

For a moment, Joan is speechless. She stares down at the buttons of the typewriter, and one part of her brain bothers, in this moment, to notice that the D and B are the most faded of the keys. She squeezes her eyes shut with thumb and forefinger, remembering for the first time the dog that had been near the porch the night they arrived, frightening Seymour, that jingling collar in the shadows: Henry, of course, just hours after his master had disappeared. "He's not here at the moment," she finally replies. She swallows. "But this is Joan Jacobs, his wife. You're calling about Henry?"

"Yes," the woman replies. "Henry. My son's dog. Is he— Do you still have him? I know it's been days, it's just that no one got the message until now, I—"

"Yes, no," Joan interrupts. "No, he's still here."

"Oh, he is," Elizabeth Favazza says gratefully. "I'm so sorry you've had him for so long. We just didn't know. There was an accident, and, well, we—well . . . Anyway, thank you."

An accident. "No, no, it's been no trouble at all," Joan says.

"I'll come pick him up this afternoon. I mean, if that's convenient. Where are you?"

"We're—" Joan gazes through the window, where outside the men have driven their trucks and trailers right up to the quarry's edge; there is no way she can allow Elizabeth Favazza to come here. "You know, we're so hard to find," she says. "Why don't you let me bring him to you?"

"I don't want you to go to any more trouble than you already have. I'm sure I can—"

"It's no trouble at all. Are you downtown?" she asks, even as she pictures the sloping hill of Magnolia Street, the off-white vinyl siding of Elizabeth Favazza's house, the three-stepped stoop, and the frosted window in the door. "Because if you are, I have to go downtown this afternoon anyway, and I could bring him then."

"I *am* downtown—but are you sure? You've already done so much, and it's just as easy for me—"

"It's no trouble at all. Where are you?"

"I'm—just a minute, I'm sorry." Joan hears muffled voices as she imagines Elizabeth Favazza holds the phone against her chest to speak to whoever has interrupted her. She watches Roscoe McWilliams consult with the other two men, who then walk around the quarry in the direction of the skimmer. Eve is out there, too, hands on hips as she surveys the scene. "I'm sorry," Elizabeth Favazza says to Joan after a moment. "Are you there?"

"I'm here. You were just about to give me your address."

"That's right. I'm at 932 Magnolia."

"Nine thirty-two Magnolia," Joan repeats, unnecessarily writing this down.

"That's a few streets off Washington, up the hill."

"Yes," Joan says. "I think I know where it is. Is there a good time?"

"Anytime. I'll be here all afternoon." Elizabeth Favazza thanks Joan again, gives her phone number, and they hang up.

For a moment, Joan only sits there, staring out the window as images real and imagined flash through her mind: Elizabeth Favazza's house, a pickup truck gurgling as it disappears beneath the surface, the dog swimming from it through the dark water, or frantically pacing at the quarry's edge, Eloise luring that same dog in circles with a stick, rubber-clad divers at night, the stained-glass windows of St. Ann's.

She blinks, turns back into the room, where the typewriter sits partially dismantled on her desk, where the telephone rests in its cradle, still warm from Joan's hand, and where the half-done bust regards her with its single staring eye.

The boom deflates with a long hissing sound; it looks to Eve as it falls in upon itself like a painfully dying creature, slowly surrendering air until it is a limp strip of canvas floating on the water's surface. It has worked to contain not only the gas leaking from the truck but leaves and bits of grass and the carcasses of insects, too, which are all pulled with it to the quarry's edge as a hydraulic reel on the back of a large trailer draws it in. Across the quarry, two men are maneuvering the separator from behind the shrub that's kept it partially out of view. Eve lifts her camera from where it hangs around her neck, snaps a shot of them, and then another of the oil drum beside it, which is black, with a white circle in the middle containing an image of a big black drop of oil. It seems somehow ominous.

She crouches down and scoops up a handful of

soggy leaves from the water, which she filters absently through her fingers as she watches the skimmer slithering in, oddly relishing the cool and slimy feel of the leaves against her skin. She looks down when she feels something else among the leaves, and she is mildly annoyed at first to see that it is a cigarette butt in her hand, imagining one of the policemen at the water's edge the other night thoughtlessly tossing his butt into the quarry. But then she sees that the butt is a Marlboro. Larry Stephens, she thinks, nodding slowly. It can only be his. She dips the butt into the water to rinse it free of leaves, puts it into her pocket, and stands. She finds herself tempted to go out to 16 Pine Street again, to find him, to confront him somehow. But she knows she can't, for now. She looks over at Roscoe McWilliams, who is manning the hydraulic reel. "How many gallons in that drum?" she asks cautiously; her mother has warned her against getting in the way as the men do their work.

Roscoe glances over at her. "Fifty-five. More than you had in here."

"How much do you think we had in here?"

Roscoe frowns, guiding the boom as the reel winds it in. "Hard to say," he says. "Depends on how much actually leaked from the vehicle. Depends on how much was in the vehicle in the first place."

Eve looks over at the oil drum, standing alone

now at the quarry's edge. A large dragonfly is perched on the rim, its shimmering wings slowly beating. "So," she continues, "what happens to the gas when you take it away?"

"Not gas," Roscoe says. "The gasoline evaporated."

"Then what was in the quarry? The rainbow thing?"

"The sheen. That's the light fractions of oil."

"Okay, so what happens to the oil?"

"It goes to a recovery center. For recycling."

Eve considers this. "So," she begins. "If it gets—Wait, am I bugging you if I ask you another question?"

Roscoe McWilliams shakes his head, smiling. "Nope."

"Okay, so, if it gets recycled, does that mean, like, it could one day get used in another car?"

"More or less."

Eve frowns, imagining another person driving around with James Favazza's oil in his car, and not knowing anything about it, or where it came from. "Weird," she says. "I never thought of oil as having a history."

The boom is reeled all the way in by now; Roscoe McWilliams fastens it into place and shuts it in. "I never really thought of it that way, either," he says.

By now, the other two men have gotten the separator around to the near side of the quarry;

Roscoe goes over to help them. Eve takes pictures of them as they work, her mind churning. To consider where the oil might end up has made her wonder about where James Favazza's truck might have ended up once Tim drove off with it the other day, and whether the functional pieces have been stripped and sold and are now being put to use as parts of other cars. She wonders if a pillaged skeleton is all that remains, and what they might have done with the personal contents that didn't float up for Eve to collect—the stuff in the glove box, for instance. The other flip-flop. It's possible that it's all still in there.

When the men have finished tying the separator down, they roll the oil drum on its edge through the grass, round and round, the oil drop flashing in and out of view. Eve takes a photograph, lowers her camera.

"You doing research, or what?" Roscoe McWilliams asks.

"No," Eve says. "I'm just curious."

"How about the camera?"

Eve regards Roscoe McWilliams seriously. "I'm documenting, I guess," she says. "I don't know the next time we're going to have a boom and skimmer in the quarry. And I don't ever want to forget what happened."

"So what'd you think?" Dave asks. He and Anders are peeling off their wet suits; Anders

272

feels as if he is removing a layer of skin.

"Pretty incredible, actually," Anders says. "I was nervous, I have to admit."

"You do get hooked," Dave says.

Anders pulls on his T-shirt, wraps a towel around his waist to change beneath. "What would you say's the best dive you've done?"

"Around here?"

"Anywhere. I guess you've probably done a lot of diving? Around the world?"

"Not as much as I'd like to. Been down in the Caribbean a bunch of times. Australia."

"Great Barrier?"

"Nah. West side of the country. Ningaloo."

Anders nods, though he has not in fact heard of Ningaloo before. He holds tight to his towel as he steps out of his wet trunks beneath.

"Iceland once, too," Dave continues.

"Iceland?"

"Yeah. Place called Silfra. It's actually a deep crack in the lava where the American and European tectonic plates meet. Glacier water. *Really* good visibility."

"Cold, I bet."

"Freezing, man. Literally, like two degrees Celsius. But totally worth it."

"What sort of things do you see in a . . . crack in the lava?"

"Oh, man, just *awesome* caves."

"Caves," Anders repeats, nodding. He'd been

trying to envision what living things one might encounter on such a dive; caves hadn't occurred to him. He reaches thoughtfully for his shorts from where he's left them on the front seat of the Buick.

"And sometimes, when you look up? The surface acts like a mirror. So it's like you're surrounded, like you're diving through a tunnel. Pretty crazy."

"Huh." Anders considers this, and it gets him thinking about Eve, and the quarry, and his promise that he'd ask Dave what he saw down there. "Listen," he ventures. "I've got a question for you."

"Shoot."

"You're going to think I'm crazy to ask, but . . . what did you see down in the quarry? My daughter is very curious."

"Nah—I don't think you're crazy at all," Dave waves him off. "Tell the truth, at the time I was pretty focused on the cables, and it's so dark down there it's hard to see anything except what your headlamp shows you, but . . ." He shrugs. "Who knows? Those quarries are hundreds of years old. There could be all kinds of stuff down there."

Anders nods. He thinks of the photographs he's seen from the quarrying days, of men on platforms hung alongside great slabs of granite, others on ladders leading from one ledge to the next, evermore down like an Escher print. Somehow he'd never associated that history with the quarry in their backyard. Absently, he shakes open his shorts to put them on; as he does, he hears something clatter to the pavement. He looks down; half visible beneath the runner of the car is the shell he found in Sophie's desk the other morning, which he'd slipped into his pocket and forgotten. He stares down at it now; smooth and round and bright, it seems to stare back at him from the concrete like an unblinking yellow eye, until suddenly Dave's hand swoops down upon it.

"Here, man," Dave says, and he holds the shell out for Anders to take from the palm of his hand.

Seven

After lunch, Eve climbs onto her bike and rides
the few miles back to the nursery. She drops her
bike at the edge of the lot, across which she can
see Nestor through the fogged glass of the
greenhouse, blurred and featureless, wandering
among the plants like a ghost. Four cars are
parked outside the nursery; Josie Saunders is
helping a woman load trays of flowers—
perennials—into the back of one.

But her interest this afternoon is not in the
nursery; her eyes travel to the far side of the lot,
where there is a sign mounted between two
wooden posts that reads:

BAYVIEW AUTO RECYCLING
USED AUTO PARTS
JUNK CAR DISPOSAL
OPEN WED—SUN 7AM—7PM
CLOSED MON & TUES

Beneath the sign is a dirt road that leads back a
short ways through the trees and over a small
ridge, where it disappears from view. Though
she's sweating, Eve feels a shiver of excitement
ripple through her body, and she adjusts her
backpack. She glances once more toward the

nursery as she hurries across the lot, wary of being seen, since the junkyard is closed, but then passes beneath the sign and up the road.

The road is in fairly bad shape, the sides of it eroded away by rain, which has left dry canyons in the center as it washed downhill. Eve follows it up the ridge, choosing her steps carefully; she is barefoot as usual, and there are shards of broken glass from taillights, she imagines, and headlights, and side-view mirrors. In the distance, she can hear the barking of a dog, and she pictures a ferocious Rottweiler at the end of a rusty chain, straining against it and snarling as it guards rows of junked vehicles in a wide, empty space on the other side of the ridge.

She is aware that her mission is contrary to her short-lived resolution, but once the likely location of James' truck had occurred to her, she knew there'd be no denying the urge to find it, not if it might lead to the discovery of clues, or even answers, which, once found, will prove her theory right and so absolve her in her parents' eyes, she is sure. And she's not doing anything particularly dangerous or irresponsible. It's daytime, no one needs her, and she's thought this out. In her backpack, along with the camera she found this morning, she has brought three coat hangers of varying strength and width, a hammer, a Phillips-head screwdriver, a flat-head screwdriver, and a Baggie full of paper clips, all of which might be essential for the task at hand, which is to gather as much as she can from James Favazza's truck. She's not worried about having to pick the main lock, as the driver's-side window is smashed, but she wants to get into the glove box, which could well be locked. And there could be other locked compartments; in their station wagon there is a lock on the well between the front seats, and sometimes there are storage boxes behind the cabs of pickups, though to her annoyance she didn't notice whether there was one on James Favazza's truck or not.

After several hundred yards and on the other side of the ridge, the road ends in a small dirt clearing where two low buildings sit dark and quiet. One is a cheap-looking white trailer where the sign above the door reads Office. The other building is larger, a wooden storehouse with large windows, which Eve can see houses all kinds of scrap metal and used car parts. In front is a large scale with a sign that assures "Your metal will be weighed properly on our state certified scale." Near this is a forklift, which is parked in a manner that suggests that whoever drove it last was interrupted in the middle of a job.

But the rows of junked vehicles that Eve had anticipated, among which she was sure she'd find James Favazza's truck, do not exist. Instead, parked haphazardly beyond the buildings—and some barely even in the clearing, so reclaimed have they been by shrubbery and vines—are maybe only a dozen junked cars in various states of decay. Some are rusted shells of what they used to be, stripped entirely of tires, steering wheels, mirrors, seats; the open hoods reveal that the engines have been pillaged, too. Other cars appear to have been sitting there for less time, and still retain some semblance of functionality, as if with care and effort they might be restored. There are a few as Eve would have envisioned, squished and stacked, though none of them are James Favazza's red truck. Her disappointment is crushing; she truly had assumed she'd find it here. Even if she hadn't found a single clue inside, she thinks, it would have been enough just to find the truck itself, just to see it again, to be reminded by something tangible of the reality of what has happened.

Eve sighs, gazing out at the small clearing before her. In addition to the handful of cars, there appears to be all manner of other junked objects, and despite the failure of her errand, Eve wanders among them curiously.

There is an abandoned Airstream trailer, overgrown with shrubbery; when Eve presses her face to the window she can see the linoleum peeling from the floor, the seat cushions ripped and plundered by nesting creatures. Hanging over the side-view mirror is a rusted length of anchor chain, maybe thirty inches long; Eve takes this and drapes it around her own neck, thinking it a perfect item for her father's garden wall.

Near the trailer, a rusted metal Coca-Cola cooler stands open, with embossed instructions across the front to Help Yourself, though of course when Eve peers inside the cooler is empty save for twigs, shriveled leaves, and a small pool of scummy water. There is an old shower stall on its side, the rings of the former curtain still around the rail. A claw-footed bathtub sits nearby, so filled with dirt and leaves that seedlings have taken root inside; Eve looks around for a toilet or a sink, wondering if someone has disposed of their entire bathroom here, but these she does not see. There is in fact no rhyme or reason to what has been left here, as far as Eve can discern. There's a rusted gas can, a plastic blender, and one of the same kind of cast-iron radiators they used to have in Maryland before they had heating ducts installed, and which Eve remembers being frightened of, for reasons that are inexplicable to her now. There is a rust-covered saw with teeth so dull they're nearly round, a bent pair of tongs, a portable gas grill, a scum-stained glass beaker.

Eve stops where she is and stares down at this, shot suddenly through space and time to the day of Sophie's death, the memory presenting itself with nauseating and insistent clarity at the mere sight of this small glass container in the woods.

She was in chemistry class, which she hates

that she hated because Sophie so loved, doing a lab to determine the molar volume of hydrogen gas, when Mrs. Suskin came and found her; that, in her mind, was the moment when everything derailed, the moment until which life had been its normal self. She was filling a beaker—like this one—with water when Mrs. Suskin tapped her on the shoulder and told her that her mother was waiting for her in the lobby; puzzled, Eve went downstairs. Her mother rose from the bench where she was sitting as soon as Eve entered the lobby and pulled her close with an urgency that made Eve's limbs go numb with dread.

"I need you to come home with me, okay?" her mother said, the expression on her face one that Eve had never seen before, stunned and rushed and quietly desperate.

"What's the matter?" Eve asked, feeling an odd combination of anger and fear. She thought at first that something must have happened to her father, that maybe his plane had crashed on its way to Italy, or that he'd had a heart attack, or stroke.

Her mother shook her head rapidly and brought a finger to her lips. "Not here, Evie, okay?" she whispered. "Not here. Let's go home."

Part of Eve was inclined to refuse, as if whatever had happened would unhappen if she refused to hear about it and went back to her day, but in the end she didn't even bother to go to her locker for her things, and instead immediately followed her mother out to the car, her lab coat on, her safety goggles on her head. They drove in silence; Eve was too afraid to ask again what was the matter, and able to take no pleasure in the delicious freedom she would normally feel to be out of the school building in the middle of a school day.

She saw her Aunt Sam's car in the driveway when they got home; while Joan had gone to pick up Eve, Aunt Sam had evidently gone to pick up Eloise, and the two were sitting at the kitchen table when Joan and Eve came inside, Eloise sipping the orange soda she would later drop to the floor. Eve had assumed that Sophie, having the lucky schedule and privileges of a senior, would also already be at home when they got there, and it was when Joan ushered the two girls into the living room alone and sat them down on the sofa that Eve began to understand that it was not their father that something had happened to, but Sophie.

Eve stares down at this beaker in the woods, unwillingly remembering, thinking how foolish it was to be determining molar volume when her sister was dead. Part of her would like to lift the beaker from the ground and smash it for what it stands for; the childish, superstitious part of her is afraid ever to touch a beaker again, as if it were the beaker's fault, if only it were that easy to explain.

• • •

Though he meant to go directly home after his dive and spend the afternoon in his garden, Anders can't resist the urge to drive to Beverly, one of the many small towns on the north shore. Beverly, Salem, Marblehead, Peabody, Swampscott, Lynn—there are too many of these towns to keep straight, all haphazardly arranged and few of them accessible by highway, though from Gloucester, Beverly isn't far. Less than twenty minutes after he has left Cape Ann, Anders is driving down Cabot Street, the main drag, which is lined with trendy new restaurants, health food stores, an independent cinema, all by-products of the art college in town, places with names like The Organic Garden, and The Atomic Health Café, Kamasinki, Kame, and Soma. He hasn't been down Cabot Street in years, and he is surprised by how much it has changed since he was last here, particularly in contrast with Gloucester, which is still refreshingly dominated by sub shops and pizzerias, places with names like Destino's, Sebastian's, Trupiano's, Valentino's.

He follows Cabot slowly north, the orange shell from Sophie's desk out on the dashboard. Earlier, when he'd taken it from Dave's hand and returned it to his pocket, he'd discovered there the scrap of paper that had been at the bottom of his daughter's wastebasket the other day, the scrap of paper with the doodled stars, the street address in Beverly: 588 Cabot, to which he's yet to come. He thought he'd thrown the scrap of paper out. He thought he'd tossed it along with the movie ticket stub, the broken barrette, the chewed toothpick, the Kleenex, and the Twizzlers wrapper, those items—items he can still name—which with a sweep of his hand he'd gathered from where he'd set them out on Sophie's desk, shoved into his pocket, and brought out to the garage to toss into the fifty-gallon trash can they keep there. It had been a pointed decision not to keep them. The shell was one thing; the shell had been in her desk drawer, was something *she* had decided herself to keep. But these other things were things she'd thrown away—they were *garbage*—and he denied himself the urge to keep them; he'd refused to give in to sentimentality.

Somehow, though, this scrap of paper had escaped, and as he stood there by the car looking down at it, he felt his mind lapsing into the magical type of thinking he tries so hard to avoid, and he knew that there was no way he could withstand the impulse to seek out the address written there, as if there were a reason that it was this scrap of paper, and not another item, that was spared.

He peers now out the window, reading the numbers above doorways and looking for 588. He doesn't know what to expect at 588 Cabot, and in truth the rational side of him expects nothing in particular; at this point, though his heart is skipping nimbly in his chest, he is simply curious. He imagines his daughter driving down this very street around this time last year, in the old VW Fox she'd bought with her life savings —the old VW Fox in which she died.

The business stretch of Cabot ends around the four hundred block, and soon Anders is in a more residential area, the road lined by older colonials, placards marking a revolutionary battle site on one side, a historic church on the other. Puzzled, he pulls the scrap of paper from his pocket; it confirms that 588 is the address he is looking for. Various unlikely scenarios begin to flash unbidden through his head: this far off the main drag, who knows what 588 could be? A drug dealer. An abortion clinic. A psychic. Anders frowns, annoyed with himself. Probably, he tells himself, 588 is simply someone's home, the place where a party was held one night, or a friend's address. He begins to wonder what he should do when he gets there, whether he should go and knock on the door, find out whose house it is, or whether he should simply drive away. He pictures both scenarios from the outside in, as if he were watching himself in a movie. The bereaved father, unhinged, knocking on a stranger's door—for what? The bereaved father, helpless and hapless, driving forty minutes round-trip to stare at a house and leave. Both scenarios make him cringe.

Soon, though, Cabot leads out under the highway overpass, and Anders finds himself back in familiar territory, at a five-way intersection near the exit where there is a gas station, an art store, Nick's Roast Beef, and in the center, 588 Cabot Street. Joseph's. This is a gourmet grocery store where Joan shops at least once every two weeks for the items she cannot get from the grocery store in Gloucester: good marinated meats, imported cheeses, homemade sauces and salsas and dips. He himself has been here many times before as well, but it's one of those places he's simply known how to find without knowing the exact address; he's never associated Joseph's, on one side of the highway, with the Cabot Street of boutiques, galleries, and cafes several miles down. He pulls into the parking lot, unsurprised, yet oddly disappointed. Joseph's—that is all. It's not that he expected any clues or explanations; it did not take him too long to decide that these do not exist, were scratched away by the pen that lay across the to-do list Sophie left out on her desk before she died. Still. Joseph's offers him as little to go on as anything else.

Anders sits in the Buick, staring through the window at the store, at his own self reflected in the glass of the dark-paned door; every time a customer goes in or out, he sees himself go reeling.

There is an American flag mounted outside Elizabeth Favazza's front door. This is the first thing Joan notices when she turns onto Magnolia Street, the car windows rolled down and James Favazza's dog in the passenger seat beside her. Back at the house, she had loaded him into the car as soon as Eve had taken off on her bike— she's decided not to mention to the girls whom the dog belonged to, for fear of upsetting Eloise and egging Eve on. Over the course of the drive downtown, Henry has made his way slowly forward, settling for a few moments in the backseat before climbing all the way into the front, where he sits now with his chin resting on the sill of the open window, looking as pensive as Joan feels.

It is almost the Fourth of July, and there are American flags mounted outside front doors all up and down the street, but the fact that there is one outside of 932 Magnolia is a detail that particularly strikes Joan. It was not there when she drove down this street a week ago, she is certain, because there are also wind chimes by the door, and she clearly remembers these. She wonders whether Elizabeth Favazza was the one to set the flag out, and if so what she'd been thinking when she did, if it was a concession to the exhausting fact that life goes on. Joan can't remember exactly how or when it happened that they themselves surrendered to the flow of living in the days and weeks after Sophie's death. It was a slow process, she supposes, during which they gave themselves over to the elements of life one thing at a time: first the necessities, like showers and meals; and then things like grocery shopping, and putting gas into the car; and then, finally, the superfluities: filling the birdfeeder, or making a birthday cake, or putting out an American flag. It is a process that is ongoing still, she supposes, but when she thinks back to those first days of numbed shock and sorrow, she is amazed by how far they have come without being fully aware, amazed by the relative normalcy of now, which then had seemed so impossible.

Most residents of Magnolia Street park their cars in small driveways that separate one house from the next; there are few cars parked in the street itself. Joan parks a short ways down from Elizabeth Favazza's house, preferring to walk the rest of the way than announce her arrival with the sound of the car's engine and the slamming of its doors, which might summon Elizabeth Favazza to the window to watch as Joan approached, the idea of which would make her overly self-conscious. Unseen, she approaches slowly, letting Henry dawdle at the end of the homemade leash of rope she's tied to his collar so as to allow him a chance to do his business.

Though at first the street appeared mostly

sleepy, now that she is out of the car Joan can hear the laughter and voices of people gathered in various backyards; she can smell something grilling. At the end of the block, a couple of kids are tossing a ball around in the middle of the street, and across the way a man stands in the small strip of lawn before his house, yanking the cord of an old lawnmower over and over again in unsuccessful attempts to get the engine going.

After Henry has peed, Joan leads him up the three steps of Elizabeth Favazza's stoop, where she makes sure to press the doorbell firmly and so avoid those awkward moments when you're not sure whether the bell inside has sounded, or whether you should ring again. In this case, there is no doubt that the doorbell sounds; she can hear the four or five notes of a cheerful melody inside. She waits, listening to the tinkling of the wind chimes as the American flag flaps gently against her head every now and then in the breeze, reminding herself that as far as Elizabeth Favazza knows, Joan is just a stranger who has found a missing dog, nothing more. It makes her feel fraudulent to deliver the dog under such a pretense, but she's not sure Elizabeth Favazza would even want to know otherwise, nor what use that information would serve.

In a minute, she hears noise on the other side of the door as Elizabeth Favazza works the lock and turns the knob. She has done her best not to imagine what the woman might look like, because she hadn't wanted to be unsettled when she inevitably got it wrong; she is unsettled anyway when the door opens and it is not Elizabeth Favazza at all, but a man standing on the other side of the screen door. He looks out at Joan from the shadows within, then glances down at the dog. He sniffs, and pushes the screen door open, letting it go only after Joan and Henry have stepped inside; it hisses slowly shut on its hydraulic spring.

They stand just inside the door, in a small, green foyer at the base of a set of stairs; the first thing Joan notices is the sweet smell of something baking.

"My sister's on the phone," the man says. "She'll be off in a minute."

Joan nods. "I'm Joan," she says. "Joan Jacobs."

The man looks at her for a moment and then nods curtly, but he doesn't introduce himself, instead fixing his gaze on Henry, who is sniffing around the base of the umbrella stand by the door. He is a large man, in his late fifties, Joan would guess, his tanned face etched with deep lines that seem borne of weather more than age, as if during his life he has spent a good deal of time outdoors. He gestures at Henry with his chin. "Where'd you find him?" he asks.

"He found us, really," Joan says. "He's just been hanging around the house."

The man grunts. "My nephew's dog," he says. He motions in the direction of the living room adjoining, again with his chin. "May as well have a seat," he says.

Joan follows him into the living room, which is painted the same color green as the foyer. The floor is wood, and though it is covered in large part by a patchwork carpet of mutely colored squares, it yet creaks beneath their feet.

"Sit anywhere," the man instructs without looking at her, passing through the living room and through a door in the far wall that appears, from the tiles of the room beyond, to lead into the kitchen. Henry does not follow him.

Joan looks uncertainly around the room. There are only two places to sit: a rocking chair by the window in the front corner of the room, across from a large TV on a wooden stand, and a leather couch against the far wall, in front of which sits a coffee table trunk similar to their own. Joan decides to take a seat on the couch; she does not want to have to rock—or to have to fight rocking. She sits on the edge of the couch, feeling oddly grateful for Henry's presence beside her; she pats him with a new fondness, hopeful that Elizabeth Favazza is less unfriendly than her brother.

After she has waited a minute or two, Joan hears a door close loudly somewhere off the kitchen, and then a moment later the chirping sound of a car lock just outside the window near where she is sitting; she looks out and sees the brother getting into the car parked in the small driveway beside the house. He turns the engine on, and for several seconds he idles there, fiddling with something that Joan can't see. Then he wraps his arm around the back of his seat, backs abruptly into the street, and pulls away. Oddly, with his departure Joan feels even more uneasy. She hopes that he has at least informed Elizabeth Favazza of her arrival, and wonders how long she should wait before either going to find the woman herself or leaving.

She takes a breath, wishing there were at least a book on the coffee table for her to pretend to occupy herself with. She lets her eyes wander around the room, from the TV to the rocking chair to a bookshelf she hadn't noticed from the doorway, atop which sits a large fern, its leaves browning at the edges. On the wall on one side of the bookshelf is a framed print of a Hopper painting, one of sunlight on the side of a white house. On the other side of the bookshelf hangs a mirror, which has the effect of making her feel as if she were looking not *at* it, but *through* it into another identical room, where she sees the same TV on a stand, the same rocking chair, the same bare coffee table, and herself on the same leather couch, framed photographs propped neatly on the table beside it.

Joan looks away from the mirror to look at these. One photograph is of a woman with short, dark hair, maybe in her thirties, holding a small, unhappy-looking child on her lap; Joan thinks this must be Elizabeth Favazza. Another is of this same woman, but older, and with longer hair, standing beside a man on what Joan recognizes as the boulevard downtown; they are leaning back against the railing at the water's edge, their hair whipping in the wind. Another photograph is of two boys, maybe twelve or thirteen years old, grinning as they dangle a large fish between them in the air, and another is of these same two boys some years before, sitting at a picnic table as they share half of an enormous watermelon. One of these boys, Joan thinks, must be James, but she can't tell which based on the photograph that ran with his obituary.

The last photograph on the table is of two young men, who Joan supposes must be the boys grown up—they, too, are slender and dark haired. In this last photograph, they are seated on the edge of a dock, bare chested, their feet hanging in the water, and they look into the camera with similarly distracted smiles, as if they had been in the midst of some engrossing conversation when the photographer interrupted them.

"I'm sorry to keep you!"

Joan turns in her seat; a small, exhausted-looking woman has appeared in the doorway. Joan stands. "That's all right," she says. "Don't worry at all."

"I just—I had this phone call, and I couldn't get off . . ." She shrugs. "I'm Elizabeth Favazza." She gives Joan a tired smile.

"Joan Jacobs," Joan says, feeling awkward and off balance in the small space between the sofa and the coffee table.

"Yes, Joan," Elizabeth Favazza says, somewhat distractedly, it seems. She glances down at Henry, who has gotten up from where earlier he'd settled at Joan's feet and come over to her, his rope-leash trailing. "Thank you for bringing him."

Joan steps out from behind the coffee table as Elizabeth Favazza greets the dog, and positions herself a few feet away from them, watching. Elizabeth Favazza is undoubtedly the woman in the photographs, though an older version; the lines in her face are more pronounced, and her dark hair has gone partly gray. She looks smaller now than she did in the photographs from when she was younger, as if time has whittled her away; her body is angular beneath her T-shirt, and ropy veins river her forearms and her hands, which work now to untie the rope from Henry's collar. When she has gotten it loose, she stands, and holds it out for Joan to take. Joan is just about to do so when it occurs to her that since Henry is not her dog the woman might not have a replacement leash. "You can keep it," she says.

Elizabeth Favazza lets the hand holding the rope drop to her side, regarding Joan bemusedly.

"Thank you again," she says, and she lets her eyes fall to the dog. "And for keeping him all this time. I'm sure many people would have quit waiting and called the pound . . ."

"It was no trouble at all, really."

The two women stand quietly, both watching the dog gnaw at a spot on his rump, until outside there is the sudden sound of a lawnmower; when she glances out the window, Joan sees that the man across the street has finally gotten the machine working.

Elizabeth Favazza looks out the window at him, too. "He mows that lawn every day," she says softly. "I'm surprised there's any grass left." She blinks, and then looks at Joan, and suddenly her expression changes. "Before you go," she says. "Wait here for just a minute."

She disappears into the kitchen; Joan can hear the sound of a drawer or cabinet opening, and the tear and crackle of aluminum foil, and in an another minute Elizabeth Favazza comes back into the room with a foil-covered plate. "Brownies." She offers the plate to Joan. "Ready just in time."

"Oh," Joan says. "You didn't have to do that."

"You didn't have to keep the dog," she says.

"Thank you." Joan takes the plate; she can tell by the bottom that the brownies are still warm. "They smell wonderful. I have a couple of girls at home who I know will be very happy." She feels her heart speed up just a little as she says this, which is as much in that conversational direction as she dares venture. "Actually," she says, glancing at the watch on her wrist, "I've got to go get one of them from camp right now."

"Of course," Elizabeth Favazza says. She nods toward the door. "I'll show you out."

Joan follows her to the door; Henry trails them. She gives Henry a quick rub good-bye and then starts down the steps.

"Have a good afternoon," Elizabeth Favazza says, as she goes, and though it feels like a lie to say the same when she imagines Elizabeth Favazza going back into the house to spend the rest of the day with her dead son's dog, Joan turns and tells Elizabeth Favazza to have a good one, too.

Nobody is there when Anders gets home. He goes in through the kitchen door and calls out; no one answers him. Not even the dog is around. He drapes his wet suit over a kitchen chair and puts away the groceries he ended up bringing home from Joseph's: fat red tomatoes with fresh basil and mozzarella cheese, native corn, teriyaki steak tips, and a loaf of fresh baked ciabatta; he's decided he'll cook dinner tonight.

He finds a plastic bag for today's dead rose leaves and brings it out with him to the garden; of the dozen bushes there, he counts seven that have blooms, which might be some improvement since he began applying the fungicide, though he can't be sure. One of the bushes, he notes with a frown, appears to have succumbed to the disease completely; it is a bloomless, leafless, thorny shrub. At least the lilies around the quarry are thriving, he thinks. He looks over at them, just starting to bloom; in a couple of weeks' time what now are pale green slender wicks will have opened into glowing yellow trumpets, their reflections shimmering on the surface of the water. He squints out at things, trying to picture the quarry empty, the steep granite walls and ledges plunging over a hundred feet down. He finds himself wondering who the men who worked within it were, and what indeed they might have left behind.

In a minute he hears the slow crunch of gravel behind him, and he turns around in time to see Eve appearing on the lip of the driveway on her bike, wearing a backpack and a rusted length of anchor chain around her neck. Between the incline of the driveway, the uneven surface of the gravel, and the combined weight of the chain and her pack, her bike veers sharply this way and that, and of course, despite the fact that he left out several helmets that he found in the closet for her to choose from, her head is bare. At the edge of the driveway, she drops her bike, and then makes her way toward her father across the lawn.

"So," she says, when she has reached the edge of the garden. "Did you get nitrogen narcosis?"

"No," he says. "But I saw squid. They glowed."

"I didn't know we had squid around here."

"There's a lot I didn't know we had around here," Anders says. He regards his daughter. "No helmet?"

"Nope."

"Not one of those worked?"

"Not a one." Eve surveys the roses, scratching her calf with a toe. "How're your perennials?" she asks. "They don't look very good."

"No," Anders agrees. "They may not be perennials after this year."

"That sucks." Eve wrinkles her nose. She undrapes the chain from around her neck. "But I have this for you. It's for your wall. I thought it would be a good addition." She walks carefully through the roses and gives the chain to her father.

"Thank you," he says. "Where'd you find it?"

"Junkyard."

Anders gives her a puzzled look.

"The one by the nursery," she explains. "The one that calls itself a *junk car disposal,* even though it's technically not."

Anders raises an eyebrow. "And what were you doing there, pray tell?" he asks, though he's fairly sure of the answer.

Eve shrugs. "Trying to find James Favazza's

truck." She says this as if it were a perfectly ordinary thing to do.

Anders looks at his daughter thoughtfully, nods. "I see." He turns and scans the wall for a spot to rest the chain. Eve watches as he weaves it between a couple of rocks like a giant sideways S. At first, it falls out of place, knocking a small glass bottle from its nook as it goes, but on his second attempt to arrange the chain among the rocks, it stays put. He looks at Eve. "What do you think?"

She nods. "That works."

They survey the wall quietly, as if it were an intricate painting, Eve's hands on her hips, Anders' arms crossed before his chest. A chainsaw whines in the distance.

"So," Anders says, after a moment. "I'm assuming you didn't find the truck."

"No."

"What if you had?"

Eve thinks about this. "I don't know," she says.

"Well, what were you looking for?"

"I don't know, exactly. I would have wanted to see what was in the glove box and stuff. I was looking for . . . evidence." She frowns, bends down to lift a rock from the soil, which she begins to toss from hand to hand.

Anders waits for her to go on.

Eve sighs. "I don't really know *what* I'm looking for," she says finally. "I just—you're going to think I'm crazy, but I'm pretty sure I know what happened, and I just want to prove it. I just want to know for sure." She sighs heavily. "But also, it was more than that, I guess. I mean—all that stuff, the EMS bottle, the flip-flop, even if it doesn't mean anything, it's still" —and here she tosses the rock back down into the dirt—"it's his *stuff*. It shouldn't just—" She makes a vanishing gesture with her hand, looks up at her father almost desperately. "You know?"

Eve hasn't offered her theory of what happened, and Anders doesn't ask her. He's not sure he'd be able to help her there, but about James Favazza's stuff, he gets it. He understands. He thinks of the yellow shell, the movie stub, the chewed toothpick, the scrap of paper with the Beverly address. "Yeah," he says. "I think I know."

Eve stands. "Why did you assume I wouldn't have found the truck there, anyway?"

Anders scratches his cheek. "Well," he says, "for one thing, that place isn't really that sort of place. And the wrecking service, if I remember correctly, came from Rowley."

Eve blinks. "So . . . the tow truck . . . oh," she says slowly. "I guess I wasn't really thinking they were all part of the same business. I guess I thought the tow truck would have just taken it to the closest place . . ."

Anders pulls his lips in; he hadn't meant to put ideas into Eve's head, but he can tell her wheels are turning. "No riding your bike to Rowley," he says firmly.

Eve holds his gaze.

"Do not even *think* about it."

"Then drive me."

Anders folds his arms across his chest.

"You said, I should've asked about Georgetown. So I'm asking about Rowley. Will you please drive me." She states her request more than asking.

Anders takes a deep breath, realizing that he has no real choice but to comply, that otherwise his daughter will no doubt find a way to get there herself. "Fine," he says. "But we have to make a deal."

"What kind of deal?"

He looks at Eve seriously. "A fair deal. *I* only make fair deals."

Eight

They have Elizabeth Favazza's brownies for dessert that night. Joan debates whether it would be right to bring them to the table, but in the end she can't put her finger on a real reason for not doing so, as strange as it makes her feel, and there seems no point in letting them go to waste. And it's true, the girls do love brownies; even Eloise, who sat sullenly through dinner, upset about Henry's departure, can't resist.

It is only afterward, while she's covering them up in tinfoil, that Joan recognizes the problem of the plate. What catches her attention is the delicate blue design of the china, newly exposed by the relative dearth of brownies; all of a sudden the fact that should have been obvious all along presents itself in alarming clarity: they now have Elizabeth Favazza's plate. Joan can't believe it hadn't occurred to her until now, even as she took the plate from the woman's hands, set it beside her in the car, carried it into the house, and later set it on the table; somehow, even as she must have been aware of the firm feel of china instead of paper or plastic, she hadn't registered the implications. And now they have the woman's plate.

For a moment, Joan only stands at the kitchen

counter, staring down at the plate half covered in foil, the cobalt pattern, the tiny chip along the edge. Seymour, having vanished for the past few days while Henry was around, rubs himself purringly against her legs. She can hear the sounds of water running in the pipes overhead as Eloise gets ready for bed, and the thud of laundry spinning in the dryer, and footsteps on the floorboards as Anders makes his way down the upstairs hallway; she stares at the plate, lulled by all these sounds, looks up only at the sound of a moth alighting on the window screen. She blinks.

Earlier, as she sat with Anders as he cooked, he'd asked out of the girls' earshot what it had been like, returning Henry to James Favazza's mother. But Joan had only shrugged, pointed at the plate of brownies as if they explained it all. He didn't press her on the issue, for which she's grateful; she herself hasn't quite processed the encounter, which seemed somehow both uneventful and profound.

She thinks back to the night they arrived, when all they knew was that a vehicle, with a body, had gone into the quarry; curiously, the more she's learned and the closer she's gotten to it all, the more she doesn't know and can only imagine. When several days ago, for instance, Anders called the number on Henry's collar, he'd unwittingly left a message on a dead man's answering machine, which someone, sometime, had taken it upon himself—or herself—to listen to. Someone had entered his apartment or his house, saw the message light blinking, and pressed play. But who? And why and how? Joan imagines Elizabeth Favazza wherever her son lived, there to—what? to pack away his things?—and listening to messages left by whoever may have called: Anders' message, of course, but also now-irrelevant messages, from a friend calling to say hello, or the bank about an overdraft fee, or the dentist's office calling to confirm some appointment in the future—the kinds of messages that would have seemed a sort of mockery, like the college brochures and the clothing catalogues that continue even now to come for Sophie in the mail.

She imagines Elizabeth Favazza having to sort through her son's things, having to decide what to keep, what to toss, and what to give away. She imagines a pile of clothing for Goodwill, another table top of things like James Favazza's coffeemaker, his toaster oven, his bedside lamp —things she wouldn't need a second of herself, having her own, but that would be wasteful to throw away. And then Joan imagines a bag of the things that nobody would need: his razors, a pair of shin guards, an old backpack, a sweat-stained baseball cap—a bag that may have been intended for the Dumpster, but that would instead live in the back of Elizabeth Favazza's own closet, the mother unable to throw it away. Joan is grateful that all she has had to do so far is close the door to her daughter's room.

Joan looks down at the plate once again and finishes wrapping it in foil, slowly accepting what she knows she has to do, which she has been doing all along in her mind. Until now she's refused to act on it, loathe to use someone else's tragedy as material; she's not even tried to write about her own. But it's not the tragedy itself she's interested in. She realizes this now. It's everything else that is attached: messages on machines, American flags, toothbrushes and razors and lost dogs and yard sales where toasters and kitchen tables are sold. The everything else, she realizes, is not Elizabeth Favazza's, or hers, but everyone's together, and everyone's own.

The cat bats at the kitchen door, looks at Joan demandingly. She pushes the plate gently to the back of the counter, turns off the kitchen lights, and goes to let him out into the night.

After Anders has read Eloise a section from *Alice* and tucked her tightly in, he turns off the lights and says good night, and he is just about to close her door when he hears her little voice. "Wait, Daddy?"

"Yuh."

"Can you come here?"

Anders crosses the room, pauses at the foot of her bed. "What's up?" he asks. Though the room is dim, he can see her face by the light from the hallway; she looks worried.

"I don't know."

"You don't know?"

"I don't know if I'm supposed to say."

Anders sits down on the edge of the bed.

"Did someone tell you not to?"

Eloise shrugs. "I don't know. No. But . . . sort of. I think it's supposed to be a secret."

"Well then maybe you shouldn't tell me. Unless you think it's something I should know."

"No, but. Well, I don't know if he wants it to be a secret."

Anders frowns. "Who?"

Eloise takes a deep breath, looks at her father plaintively. "His name is Hobbster," she says finally.

It takes Anders a moment to find his voice. "Hobbster?" he repeats. He clears his throat. "Tell me about Hobbster."

Eloise kicks herself free of her sheets and climbs out of bed. "I have to get something," she says, and she slips out of the room.

Anders stays seated on the edge of her bed as he awaits her return. In the darkness, the ticking of the clock's second hand seems magnified, and strangely in keeping with the thud of his heart. Hobbster. It was a curious rush of emotions that coursed through him when Eloise said the name; for the briefest of moments, the only way to explain this seeming impossibility was with the impossible, and he allowed himself the impossible thought that Sophie must be responsible, and somehow writing from the other side. But this was only fleeting; his next thought was that she had left the Hobbster notes for Eloise last summer, though this made no sense, either. He arrived at the most likely explanation last; it is also the one that makes his heart ache most. Eve, trying to fill her sister's shoes. He feels a surge of heat behind his eyes, tears that he can't contain; he catches them with the back of his wrist, stops them before Eloise returns.

She does so momentarily, a few sheets of paper in her hand. "I hid them in the mothball closet because I didn't want them in my room," she says. "But *he* leaves them under my pillow."

Anders takes the notes, first turning on the bedside light so that he can see. There are four altogether, all clearly in Eve's hand; the last one suggests to Anders that the first three notes have gone unanswered.

I think you don't like me very much. Maybe you are just afraid, but I promise I am not scary. I am really very friendly, and I just want a friend. But if you do not want to be my friend, I understand, and this will be my last note. Tomorrow is my birthday, and Kermit is making me Moose Tracks ice cream from scratch. It is my favorite kind of ice cream. Love, Hobbster

Anders rests the notes on the bed beside him. "It sounds like you guys have a lot in common."

Eloise looks at her father uncertainly.

"I don't know that many people whose favorite ice cream is Moose Tracks."

Eloise shrugs. "You know at least two. Me and Evie."

"He's got pretty good taste in books, too." Anders gestures toward the Lewis Carroll on the beside table. "I mean, if *Alice* is his favorite."

Eloise shrugs again.

"Did you write him back?"

"No."

"How come?"

"I don't like him leaving notes under my pillow. I don't like him coming in my room."

"I see." Anders pretends to think, fingers on his chin. "Maybe," he says, "you could write him back and let him know that you'd prefer it if he left them in the hamper instead, like how *you're* supposed to."

"What if he says no? What if he comes in my room anyway?"

"I don't know why he'd do that. It sounds like he just wants to be pen pals."

Eloise looks at her father skeptically.

Anders shrugs. "Maybe *I'll* write him. I'm sort of curious about what it's like living on a star."

Eloise narrows her eyes. "But he didn't write to *you*. He wants to be *my* pen pal."

"This is true. But to be pen pals, you have to both write each other, right?"

"Yeah," Eloise admits reluctantly. They are quiet. The second hand tocks.

"So what do you think?" Anders asks finally. "Shall I go find a pen and paper?"

Eloise nods.

Anders finds a notepad and a pencil in the drawer of the desk in the hall and returns to his daughter's room. "Here," he says.

Eloise sits with the paper and pencil on the floor. "What should I say?"

"Whatever you want. I don't know. What's on your mind?"

"The dog. And how I was getting so used to him and then he had to go home and I didn't even get to say good-bye."

Anders nods. "So tell him about that," he says.

"Will you wait here?"

Anders nods. "I will.

Eloise bends over the paper, her hand curled around itself in the odd posture of a lefty; shielding her words with her right arm so her father cannot see, she begins laboriously to write.

Anders goes and stands by the window. The

moon is nearly full tonight; outside, he can see its golden crown just beginning to rise from behind the treeline. He watches; the trees' topmost branches seem, like fingers, to uncurl and let it slowly go, and soon it is a whole, looming orange globe, dim still yet with the power as it rises high to make the trees cast shadows in the grass and turn the surface of the quarry molten silver. Anders searches it for the face that he can never find; tonight, like all nights, it eludes him.

After dinner, Eve takes the camera up to her room to document the evidence stored beneath her bed, which, to her relief, her father had returned to her the other night. One at a time, she photographs each item: the EMS bottle, the flip-flop, the collection of bottles and cans, the Vic's T-shirt, the purple plastic bowl, the Marlboro cigarette butt she found among the leaves in the quarry, and the last remaining Marlboro of the three she found on the rock by the road the night of James Favazza's death. Earlier, after Roscoe McWilliams and his crew had left, she had also photographed what she thinks of as the crime scene. She photographed from various angles the ledge off of which the truck went in, and the trees the truck had managed to squeeze between, and the nick left on one by the side-view mirror. She photographed the general area of the lawn where the grass had been briefly flattened by his tires, which is what had suggested to her in the first place the night that they arrived that somebody had driven in. She wishes she'd had a camera all along, to document the grass when it was actually flattened, and the divers by night pulling the body from the quarry, and the tow truck the following day as it raised the truck from the quarry floor. She thinks of how she explained her motives to Roscoe McWilliams when he asked—that she was documenting, so that what has happened here will be impossible to forget. She doesn't think it's likely that she ever will, though, kind of like the moment with the beaker, the memory of which earlier today has left her generally out of sorts; not even all her documentation tonight has been able to distract her from the persistent thought: *your sister is dead, dead, dead.*

Glumly, she bags the evidence and makes her way down the hallway to the bathroom, where she avoids eye contact with herself in the mirror as she brushes her teeth. She lets her shorts fall down around her ankles, then lifts them with a toe and opens the hamper to drop them in; it is only as an afterthought that she glances inside for a note from Eloise, having just about given up hope. But there at the bottom of the hamper she sees a piece of paper neatly folded into thirds, with Hobbster printed in big block letters along the back. She pauses with her leg half raised, shorts dangling from her big toe. She lets them drop to the ground, and then tentatively, as if the note might disappear if she moves too fast, she reaches in to retrieve it, her gloom suddenly replaced by the same nervous and excited anticipation she remembers feeling when years ago she received notes from Hobbster.

She lowers the lid of the toilet and sits down, unfolds the note, and starts to read.

Nine

Anders wakes the next morning to the sound of Eve getting ready for the day. He lies awake, listening to the sound of water in the hallway bathroom as she brushes her teeth, of the toilet being flushed; he smiles to himself when he imagines her discovering the note that finally awaits her at the bottom of the hamper. Soon he hears her disappear downstairs, and shortly after that he hears the slam of the kitchen door; he imagines he can almost hear the crunch of gravel as she pedals off barefoot down the driveway, probably bareheaded.

Though it is yet early, there seems no point in falling into the brief sleep that Anders knows would only leave him groggy when, in half an hour, the alarm goes off. Quietly, so as not to wake Joan, he slips out from beneath the sheets and walks as lightly as he can over the creaking floorboards into their own bathroom. He changes into the clothing he has left on the chair by the sink, where Joan has also left her clothing, and the same pocketbook she's used for twenty years—one of his most successful gifts to her, he thinks, though at this point it shows its age. He gazes down at the pocketbook as he brushes his teeth, wondering if it might be time for a new one, even as he knows that Joan would never have it. The strap by which it hangs from the back of the chair is worn and slender, the leather of the purse itself soft and creased with age, and the clasp, he sees, no longer holds; it hangs open, revealing the myriad contents inside: wallet, planner, change, notebook, hairbrush, emery board. But something else inside the pocketbook catches his eye, a pamphlet that is wedged between the wallet and the planner; rising from behind the wallet he can see the printed etching of a steeple and a spire.

Puzzled, he sets his toothbrush down and rinses out his mouth, dries off his hands, takes the pamphlet from the purse. He recognizes the church on the front as the large one downtown—St. Ann's, the printed name beneath the etching tells him, which further text informs him was where James Favazza's funeral was held the other week. Anders frowns, trying to remember where he might have been that Wednesday while Joan was at the funeral without his knowledge, but the days here seem to blur one into the next, and he can't recall. Slowly, he opens the program, scans the contents inside. They are what he'd expect—hymns, readings, eulogies, though there is no picture, nor a summary of James Favazza's life.

He closes the program and returns it to Joan's purse, precisely where it was between the wallet and the planner, guilty to have committed such a violation, as unwitting as it was; it wasn't his intention to unearth a secret. He finds himself unsettled, not by the fact that Joan went to the funeral, but by the fact that she felt she had to keep it from him, and he wonders what else he might not know. He bends down again and takes the program out, then puts it back between the hairbrush and the notebook instead, so that if Joan was even aware of where it was, she will know that he has found it.

Eve stands barefoot in mulch still cool with night, hose in hand as she makes her way methodically down the nursery's rows of plants, one row of tables at a time. Dew glints on the foliage and beads atop each table, and the air holds a faint chill untempered by the sun, which has not yet climbed above the treeline; aside from the narrow strips of sunlight that filter through the trees, the lot is still in shadow.

Although conversation between them has been limited to brief questions and Latin names, Eve feels a growing sense of kinship with Nestor, who works with her among the rows. They are an efficient team, she thinks, early risers, tending quietly and carefully to their tasks, Eve testing soil moisture and watering when needed, Nestor pruning and staking. He stands across the table from her now, staking what he has told her is a coreopsis to a cage. As she waters, Eve watches

315

him work, worrying his hands around a plant as if casting a spell.

There is something about Nestor's hands that Eve finds fascinating. The way they are perpetually stained, covered with a layer of dirt even at this hour of the morning. The way the skin, stretched taut and smooth across his knuckles, gathers in leathery folds between the joints; when he holds his hand out, it seems to Eve that you could read the lines in his fingers as you would a palm. They are big hands, and despite their arthritic look, dexterous; he tucks twine into careful knots around vines and stems with impossible speed, plucks shoots and wilted leaves with quick snaps of his ridged and brittle nails. She eyes the scar that runs from wrist to elbow, white and wide; though she is curious, she doesn't ask where it came from.

"What's this?" she asks instead, of the last plant left for her to water. It is an unruly little bush, about a foot and a half in height, with gray-green foliage and drooping conical clusters of tiny purple blossoms. If plants had personalities, she thinks, she would get along well with this one. "I kind of like it."

Nestor glances in her direction. "That," he says, "is a Buddleia davidii. Of the Lamiales order and the Buddlejaceae family."

"The Buddleia davidii," Eve repeats.

Nestor reaches for a pair of clippers and snips

a length of twine. "More commonly known as the butterfly bush."

Eve studies the plant, searching its blossoms for some resemblance to butterflies. They put her more in mind of little doilies, the edges wavery and uncertain. "Why?"

"Look over there." Nestor gestures with his chin toward another similar plant; three or four large, black and yellow butterflies are alight on its blossoms.

"They attract butterflies?"

"The tiger swallowtail, particularly."

"How is swallowtail different from any other butterfly? Like a monarch?"

"Take a look. They've got forked tails. See that? Just like the forked tail of a swallow. Hence swallowtail." Nestor frowns down at the plant before him, assessing his work.

"How come they like the butterfly bush so much?" Eve inquires.

"The nectar. Hummingbirds love the nectar, too."

"They attract hummingbirds, too?"

Nestor nods. "Keep your eyes open, and at some point you'll be sure to see one."

Eve looks toward the butterflies on the far bush, their wings beating in slow motion as they gorge themselves on nectar. "How much do you charge for a butterfly bush, anyway?" she asks.

"How much?"

"Yeah. If I wanted to buy one. How much?"

Nestor regards her seriously. "For you?" he says. "I'd say a morning's work."

The sputtering sound of a car engine encroaches on the sounds of birds, the trickle of hose water, the hum of bees; both Eve and Nestor look toward the entrance to the parking lot, waiting for Josie Saunders to appear in her old, beat-up Omni. Eve can't help but feel disappointed that her time alone with Nestor is up, that Josie is here and the nursery will open and customers soon will begin to appear. And sure enough, Nestor clears his throat, wipes his hands against his thighs. "Well," he says. "Time to get down to business." And without another word to Eve, he turns to go inside. Eve watches him, bowlegged and lean, his hair lifting with each step. When she turns back to the butterfly bush, Josie is halfway through the rows of plants, walking in her direction; Eve feels herself stiffen in an inexplicable and reflexive self-defense.

"Hey, Eve," Josie says.

Eve keeps her attention on her watering. "Hey."

"How was your weekend?"

At this, Eve glances up. "It's Tuesday." The words are out before Eve can stop them, and she feels herself blush; she has nothing against Josie, and the petulant tone was not what she intended.

Josie looks at her. "I know it's Tuesday," she says. "I just didn't see you yesterday. You were gone before I got here."

"Sorry," Eve says. "I know. It was fine. The weekend. How was yours?"

Josie shrugs. "It was okay." Absently, she deadheads a petunia. "Listen," she says, "the bonfire for the Thunder Moon is tonight, down at Lanes Cove, and a bunch of us are going to go, set up some chairs, and grill." She looks at Eve questioningly. "You want to come?"

Eve imagines the massive pyramid of lobster pots and wooden pallets that they pile each summer at the water's edge and set alight on July's full moon—the Thunder Moon; she hadn't realized that tonight was the night, and of course she wants to go. At the same time, she is acutely aware that this invitation would never have been extended last year, or for that matter any year before, that Josie is motivated not by an interest in Eve herself, or her friendship, but by a pity Eve is weary of. Sometimes this is why she resents Sophie the most; she is tired of the new, pitiable identity she's saddled with. She shrugs. "I don't know," she says. "I mean, I think have to baby-sit my little sister. Thanks, though."

Josie shrugs. "Well if you don't," she says. "Or when you're done? We'll be right down the hill. You know where to find us."

• • •

After breakfast, Anders carries his coffee out with him to examine the Buick's antenna. He called Rowley Auto Salvage this morning, and they are fairly sure they can find him a replacement; if he's going to drive Eve over to Rowley anyway, he figures he may as well make the trip worthwhile. The antenna is a particularly tall one, of a sturdy, thick gauge; before Anders unscrews it he strums it with a finger, and diminishing waves continue to ripple its length for several seconds, emitting an eerie cosmic sound. Then he opens the hood to see if there are any rusting parts inside, if there is anything loose or failing that might also need replacing while he's at it.

He scans the coils and wires of the engine, the belts and fans, though in truth he doesn't really know what he's looking at. All of it is fairly rusted and old aside from the air filter, which he'd had to replace last year; the winter before, mice had made a nest beneath the hood and chewed through the filter completely. Otherwise, nothing has lately been replaced. Most of the parts are original, the same parts that took him and Joan thirteen thousand miles around the country the summer before they were married—although at the time, he remembers now, he didn't think that would ever happen.

In a minute, Anders hears footsteps coming up the driveway behind him; when he turns, he sees Eve on foot, her face partially obscured by the plant she's carrying in her arms. "Hi, Dad," she says, from behind the leaves.

"What do you have there?" he asks her, lowering the hood. "And where's your bike?"

"I had to leave it at the bottom of the hill. There was no way I could ride all the way up trying to balance this on the handlebars." She sets the plant down on the gravel.

"And I assume that came from the nursery?"

"Yeah. I earned it. It's a Buddleia davidii. Aka a butterfly bush."

"Ah."

"I'm thinking of maybe starting a garden. A creature garden, where I only plant things that attract creatures. Eloise'll be excited. Butterflies and hummingbirds and things." Eve turns around, surveys the lawn. "But where?"

Anders scans the lawn himself; all along the edge, where there aren't things already growing, like the lilies, are rocks and slabs of granite. "I suppose I've monopolized the best gardening space, haven't I?" he says. He nods toward his rose garden. "Tell you what," he says. "Why don't you plant it in there?"

Eve follows his gaze. "In your rose garden?"

"Sure. There's room. And at least one of them needs a replacement anyway."

"Really?"

"Really."

They look across at the failing garden, where a squirrel is making its furtive way along the top of Anders' wall. It heartens Anders to imagine the spot alive with winged color, resurrected. "If you want," he says, "I'll help you get it in the ground right now."

Eve nods. "Cool. Okay."

"And after that," he says, "we can get going, if you're still interested."

Eve gives her father a puzzled look. "Get going?"

"Yes. To Rowley. Remember? I thought we had a deal."

Joan is passing through the kitchen with an armful of dirty sheets when she glimpses Eve and Anders out in Anders' garden; at the sight of them, she pauses there in the middle of the room, still, just looking out. Eve is watching her father intently as he works, standing on the blade with all his weight to sink it deep into the earth, once and then again, moving in a circular direction around a dying rose bush. After a few minutes, the circle is complete, and Anders hands Eve his shovel. He bends down and grips the rosebush by its base, and with the help of a spade, uproots it. Then he stands and tosses it from the garden; father and daughter follow its trajectory with their eyes.

Joan frowns, feeling deep within her chest the

vague, fluttering sense of despair she sometimes has when she sees the two of them together, if only because it makes her think of how she fears her own relationship with Eve has suffered by contrast. It isn't that Eve is unkind to her mother, or prickly, or rude, at least not most of the time— Joan would almost welcome these as inevitable signs of adolescence. It is instead her daughter's ostensible indifference that Joan finds troubling, the arm's length at which Eve lately holds her mother at bay. Joan believes she understands; she thinks of the days immediately following Sophie's death, how until Anders had returned home Eve had stubbornly refused to leave her mother's side; Joan worries that it might have been too much. She fears she may have shown too much; she worries that Eve fears the same.

Joan gazes out the window for a moment more and then continues into the laundry room. She is folding the clean load, trying to forget her niggling unease by focusing instead on the thunk, thunk, thunk of the wash, when she hears Eloise behind her. "Mom?" Joan sets a shirt down and turns at the sound of her daughter's voice; Eloise has appeared in the kitchen, ready with her things for camp. "You forgot something *really* important." Eloise thrusts her arm out; Joan sees, to her dismay, the old pig-shaped dog toy of Buster's that Eloise had dug out of the closet for Henry the other day. She drops the shirt she'd been folding onto the dryer and steps into the room. "His *pig*," Eloise says. "He *loves* his pig."

"I'm sure he has loads of toys that he loves at home," Joan says. "Actually, I *know* he does," she fibs. "I saw them."

"I don't care," Eloise says, adamant. "It doesn't matter if he has other toys, because he loves his pig. He *needs* his pig."

"I don't think he *needs* it, sweetie. And isn't it nice to have something to remember him by?"

"I have my *memory* to remember him by." Eloise blinks at her, wide-eyed and irate. "If you had *waited* in the first place to bring him home so I could have said *good-bye, I* would have remembered his pig. But you didn't wait. And you forgot. And now we have to bring it to him."

Joan takes a deep breath, pulls her lips in; the washing machine thunks behind her. Eloise's eyes have begun to fill with tears.

"*Please*, Mom. I'm asking nicely. Please, please, please please please let's bring it to him. I really want to say good-bye."

Joan nods; there is the plate to return anyway. "If it means that much to you—"

"—It does!"

"Then we will."

Rowley Auto Salvage is located just off the main road several miles north of Rowley proper, in a large, open lot hemmed in by a chain-link fence.

Although it takes Eve and Anders only half an hour or so to get there, Eve is glad not to have had to ride her bike all the way; while it's not far by car, she thinks, it would be a hike on a bike, and the unintended rhyme amuses her enough that she repeats it aloud as they pull into the driveway.

Her father glances at her. "Yes, it would," he agrees, squinting out again through the windshield.

"But would I be allowed, now?" she asks, referring to the new helmet she has worn for the entirety of the drive, which they stopped off for at the bike store in Gloucester on the way. *If you want to go Rowley, this is your half of the deal,* her father had insisted, to her chagrin.

"Absolutely not," he says.

Eve unbuckles her seat belt and removes the helmet from her head, surveying the place as they approach. Rowley Auto Salvage is much more in keeping with what Eve had envisioned on her way to the junkyard yesterday, with hundreds of junked cars parked in semi-ordered rows, large piles of rusted scrap metal, stacks of wheels and tires, Dumpsters filled to capacity. Off to one side of the lot is a large brown machine that looks like a giant veterinary scale, but with a roof that slides up and down two fat poles on either end. This, Eve guesses, is the car squisher, and the reason that some of the vehicles here are flattened versions of their former selves. Beyond this machine, parked in a second lot of its own, is a fleet of tow trucks, among which Eve spies two, which are identical to the one that came to the quarry the other day. She returns her gaze to the endless rows of cars, wondering if James Favazza's truck might really be among them.

Anders parks in front of the main building. Through the nearest door, Eve sees two men working beneath a car mounted up on a lift, likely removing any worthwhile parts. She snaps a shot with the old Pentax, which she's brought along for the sake of documentation, then reaches for the door handle.

"Evie." Anders grabs hold of her wrist as she is getting out. Eve turns, looks at her father expectantly. "You let me do the talking," he says firmly.

"I will, but—"

"No buts about it."

"No but, Dad—" Anders interrupts her with a look and a raised finger. "Fine," she says. Anders nods once, touches her lightly on the nose.

They approach the warehouse door where the men are working, Anders guiding Eve with a hand on the base of her neck, both gentle and warning at once. They pause in the doorway, their shadows squat versions of themselves on the oil-stained floor, Anders' shadow headless, decapitated by the line where the sunlight ends. The shadow of his outstretched arm reminds Eve of his grip, and she shrugs him off as she peers into the shadows within. The shelves, she sees, rise ceiling high, and the auto parts they hold are evidently organized by type and brand of car: transmissions, steering columns, axles, doors, Honda, Volvo, Nissan, Ford. The car the men are pillaging now is a Subaru, its windshield a shattered web, the front of the car a mangled mess of what it used to be. As Eve stares at it, Anders clears his throat; one of the men working beneath the car looks over his shoulder, his arms raised up as he loosens something with a wrench. "Help you?" he asks.

"Yes. I called this morning about an antenna," Anders replies. "For an '82 Buick Riviera?" He gestures over his shoulder in the direction of the car.

"Right. You spoke to me." The man puts the wrench down on a worktable nearby and steps toward them. "Believe it or not," he says, "I found one that did come from a Riviera. A '74, not an '82, but the mounting hole would be the same—they're pretty standard. To be honest, most any old antenna would do the trick. But if you want authentic."

"I do," Anders says. "Great."

The man jerks his head toward the back of the warehouse. "I got it back in the office," he says. Anders follows the man in that direction; Eve starts to follow them both, but remains where she is, transfixed by the car on the lift. The front of the car is so smashed it appears about half the length it should be, the hood bent back like a hairpin, revealing an engine that looks as if it had been rattled by an earthquake. From her vantage on the ground, she can see the tips and sides of different parts that should be lying flat instead protruding from within. The front fender is gone completely, and the right front wheel is bent weirdly on its axle. She looks down at the man still standing underneath the car, who is looking upward with a grimace of concentration as he removes the rear muffler. His name tag reads Robert. "Um," Eve begins, despite her father's admonition not to speak.

The man looks over at her.

"What happened?" she asks, nodding toward the car; she cannot help herself. "It looks pretty bad."

"Sure does," he says. "Head-on into something, that's for sure."

"But you don't know what happened?"

Robert shakes his head. "Nope," he says. He sets the muffler on the table and steps out from beneath the car, folds his arms across his chest as he looks up at it. "But I betcha whoever it was didn't get out of that one alive." He sniffs.

Eve blinks, picturing the car on the side of the road, smashed into a tree, the driver's head against the windshield. She pictures the row of ambulances, fire trucks, police cars lined up on the shoulder, the line of curious traffic crawling by, mist rising from the pavement, because, she thinks, it would have been a rainy day. She pictures firemen in their big black boots standing in groups of two or three, paramedics trudging down the grassy slope to where the car sits steaming in the rain. She wonders if they'd had to use the Jaws of Life, or if it was too late for that. It was a man; for some reason she feels as certain of this as she does that it was raining. She wonders if he had a family, kids. She wonders if they'll always think about what they were doing while their father lay trapped and dying or even dead behind the wheel of a car, or if maybe they were there, unscathed. The backseat looks okay.

She swallows as it dawns on her with sickening rapidity that she has no idea what became of Sophie's car. How, she thinks, could she have never wondered, not back in October, and not even this week, after James Favazza? How had its fate not have once crossed her mind? She is ashamed when she thinks of the effort she's put into finding James' truck by contrast, though it's true that she's been looking for evidence and artifacts, not searching out a grave.

"Why don't you just smush the thing?" she asks. "There can't be a lot left to take. I mean, a muffler?"

"Most of the engine's a loss. But everything else—oil pan, headers, axles." Robert shrugs. "Why let that go to waste?"

Eve turns to him, her face hot. "Because someone *died* in that car."

Robert looks at her, bemused. "Or they didn't," he says. "It's a car, either way."

Joan and Eloise stop at Magnolia Street on their way to Eloise's camp, and the first thing Joan notices is the pot of flowers on Elizabeth Favazza's stoop. It wasn't there yesterday. They are yellow mums, an ironically cheerful explosion of color beneath the American flag, which, in the day's quiet, hangs unmoving. The wind chimes are also still, and as they wait on the stoop after she has rung the bell, Henry's pig and Elizabeth Favazza's plate in a plastic bag at her side, Joan finds herself wishing for their tinkling melody; the only other sound is the grind and thunk of a garbage truck making its way down the street. She watches the huge levers shovel and shift inside the back, devouring loads of trash like so many mouthfuls of food. Eloise stands beside her, eyes intent on the front door.

It wasn't much of a concession to bring the dog the pig; whether or not Elizabeth Favazza expects it, whether or not the woman is even aware that she has given it away, Joan knew already that at some point she would have to return the plate to her. Once the brownies were eaten, it was either that or else put the plate away among their own as a constant, awful reminder

330

of what has passed. She was almost grateful when Eloise demanded she return the pig, relieved to transfer the brownies onto a plate of their own and pack the plate away today, and so spare herself the hours she knows she'd otherwise spend anticipating its return.

After a minute, no one has come to the door. Eloise tugs on her mother's shirt. "Ring it again," she says. "I think I heard Henry in there."

Joan complies, even though it seems unlikely to her that anyone inside would not have heard those four cheerful notes sound the first time. Still, she counts to thirty before leading Eloise back to the car. "We'll leave a quick note before we go," she says.

"What about the toy?" Eloise asks, following her mother across the sidewalk.

"We'll leave that, too, of course."

"But what if it gets stolen?"

Joan opens the back so that her daughter can get in. "I don't think anyone's going to steal it, sweetheart." She gets into the passenger seat, leaving the door open, and rummages through the glove box for a working pen, then takes a receipt from the floor of the car and flattens it against the dashboard, backside up. *"Here is your plate,"* she reads aloud as she writes for Eloise's approval, *"and a toy from my daughter for Henry. Thank you again for the brownies.*

Joan Jacobs." She looks at Eloise in the rear-view mirror. "How does that sound?"

Eloise's two eyes blink in the mirror. "Can I put my name, too?"

Joan concedes and gives her daughter the note and the pen. "Okay," she says when Eloise has finished. "Sit tight." She drops the note into the bag and again she climbs the three steps of the stoop, and she is just about to loop the bag's handles over the doorknob when suddenly the door opens; when Joan looks up, she sees Elizabeth Favazza's face in the shadows on the other side.

"Oh! I didn't think anyone was home," Joan says in surprise.

"I was on the telephone," Elizabeth Favazza says.

Joan wonders if this is true, or if she had been watching Joan and Eloise through the window all this time. The woman steps out onto the stoop; she is again wearing a T-shirt that is slightly too large, though it could just be that she is so petite she seems to disappear in anything she wears—her loose linen pants seem large for her, too. She looks at Joan quizzically, almost with an air of mistrust.

Joan lifts the bag in explanation. "I was just going to leave this for you." She extends it forward. "Your plate. And a toy my daughter wanted Henry to have."

"My plate?" Elizabeth Favazza repeats; she appears confused.

"The brownies," Joan explains.

"Oh," the woman says, and her expression softens with comprehension. "I wondered why you were back. I didn't even think about the plate when I wrapped those up—I would have forgotten completely." She takes the bag from Joan's hand. "But thank you."

"Of course," Joan says. "I'm sorry to bother you."

"Not at all." Elizabeth Favazza reaches into the bag and takes the pig toy out; its ropey limbs dangle. She stares down at it with a calm distraction, as if lost in thought, and then she looks up at Joan, regards her in an appraising manner that makes Joan feel like some sort of specimen.

"She's seven," Joan says, as if to explain. "She felt strongly."

Elizabeth Favazza nods. "Well thank her, too," she says. She looks toward the car, where Eloise sits peering out the window. "That must be your daughter there," she says.

Joan glances back at the car herself. "Yes," she says. "One of them," she adds.

Just then, Henry appears in the doorway, and before Joan has time to ask if it's okay, Eloise has sprung from the backseat and is hurrying toward them; Henry meets her at the bottom of the stoop.

"Henry!" Eloise coos, crouching down beside him. She kisses his mangy fur. "I almost didn't get to say good-bye!"

Joan and Elizabeth Favazza watch her for half a minute, and then Joan touches her daughter on the head. "Okay, sweetheart, one more kiss and we should get going."

Eloise wraps her arms around Henry's neck; the dog wriggles free and runs back into the house.

"We'll leave you," Joan says. "We just wanted to leave those off, and . . ."

"Thank you," Elizabeth Favazza says. "And thank you for taking such good care of Henry," she adds, looking down at Eloise.

Eloise smiles, eyes downcast, but she is clearly pleased. She turns and runs back to the car, where she has left the back door open.

Joan follows, and she has just reached the bottom of the stoop when Elizabeth Favazza calls out quietly behind her. "I know who you are," she says.

Joan freezes where she is, feeling suddenly hot and cold at the same time, nearly dizzy. She composes herself and turns around. "I'm sorry?"

Elizabeth Favazza stands on the stoop, her head tilted slightly to the side. "I know who you are," she repeats. She runs her forearm across her brow, the pig toy in her hand. "Joan Jacobs. I mean, I read the police report. I know where it happened. I—I thought that might have been why you were back."

Joan opens her mouth, unsure of what to say. "Oh," she says, finally. "No." She takes a breath.

She casts a quick look toward the car, where Eloise sits buckled in the backseat. "I'm sorry. I—I don't know what to say." She looks at Elizabeth Favazza beseechingly. "I didn't say anything because . . . I don't know."

"I probably wouldn't have mentioned it if I were you, either. I just had to let you know. That I know who you are. And that I know you know who I am."

Joan feels her eyelids twitch; she tries to blink the sensation away. "Well, I'm sorry," she says.

Elizabeth Favazza shakes her head. "Don't be sorry."

"No," Joan says. "I am. I'm sorry about your son." She swallows "I'm sorry about James."

Elizabeth Favazza looks at Joan quietly. She nods. "Thank you," she says. "I am, too."

They find James Favazza's truck at the far end of the lot, parked in tall grass between an old Honda sedan and a Volkswagen Dasher, the likes of which Anders hasn't seen in years. The men inside gave them permission to take a look around, which Anders requested after he'd installed the new antenna; they have done so quietly, Anders trailing Eve up and down each row of cars.

He stands now several feet back from the truck, watching as his daughter slowly circles it, snapping pictures. The wheels have been removed, as have most other useful parts: the steering wheel, antenna, likely the transmission inside, although this may have been water damaged. Anders is mildly perturbed to realize how little about the truck he'd registered the other week, when it was first pulled from the quarry; he looks closely at it now, trying to see the truck as Eve must, with an eye to every detail. The smashed window on the driver's side. The Red Sox bumper sticker. The rust spots on the door, which stand out only slightly from the color of the truck itself. The dent in the front bumper; he would wager Eve wonders whether it was there before the truck ended up in the quarry, or whether it was dented when it hit the quarry floor; likewise for the cracked red taillight case. All details, in the end, that don't explain a thing.

"I can't believe it's really here," Eve says, standing at the rear of the truck. She crouches down to take a picture, brushing absently at the tall blades of grass tickling her ear.

Anders does not respond, only watches as Eve stands, walks around to the truck's far side. She stops at the passenger-side door and looks inside; Anders can see her through one window, then the next, framed there. After a moment she lifts her eyes to meet his; she looks serious, pensive. She sighs, then comes around the hood of the car to where her father is standing, folds her arms.

"They took everything," she says. "There's nothing in there."

"No."

"Even the glove box is gone."

They stand looking at the truck without speaking. Cicadas sizzle in the grass around them, and seagulls caw overhead. Anders puts a hand very gently on Eve's neck; this time, she does not shrug him off.

The typewriter is as Joan left it yesterday when Elizabeth Favazza called, the lid removed, the experimental piece of paper blank behind the platen. She lifts the spool from its posts, even though she hasn't yet gotten a new ribbon to replace the old one; she realizes that a replacement might be hard to come by anyway these days. She flips the ribbon over to see if there is any ink left on the other side, but when she replaces the spool and lid and tries again to type, the paper remains blank beneath each typebar's strike. She sighs, sits back in her chair, and looks out the window, where innumerable black starlings flit restlessly from branch to branch in the trees, preening and calling and swooping. Yesterday she'd admired these birds and the pattern they made against the sky; today they seem ominous, all of them together like a big black cloud in the trees, and she is struck with a surprising certainty that they were there in the branches the day James Favazza drove his truck into the quarry, screeching him to his death.

She sits forward and puts her chin into her hands, remembering Elizabeth Favazza's words: *I know who you are,* and then, *I know where it happened.* It turns her perception of yesterday's encounter with the woman on its head—*Joan* was the one in the dark, even as she'd approached the situation thinking the opposite, and Elizabeth Favazza knew just who she was dealing with. It makes Joan feel self-conscious to think back on, almost annoyed; she'd gone to such lengths to protect the woman from knowledge she already had: *I know who you are.* Joan frowns; Elizabeth Favazza does not know who Joan is, not really. She has no idea how much they actually have in common, and Joan did not take the opportunity to tell her, though part of her now wishes that she had, as if to forge this bond would relieve her of her isolation. But she hadn't been prepared. And there had been Eloise waiting in the car.

She gazes out the window at the quarry, black and glossy and deep. *I know where it happened.*

Slowly, she stands and walks down the hallway to Eve's room. The door is open; clothes are piled on the wicker chair in the corner of the room, where the cat lies sleeping, contented to have the house to himself again. A book sits open and facedown on the bedside table—her daughter, she sees, has gotten all of twelve pages into *Northanger Abbey*, a book she'd started weeks ago. But Joan can understand Eve's distraction. She gets onto her knees between the twin beds and peers beneath the one Eve sleeps in, where she sees the bag of "evidence" her daughter has collected from the quarry. When Anders brought it downstairs on Trivia Night, she hadn't even bothered to look at the contents; to her, at that time, it was only so much junk.

She empties the bag onto the floor and sits down on the edge of Eve's bed, looking down at all the items her daughter has gathered. There are beer cans and bottles, the Vic's T-shirt, a flip-flop, a bowl, a water bottle. She wonders what of Sophie's might have been left behind at the tracks, what items, if any, might be lying even now at the base of the embankment: the miniature troll that dangled from her rearview mirror, a shred of clothing, an elastic band, all things that Joan has never considered before, things, like these before her, that she wouldn't think to miss.

She looks out Eve's window at the quarry, remembering the bubbles that had risen glug by glug the other night, the residue of oil, the black-clad divers, the horror of it all. She wonders *what* exactly Elizabeth Favazza thinks happened, whether she thinks it was an accident or intentional that her son ended up in the quarry. While they both must live with the *why* of things, Joan isn't sure that she could live with that uncertainty—the uncertainty of *what*—herself, though the moment the thought occurs to her, she feels guilty for it, guilty to feel grateful to be sure of what she's sure, which is, without a doubt, that her daughter chose to leave her.

Ten

Just before dinnertime, Eve marches into the kitchen to announce that she won't be eating with her family tonight; she's going down to Lanes Cove for the bonfire and a cookout with some friends. Anders is sitting at the kitchen table, reading about the various shipwrecks said to have occurred at the reef where his class will dive tomorrow, and Joan is at the counter slicing radishes for a salad; both look at her with blank surprise. "Oh," Joan says, finally. "Okay," and they watch, otherwise speechless, as Eve passes through the kitchen and out the door, which she lets slam shut behind her.

She can feel her parents' eyes upon her as she crosses the driveway, dutifully dons her new helmet, and mounts her bike, but she does not look back, nor does she allow herself a moment to pause and reconsider her decision, which is as surprising to her as it clearly was to her parents. She's not even sure exactly how it came about; one minute she'd been stretched out on her bed, staring at the ceiling, and the next she was striding downstairs and out the door, damned if she'd miss out on the bonfire just because she's a dead girl's sister.

It troubles Eve a bit that she had no idea that

tonight was the night of the bonfire, not because of the fire itself, but because it takes place on the full moon. Normally, in summers, she pays close attention to the phase of the moon, to the timing of the tides, to the movement of constellations across the sky, as if meting out the summer one day at a time, and relishing each day for its distinctive character. But she has no idea what the tides are doing now, nor has she really considered the moon or stars since the night that they arrived.

Lanes Cove is just down the hill from their quarry, at the end of a short spur off the main road around the corner from Arthur's store; the closer Eve gets, the less sure of her decision she becomes, and by the time she reaches the main road, her ambivalence has become full-blown intimidation. She plants a foot on the ground for balance and looks around her. Cars are parked haphazardly all along the shoulder as far as she can see, and groups of people are making their way down to the cove with chairs and blankets and coolers and beers. One guy has painted his body blue, and another guy is wearing a clown suit. One couple is struggling down the street with a particularly enormous cooler, the girl walking backward and giggling loudly every time she stumbles. Eve doesn't see what's funny, or why the girl doesn't just set the cooler down for a second and turn around, and she watches their slow progress until they, like everyone else, have disappeared around the corner.

She takes an unhappy breath, picturing that couple and their like gathered in groups along the water's edge, playing music and dancing and drinking. Last year, she went to the bonfire with Sophie and Eloise and Saul, and they watched from a safe distance, in a little row of their own atop the breakwater that walls the harbor in. In years before that, when she was young, her father would bring them down, if they went at all; for a few years in between, the city outlawed the event, claiming that it drew too raucous a crowd. She has never gone to the bonfire as an insider, and even though Josie has explicitly invited her, she doesn't feel like one. She pictures the group gathered around the public quarry the other night, the beer bottles, Ms. Rolling Stones, the way they all would look at her; all pity aside, she can't picture herself among them anyway.

She looks toward Arthur's store, which stands like a safe haven across the road, and she pedals over; even though there's nothing she particularly wants inside, it is somewhere to go other than down to the cove, which she isn't sure she has the nerve to do, and after her announcement of intent she can't just turn around and go home. It's been awhile since she's seen Arthur anyway, though she's been just as happy not to have to go each morning and get the paper alone.

She has just propped her bike against the telephone pole outside the store when she hears the bells on the door jangle, and when she turns, she sees Saul coming through the door, a bag of ice under his arm. Immediately, she feels herself turn red. She hasn't seen Saul since Trivia Night, the memory of which encounter fills her with a combination of embarrassment and anger, though she's not sure whether that anger is directed more at Saul for his girlfriend or at herself for being a fool.

"Hey, Evie," Saul says.

Eve glances over Saul's shoulder, waiting for the girlfriend to follow him out the door, but he appears to be alone. She pulls her helmet off her head. "Hi."

"You going down to the bonfire?" he asks.

Eve shrugs. "No," she says. "I was just going to the store. I'd kind of forgotten about the bonfire until now, so . . ."

Saul studies her, shifts the bag of ice from beneath one arm to the other. "How's it going, anyway?" he asks.

"Fine."

"Any progress?"

"What do you mean, progress?"

Saul shrugs. "The quarry. Vic's. All that."

Eve narrows her eyes, feeling teased. "Don't be a jerk, Saul."

"I'm not being a jerk. I'm honestly just asking."

"Well, no. No progress." She looks him in the eye, still thinking of their encounter in the woods. "How's your girlfriend?"

Saul's face falls. "Evie."

Eve drops her gaze to the sidewalk, stares down at a black gum spot on the pavement. "Sorry," she says, wishing she had held her tongue. It occurs to her that maybe Saul really *was* curious, which is more than she can say for anyone else, and she has no right to punish him for being alive, even when Sophie's not. She lifts her eyes. "I really am," she says. "I didn't mean it."

Saul nods. "I know," he says. "It's all right."

Eve sighs, gazes absently down the street at nothing in particular.

"Hey," Saul says, punching her lightly on the shoulder. "If you're not doing anything you should really come down to the bonfire. I heard it's huge this year."

Eve looks back at him. "I don't know," she says.

"What else are you going to do?"

Eve shrugs, though it *is* the bonfire, and the idea of having Saul as a chaperone does make the whole thing seem somehow easier.

"If it makes you feel any better, Mona isn't going to be there."

Eve blinks at him. "That's her name?"

Saul nods. "Yeah." He shifts his bag of ice again, this time to his shoulder. "Come on," he says. "My hands are freezing. I've got a cooler in the car and when it's full of ice I'll need a hand getting it down there anyway." He turns and walks toward his car, which is parked several cars away. Eve watches him go; he is familiar, and safe, and suddenly it makes no sense to do anything but follow.

After Anders has read Eloise a chapter from *Alice* and waited as she composed this evening's Hobbster note, he goes into the kitchen for a bottle of wine to take outside, where Joan is out on a lawn chair waiting for him. They are out of red, but he finds a bottle of cold white in the refrigerator; as he uncorks it, his eye falls to the brochure that describes the dive his class will take tomorrow, at a reef called Norman's Woe. It is the site of many shipwrecks over the years, though the brochure describes only two in detail. One was the wreck of the *Rebecca Ann*, in a snowstorm in 1823. All of the ten crew members but one were swept out to sea; the lone survivor managed to stay alive by clinging to an icy rock. The other shipwreck was that of the schooner *Favorite*; twenty bodies washed ashore, among them that of a girl tied to a piece of the ship, supposedly the captain's daughter. According to the brochure, this wreck was the inspiration for Henry Wadsworth Longfellow's poem *The Wreck of the Hesperus*, though only a verse is reprinted:

And fast through the midnight dark and drear
Through the whistling sleet and snow,
Like a sheeted ghost, the vessel swept
Tow'rds the reef of Norman's Woe.

Though one might expect to find the wooden ribs of ships and forms of rusted anchors at the site, the photographs of the dive feature marine life similar to what Anders saw at Plum Cove. Part of him wishes that the history of the reef had not been included in the brochure; he worries that the knowledge might take away from the experience. It seems odd to consider diving in a place where so many have died, even as he knows that in the past he has wandered without a second thought through Civil War battlefields, and over the beaches at Normandy. Still. One of the things he has found strangely difficult to understand since Sophie's death is how trains— filled with oblivi-ous commuters reading their newspapers or magazines or sipping their coffees —continue to pass several times daily over the spot on the tracks where she was killed, without ceremony or recognition. Of course, he under-stands this intellectually, just as he does the acceptability of tomorrow's dive, but on another level it is difficult for him to accept; for him, the spot is sacred, heavy with meaning. When he finally made it home from Italy shortly after she died, visiting the spot seemed, to him, of great importance. Joan felt no similar need or desire, but for her, he supposes, their daughter's death already seemed real.

He looks out the window at his wife at the quarry's edge, thinking not for the first time about the fact that their quarry is now that spot for someone else.

Joan looks up at the sky as the last daylight fades, watching as the full moon rises above the far horizon. The stars have started to appear one by one, as if someone were drilling holes in the firmament from some bright other side. Somewhere along the quarry's edge, bullfrogs are in croaking conversation, and the trees are electric with cicadas, invisible and roaring. She spent the afternoon writing—longhand—and for some reason it came out easier that way than writing has for years, or perhaps it was easy because she has found material that finally compels her; either way, she feels fulfilled in a way that she hasn't in some time.

She doesn't hear Anders' footsteps behind her in the grass, but she can somehow sense when he's approaching, and indeed after a second he sets a wine bottle down on the table between her lawn chair and his own, where their wineglasses from dinner sit empty.

"We didn't have any more red," he says, sitting down.

"That's okay," Joan says. "White's refreshing."

Anders pours them each a glass, then leans back, balancing his wineglass on his chest, bracing it in the crevice of two fingers.

"It's like white noise," Joan says after a moment.

Anders looks over at his wife. "What is?"

"Listen."

Anders is quiet. "What am I supposed to hear?" he asks.

"Crickets. Frogs. Cicadas. That's the thing. They're like white noise. You don't even realize how noisy they are until you pay attention. But listen to those guys in the trees especially."

They listen.

"They are loud," Anders agrees.

Joan looks at her husband. "I thought you maybe weren't coming back out," she says. "Did you read an extra chapter?"

"No." Anders takes a sip of wine. "She also had to compose a note to Hobbster."

"Of course." Joan shakes her head. "Evie. She never fails to surprise me."

"No," Anders agrees.

"Who do you suppose she went to the bonfire with? As far as I know she's done nothing with anyone since we got here—or should I say she's done nothing to do with anything aside from . . ." She gestures with her chin toward the quarry, then looks over at her husband. "I hear you found the truck, by the way."

"We did."

"And?"

Anders shrugs. "Nothing garnered," he says. "But I don't think she'd have been satisfied until we'd at least gone looking."

Joan takes a sip of wine. "I wonder what's next. What her next expedition might be. The junkyard yesterday, Rowley today, Saul the other night . . ."

"And Georgetown," Anders adds automatically.

"Georgetown?"

"Oh. Yuh." Anders takes a breath. "That was the first. She wanted to return a cooler that she found in the quarry. It had a name on it, and I guess whose ever it was lived in Georgetown."

"You drove her to Georgetown, too? Aiding and abetting."

"Oh no," Anders says. "I didn't drive her. She rode her bike."

"She rode her *bike?* Jesus." Joan frowns. "Why didn't you tell me?"

"I know," Anders says. "Sorry. I promised I wouldn't if she wouldn't do something like it again. Hence the lift to Rowley," he adds.

"I see."

They are quiet for a moment, and then Anders looks over at his wife; she is looking upward, at the sky. "You didn't tell me you went to James Favazza's funeral," he ventures. "I saw the program in your pocketbook."

Joan meets his gaze, feeling caught at the same time that she is somehow unsurprised. "I didn't, really," she says. "I went to the church beforehand. But not to the funeral."

Anders waits.

Joan takes a breath. "I didn't plan it, exactly," she goes on. "I was in town, and . . . I don't really know why I went." She knits her brow.

"But you didn't want to tell me?" Anders asks.

Joan is quiet for a moment. "I don't know," she says finally. "I suppose I worried you'd find it . . . upsetting."

The sound of a car engine grows, then fades, as a car passes on the road nearby.

"Why?" Anders asks when it has gone.

"I don't know."

Anders looks at his wife, her furrowed brow and worried eyes. "You're allowed, you know," he tells her.

She looks at him questioningly.

"You're allowed your own response to things," he goes on. "You're allowed not to be a rock. God knows you allow it for everyone else." He holds her gaze. "We're all okay," he says. "And I understand."

"You do?" Joan laughs lightly. "I don't know if I understand, myself. *I* don't know why I went."

"The other day," Anders says. "I found a scrap of paper with an address in Sophie's garbage."

Joan looks at her husband, waits.

"It was a Beverly address, and I went and found it. I don't know why *I* went, either, really." He looks over at his wife. "But that's what I mean when I say I understand."

Joan holds his gaze, surprised by this admission. She recognizes how difficult it must be; it is difficult for Anders to talk about their daughter at all. "What was the address?" she asks.

Anders looks at her, a curious expression on his face. "Joseph's," he replies. "It was Joseph's." He sighs, and sits back. Joan reaches across the space between them for his hand; finally, it seems, he is there.

The bonfire truly is the largest Eve can remember seeing. She sits on a picnic blanket spread across a rocky ledge at the edge of the cove, her face warm in the light from the bonfire, which towers maybe fifty feet in the air, licking against the sky and sending up great sputtering showers of sparks. Josie Saunders is dancing with a couple of other girls nearby; the three of them spin slowly to reggae playing from a stereo that someone has brought along. Saul has gone off with a couple of guys to find more beer. Steve Busman and a girl whose name Eve didn't catch are hovering over the grill, cooking up yet another round of hot dogs, though Eve doesn't think she could eat another thing. She is both satiated and satisfied, and content to sit where she is and watch the scene. All around the cove, the rocks and shore are packed with revelers. People stand in a jagged line atop the breakwater along the cove's outer edge, shooting off flares and small whistling fireworks. The clown she saw earlier dances in front of the bonfire, the fabric of his suit translucent against the flames. Dark heads bob on the molten surface of the water.

It was easy, in the end, coming down here. She and Saul had lugged his cooler down between them, and as they approached Josie and the others, no one had muttered about her presence, or exchanged looks; they'd only waved in welcome, offered them hot dogs and beer. She'd talked to Josie about the nursery, and about Nestor, who Josie thinks is weird, and she'd talked about forensics with another girl named Maura whose dad works for the FBI. And though she wasn't interested in the beer, which tastes to her like soap, she did out of sheer curiosity eat a couple of pot brownies, which have put her in a calm and thoughtful mood.

She keeps on picturing James Favazza's truck, parked so forlornly at the edge of that lot all pillaged of its parts, how its grill had almost seemed to grimace at her when she looked at it headlong. Even though there was nothing worth noting in James Favazza's truck—not a shred of evidence or a personal effect—the fact that they found it at all was hugely gratifying. It made her feel like she'd found something to hold onto, had somehow nailed down for her the increasingly nebulous feel of the whole event of James Favazza's death with its sheer physicality. *Someone died here,* it said to her. *Your search is valid.* And all those pillaged parts! She can only imagine what will become of them; it is curious to think that someone, someday, will hold James Favazza's steering wheel beneath his hand, and someone else will adjust his rearview mirror. Sophie's, too, probably. She's not sure if she's more comforted or troubled by the notion.

"Hey," she hears, and Saul sits down beside her with a fresh beer.

"Hey."

"How you doing?"

"Good," she says. "Just people watching."

"This is a good scene for that," Saul says. "That clown guy's going to combust, though."

They watch him dance ever closer to the flames; finally, he swan dives into the water.

Eve looks at Saul sidelong. "So," she begins tentatively; she cannot help herself. "We did find the truck."

"The what?"

"The truck. James Favazza's truck? In the car salvage place in Rowley."

"Oh yeah?"

"Yeah," Eve says. "Me and my dad went. Just

since you asked about progress. Even though I guess it's not really progress."

"Yeah, but it must have been kind of cool to see. Or creepy."

Eve nods. "Both," she says.

"And they still don't know what happened to the guy?"

Eve shakes her head. "Nope," she says. "And they never will because they're not doing a thing about it. But." She sighs, watching the top of the fire, where flame transforms to smoke, mesmerized. "It's crazy," she goes on. "All those recycled car parts they have? They took *everything* from the truck, and they're going to sell it all. And Dad? He got a new antenna for the Buick, and the guy said it came off of a '74 Riviera. So it just makes me wonder where it really came from."

"What do you mean?"

"Like, what car it might have come from. Who it belonged to. If it went to drive-in movies in its past, or if it picked up only classical because it was on the Buick of some old lady who wore a lot of perfume and smoked cigarettes with the roof on and the windows up."

"A chain-smoking granny in a Riviera." Saul nods, amused.

Eve shrugs. "I don't know, that's the image that came to mind. But seriously. All those auto parts that came from different cars. It's like their history is living on. Or like a transplant or something. It's kind of creepy, but it's kind of cool, too, don't you think?"

"I guess."

"It actually kind of makes me want to be an organ donor when I get my license."

Saul looks at her, grinning now. "How many of those brownies did you eat, anyway?"

"I don't think it's the brownies," Eve says. "I think it's just me." But something about the notion makes her start to giggle, and she finds that she can't stop, which makes her laugh harder, and the look on Saul's face makes her laugh harder still, until finally she collapses back onto the blanket and she is face to face with the moon overhead, whose face seems tonight to be laughing not at, but with her.

Eleven

The next day it rains—not in a series of the short-lived, wind-driven squalls they've grown accustomed to, but with a tireless insistence, battering and heavy. Joan stands at the stove, listening to the pelting sound of drops against the roof and windowpanes; she imagines she can almost hear the raindrops slapping at the surface of the quarry. Bacon sizzles a duet with the weather in a skillet before her, and pancakes are slowly cooking on the griddle; a few more bubbles around the edges, and they will be ready to flip. Joan stands ready, spatula in hand.

Behind her, Eloise sits at the kitchen table, watching Anders lay out the gear he'll need for his dive, and peppering him with questions; right now they are discussing methods of entering the water.

"Did you walk backward like I told you?" Eloise inquires.

"Well, we didn't have to, because we didn't put our flippers on until we were already in the water."

"What about today?"

"Today we go in off of some rocks."

"So you have to jump in?"

"Well," Anders explains, "it's more like

stepping in. Like taking a big, giant step right into the water."

"Oh."

Joan lifts the edge of a pancake with the spatula. She is surprised that Anders is as game as he is about diving; when she'd signed him up it had been more of a desperate, last-ditch attempt to engage him in *something,* after her failures to do so with anything else. Though she wouldn't ever admit it, or discourage him, in truth the thought of her husband scuba diving makes her mildly anxious; like mountain climbing or bungee jumping it doesn't strike her as overly safe, and part of her wishes he'd taken to yoga or painting instead. She flips the bacon, one piece at a time.

"Can I try that on?" Eloise asks behind her.

"Sure," Anders replies.

After a few seconds, Eloise laughs. "Mom, look!" she cries in a muffled voice.

Joan glances over her shoulder; Eloise's face is covered almost entirely by Anders' mask. "You look like an astronaut!" she says.

Joan peeks under a pancake again; they are ready to be flipped. She thinks of the time maybe twenty years ago when they were in Colorado and Anders went helicopter skiing. She was apprehensive at the thought in the same way that she is now, and in the end rightly so; one of the blades caught on an outcropping of rock and the helicopter crash-landed on the side of the mountain. No one was hurt, but she remembers being unsurprised when she got the call, and she remembers thinking that she should have listened to her gut and implored him not to go.

"What's that?" she hears Eloise ask as she spreads a paper towel out on a plate.

"This is called a buoyancy control device. A BCD for short."

"What is a BCD for? It looks like a life jacket."

"It does look like a life jacket," Anders agrees. "But it's not, exactly."

"Can I try it on?"

"You may."

Joan transfers the bacon from the skillet to the plate with the towel; grease spreads across the paper. She pictures her husband running out of oxygen at the bottom of the ocean, or having a heart attack—by the time they got him to the beach, she thinks, it would be too late. Her heart jumps violently at the thought. Impatiently, she checks the pancakes one more time, willing her imagination to settle down. But it bothers her that she should feel this way about today's dive, when she felt just fine about last week's by comparison, and she wonders seriously if she ought to stop Anders from going.

"It's kind of big for me," Eloise is saying. "Why do you wear a life jacket thingy if you're trying to sink?"

"Well, like I said, it's not really a life jacket.

There's this little space here, see? Which you can put air into, and take air out of, and it makes you go up and down."

"How?"

"Well, if I put air in, the air I added wants to get to the surface, and it brings me with it. So up I go. Make sense?"

"I guess."

Joan begins to transfer the pancakes onto a plate. She *should* stop him, she decides, as crazy as it might sound.

"But what's coolest," Anders goes on behind her, "is when you get to the place where you're not going up or down. If you have *just* the right amount of air, you just . . . do nothing. You're suspended. It's kind of like magic. You don't have to do anything except just be."

Joan turns around, a plate in either hand, trying to think of how to express her reservations without terrifying them all. How, after all her encouragement, she'll explain herself. But as soon as she looks at her husband, she realizes she has no right to stop him. The look on his face is one of wonder, and amazement, and she understands that he has found something that makes him come alive. No matter her imagination, she decides, and no matter her gut, she cannot, will not, take that from him.

She sets the plates on the table. "Breakfast," she says. "Fuel up for the dive."

···

Eve wakes to the sound of rain. She doesn't open her eyes at first; she only listens, and lets her senses gradually awaken to other things: the distant sound of a fog horn, the smells of must and rain, the sheets against her bare skin, the draft of air that passes over her with every revolution of the fan purring in the corner of the room. After a few minutes, she opens her eyes and looks out the window; it is raining steadily, as it was when she first awoke several hours ago, grateful for the weather, which meant she didn't have to water and could go back to sleep.

After several minutes, she untangles herself from the sheets and pulls on her clothes. She can smell bacon from downstairs, and her mouth waters. She pictures her parents and Eloise down in the kitchen, a big bowl of eggs, strips of crispy bacon, but when she gets down there, she finds the room empty, the dishes put away, the frying pan drying in the dish rack. Neither of the cars is parked in the driveway. She glances at the clock above the door, surprised to discover that it is nearly ten o'clock; she has not slept so late in she can't remember how long.

She eats a bowl of cereal standing at the kitchen counter, thinking about last night. It is like a strange movie in her memory, which she attributes to the pot; she remembers the night almost as if she'd witnessed it from above. She stayed until well after midnight, happily watching the bonfire smolder as people milled about and danced and drank around her, and afterward Saul had loaded her bike into the back of his car and driven her home. She glances guiltily at the diminished plate of brownies on the counter, both amused and somewhat horrified to consider the amount of brownies she must have consumed in total last night, between the pot brownies she had at the bonfire and the brownies she devoured when she got home later.

She finishes her cereal and brings her empty bowl over to the sink. Out the window, the rain is slantless and unrelenting. Steam rises from the quarry, which is nettled with endless rings, and the trees stand in solemn stillness at the quarry's edge. Without really thinking about what she feels compelled to do, she pulls off her shirt, steps out of her shorts, which she leaves pooled on the kitchen floor, and goes outside in her underwear.

The rain is warm against her bare skin, and in only seconds she is soaking wet, her hair flat against her head, raindrops dripping from her eyebrows. She hurries across the lawn to the water's edge, where without a moment's hesitation she plunges headlong in. Suddenly, the slapping sound of rain on water is a distant echo, and the day's gray light is replaced by a velvet darkness, and she keeps her eyes open to it, wondering what it might have been like for James Favazza as his car plunged down, down, down through the infinite darkness, and if he was conscious when he hit the quarry floor. She hopes not, she decides; she hopes the black tunnel of the quarry's water was seamlessly replaced by the fabled white tunnel of heaven. It's an interesting thought.

She swims forward, propelling herself as powerfully as she can through the black water toward the center of the quarry, where she comes to a breathless stop. There she lifts her head and looks around her. The rocks and trees along the quarry's edge are faint, colorless shapes through the hovering mist. Raindrops seem to bounce upon the water; silver drops of water leap up from the center of every ring, almost as if it were raining in reverse. She floats onto her back and lies completely still, stares up at the gray sky, dares raindrops with her eyes. She feels very much at a convergence point, where raindrops fall and rise, where air and water collide, and when she considers the depths below her, she is struck for once not by the possibilities of what might lie beneath, but by the idea that she is above it all, that though she is level with it, she is also one hundred feet above the surface of the hard earth, that the quarry is like gravity defied.

Joan goes to the florist after she has left Eloise off at camp; the flowers she bought and distributed around the house when they first arrived have passed their prime, the silky ruffle of the peonies collapsed, the manes of sunflowers drooping around each black face, all of them looking earthward like so many defeated lions.

She parks out front and darts to the door through the rain, not bothering with an umbrella for such a short distance, and soon she is enveloped in the shop's steamy, floral warmth. The store has been here for as long as Joan can remember; summers when she was a little girl, she would come here with her grandmother for the bouquets that they would set around the house each week, as Joan still does today. Cut flowers, her grandmother told her, were fundamental components of civilization, like manners; no matter what the circumstance or situation, one should always have them around. Though she is not quite as diligent as her grandmother was— her grandmother would never have allowed her flowers to get to the point of decay that Joan will tolerate—Joan did take this lesson to heart, and it is rare when there are not flowers of some kind spaced around the house, whether here or back in Maryland, just as there is always food in the fridge, or gas in the car.

She wanders around the shop, scoping the offerings to see what looks best—hydrangeas, iris, freesia, Asiatic lily—but any of them, in the end, would do. What most people do not know, which Joan also learned from her grandmother, is that there is a language of flowers, that the modern practice of sending flowers for birthdays, deaths, or weddings began in the Victorian era as an entirely different thing, as a method of communication in which different flowers were used to express those sentiments that could not be otherwise spoken. When a woman received a flower, she could either accept or reject the sentiment expressed by wearing the flower on her afternoon call, face up for acceptance, face-down for denial. Certain types of flowers had very specific meanings; Joan can't remember many of them now, but her grandmother had a list—ambrosia was love returned, she remembers this; the foxglove insincerity; the heliotrope devotion. Joan rarely bases her selection on a flower's supposed meaning; she remembers also that the peony is shame, and that is one of her favorite flowers.

Today, Joan chooses a bunch of cornflowers—she cannot resist the blue—and one of yellow iris, even as she also remembers that yellow represents jealousy. She looks around her for one more selection, and she is just about to reach for another bunch of sunflowers when the irresistible fragrance of a potted lily of the valley arrests her. She looks down at the unassuming thing, the fragile white bonnets of the tepals clinging to its slender stems, the broad green fan of its leaves, and she chooses this, which is so humble in appearance and yet powerful in scent; nor is it far from her mind that in the language of flowers the lily of the valley stands for the return of happiness.

Norman's Woe is located on the coast of the mainland just south of downtown Gloucester. Anders drives out over the drawbridge, where he picks up the twisting, tree-lined road that after several miles will lead to the designated parking area for the reef. The road generally follows the contours of the coast, though the ocean is not visible through the trees, and if Anders didn't know any better, he might think he was on some landlocked country road. He realizes, as he drives, that it is the first time he's taken the road this summer. Since last year, things have changed only incrementally; a Slow sign nailed years ago to the trunk of a tree has become slightly more engulfed in bark as the tree grows around it; more clutter has accumulated in the yard of a long-rooted mobile home; someone has painted the old boat that has sat for years on its trailer at the edge of a driveway. Everywhere else in the world, it seems to Anders, things change at such a rapid pace it's hard to keep track of anything; he takes great comfort in the sameness here from year to year.

He tries not to think about his impending dive,

because he knows from the last dive that the anticipation is by far the worst part; once he was actually in the water, he reminds himself, he didn't ever want to surface. He thought when he first woke up that the dive might be canceled due to the rain, but apparently they only cancel when there is lightning involved, and when Anders thinks about it, this makes sense; if you're underwater, what difference does it make if it is raining above?

By the time he reaches the parking area, the rain has begun to let up anyway. He pulls into the small lot along the side of the road, where he sees that he is last to arrive; Dave, Caroline, and Pete are all already there, Dave in foul-weather gear, Pete in a raincoat, and Caroline beneath an umbrella, looking less than thrilled. Anders climbs out of the car wearing a raincoat himself. "Sorry if I'm late," he says.

"No worries," Dave says. "You're right on time." He squints up into the rain. "We chose a nice one for it, huh?"

"It looks like it's letting up," Anders offers. "The sky is a little brighter over there."

"It's supposed to stop," Caroline says. "I hope it does."

"Well," Dave says. "We're all going to get wet anyway." He gestures over his shoulder toward a dirt path that leads off through the trees in the direction of the water. "The dive site is about a quarter mile down that path. It's an easy walk, but it feels farther than it is when you're carrying all your gear, so we'll take it slow. If you want, you can get into your wet suits here. Otherwise, you can change out on the rocks."

All opt to get into their wet suits later, and after each has gathered his gear, they follow Dave down the path through the trees. No one speaks, and it seems to Anders almost eerily still, silent but for the pattering of rain on the canopy and the rustle of shrubbery and undergrowth brushed by a leg. He listens for a white noise he may be missing—birdsong or the buzz of insects —but the birds and bugs are silent, too.

By the time they reach the shoreline, the rain has fully stopped, and Anders finds himself wishing that it had not; he is sweating under the weight of all his gear, and would welcome the cooling effect of rain against his skin. He sets his gear down on the rocks, which descend in sloping shelves toward the water. Here is a jagged union between land and sea, Anders thinks, when compared to their tidy meeting at the beach, or the symbiotic interweave of river and marsh. The last rocky ledge ends about three feet above the waves, which roil and froth beneath, menacing and gray, sending up great sprays of foam each time they crash against the shore.

"Are you kidding me?" Caroline says in disbelief.

"I told you guys," Dave says. "It's a toughie, but trust me, it's not as bad as it looks. I'm confident in you guys. You'll be fine."

"I get it that we have to giant-stride in," Pete says. "But how exactly do we get out?"

Dave points. "Over there," he says. "There's a rock with a good foothold just under the surface. You can't see it today—the tide's super high because of the moon."

Anders looks uncertainly in that direction, but all he can see are waves hurling themselves against the rocks. "Is it always this rough?" he asks.

"It's generally on the rougher side," Dave allows. "But it doesn't make any difference once you're submerged, right?"

Anders raises his eyebrows in response, the words of Longfellow's poem repeating in his head: *Like a sheeted ghost, the vessel swept tow'rds the reef of Norman's Woe . . .*

When the rain lets up, Eve decides to ride into town to pick up the film she and her father dropped off yesterday on the way home from Rowley—both the roll she took, and the rolls she found. She goes up to her mother's study for a pen and paper, scrawls a quick note explaining where she's gone. She is just putting the pen back into the mug on her mother's desk when the open spiral notebook beside the dismantled typewriter catches her eye. It is, of course, the word quarry that draws her attention. She glances over her shoulder toward the doorway, even though she knows she is alone in the house, and pulls the notebook toward her; she cannot help herself.

They stand at the quarry's edge: Catherine, Jake, and their youngest girls, Claire and Genevieve, who will not go to bed. The water below them is black and looks thick as tar; reflections of light from the house are wavering rectangles on its surface: window, window, door. Now and then, debris will bob through the light. An empty beer can. A flip-flop. A plastic bag.

Eve blinks, wide-eyed, and sits down to read further, though of course it is all familiar—it is almost exactly an account of the night they arrived. Of course, it is not exact—Claire does not, in her mother's account, hide from a car-load of teenagers in the shadow of a tree, nor does she find three cigarettes by the side of the road. But Eve can recognize in Claire much of herself—her desperation to know what happened, her outrage at the authorities' lack of concern. And the character that is her mother—Eve didn't realize how much her mother actually cared. She'd mistaken her mother's stoicism for indifference, and beyond the fact that this

Catherine character does seem to care, the very fact that her mother is writing this story at all belies any seeming lack of interest.

The writing stops after several pages, at the end of the night; on the opposite page, her mother has jotted down some notes under the heading Chapter 2. Eve reads these curiously, wondering how her mother intends to go on. *EF getting phone call that JF is dead. Or does someone have to tell her? Brother? Same house as on Magnolia, green, dark, etc., Hopper painting. How does she react?*

Eve turns the page, hoping that her mother has made more notes on the other side, but the rest of the pages in the notebook are blank. Eve slumps back in the chair, amazed. Obviously, JF is James Favazza, but EF—who would that be? His mother, she'd assume, though there were so many surviving family members listed in the obituary that she doesn't remember them all by name. She gets up and goes down the hallway to her bedroom, where she pulls James' obituary from her bedside drawer.

James Favazza, 27, of Gloucester, died unexpectedly on Friday evening. He was born in Gloucester on Feb. 3, 1983, son of Elizabeth Favazza of Gloucester and the late Gordon Favazza. He attended Gloucester High School. James was employed at

Gorton's Fish Company in Gloucester. James was a quiet, caring person and was very loyal and well liked by all of his friends and he also enjoyed bowling. He loved his family very much and will be missed by all who knew him. He is survived by his mother, Elizabeth Favazza; two older sisters, Benedetta "Bunny" Favazza of Quincy and Jocelyn Favazza Trupiano and her husband, George Trupiano, also of Quincy; and one younger brother, Billy Favazza, of Gloucester.

Arrangements: His funeral Mass will be held at St. Ann's Church on Wednesday, June 26, at 11 a.m. Relatives and friends are cordially invited to attend. Visiting hours will be held at the Greely Funeral Home, 212 Washington Street, Gloucester, on Tuesday from 5 to 7 p.m. In lieu of flowers, contributions can be made to the family, c/o Elizabeth Favazza, 932 Magnolia Street, Gloucester, MA 01930.

So EF *is* the mother, and the house on Magnolia Street hers. Eve suddenly recognizes how little thought or attention she's given to the family James left behind, as fixated as she's been on trying to understand how his death actually occurred, but her mother's musings have made her realize that there is also what happened to

Elizabeth, the mother, and to Bunny, and to Jocelyn, and to Billy, who all have stories of their own, too—and so, for that matter, do her mother, and her father, and even Eloise. These are utterly exhausting realizations, and larger than her mind right now has room for.

Eve folds the obituary, tucks it back into the drawer, and takes the note for her mother downstairs to the kitchen.

Joan returns to the house not long after Eve has left for town. She sets the flowers from the florist on the table beside Eve's note, and then she collects last week's bouquets, which she carries a few short steps into the woods to the old compost pile. Anders does not use this compost for his garden; the pile simply came with the house, one of those things like the bust and the crystal plates and the racy books upstairs that always make Joan feel vaguely as if they are renters, that the sculptor will resume residence as soon as they have gone away for the year.

In the kitchen, she washes out three vases and then trims the stems of the iris and cornflowers. As she's placing one of the bouquets on the dining table in the bay window of the main room, she pauses to look outside. It stopped raining while she was in the florist shop, and she wonders, as casually as she can, how the dive is going. The sky seems to be brightening, though the occasional drops of rain still strike the windowpanes like so many handfuls of pebbles, shaken by the breeze from the overhead leaves. A thinning layer of mist skims the quarry, which is swollen with rain, the rocky ledges suddenly much lower to the surface. At the water's edge, the wine bottle and glasses from last night are still out on the table between the lawn chairs, where she and Anders left them last night to lead each other through the dark indoors and up to bed, where they came together for the first time in a long time. Joan gazes out the window, remembering, though the memory has the distant quality of a dream, less a discrete series of actions than a broader experience, almost a notion.

She slips off her sandals and goes outside to retrieve the bottle and glasses. The wet grass is cool against her feet. The air feels cooler, too, now that the rain has ended, and she wonders if it will begin to rain again, if this is a lull between storms or if the system has passed; while the sky has indeed brightened considerably toward the west, the eastern sky looks ominous. She gathers up the glasses and the half-drunk bottle of wine, which she empties into the grass, vaguely aware of the growing sound of a car engine. The sound always fills her with a sense of expectation, even though more often than not the sound continues past their driveway down the road. This time, though, the sound gets louder, and she glances up at the eastern sky as she makes her way across the grass, wondering if its threat is indeed imminent, wondering if maybe Anders' dive is canceled after all and he is home. The notion fills her with relief.

In the kitchen, she sets the glasses in the sink and looks out through the window above, and she is more disappointed that it is not Anders than surprised when she sees pulling up the driveway the same maroon car that has appeared here twice before, as if she'd been actively anticipating its return. She feels her heart pick up speed, though she is not necessarily afraid; her instinct is to feel more curious than threatened. She cannot see the driver through the glare of the windshield, but she remembers his scrawny appearance, his deep-set eyes and narrow features, the shadows cast by his cheekbones. Just as it has before, when the car comes near to the house it comes to an idling halt. Joan debates going out to find out what the driver wants, and she wishes that the car were at such an angle that she could see him inside and so read his expression.

She wonders again if whoever the driver is might have something to do with James Favazza's death, even as she realizes that lately she has been seeing everything through that lens. Still. It occurs to her briefly that this young man could be a private investigator, hired by Elizabeth Favazza to inquire into all that the authorities are not, though she dismisses this possibility as unlikely, given the young man's appearance, and given the fact that he doesn't simply come and knock on the door. She thinks of Eve's theories, of the possibility of foul play. Perhaps there is some sort of evidence lying around that they have overlooked, that this young man has come back in order to retrieve. Or perhaps he, too, was here the day of the death, and left something of his own behind. Perhaps he has come up the driveway three times now in the hopes of sometime finding the driveway empty, so that he can get out and find whatever it is he might be looking for. In any case, Joan has concluded that he knows what happened here, and how, whatever role he may have played.

All of these thoughts flash through Joan's mind in only a few seconds, during which time the car begins to back down the driveway. Joan hurries out the door, remembering her regret for not confronting the same young man the other day. "Hello!" she calls, waving. "Can I help you?" The young man gives a quick glance in Joan's direction before returning his eyes to the driveway behind him, picking up speed instead of stopping. "Wait!" she calls. "Stop!" But he does not, and soon the car has disappeared from sight, and Joan is alone in the driveway. But this time, she does not simply stand and stare and wonder; without bothering to return to the house for her flip-flops or her purse, she gets into the car, takes the keys from the floor, and follows him, her curiosity unwilling to let him get away.

The waves may be irrelevant once submerged, but it is not without trepidation that Anders plunges the three feet from the rocks at Norman's Woe into the seething waters below. Immediately, he swims away from the shore to wait for the others a few yards out, so that the waves will not toss him against the rocks, though with every large swell he finds he is swept shoreward and must swim out again. The smaller chop within the swell surprises him again and again with facefuls of water, which blur the window of his mask, adding to the general sense of dizziness he feels in the waves. Pete, Caroline, and Dave appear to be in conversation at the water's edge; Anders wishes, as he struggles to maintain a safe distance from the shoreline, that they would hurry up and get in.

He tries to picture what this place must look like in winter, when the *Rebecca Ann* and the *Favorite* went down, the rocks white with ice, the tide pools frozen over, the sea and sky both dark and bitter cold, as if the contrast might provide some comfort, but the accompanying images of bloated rag-doll bodies tossing in the surf has the opposite effect. Instead, he tries to forget about these things, though the more he tries to banish them from his mind, the more insistent they become. Finally, he sees Pete enter the water with a splash. He swims competently in Anders' direction and removes his mouthpiece. "Caroline's a little freaked out," he explains. "But she's coming. She's fine."

And in a moment, Caroline does indeed leap into the water, followed shortly by Dave, and the two swim toward where Pete and Anders are waiting. Dave removes his mouthpiece. "All right," he says. "We're going to swim out a little bit farther, right around where that lobster pot is out there, and then we'll descend. Everyone good?" The three nod, and then they all swim in the indicated direction, where Dave gives the signal to deflate their BCDs.

In the time since she first noticed the bar from the window table at George's, it has not ceased to amaze Eve that Vic's is so central in town, that she has been oblivious to it for the years and years she's gone to the car wash, the grocery store, Salah's, George's, the CVS. And yet, there it is. After she has picked up her film, she pauses on her way out of the pharmacy and looks over at the bar, which sits squat and solid and nearly facelike, its windows like glassy eyes on either side of the nose of a door. She'd eyed it yesterday when she and her father dropped the film off on the way home from the junkyard, though she hadn't dared suggest that they go check it out, and it had been crowded besides, a group of smokers banished to the curb, music emanating from within. But now, still late morning, Vic's appears to be closed; the two opposing doors in the entryway are shut, and the beer signs in the windows are colorless shadows of their glowing, neon selves. The sidewalk is empty but for a red paper Coke cup with a plastic lid and straw, which rolls gently across the concrete in the breeze.

But what really stops Eve cold now, and makes leaving without investigation absolutely impossible, is the sight of Larry Stephens' blue Camaro parked on the street a few doors down from the bar.

Eve stares, dumbfounded; she is right, then, and has been all along. The cooler bag, Larry, James Favazza, Vic's—all of it is related, just as she's thought; it has to be. What could the car's presence there mean otherwise? Even if Larry Stephens isn't the murderer she's quite certain he is, there is no doubt in her mind, given the evidence she's amassed—the cooler bag, the Vic's T-shirt, the cigarettes and the cigarette butt, the beer bottles from New Hampshire, like Larry Stephens' car—that he was there at the time James died and that he knows what happened. And she'll be damned if she's not going to confront him and find out what it was. People don't just *die*.

Eve hangs the bag with the photographs over the handles of her bike, which is propped against the side of the CVS, and hurries across the street, where she pauses in the shelter of an empty bay of the car wash near the bar. Eve glances around her; everyone around seems to be occupied with their own tasks; the man in the next bay over is busy with a vacuum deep inside his car, and the people in the parking lot of the grocery store behind her are loading groceries. No one is paying her any attention, though really, she asks herself, why would they?

She crosses the street that separates the car wash and the bar; as she steps onto the sidewalk, she feels as if she is stepping into a photograph, or out of one reality and into another, which, flat from a distance, suddenly comes alive. She is acutely aware of the sounds of the Coke cup scuttling on the concrete and the humming of the power line overhead, the rank scent of vomit mingling with beer. Cigarette butts litter the sidewalk, even though there is a standing ashtray by the doors. Eve wrinkles her nose, silently agreeing with Saul that Vic's is a dump. She stands for a moment on the concrete, suddenly realizing the implications of the fact that the bar is closed. If the bar is closed, then Larry Stephens cannot be inside. Perhaps, she thinks, he left his car here overnight and took a cab home instead, too drunk to drive. Or he arrived here early, parked outside, and went off to George's or somewhere else nearby for a bite to eat, to kill time until the bar opens in an hour. She takes a few steps in the direction of the Camaro—close enough that she can see inside it, yet not so close as to seem suspicious.

From where she pauses several feet away from the car, there does not appear to be much to see inside anyway; it is surprisingly clean, the backseat and floors devoid of any interesting items or telltale bits of junk. There is a single CD case on the passenger seat: Paul Simon, she can tell by the familiar cover; she's got the same CD at home. Eve frowns. She's not sure what sort of music she'd expect Larry Stephens to listen to, but it wouldn't be Paul Simon.

But aside from the CD, there's nothing of note. Just one of those Christmas tree air fresheners hanging from the rearview mirror. Eve looks up and down the street. Wherever he is, and for whatever reason he's left his car here, Larry Stephens has to come back at some point, she knows that, and in the meantime—she turns around—Vic's is here before her, begging to be explored. It occurs to her that it's possible that even though the bar is closed he's in there anyway, talking to the bartender, who could well know something himself about what happened to James, judging from their brief conversation on the phone the other night. It's also possible, she thinks suddenly, that Larry *is* the bartender. Why not?

She scans the bar again slowly, taking it all in. Two posters hang in the left-hand window. The larger poster is the nightly schedule of bands that will play at Vic's this week—Shang-reg-gae-la, the Jax Scags Band, and the Obtuse Angles, among others. The smaller poster advertises a bluefish tournament sponsored by the bar, which is set to take place in August. Eve studies these posters carefully, and then she steps right up to the rain-streaked windows, and with a mild feeling of recklessness she cups her eyes against the glass.

To her combined relief and disappointment, the bar appears empty. It is dim, but Eve is able to get the general sense of the place. Lamps with darkly colored shades hang from the ceiling, where pipes run between exposed beams. A row of small booths recedes into the shadows at the back, installed against the wall opposite the bar. The bar itself seems to horseshoe around into another room that Eve supposes must be accessed by the door in the right side of the entryway, whereas she can see from here that the room she is looking into now is accessed by the door in the left side. She takes in the space greedily. Seeing Vic's for real feels as unbelievable as actually finding James Favazza's truck, even if there are tantalizing details that she can't make out from here: the figures in the photographs on the Peg-Board on the wall, the names in the boxes on a betting pool chart behind the bar.

She goes to look through the window on the other side of the entryway, which she finds has no posters hanging in it for her to read, and again cups her face against the glass. This room, she sees, would be a mirror of the room on the left-hand side of the bar except that a pool table stands in the middle, to accommodate which there are two fewer booths against the wall. A large, triangular Budweiser lampshade hangs above it, and pool balls are scattered on the felt. The other main difference between the rooms is the hallway at the back of this one, which Eve guesses is where the rest rooms are located, and at the end of which is a door that appears to lead outside.

Eve steps back from the glass, noting with satisfaction the alleyway separating the thrift store from the bar. She walks over to investigate; a ladder lays propped against the bar on its side, and an AC window unit hums in a window above the thrift store, dripping into the alley's overgrown grass. There is no gate or fence, no sign that warns to keep out, and so after a moment of hesitation, Eve ventures down the alley and around to the back of Vic's to see where the back door leads.

Behind the bar, she discovers that whatever

outdoor seating area is accessed by that rear door is walled in by a fence of wooden two-by-fours about eight feet in height, with lanterns mounted to the top of each main post. Between this fenced-in area and the more residential street beyond is a dusty lot, where a single car is parked right now, but which Eve imagines is jammed with cars on a busy night; probably, she thinks, James Favazza's truck was parked right here many times before. She tries to picture it here, but the images that keep coming to mind are of the pickup front end down and dangling, water streaming through the cracks around the doors and windows, and of the same truck where it is now, pillaged in a crowded lot. She turns back to the fenced-in area, where a door on hinges leads out into the parking area; Eve can't resist giving it little push to see whether it will open, and to her surprise, it does. Having come this far, she knows she can't stop. She pushes it open the rest of the way, and steps through.

Inside, she discovers green plastic chairs and tables scattered across a concrete patio; it is somewhat uneven at the edges, as if whoever owns the bar had simply dumped a pile of concrete and spread it out to harden into solid ground. She wonders how often James Favazza sat out on this very patio, if he might have even been here the day of his death, and she is contemplating the industrial-size cooler along the wall and wondering if inside it there might be Smuttynose Old Brown Dog Ale or Tucker-man's Headwall Ale, the New Hampshire brews that Larry favored, when she hears the bar's back door being unlocked from the inside.

For the first time Eve truly understands what it means for your heart to skip a beat. She takes a step back, her mind racing, but before she can decide on the best course of action—run away? Smile and say hello?—or come up with any good excuse for being here, a man is standing in the entryway. He is stocky and balding, with a soul patch beneath his lower lip that looks to Eve more like a chocolate stain. His build is like that of someone who spends a lot of time in the gym, not in the sculpted sense, but in the sense that he looks like he could pick up a car. Eve imagines a heavily tattooed torso beneath his T-shirt, even if his skin presently exposed appears to be ink-free.

"Can I help you with something?" he asks, without a hint of friendliness.

Eve gives him a nervous smile, wondering if he was the one she spoke to when she called up here the other night. "I . . . I didn't think anyone was inside. Sorry."

The man stares at her. "Can I help you with something?" he repeats.

Eve shakes her head. "No, sorry," she says, taking another step back toward the door. "I was just looking."

"I know you were looking. I saw you looking through the windows up front, too. But I don't know if you were *just* looking."

"I was," Eve says. "Honest. I really was."

"Seems to me you're trespassing."

"No!" Eve insists, though she hesitates just a fraction of a second, since she supposes technically she might be.

"No? Bar's clearly closed, and not only are you on the premises anyway, you're also under age."

Eve blinks at him. A raindrop lands on her cheek, but she does not wipe it away.

"It's against the law for a minor to enter a bar, or be on the premises of one. It's against the law for a minor to drink, and it's against the law for anyone to steal alcohol at all."

"I wasn't!" Eve cries. "I don't even drink!"

"Yeah, then what exactly *were* you doing?"

Eve swallows, racking her brains for a legitimate excuse aside from curiosity. "I—"

"Huh?"

"I—"

"Hm?"

"I—"

"Yeah?"

Eve looks at him bewilderedly, beginning to feel mildly indignant. She narrows her eyes. "You shouldn't ask a question if you don't really want an answer," she says, her face hot. "I was just *looking*. I was curious, I'm sorry, and I'm leaving."

"No, you're not," the man says, coming down the steps to the concrete. "You're not going anywhere till your ma comes to get you. Either your ma, or the police."

Eve swallows. A raindrop lands on her head, and another on her shoulder.

"You got a phone on you?" the man demands.

Eve shakes her head.

The man gestures over his shoulder toward the door. "Get inside," he says. "Use the phone in there."

Eve realizes that she has no choice but to comply, and she picks a path through the plastic chairs toward the bar. The man opens the door; she glances at him nervously, and again he gestures inside with his chin.

Though it isn't particularly bright outside today, it still takes a moment for Eve's eyes to adjust to the darkness of the bar, especially in the windowless back hallway. She waits for the man to come inside, and follows him down the corridor, briefly through the room with the pool table and into the first room she looked into. In the backmost booth, there are papers, pen, and calculator out on the table, and she realizes that the man must have been sitting there earlier doing paperwork as she pressed her face against the glass. It gives her an uncomfortable feeling to consider being watched without her knowledge. Otherwise, the only real difference between looking inside and being inside is the smell; she had imagined the mingling smells of beer and stale smoke, but it smells oddly more as if something had recently been fried. The man lifts a folding segment of wood and steps behind the bar; Eve begins to follow, but the man shakes his head.

"Uh-uh," he says. "You stay on the other side."

Eve stays where she is, watching as the man walks up to the front of the bar, where there is a phone mounted against the wall perpendicular to the mirror, above three rising rows of liquor.

"Here," the man says, handing her the receiver.

She takes it from him, looks down at it skeptically. While she doubts that either parent would believe that she had been there intending to steal beer, she's not sure how much more tolerance either one has left at this point with her fixation, and she feels a sudden sense of injustice at her current situation; it's not as if she came to town specifically in order to search out the bar, it just happened that she'd ended up here. Reluctantly, she turns the phone on and dials the number to the house, figuring her mother must have returned from leaving Eloise at camp. It rings once, twice, three and then four times before the machine picks up, and her father's voice tells her that no one is home. "Mom?" she says into the machine, picturing her mother writing up in her study, ignoring the phone, as she sometimes does. "Mom?" she says, louder, realizing that the machine is downstairs and her mother might not be able to hear her. "Mom!" she half yells, one last time. She waits several seconds. "Never mind," she says, "I'll try your cell."

She looks up at the man behind the bar uncomfortably. He regards her with a look of disdain, his burly arms folded across his large chest. "Sorry," she says. "I'm trying her cell." The man's eyebrows flicker a response, up then down.

Eve anxiously dials her mother's number, sure she will pick up. If she is not yet back at the house, it's likely that she is doing errands around town, which gives Eve some measure of comfort; it's possible that at this very moment her mother is just minutes away, and can get her out from under this man's withering gaze that much faster. And it's possible, given the pages of writing Eve read in her mother's study, that her mother just might understand. But in the end Eve gets her mother's voicemail on the cell, too. She hangs up without leaving a message, and gives the man behind the bar a sheepish look. "She didn't answer," she explains, "but I'll try my dad."

She dials her father's number, hoping against hope that maybe his dive was canceled; it is raining again outside, she can see through the window, and hard. Despondently, she listens to it ring, picturing the phone ringing away in the side well of the Buick, the car parked on the edge of some road in the rain, and she is not surprised when she gets his voicemail.

She hangs up without leaving a message. "I can't reach either of my parents," she reports. "I promise I was just looking. I was curious." She glances out the window, where she sees the blue Camaro still sitting along the curb. But now she doesn't dare ask about Larry Stephens, or James Favazza. "I'm really sorry I trespassed, and it will never happen again. Can I just go?"

"No," the man says. "Your parents can't come get you, the cops will." He holds his hand out to take back the phone.

"Wait a second!" Eve says, pleadingly, desperate. "Just wait a second. My dad didn't pick up his cell because he probably left it at home. But I know where he is. All I need is a phone book."

To Anders' relief, descending does indeed provide immediate reprieve from the lurching swell, and he feels his nerves begin to calm as the weights in his belt pull him slowly toward the bottom. The water is a deep and somewhat murky blue; he can make out little around him beyond the other divers. When he looks up, the surface above looks like a ridged glass ceiling, the light of the upper world filtering through in weak rays. The lobster pot near which they descended is a small, black, silhouetted oval overhead; that the scum-fuzzed rope attached descends beside them provides Anders with an odd sense of comfort, as a tangible connection to the world above.

Partway down, they pause to check each other's equipment for leaks, as diving protocol demands, and to clear their ears, and then they continue down; only after they have reached a depth of maybe forty or fifty feet do the boulders at the bottom gradually start to come into view, and then quite suddenly the four find themselves in a labyrinth of large granite shapes. The boulders of the not-so-distant shore evidently drop off quickly to this depth, the tumbled rocks creating crevasses and crannies interspersed with a few spots of sandy bottom. All in all, it seems to Anders, the underwater terrain isn't much different from what lies above, except that it is full of life. All manner of kelp grows from the rocks: clusters of long yellow strands that vaguely resemble linguine, climbing vines with green transparent leaves, beds of purple moss. One rock is covered with patches of what look like furry pink balls wavering at the end of slender yellow strings. These put Anders in mind of the speaking flowers in *Alice in Wonderland*, and it occurs to him briefly—and not entirely seriously—to pick one of them for Eloise, though he knows it would only languish if taken out of its element.

They swim as a group slowly among the rocks, where creatures go about their business with seeming indifference to the divers' presence. An eel-like fish with remarkable teeth hides in the shadows of a nearby boulder, where a colony of frilled anemone glows like a field of yellow flowers. Bait fish flit like fireflies, and larger fish—a red one like a giant football, several bluefish, and others that Anders can't readily identify—swim more slowly through the rocky avenues; jellyfish hover like neon ghosts. Below him, a giant crab scuttles sideways over a stretch of sandy bottom, which Anders searches unsuccessfully for chameleon flounders, willing his eye to find that vague, round figure against the sand. The sand itself is striated with the familiar lines of glass and shells and pebbles along which he's often walked with the girls at their local beach at low tide, searching for blue or red sea glass, or for small clamshells with holes to be worn on necklaces. Anders finds himself briefly scanning now for the same, out of habit, when Dave touches him on the shoulder and points overhead, where a swirling school of silver pollack is shimmering quickly by. They seem to Anders to move in a single mass, much in the manner of flocking sparrows, which somehow all can turn at once on a dime, and he watches them dart this way and that until they are out of sight.

Suddenly he is overcome by a curious feeling, as if he were telescoping deep into himself. He becomes acutely aware of the sounds of his inner workings: the dutiful plodding of his heart, the tireless rivers of blood coursing through his veins, each breath rushing like a great wind into his lungs, all of these functions calling attention to the machine that is his body, which soldiers on without his will or effort. He finds himself as amazed by that as he is by the life around him, and bound to that life by a common energy that animates them all, that gives these rocks their kelpy covering, the creatures their ability to be, the machine of his body its power. He looks with wonder at all of these creatures coexisting in their rocky city, more than he'd ever have imagined, even after the dive at Plum Cove, and he allows himself to arrive at an enchanted explanation for all this life. This place is no graveyard, he thinks; it is a place where the energy of those who died here has infused what lives here now, it is *because* so many have died here that so much else now lives.

In all the thinking he's done about death over the past year, he's been able to find no solace in any concept he has considered; the scientific reality depresses him, and the notion of heaven is impossible to believe. But down here, he comes to his own understanding of a single energy that inhabits all living things, an energy that is both fleeting and eternal; we each are given it only for a time before it passes on to give life to something else. What is comforting, at last, is the idea that while the energy might indeed pass on, it still exists somewhere, and it cannot be destroyed. The notion is a simple one, but it fills him with a sense of euphoria that makes him wonder if he might be suffering from nitrogen narcosis, because what this feels like to him is truly rapture of the deep.

Joan follows two cars behind the maroon car, not as much for the sake of stealth as because she had to wait for a car to pass before she could turn onto the main road at the bottom of their hill. It has begun to rain again; despite the wipers' manic dance across the windshield, sheets of water blur Joan's view, and in spots the road is narrowed to a single middle lane by the growing puddles collected in the curb. One part of her finds this pursuit verging on absurd, akin to one of Eve's recent missions; another part of her thinks it not unreasonable at all to demand an explanation for the young man's repeated appearances at the quarry, particularly given that he ignored her earlier attempt to do so at the scene. To reconcile her two conflicting views, she tells herself that she will continue to follow him only if he takes the exit off the rotary that leads into town, and will confront him at his destina-tion there; if he takes the exit that leads out over the river on the highway, she will complete the rotary's circle and return home. Even if she is acting somewhat crazy, she's not so crazy that she's going to follow him into Boston, for instance, or even as far as Rowley or Georgetown; there are limits.

The rotary is flooded, and the cars circling drive slowly, sending up winging panes of water in their wake; Joan drives cautiously, hating those moments when her tires lose traction with the road, and she is both gratified and anxious when the maroon car takes the exit that leads into town. The car that had been between them took a different exit off the rotary, and though she thinks he must know her car from having seen it in the driveway, she is unconcerned and follows directly behind him, picturing in her mind how this confrontation might play out, imagining the backdrop of a parking lot, or Main Street, realizing with dismay that she doesn't have her shoes. But instead of heading into the commercial part of town, he turns off Washington onto Commonwealth, and it is with the same dawning sense of unsurprise that she felt when he first appeared in the driveway twenty minutes ago that she follows him on a now familiar route from Commonwealth to Maple, from Maple to School, and ultimately to Magnolia Street, where he parks in front of Elizabeth Favazza's house.

As she'd gradually come to understand where he was going, even as, once realized, it felt as if the knowledge had been there all along, Joan had increased the distance between the two cars; she didn't want to call attention to herself, and she knew the way. Now she pulls over several yards down the street before Elizabeth Favazza's house, turns the engine off. Water slides in sheets down the windshield; as she looks out through the glass, the young man is a mere shape in the rain, climbing the stairs to his mother's house, and disappearing inside.

Of course, Joan thinks, of course. She remembers all the photographs of two boys together on Elizabeth Favazza's side table, all the photographs of those same two boys grown into young men, and she wonders at herself that it had not occurred to her before that this young man might be James Favazza's brother. She thinks of the days and weeks following Sophie's death, when Eve would venture off on foot for hours at a time; once, Joan followed her. Her daughter meandered through the gray streets without a coat, oblivious to the crisp autumn chill, and ultimately she came to the railroad tracks where they passed through town near the park, where she simply stood for some minutes, unmoving. Joan watched from a distance, unwilling to intrude on her daughter's private grief until she heard the distant whistle of a train, at which she ran to Eve in panic, and pulled her close, and held her hard against her body until the train had roared by with a power that Joan hated to consider. When she let Eve go, her daughter looked at her with a peculiar expression on her face. "I was just looking," she said. "That's all."

Joan looks toward Elizabeth Favazza's house, imagining Elizabeth Favazza and her surviving son sitting together in the room where Joan herself sat the other day. She could go to them, she thinks. She could knock on the door and demand of the young man what he was doing at the quarry, but she knows, and she knows that he likely has no more idea what happened to his brother than anyone else. Perhaps in her book things will turn out differently. The man in the maroon car will lead her somewhere else and she'll learn from him what happened, or the character of Joan will knock on the door and go inside and tell them her own family's story, and they will become friends; this is what she has wanted to do all along. But in real life she understands that what has happened, happened, and it wouldn't make a difference. And after all, she reasons, she *doesn't* have her shoes.

Eve waits by the window of the bar, anxiously peering up and down the street, while in the back booth behind her, Guy—she learned his name when minutes ago he'd talked with someone about a missing Heineken order on the phone—continues to do his paperwork, or pretends to; she is sure that she can feel his eyes upon her back, though she does not dare turn around to find out. Raindrops run in crooked paths down the window's glass, and when she presses her palm to the window, it fogs around the shape of her hand. Across the street, she can see her bike still propped against the side of the CVS, and she worries for her photographs in the rain, hoping that between the plastic of the sleeve of each set and the plastic of the bag that they will be protected.

In front of the bar, a few cars down, Larry Stephens' blue Camaro also sits in the rain. Eve can tell by the way the raindrops seem to shrink into themselves and roll in discrete balls down the windshield that Larry Stephens has treated the glass with Rain-X. She knows this because Sophie tried the stuff out on her VW Fox last summer, and the source of this information, plus the uselessness of it, plus the overall injustice of her predicament all combined make Eve's eyes suddenly well with tears. She quickly wipes them away. She'll be damned if anyone, but especially this man, this Guy behind her, should see her cry.

She blinks hard, stares out through the glass, the skin of her cheeks firmly gripped between her teeth. She watches a man guide his child down the street out front, the two of them sheltered beneath a huge golf umbrella, the little girl pausing to stand in a shallow puddle, evidently pleased to be putting her rain boots to work. Next she watches another man as he passes down the street, his T-shirt wet against his shoulders and his shorts stuck to his thighs, though he seems oblivious to what Eve always finds the itchy discomfort of wet cloth against skin, the squelch of wet sneakers. This man nods as he passes a youngish woman in flip-flops and a waterproof windbreaker, the hood cinched up around her face, her exposed tendrils dripping. Eve shifts her focus from man to woman as they pass by each other, follows the woman with her eyes in the other direction. The woman carries a pie from Jim's Bake Shop in one platformed hand, key lime, it appears through the domed plastic of its lid, on which the raindrops bead in much the same way they do against the windshield of Larry Stephens' car. Three or four shopping bags dangle from the woman's other hand, which is hidden in the sleeve of her windbreaker.

To Eve's surprise, the woman slows, and then comes to a stop by Larry Stephens' blue Camaro, hooks the grocery bags over a finger of the pie hand. She reaches into her pocket for a set of keys, which she uses to open the Camaro door. Eve stares as the woman opens the back door and sets her things onto the seat inside, her mind racing. Wife? she wonders. Girlfriend? Who might this woman be, and why is she getting into Larry Stephens' car? The woman pulls off her raincoat and tosses it through the open driver's door onto the floor, gets into the driver's seat, and shuts herself inside. Exhaust curls from the pipe as the woman turns the engine on; inside the car, she reaches over, and Eve imagines her taking Paul Simon out of its case, the first notes of "Graceland" starting to play from the stereo.

Eve glances over her shoulder in Guy's direction, wanting to ask the man if she can just run outside, just quickly, just for a minute, so that she can find out . . . what? She's not even sure what she would ask at all, and the look Guy shoots her from his corner—withering and disgusted—causes any such request to catch in her throat, and by the time she has turned around again, the blue Camaro has pulled away from the curb. She watches it pass by the bar and drive down the street, the Massachusetts license plate staring back at her through the rain like a cruel joke—one that causes the weakened scaffolding of her suspicions to fall further away. Defeated, she lowers herself onto a plastic chair against the window, tucks her leg beneath her, and settles in to wait.

After another fifteen or twenty minutes, during which time Eve stares with exhaustion at nothing at all, an old blue pickup pulls up outside the bar, and Nestor climbs out. Eve isn't sure she's ever been so grateful to see someone in her life. She lifts herself from her plastic chair, not caring that her leg is asleep. "He's here," she announces, as outside Nestor walks stiffly toward the bar, not bothering to alter his gait in the rain. Guy gets up from the booth and goes to unlock the door just as Nestor has reached its other side. Eve swallows anxiously, unsure of exactly how this will play out; she'd been vague on the phone, but urgent enough, she hopes, that Nestor will have the sense to play along. Luckily enough, when she dialed the nursery's number, Nestor had been the one to answer; she hadn't had to go through Josie, which only would have complicated things. "It's Eve," she'd said. "I'm in a bit of trouble, and right now you're the only one who can help."

There had been a pause on the other end of the line. "Go on," Nestor had said.

"I'm at a bar called Vic's in Gloucester, and I need you to come get me."

"Seems to me something your parents might be the appropriate ones to deal with."

Eve swallowed. "I know. That's the thing. I tried. No answer."

"It's not my place, Eve."

"Please."

"What if I say no? I've got a business to run here."

"Then I'm *stuck*," she whispered frantically. "I'm going to get *arrested*. It's bad."

She could hear Nestor sigh heavily. "You say you're at Vic's?"

"Yeah. It's—"

"I know where it is." And he hung up the phone.

"Okay, Dad," Eve had said into the emptiness.

Now Guy opens the door, but Nestor does not come inside, choosing instead to remain on the doorstep.

"You the father?" Guy demands.

Nestor's eyes flicker; behind Guy, Eve gives him a beseeching look. "Yuh," he says.

"Your kid was on the premises, looking to take some liquor."

"I was—" Eve begins.

"You keep quiet!" Guy interrupts her, whirling around. He turns back to Nestor. "She was trespassing out back."

"That so," Nestor says.

"Yeah," Guy says. "That's so. Thought you oughta know that."

Nestor nods. "I see."

"That's it? You see?"

"I see," Nestor says. "And we'll discuss it at home. Thank you for your concern." He looks over Guy's shoulder toward Eve, nods once. "Let's go," he says.

Eve looks at Guy uncertainly; Guy steps away from the door so Eve can pass through. "I don't ever want to see you around here again," he says.

Eve stalks by him, and the feeling of freedom she has as she steps out into the rain is exhilarating. She turns around and glares at the man. "I wouldn't set foot anywhere near your dirty hellhole again if you paid me," she says defiantly, and she marches to Nestor's truck and clambers in, her blood coursing hotly through her veins.

In a moment, Nestor climbs in the other side, and wordlessly he drives away. Despite the fact that her bike and photographs are still sitting in the rain, Eve does not ask where he is going, and he does not go far; he turns right onto the next possible street, drives a hundred yards down, and pulls over. Eve waits for him to talk, but he says nothing; the only sounds are raindrops clattering against the roof of the cab and the splashing sounds made by each infrequent passing car. They are on a residential street; small houses sit quietly in the rain, their small yards empty. Everything seems to Eve to be in shades of gray.

"Thank you," she says. "I would never have bothered you, but he wasn't going to let me leave and I couldn't get either of my parents and I couldn't stand to be stuck there with that guy and—thank you. And I'm sorry."

Nestor looks at her expectantly.

"I wasn't trying to steal liquor or anything else," Eve goes on.

Nestor waits.

"I was just . . . looking. I'm an idiot." She shakes her head. "It's a long story."

Finally Nestor speaks. "I'm in no rush," he

says. "Rainy days are always quiet at the nursery. Josie can manage."

Eve shakes her head again. "You don't want to hear it."

"I'd say I'm a better judge of that."

"You really don't."

Nestor looks at her. "I believe I'm *owed* an explanation, actually," he says.

Eve looks him in the eye, noticing how blue the irises are against the stark white, like endlessly deep pools. She takes a breath. "The night we got here, I noticed that there were tire tracks leading into the quarry in our yard. No one believed me at first, but then my parents called the police, and divers came, and just like I thought, there was a truck at the bottom of the quarry, and there was a guy inside. He was dead. James Favazza. He was only twenty-seven." Eve pauses, exhausted by all there is to tell.

"Go on," Nestor urges.

And Eve does. She tells Nestor about all the items she collected from the quarry, about the cooler bag and L. Stephens and his Camaro, about the three Marlboros on the rock and the butt in the water, about the boom and the skimmer and the recycled oil, about her trip to the junkyard across the lot from the nursery, about finding the truck in Rowley. All the details together, the way she hasn't even told her parents, or Saul. She tells him about the preliminary findings, and the failure of the authorities to investigate, and how no one really seems to care. "They just shrug it off as either accident or suicide and don't even bother to look into anything. But if you're as drunk as he was, how do you manage to drive all the way to the quarry and then accidentally drive in? And suicide—well, the windows of his truck were rolled up, which doesn't make any sense, 'cause you'd want the water to get in faster, and . . . well, I mean, I just don't think you can *assume* it was suicide. But *no one* has looked into any foul play at all."

"What sort of foul play are you envisioning?"

Eve sighs. "I don't know, exactly," she says. "I mean, I *do,* or I thought I did, but—it just drives me crazy that no one wants to know what really happened, whatever it was."

Nestor is quiet for a moment. "I don't see how Vic's factors into all of this."

"The T-shirt! I told you. There was that Vic's T-shirt in the quarry, which means he hung out there a lot, maybe even the day he died!"

"Possibly. But are you sure it was even his?"

Eve can't allow herself to consider this. "Well, anyway, today I didn't even mean to go find the bar at all, I was just picking up some photographs from CVS and I saw the Camaro—except that it wasn't the right one—so I went over, now here we are. But I was *not* after any booze."

"What *were* you after, really?"

Eve is quiet for a moment. She sighs. "I was curious," she says. "I mean, I was after Larry at first, but then I wasn't really after anything. I was just *curious*." She looks over at Nestor. "Do you believe me?"

He nods. "I do."

A car drives slowly by, the bass on the radio thudding. It comes to a stop in front of one of the houses across the street, the door of which immediately opens, and a kid in an oversized mesh basketball tank comes out. He leaps the stoop in a single bound and slides into the car, which continues on and away, leaving a vague thudding echo in Eve's ears even after it has vanished around the corner, like the glowing imprint of the sun in your eyes even after you have looked away.

"It must have been a particularly difficult thing to arrive to, after what happened to your sister."

The statement knocks the wind out of Eve; she finds she cannot respond.

"The whole situation is possessed of a rather cruel irony. I can understand why it would hold such interest for you."

Eve's breath trembles, and she grits her teeth to contain herself. "How do you know what happened to my sister?" she asks.

"Josie told me," Nestor says. "It must be hard to live with."

"Why didn't you say anything before?"

"What is there to say aside from sorry, which you must have heard now countless times?"

Eve is quiet. She knows Nestor is right.

"I figured if you wanted to talk about it, you would."

"Then why did you just bring it up now?"

Nestor looks at her. "Think about all you just told me."

Eve remains quiet.

"My wife killed herself," Nestor continues.

Eve looks at him with surprise; he gazes distantly through the windshield.

"It was many years ago, but the question I still struggle with is *why*. For the living, for those left behind, there is no answer that is good enough." Nestor looks at Eve. "I imagine you feel the same way."

Eve blinks rapidly, trying not to cry.

"And I understand that. But sometimes, there simply are no answers. And when there aren't, you have to give up the search and live with the mystery. It's hard, I know it well."

"Sometimes I think that nothing will ever be the same again," Eve says, crying openly now.

"It won't," Nestor says, and he takes her firmly by the hand. "But you, Eve, will be okay."

Epilogue

SIX WEEKS LATER

They stand at the quarry's edge, Joan, Anders, Eve, and Dave. Eloise floats in an inner tube nearby. Anders and Dave are wearing wet suits, BCDs, and headlamps, and each has a cylinder strapped to his back. It is morning, and a cool breeze ripples the surface of the quarry, which is still warm from long summer days in the sun; Eloise has reported from the water that it is warmer than the air. Now late August, the season has started to change; the nights are chillier, the air more clear, and though not quite orange yet, the leaves of the trees around them have lost their summer green. The lilies along the quarry's far edge have blossomed and languished, though Anders' garden is still aglow with clusters of tiny flowers: the purple of the first butterfly bush, the yellow of the next, and the orange and pink and white of the rest that Eve has brought home from the nursery one by one as Anders' rose bushes died.

Unlike the night they arrived here, they are not gathered by the high ledge of the quarry, where James Favazza's truck went in; they are instead almost directly across from that spot. Joan has directed them here; it is here where the people in the photographs from the old film Eve found were mostly gathered. She holds the photos in her hand now; they are rippled and waterstained, but in several you can make out a small barge in the middle of the quarry, which is anchored to the shore with a line attached near to where earlier in the summer the skimmer stood. Though they are not the grand band Joan had always imagined when she considered the sculptor's fabled parties, there is on board the barge a man with a guitar, a man with drums, and a woman without an instrument who Joan assumes must be a singer. Other photographs are of clusters of people gathered where Joan and her family are gathered now, many with wineglasses and cocktails and cigarettes, some in laughing conversation, some dangling bare legs into the water. Interspersed among them, as if guests of the party themselves, are dozens of varied sculptures: busts like the one in her study, body parts, and abstract sculptures of all kinds.

Joan had always incorrectly imagined these parties as taking place in the thirties or forties, though in reality they appear to have occurred sometime in the seventies; most of the crowd appears to be in bohemian garb—long dresses, flared pants, large round sunglasses—as one might expect from the type to associate with an artist. When Eve first showed her parents the photos, Joan was amazed that a roll of film could have lasted so long, and when she took the negatives to be archived, the man at the photo store attributed the film's preservation to the fact that the two unspoiled rolls had been rewound and stored in a canister; the other roll of film, which had been stored unwound and in the camera, was destroyed, much to Eve's dismay, since that was the roll that she had added to. In the weeks since, Joan has done some research in the town hall archives, looking for more information about this sculptor who once inhabited their house, and for photos of the man so she might identify him in these, and to find out what became of all his work. It is her secret hope and theory that Anders and Dave will find some of it at the bottom of the quarry; in the book that she is writing, she knows they will.

Anders himself isn't sure what they will find. He imagines it's likely they'll find various items left over from the quarrying days—maybe iron picks, or the pieces of metal that would have held together now disintegrated wooden platforms. No doubt they will find junk—an old bathtub, maybe, car parts or whole other cars, unidentifiable scraps of rusted metal. He looks through his mask at the water beneath him nervously; never before has he dived as deep as he will today. Dave has brought cylinders with larger volumes of breathing gas to compensate for the increased gas consumption at greater depths, and the gas for this dive is helium based, to reduce the risk of nitrogen narcosis. Anders has also received private training from Dave over the past two weeks in preparation for this dive, and he's been officially certified for greater depths than those his class training prepared him for, but he is anxious nonetheless. But he is interested, too. All of the dives he's taken this summer have been saltwater dives, and he is curious to see what different sort of life they'll find down here: slow-swimming bass, freshwater algae, the turtles they see occasionally at the surface; as black and uninhabitable as the water looks from above, he has no doubt they will find life.

Eve doesn't care what her father finds; she just wants him to find it. It was her idea for him to attempt this dive in the first place, and that he has agreed is nothing short of miraculous. She has spent her whole life wondering what could be down there; she and her sisters have spent countless hours speculating, and finally, finally, she is going to find out.

Eloise is equally curious; when she asked Hobbster in a note earlier this summer, he admitted that he didn't know, which amazed her, because Hobbster knows everything. He told her that sometimes you have to just live with a mystery. But she suspects that there are things down there that none of her family would even imagine, because what they don't know is that Hobbster has cleaned it with a magical chlorine, which in her mind could have given rise to all sorts of otherwise impossible things. For all Eloise knows, there could be mermaids down in the water. There could be talking fish, or singing flowers. There could be a whole miniature magical city of gold. There could be friendly ghosts, which Hobbster has assured her are the only kind. There could be anything down in the quarry. Anything, it seems, is possible.

Acknowledgments

Thanks first and foremost to my brilliant editor, Millicent Bennett, who helped me to make this book what it is. I am grateful for your careful thoughtfulness, your patience, and your wisdom.

Thanks, as always, to Amanda Urban, who stuck with me and found this book its home.

Thanks to Uncle Woody for creating the magical place Twin Quarries has become, and for allowing for the hours of laps during which much of this book was thought out.

Thanks always to my parents for their endless love and encouragement. Your support means more than I can say.

Thanks forever to Nan and Char, my sisters and my best friends.

Finally, thanks and love to Adin, my husband and soulmate, for reading this book with such care again and again in all its incarnations, and for pointing out the way when I lost it. Knowing I could talk to you each night at the table at 205 made the day's frustrations tolerable, and our brainstorming motivated me the next day to go on.

Hazel and Mona: Waah and woof.

About the Author

ELIZABETH HARTLEY WINTHROP was born and raised in New York City. She earned her BA from Harvard University, graduating Phi Beta Kappa and summa cum laude, and earned her MFA in fiction from UC Irvine, where she was the recipient of the Schaeffer Writing Fellowship. She is the author of two novels, *Fireworks* (Knopf 2006) and *December* (Knopf 2008), and her short fiction has appeared in *Wind*, *The Evansville Review*, *The Missouri Review*, *The Red Rock Review*, and *Indiana Review*. She currently lives in Massachusetts with her husband, daughter, and Saint Bernard.

Center Point Large Print
600 Brooks Road / PO Box 1
Thorndike ME 04986-0001 USA

(207) 568-3717

US & Canada:
1 800 929-9108
www.centerpointlargeprint.com